RILLA

of

INGLESIDE

Anne of Green Gables
Anne of Avonlea
Anne of the Island
Anne of Windy Poplars
Anne's House of Dreams
Anne of Ingleside
Rainbow Valley
Rilla of Ingleside
The Blythes Are Quoted

Chronicles of Avonlea
Further Chronicles of Avonlea

Emily of New Moon
Emily Climbs
Emily's Quest

Kilmeny of the Orchard
The Story Girl
The Golden Road
The Blue Castle
Magic for Marigold
A Tangled Web
Pat of Silver Bush
Mistress Pat
Jane of Lantern Hill

L.M. MONTGOMERY

RILLA
of
INGLESIDE

Edited and with an Introduction by
Benjamin Lefebvre and *Andrea McKenzie*

VIKING
CANADA

VIKING CANADA

Published by the Penguin Group

Penguin Group (Canada), 90 Eglinton Avenue East, Suite 700,
Toronto, Ontario, Canada M4P 2Y3 (a division of Pearson Canada Inc.)

Penguin Group (USA) Inc., 375 Hudson Street, New York, New York 10014, U.S.A.
Penguin Books Ltd, 80 Strand, London WC2R 0RL, England
Penguin Ireland, 25 St Stephen's Green, Dublin 2, Ireland (a division of Penguin Books Ltd)
Penguin Group (Australia), 250 Camberwell Road, Camberwell, Victoria 3124, Australia
(a division of Pearson Australia Group Pty Ltd)
Penguin Books India Pvt Ltd, 11 Community Centre, Panchsheel Park,
New Delhi – 110 017, India
Penguin Group (NZ), 67 Apollo Drive, Rosedale, North Shore 0632, New Zealand
(a division of Pearson New Zealand Ltd)
Penguin Books (South Africa) (Pty) Ltd, 24 Sturdee Avenue, Rosebank,
Johannesburg 2196, South Africa

Penguin Books Ltd, Registered Offices: 80 Strand, London WC2R 0RL, England

First published 2010

1 2 3 4 5 6 7 8 9 10 (RRD)

Rilla of Ingleside copyright © 1921 McClelland & Stewart Ltd.

This edition copyright © 2010 Heirs of L.M. Montgomery Inc., Benjamin Lefebvre,
and Andrea McKenzie

Introduction copyright © 2010 Benjamin Lefebvre and Andrea McKenzie
Maps copyright © 2010 Andrea McKenzie and Edward Devereux Sheffe III

The poem *Our Women*, by L.M. Montgomery is reprinted with the permission
of Heirs of L.M. Montgomery Inc.

L.M. Montgomery and *L.M. Montgomery's signature and cat design* are trademarks
of Heirs of L.M. Montgomery Inc.

Anne of Green Gables, *Rilla of Ingleside* and other indicia of "Anne" are trademarks and
Canadian official marks of the Anne of Green Gables Licensing Authority Inc.

Manufactured in the U.S.A.

Library and Archives Canada Cataloguing in Publication data
available upon request to the publisher.

ISBN: 978-0-670-06519-6

Visit the Penguin Group (Canada) website at **www.penguin.ca**

Special and corporate bulk purchase rates available; please see
www.penguin.ca/corporatesales or call 1-800-810-3104, ext. 2477 or 2474

CONTENTS

Introduction by Benjamin Lefebvre and Andrea McKenzie ~ IX

A Note on the Text ~ XX

The Origins of the First World War ~ XXI

CHAPTER I
Glen "Notes" and Other Matters ~ 5

CHAPTER II
Dew of Morning ~ 18

CHAPTER III
Moonlit Mirth ~ 25

CHAPTER IV
The Piper Pipes ~ 39

CHAPTER V
"The Sound of a Going" ~ 53

CHAPTER VI
Susan, Rilla, and Dog Monday Make a Resolution ~ 69

CHAPTER VII
A War Baby and a Soup Tureen ~ 78

CHAPTER VIII
Rilla Decides ~ 89

CHAPTER IX
Doc Has a Misadventure ~ 98

CHAPTER X
The Troubles of Rilla ~ 105

CHAPTER XI
Dark and Bright ~ 118

CHAPTER XII
In the Days of Langemarck ~ 130

CHAPTER XIII
A Slice of Humble Pie ~ 138

CHAPTER XIV
The Valley of Decision ~ 149

CHAPTER XV
Until the Day Break ~ 158

CHAPTER XVI
Realism and Romance ~ 166

CHAPTER XVII
The Weeks Wear By ~ 181

CHAPTER XVIII
A War Wedding ~ 196

CONTENTS

CHAPTER XIX
"They Shall Not Pass" ~ 210

CHAPTER XX
Norman Douglas Speaks Out in Meeting ~ 220

CHAPTER XXI
"Love Affairs Are Horrible" ~ 227

CHAPTER XXII
Little Dog Monday Knows ~ 234

CHAPTER XXIII
"And So, Goodnight" ~ 242

CHAPTER XXIV
Mary Is Just in Time ~ 248

CHAPTER XXV
Shirley Goes ~ 260

CHAPTER XXVI
Susan Has a Proposal of Marriage ~ 269

CHAPTER XXVII
Waiting ~ 281

CHAPTER XXVIII
Black Sunday ~ 298

CHAPTER XXIX
"Wounded and Missing" ~ 304

CHAPTER XXX
The Turning of the Tide ~ 309

CHAPTER XXXI
Mrs. Matilda Pitman ~ 315

CHAPTER XXXII
Word from Jem ~ 327

CHAPTER XXXIII
Victory!! ~ 336

CHAPTER XXXIV
Mr. Hyde Goes to His Own Place
and Susan Takes a Honeymoon ~ 339

CHAPTER XXXV
"Rilla-my-Rilla!" ~ 344

Canadian Women's Poetry of the First World War ~ 351

Glossary ~ 354

Further Reading ~ 388

Acknowledgments ~ 390

INTRODUCTION

by Benjamin Lefebvre and Andrea McKenzie

Since the publication of her bestselling first novel, *Anne of Green Gables*, in 1908, L.M. Montgomery's readers have included both women and men, adults and children, of all backgrounds and in all places. More than a century later, readers around the world continue to respond to her domestic comedies set primarily in rural Prince Edward Island, which she continued to write even after her marriage and move to Ontario in 1911. Today, many readers associate Montgomery's work with small communities, the trials and tribulations of girls and women, and the slower pace to be found in the years surrounding the turn of the twentieth century, all of which are found in *Anne of Green Gables* and its first sequel, *Anne of Avonlea* (1909), about Anne's two years as a schoolteacher, and in *Chronicles of Avonlea* (1912), a collection of short stories set in the same location. These elements appear as well as in Montgomery's personal favourite, *The Story Girl* (1911), and its sequel, *The Golden Road* (1913).

And yet, while these themes are continually found in some form in all her work, her subsequent Anne books are all touched by the atmosphere of the First World War of 1914–1918: *Anne of the Island* (1915), about Anne's university education, was completed three and a half months into the war; *Anne's House of Dreams* (1917), depicting Anne and her husband, Gilbert, as newlyweds, marked Montgomery's attempt to establish herself as a bestselling author with a new publisher, struggling to survive the uncertain wartime market; and *Rainbow Valley* (1919), a novel about Anne's children that Montgomery finished six weeks after the war's end, portrays the pressures, challenges, and rewards of the young people whose duty it will be one day to serve in the "great conflict" overseas. These three novels are all set long before the war broke out, but their initial readers would have noticed the marked contrast between the pre-war era they depict and the reality of the time of their publication. When Anne's oldest son, Jem, at the end of *Rainbow Valley*, responds enthusiastically to his brother Walter's prophecy of a shadowy figure named the Piper that would lure them, their siblings, and the neighbouring Meredith children to an uncertain future, the young characters in the book had no idea of the conflict ahead of them. But Montgomery's readers in 1919 certainly did.

Although the war is not mentioned directly in these three wartime novels, the anxiety and anguish that it caused was omnipresent in Montgomery's life during these years as a minister's wife with two young children. Although Montgomery had no son or husband at the front, the beginning and the ending of the war were marked for her by personal tragedies. In August 1914, within days of war being declared, her longed-for second son, Hugh Alexander, was born dead; two and a half months after peace was declared in November 1918, her beloved cousin and best friend Frederica died in Montreal in the influenza epidemic that swept the world in 1918 and early 1919. More was to follow: grieved by Frederica's death and perhaps worn down by the complex emotions engendered by the war, Montgomery's husband, Ewan Macdonald, lapsed into a severe and prolonged depression that was eventually diagnosed as religious melancholia, an illness not well understood at the time, and a stigma that

Montgomery strove to hide from his small-town Presbyterian congregation. Instead of peace, Montgomery faced an ongoing personal battle following the end of the war overseas, and her journal for 1919 bears the same emotional hallmarks as her entries for the war years: grief, endurance, and unending suspense. These events contributed to her understanding of what women and families endured during the war years.

Rilla of Ingleside, her next book, was born out of this difficult aftermath. She began writing it in March 1919, less than two months after Frederica's death, and persevered under increasingly difficult circumstances to finish it in August 1920. This novel, written to be the final sequel to *Anne of Green Gables*, documents the complex web of emotions that those who worked and waited for news in Canada, far from the trenches, endured for those long four years. Considered in the context of First World War literature, *Rilla* is a remarkable work: in 1921, when it was published, the great wave of war literature—the poetry, novels, and memoirs that would attempt to find meaning in the war or to condemn it as meaningless—was still largely in the future. In Canada, although mothers were sanctified for sending and sacrificing their sons, the war was considered a male enclave, and its documenting was largely confined to regimental diaries and histories of battles. Canadian men had triumphantly stormed Vimy Ridge in April 1917 to win a victory for the Allies that would become legendary for uniting Canada and shaping its future as an independent country. In this history, women seemingly had little place, an attitude that is still prevalent today.

The version of the war that Montgomery shows us in *Rilla of Ingleside* transforms this male, battle-dominated enclave into a lively community where men and women support one another through what Carol Acton has termed "shared war stories," even from a distance, and the women working on the home front are as heroic as the men fighting overseas. Montgomery venerates the Canadian soldiers who fought and died overseas, but she also illuminates the sacrifice that Canadian women and their families made through giving their men to the war. "*Our* sacrifice is greater," cries Rilla Blythe when the first young men enlist. "Our boys give only *themselves*. *We* give them." As few other contemporary war books do, *Rilla of Ingleside* vividly depicts the impact of the war on those at home. Montgomery contrasts the "anguish" in Anne Blythe's eyes when Jem decides to enlist with her courageous smile when he leaves, and Gertrude Oliver's stoic determination to carry on teaching when her fiancé is reported killed with her collapse when he is reported safe. Montgomery's fictional account of the small community of Glen St. Mary vividly depicts the suspense, the fears, and the grief that transformed many Canadian families, while emphasizing the courage that it took to "carry on."

Montgomery's war is also a complex and troubling account of how the violence in Europe bred conflict and extremism at home. We experience Rilla's confusion about her brother Walter and her struggle with the conflicting emotions of patriotism and her wish to keep him safe at home. Sympathetic to his fears about killing others and being wounded or blinded, she fiercely defends him against charges of cowardice when he doesn't enlist. Yet she has an "odd feeling of relief" when he finally does enlist, because "*no one* could ever call Walter a slacker now." But Walter's former fears become Rilla's burden; her imagination, as sensitive as his, pictures him "cold and dead under the stars" with "the light of his eyes blotted out." Yet she, like he, overcomes her fears, continuing her own work bravely, and the two actively support one another, their love reaching across the distance between them after he goes overseas. Each is heroic; each depends on the other; and it is Walter who endows Rilla with the resolve to continue the work he has begun in building for Canada's future in this time of horror, which makes her wartime contribution equivalent to his.

Rilla's patriotism, then, is based on a thoughtful and realistic assessment of the horrors of war and its possible consequences for her brothers' lives and her own; she becomes a shining example of support for community, nation, and Empire. But Montgomery also shows us the darker side of war and the cruelty it can breed. To be against the war was considered, in many parts of Canada, to be pro-German and a legitimate target for contempt and violence. Thus, Walter, before he enlists, is sent a white feather as a symbol of his presumed cowardice, and Mr. Pryor, Glen St. Mary's sole pacifist, has his windows broken by a mob of boys after the *Lusitania*, a British passenger ship, is sunk by a German U-boat, causing hundreds of civilians to drown. As Montgomery's vision of the war makes clear, the binary oppositions engendered by the war invaded even small communities at home.

Montgomery also shows us that the war has its lighter side, especially in its domestic details: Susan's struggle to make a cake that is not just "a slab" when voluntary food rationing urges women to reduce or eliminate butter and sugar; Rilla's elaborate green velvet hat of 1914 "conspicuous" against the much plainer, smaller-brimmed models of 1917 and 1918; Mary Vance's satisfied grin as she pioneers trousers for women in Glen St. Mary by donning a pair of overalls to help with the harvest; Miss Cornelia's reconciliation to Methodists; and Susan's mangled attempts to pronounce

"Rheims" and "Joffre." Montgomery's portrait of the teenaged Rilla, desperate to appear grown-up in front of her beau, only to be utterly embarrassed and undone by Susan, still makes us laugh today. Humour can leaven suspense and grief. Montgomery's insights into human nature, her capturing of small sly details that hilariously undercut sentimentality, create universal laughter and hope, even in a world at war.

Rilla is also remarkable for its accuracy about the events of the war. Through Susan and Rilla, especially, we can follow the battles and the political controversies throughout the war years as they happened; we also follow the journey of the main contingent of Canadian troops, from the mud of the training camp at Salisbury Plain to the poison gas attack in the trenches on the western front in April 1915, the triumphant assault on Vimy Ridge in April 1917, and the demobilization of troops in 1919. Borrowing extensively from her own war diary, Montgomery recreates the continuing atmosphere of suspense: of not knowing which army would win a battle, whether or not a town would fall, who would be injured or killed, and which side, eventually, would win the war. She also had few illusions about the ways that soldiers lived: the Blythe and Meredith boys' letters home vividly and authentically describe the mud, rats, and lice that were inevitable in trench conditions—and the ever-present risk of sudden death. By the war's end, few men are left unscarred, and all the characters—soldiers and families alike—have been transformed by the fires of war.

Montgomery appears to give us a narrow scope for the work women did during the war, but Rilla's war work is largely drawn from Montgomery's own experiences: president of the local Red Cross chapter, mother bringing up two small children, speaker at recruiting meetings and concerts, minister's wife who worried about enlisted parishioners and tried to comfort their families when their sons died. This work—and Rilla's—was typical for a woman living in a small rural community. But Montgomery also shows us how Rilla, like many of her real-life counterparts, gains in independence and organizational abilities through this work; Rilla's scope, like Susan Baker's world knowledge, is greatly expanded as a direct result of the war.

Yet Montgomery's depiction of women's war work, though representative of those who stayed at home in small communities, speaks to a certain perspective about work suitable for young women. Faith Meredith, who trains as a voluntary nurse, is the most adventurous, serving in hospitals in England, while Nan and Di do Red Cross work in the fictional city of Kingsport. Montgomery does not mention the non-traditional work women undertook, from making munitions to running farms in their husbands' absence, driving and maintaining ambulances overseas, and doing skilled factory work. Perhaps Montgomery was constrained by thoughts of her readers and what they would consider "suitable" occupations for women; perhaps, too, she wanted the focus to remain on Rilla and her work in sustaining the home as representative of the many Canadian women who, like Rilla, courageously kept the home fires burning despite their own suspense and grief.

In all of her books, Montgomery depicts communities of well-read individuals who have a shared literary heritage and who allude to the work of her favourite writers from Great Britain, such as Byron, Tennyson, Milton, Scott, Kipling, Shakespeare, Browning, and Wordsworth. These literary allusions to past works extend the reading experience of those readers who recognize the texts alluded to and can place the allusions in their larger context. In *Rilla of Ingleside*, however, allusions to British poets are relatively infrequent, as though Montgomery shared Gertrude Oliver's assertion that the calm, pastoral scene evoked by a poet such as Wordsworth is incompatible with the anxiety and anguish of the Great War period. Perhaps not unexpectedly for a novel about Canada's growth as a nation, the two poets who take pride of place in *Rilla of Ingleside* are Canadians: John McCrae, whose famous poem "In Flanders Fields" is echoed in Walter's "The Piper," and Virna Sheard, whose poem "The Young Knights" Montgomery quotes as the epigraph for her title page. Both poems are a tribute to the young people who gave their lives to the war effort and the call to patriotism, a tribute that is reflected in the descriptions of Walter's poem and the quoted line "keep faith." These few allusions do not give a sense of the range of war poetry that Montgomery had read by the time she wrote this novel, however, and it is worth noting that the novel includes over forty allusions to the Judeo-Christian Bible and the Book of Common Prayer, implying that the call to "keep faith" has both patriotic and religious dimensions. (We include the full text of Sheard's poem in "Canadian Women's Poetry of the First World War" and identify as many of Montgomery's literary allusions as possible in the Glossary that follows the full text of the novel.)

On November 11, 1918, when the Armistice was signed and the fighting stopped, Montgomery was at Park Corner, in her beloved Prince Edward Island, helping her cousin Frederica to nurse her family through the influenza epidemic. "The Great War is over," Montgomery wrote in her journal, "the world's agony has ended. *What has been born?* The next generation may be able to answer that. *We* can never fully know." Like many others around the world on that day, Montgomery gave meaning to the millions of men and women lost in the war, to the pain and the suffering felt almost worldwide, by looking to the future for some great blessing. But in the postwar years, the peace Montgomery longed for never emerged, either in world affairs or in her personal life.

In 1935, driven by the financial stress of the Depression and of her husband's recurrent and worsening mental illness, Montgomery changed her mind about *Rilla of Ingleside* being the last of the Anne books. Although she had introduced her readers to several new heroines in the intervening years— Emily, Valancy, Marigold, and Pat—*Anne of Green Gables* and its sequels continued to outsell her later books. In two of her last three books published in her lifetime, Montgomery returned to earlier periods of Anne's life: in *Anne of Windy Poplars* (1936), Anne is the principal of Summerside High School in the three years leading up to her marriage to Gilbert, and in *Anne of Ingleside* (1939), she is the young mother of five children (soon to be six, with the birth of Rilla).

But in September 1939, within a few months of the publication of *Anne of Ingleside*, war was again declared. Montgomery, who had agonized over the rise of Hitler in the 1930s, dreaded the prospect of repeating the years of anguish and uncertainty she had lived through two decades before. Unlike the previous war, she feared that the call to action she had depicted so vividly in *Rilla of Ingleside* would claim her two sons. And, too, the shift from the term "Great War" to "First World War" meant an implicit acknowledgment that the "better" world she had predicted through the characters in *Rilla* had not come true, making her question the optimism and patriotism she had believed in so strongly twenty years before.

The Blythes Are Quoted, her last book, delivered to her publishers the day of her death in April 1942, reunites the Ingleside characters for an experimental blend of prose, poetry, and dialogue. It is in many ways a welcome return to the community of Glen St. Mary, but the title indicates a shift in focus: the Blythes are no longer at the centre of the action, as they are in *Rilla of Ingleside*, but are onlookers who comment upon the action from the sidelines. Montgomery's humour is as sharp and alive as ever, but the divides are deeper and the currents darker. Although she includes a poem called "The Piper" in *The Blythes Are Quoted*, this poem omits Walter's call to "keep faith," and the final poem included in the book, "The Aftermath," portrays the war and survival for the men who fought in it as a bleak and traumatizing hell that does not end with the Armistice. *The Blythes Are Quoted* forms an equally unique perspective about how the questions left by the First World War were answered for the Blythe family and for Canada in the decades that followed.

Like many of her contemporaries in the years immediately after the First World War, Montgomery created meaning from the horrific sacrifice of a generation by believing that the blood spilled and the grief endured must create a more idealistic, uplifted, and uplifting world. She also believed that the war had created a mature Canada, ready to take its place on the world's stage as an independent nation, and highlighted the role of the generation of young women who had lived through the war and would become the mothers of the future. In a 1921 autobiographical sketch titled "How I Became a Writer," Montgomery made a remarkable revelation about her work, her readers, and her nation: "In my latest story, 'Rilla of Ingleside,' I have tried, as far as in me lies, to depict the fine and splendid way in which the girls of Canada reacted to the Great War—their bravery, patience and self-sacrifice. The book is theirs in a sense in which none of my other books have been: for my other books were written for anyone who might like to read them: but 'Rilla' was written for the girls of the great young land I love, whose destiny it will be their duty and privilege to shape and share." *Rilla of Ingleside* thus pictures, as no other war novel of its time does, a uniquely Canadian perspective about the women and families who battled to keep the home fires burning throughout this tumultuous era.

A NOTE ON THE TEXT

This present edition is based on the full text of the first Canadian edition of *Rilla of Ingleside*, published by McClelland & Stewart (Toronto) in 1921. Although later Canadian editions of the novel contain a copyright date of 1920, the novel was published simultaneously in the United States (by Frederick A. Stokes Company) and in Canada in fall 1921 using the same plates. In 1976, the American Reprint Company issued a new hardcover edition that silently cut 4,530 words, a total of 4 percent of the original text. It was this version of the text that was reissued in paperback form by Bantam-Seal in 1985.

We have regularized spelling, punctuation, capitalization, and hyphenation to be consistent throughout and corrected obvious typographical errors. We corrected occasional errors with character names ("Jem Meredith," "Olive Keith," "Mrs. Alec Douglas") and the date of Rilla's March 23, 1917, journal entry, which should be 1918. We have incorporated three handwritten corrections made by Montgomery in her personal copy of the book (a first Stokes edition, held in the L.M. Montgomery Collection, University of Guelph archives): on page 186 of our edition, "shrill sound" has been replaced by "shrill song"; on page 240, "silvery-pink shadows" has been replaced by "silvery-pink shallows"; on page 329, "shadow army" has been replaced by "shadowy army." We have avoided correcting names of historical personages, events, and battles, but comment on irregularities in the Glossary.

THE ORIGINS OF THE
FIRST WORLD WAR

In 1914, Europe was governed by a complex set of treaties that served to maintain the balance of power among the major countries. In 1907, Britain had joined France and Russia to form the Triple Entente: the three countries had a "moral obligation" to support each other, but were not required to go to war if an ally's country was attacked. Britain had also signed an agreement in 1867 to uphold Belgium's neutrality if Belgium was attacked, and Russia, similarly, had agreed to protect Serbia, one of the small Balkan states. Germany, the Austro-Hungarian Empire, and Italy formed the Triple Alliance, but their agreement called for military support if an ally's country was attacked. Ironically, the royal houses of three of the major powers were related to one another through Queen Victoria. George V of Great Britain was her grandson, as was Kaiser Wilhelm II of Germany. Nicholas II, Czar of Russia, was cousin to both George V and Kaiser Wilhelm II. (For a description of the personalities, major battles, and European towns involved in the war, see the Glossary.)

The Balkan countries contributed to the complexity of the situation. These small states, including Serbia, had fought for independence from the major powers (Austria, Russia, and Turkey), and had also fought each other. Austria had annexed Bosnia and Herzogovina and was eyeing independent Serbia before the war broke out.

On June 28, 1914, Gavrilo Princip, a nineteen-year-old Serbian student, shot Archduke Franz Ferdinand, heir to the

Austro-Hungarian Empire, and his morganatic wife, in Sarajevo, the capital city of Bosnia. Princip, a member of the Serbian secret society The Black Hand, and his fellow conspirators wanted to free Bosnia from Austrian rule, then unite Bosnia and Serbia into the free state of Yugoslavia. Austria saw the Archduke's assassination as an opportunity to obtain control over Serbia, so held Serbia responsible for the shooting. After receiving Germany's assurance of support, Austria-Hungary issued Serbia an ultimatum: meet a list of harsh conditions or face war. Although Serbia agreed to most of the conditions and tried to negotiate the remaining items, Austria-Hungary declared war on Serbia on July 28 and invaded the smaller country the next day.

Russia, bound by treaty to protect Serbia, then mobilized; Germany, bound to Austria-Hungary, also mobilized. Germany's Schlieffen Plan, a military strategy drawn up years earlier in case France, Russia, and Britain threatened to attack, called for German troops to make a wide sweep through Belgium into France (morally obligated to uphold Russia), to defeat the French army, then turn east to engage Russia. Germany called on Belgium to let the German troops through without hindrance, but King Albert and the Belgian government would not agree; if German troops entered the country, Belgium would fight.

Germany did invade Belgium on August 2, 1914, causing Britain to come to Belgium's aid by the terms of the 1867 agreement, and to help France, the object of Germany's attack. On August 4, Britain declared war on Germany, and Canada, as a British dominion, was thus automatically at war with Germany. War fever swept Canada, and the first twenty-five thousand volunteers joined up and were sent to the new training camp at Valcartier, Quebec, close to Quebec City.

This First Canadian Contingent of soldiers and medical staff sailed in a convoy of ships for England in October 1914, and camped on muddy Salisbury Plain for the autumn and winter. The main body of Canadian troops entered the trenches in February 1915. They earned accolades for their fighting spirit, their efficiency and organization, and their contributions to battle victories throughout the war.

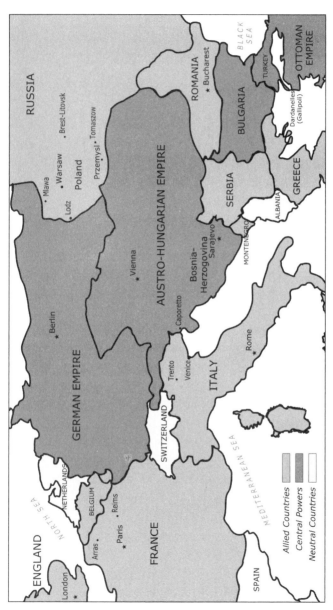

Europe during the First World War

The Western Front

RILLA

of

INGLESIDE

Now they remain to us forever young
Who with such splendour gave their youth away.

—SHEARD

To
the memory of
FREDERICA CAMPBELL MACFARLANE
who went away from me when the dawn broke
on January 25th, 1919—a true friend, a rare
personality, a loyal and courageous soul.

$\mathscr{G}$len "Notes" and Other Matters

It was a warm, golden-cloudy, lovable afternoon. In the big living room at Ingleside Susan Baker sat down with a certain grim satisfaction hovering about her like an aura; it was four o'clock and Susan, who had been working incessantly since six that morning, felt that she had fairly earned an hour of repose and gossip. Susan just then was perfectly happy; everything had gone almost uncannily well in the kitchen that day. Dr. Jekyll had not been Mr. Hyde and so had not grated on her nerves; from where she sat she could see the pride of her heart—the bed of peonies of her own planting and culture, blooming as no other peony plot in Glen St. Mary ever did or could bloom, with peonies crimson, peonies silvery pink, peonies white as drifts of winter snow.

Susan had on a new black silk blouse, quite as elaborate as anything Mrs. Marshall Elliott ever wore, and a white starched apron, trimmed with complicated crocheted lace fully five inches wide, not to mention insertion to match. Therefore Susan had all the comfortable consciousness of a well-dressed woman as she opened her copy of the *Daily Enterprise* and prepared to read the Glen "Notes" which, as Miss Cornelia had just informed her, filled half a column of it and mentioned almost everybody at Ingleside. There was a big, black headline on the front page of the *Enterprise*, stating that some Archduke Ferdinand or other had been assassinated at a place bearing the weird name of Sarajevo, but Susan tarried not over uninteresting, immaterial stuff like that; she was in quest of something really vital. Oh, here it was—"Jottings from Glen St. Mary." Susan settled down keenly, reading each one over aloud to extract all possible gratification from it.

Mrs. Blythe and her visitor, Miss Cornelia—*alias* Mrs. Marshall Elliott—were chatting together near the open door that led to the veranda, through which a cool, delicious breeze was blowing, bringing whiffs of phantom perfume from the garden, and charming gay echoes from the vine-hung corner where Rilla and Miss Oliver and Walter were laughing and talking. Wherever Rilla Blythe was, there was laughter.

There was another occupant of the living room, curled up on a couch, who must not be overlooked, since he was a creature of marked individuality, and, moreover, had the distinction of being the only living thing whom Susan really hated.

All cats are mysterious but Dr. Jekyll-and-Mr. Hyde— "Doc" for short—was trebly so. He was a cat of double personality—or else, as Susan vowed, he was possessed by the devil. To begin with, there had been something uncanny about the very dawn of his existence. Four years previously Rilla Blythe had had a treasured darling of a kitten, white as snow, with a saucy black tip to its tail, which she called Jack Frost. Susan disliked Jack Frost, though she could not or would not give any valid reason therefor.

"Take my word for it, Mrs. Dr. dear," she was wont to say ominously, "that cat will come to no good."

"But why do you think so?" Mrs. Blythe would ask.

"I do not *think—I know*," was all the answer Susan would vouchsafe.

With the rest of the Ingleside folk Jack Frost was a favourite; he was so very clean and well groomed, and never allowed a spot or stain to be seen on his beautiful white suit;

he had endearing ways of purring and snuggling; he was scrupulously honest.

And then a domestic tragedy took place at Ingleside. Jack Frost had kittens!

It would be vain to try to picture Susan's triumph. Had she not always insisted that that cat would turn out to be a delusion and a snare? *Now* they could see for themselves!

Rilla kept one of the kittens, a very pretty one, with peculiarly sleek glossy fur of dark yellow crossed by orange stripes, and large, satiny, golden ears. She called it Goldie and the name seemed appropriate enough to the little frolicsome creature which, during its kittenhood, gave no indication of the sinister nature it really possessed. Susan, of course, warned the family that no good could be expected from any offspring of that diabolical Jack Frost; but Susan's Cassandra-like croakings were unheeded.

The Blythes had been so accustomed to regard Jack Frost as a member of the male sex that they could not get out of the habit. So they continually used the masculine pronoun, although the result was ludicrous. Visitors used to be quite electrified when Rilla referred casually to "Jack and his kitten," or told Goldie sternly, "Go to your mother and get him to wash your fur."

"It is *not* decent, Mrs. Dr. dear," poor Susan would say bitterly. She herself compromised by always referring to Jack as "it" or "the white beast," and one heart at least did not ache when "it" was accidentally poisoned the following winter.

In a year's time "Goldie" became so manifestly an inadequate name for the orange kitten that Walter, who was just then reading Stevenson's story, changed it to Dr. Jekyll-and-Mr. Hyde. In his Dr. Jekyll mood the cat was a drowsy, affectionate, domestic, cushion-loving puss, who liked petting and gloried in being nursed and patted. Especially did he love to lie on his back and have his sleek, cream-coloured throat stroked gently while he purred in somnolent satisfaction. He was a notable purrer; never had there been an Ingleside cat who purred so constantly and so ecstatically.

"The only thing I envy a cat is its purr," remarked Dr. Blythe once, listening to Doc's resonant melody. "It is the most contented sound in the world."

Doc was very handsome; his every movement was grace; his poses magnificent. When he folded his long, dusky-ringed tail about his feet and sat him down on the veranda to gaze steadily into space for long intervals the Blythes felt that an Egyptian sphinx could not have made a more fitting Deity of the Portal.

When the Mr. Hyde mood came upon him—which it invariably did before rain, or wind—he was a wild thing with changed eyes. The transformation always came suddenly. He would spring fiercely from a reverie with a savage snarl and bite at any restraining or caressing hand. His fur seemed to grow darker and his eyes gleamed with a diabolical light. There was really an unearthly beauty about him. If the change happened in the twilight all the Ingleside folk felt a certain terror of him. At such times he was a fearsome beast and only Rilla defended him, asserting that he was "such a nice prowly cat." Certainly he prowled.

Dr. Jekyll loved new milk; Mr. Hyde would not touch milk and growled over his meat. Dr. Jekyll came down the stairs so silently that no one could hear him. Mr. Hyde made his tread as heavy as a man's. Several evenings, when Susan was alone in the house, he "scared her stiff," as she declared, by doing this. He would sit in the middle of the kitchen floor, with his terrible eyes fixed unwinkingly upon hers for an hour at a time. This played havoc with her nerves, but poor Susan really held him in too much awe to try to drive him out. Once she had dared to throw a stick at him and he had promptly made a savage leap toward her. Susan rushed out of doors and never attempted to meddle with Mr. Hyde again—though she visited his misdeeds upon the innocent Dr. Jekyll, chasing him ignominiously out of her domain whenever he dared to poke his nose in and denying him certain savoury tidbits for which he yearned.

"'The many friends of Miss Faith Meredith, Gerald Meredith and James Blythe,'" read Susan, rolling the names like sweet morsels under her tongue, "'were very much pleased to welcome them home a few weeks ago from Redmond College. James Blythe, who was graduated in Arts in 1913, has just completed his first year in medicine.'"

"Faith Meredith has really got to be the handsomest creature I ever saw," commented Miss Cornelia above her filet crochet. "It's amazing how those children came on after Rosemary West went to the manse. People have almost forgotten what imps of mischief they were once. Anne, dearie, will you ever forget the way they used to carry on? It's really surprising how well Rosemary got on with them. She's more like a chum than a stepmother. They all love her and Una adores her. As for that little Bruce, Una just makes a perfect slave of herself to him. Of course, he *is* a darling. But did you ever see any child look as much like an aunt as he looks like his Aunt Ellen? He's just as dark and just as emphatic. I can't see a feature of Rosemary in him. Norman Douglas always vows at the top of his voice that the stork meant Bruce for him and Ellen and took him to the manse by mistake."

"Bruce adores Jem," said Mrs. Blythe. "When he comes over here he just follows Jem about silently like a faithful little dog, looking up at him from under his black brows. He would do anything for Jem, I verily believe."

"Are Jem and Faith going to make a match of it?"

Mrs. Blythe smiled. It was well known that Miss Cornelia, who had been such a virulent man-hater at one time, had actually taken to match-making in her declining years.

"They are only good friends yet, Miss Cornelia."

"*Very* good friends, believe *me*," said Miss Cornelia emphatically. "I hear all about the doings of the young fry."

"I have no doubt that Mary Vance sees that you do, Mrs. Marshall Elliott," said Susan significantly, "but *I* think it is a shame to talk about children making matches."

"Children! Jem is twenty-one and Faith is nineteen," retorted Miss Cornelia. "You must not forget, Susan, that we old folks are not the only grown-up people in the world."

Outraged Susan, who detested any reference to her age—not from vanity but from a haunting dread that people might come to think her too old to work—returned to her "Notes."

"'Carl Meredith and Shirley Blythe came home last Friday evening from Queen's Academy. We understand that Carl will be in charge of the school at Harbour Head next year and we are sure he will be a popular and successful teacher.'"

"He will teach the children all there is to know about bugs, anyhow," said Miss Cornelia. "He is through with Queen's now and Mr. Meredith and Rosemary wanted him to go right on to Redmond in the fall, but Carl has a very independent streak in him and means to earn part of his own way through college. He'll be all the better for it."

"'Walter Blythe, who has been teaching for the past two years at Lowbridge, has resigned,'" read Susan. "'We understand that he intends going to Redmond this fall.'"

"Is Walter quite strong enough for Redmond yet?" queried Miss Cornelia anxiously.

"We hope that he will be by the fall," said Mrs. Blythe. "An idle summer in the open air and sunshine will do a great deal for him."

"Typhoid is a hard thing to get over," said Miss Cornelia emphatically, "especially when one has had such a close shave as Walter had. I think he'd do well to stay out of college another year. But then he's so ambitious. Are Di and Nan going too?"

"Yes. They both wanted to teach another year but Gilbert thinks they would better go to Redmond this fall."

"I'm glad of that. They'll keep an eye on Walter and see that he doesn't study too hard. I suppose," continued Miss Cornelia, with a side glance at Susan, "that after the snub I got a few minutes ago it will not be safe for me to suggest that Jerry Meredith is making sheep's eyes at Nan."

Susan ignored this and Mrs. Blythe laughed again.

"Dear Miss Cornelia, I have my hands full, haven't I?—with all these boys and girls sweethearting around me? If I took it seriously it would quite crush me. But I don't—it is too hard yet to realize that they've grown up. When I look at those two tall sons of mine I wonder if they can possibly be the fat, sweet, dimpled babies I kissed and cuddled and sang to slumber the other day—only the other day, Miss Cornelia. Wasn't Jem the dearest baby in the old House of Dreams? And *now* he's a B.A. and accused of courting."

"We're all growing older," sighed Miss Cornelia.

"The only part of me that *feels* old," said Mrs. Blythe, "is the ankle I broke when Josie Pye dared me to walk the Barry ridge-pole in the Green Gables days. I have an ache in it when the wind is east. I won't admit that it is rheumatism, but it *does* ache. As for the children, they and the Merediths are planning a gay summer before they have to go back to studies in the fall. They are such a fun-loving little crowd. They keep this house in a perpetual whirl of merriment."

"Is Rilla going to Queen's when Shirley goes back?"

"It isn't decided yet. I rather fancy not. For one thing, her father thinks she is not quite strong enough—she has rather outgrown her strength—she's really absurdly tall for a girl not yet fifteen. I am not anxious to have her go—why, it would be terrible not to have a single one of my babies home with me next winter. Susan and I would fall to fighting with each other to break the monotony."

Susan smiled at this pleasantry. The idea of her fighting with "Mrs. Dr. dear!"

"Does Rilla herself want to go?" asked Miss Cornelia.

"No. The truth is, Rilla is the only one of my flock who isn't ambitious. I really wish she had a little more ambition. She has no serious ideals at all—her sole aspiration seems to be to have a good time."

"And why should she not have it, Mrs. Dr. dear?" cried Susan, who could not bear to hear a single word against any one of the Ingleside folk, even from one of themselves. "A young girl *should* have a good time, and that I will maintain. There will be time enough for her to think of Latin and Greek."

"I should like to see a *little* sense of responsibility in her, Susan. And you know yourself that she is abominably vain."

"She has something to be vain about," retorted Susan. "She is the prettiest girl in Glen St. Mary. Do you think that all those over-harbour MacAllisters and Crawfords and Elliotts could scare up a skin like Rilla's in four generations? They could *not*. No, Mrs. Dr. dear, I know my place but I cannot allow you to run down Rilla. Listen to this, Mrs. Marshall Elliott."

Susan had found a chance to get square with Miss Cornelia for her digs at the children's love affairs. She read the item with gusto.

"'Miller Douglas has decided not to go West. He says old P.E.I. is good enough for him and he will continue to farm for his aunt, Mrs. Alec Davis.'"

Susan looked keenly at Miss Cornelia.

"I have heard, Mrs. Marshall Elliott, that Miller is courting Mary Vance."

This shot pierced Miss Cornelia's armour. Her sonsy face flushed.

"I won't have Miller Douglas hanging round Mary," she said crisply. "He comes of a low family. His father was a sort of outcast from the Douglases—they never really counted him in—and his mother was one of those terrible Dillons from the Harbour Head."

"I think I have heard, Mrs. Marshall Elliott, that Mary Vance's own parents were not what you could call aristocratic."

"Mary Vance has had a good bringing up and she is a smart, clever, capable girl," retorted Miss Cornelia. "She is not going to throw herself away on Miller Douglas, believe *me*! She knows *my* opinion on the matter and Mary has never disobeyed me yet."

"Well, I do not think you need worry, Mrs. Marshall Elliott, for Mrs. Alec Davis is as much against it as you could be, and says no nephew of hers is ever going to marry a nameless nobody like Mary Vance."

Susan returned to her mutton, feeling that she had got the best of it in this passage of arms, and read another "note."

"'We are pleased to hear that Miss Oliver has been engaged as teacher for another year. Miss Oliver will spend her well-earned vacation at her home in Lowbridge.'"

"I'm so glad Gertrude is going to stay," said Mrs. Blythe. "We would miss her horribly. And she has an excellent influence over Rilla who worships her. They are chums, in spite of the difference in their ages."

"I thought I heard she was going to be married?"

"I believe it was talked of but I understand it is postponed for a year."

"Who is the young man?"

"Robert Grant. He is a young lawyer in Charlottetown. I hope Gertrude will be happy. She has had a sad life, with much bitterness in it, and she feels things with a terrible keenness. Her first youth is gone and she is practically alone in the world. This new love that has come into her life seems such a wonderful thing to her that I think she hardly dares believe in its permanence. When her marriage had to be put off she was quite in despair—though it certainly wasn't Mr. Grant's fault. There were complications in the settlement of his father's estate—his father died last winter—and he could not marry till the tangles were unravelled. But I think Gertrude felt it was a bad omen and that her happiness would somehow elude her yet."

"It does not do, Mrs. Dr. dear, to set your affections too much on a man," remarked Susan solemnly.

"Mr. Grant is quite as much in love with Gertrude as she is with him, Susan. It is not he whom she distrusts—it is fate. She has a little mystic streak in her—I suppose some people would call her superstitious. She has an odd belief in dreams and we have not been able to laugh it out of her. I must own, too, that some of her dreams—but there, it would not do to let Gilbert hear me hinting such heresy. What have you found of such interest, Susan?"

Susan had given an exclamation.

"Listen to this, Mrs. Dr. dear. 'Mrs. Sophia Crawford has given up her house at Lowbridge and will make her home in future with her niece, Mrs. Albert Crawford.' Why that is my own cousin Sophia, Mrs. Dr. dear. We quarrelled when we were children over who should get a Sunday School card with the words 'God is Love,' wreathed in rosebuds, on it, and have never spoken to each other since. And now she is coming to live right across the road from us."

"You will have to make up the old quarrel, Susan. It will never do to be at outs with your neighbours."

"Cousin Sophia began the quarrel, so she can begin the making up also, Mrs. Dr. dear," said Susan loftily. "If she does I hope I am a good enough Christian to meet her half way. She is not a cheerful person and has been a wet blanket all her life. The last time I saw her, her face had a thousand wrinkles—maybe more, maybe less—from worrying and foreboding. She howled dreadful at her first husband's funeral but she married again in less than a year. The next note, I see, describes the special service in our church last Sunday night and says the decorations were very beautiful."

"Speaking of that reminds me that Mr. Pryor strongly disapproves of flowers in church," said Miss Cornelia. "I always said there would be trouble when that man moved here from Lowbridge. He should never have been put in as elder—it was a mistake and we shall live to rue it, believe *me*! I have heard that he has said that if the girls continue to 'mess up the pulpit with weeds' that he will not go to church."

"The church got on very well before old Whiskers-on-the-moon came to the Glen and it is my opinion it will get on without him after he is gone," said Susan.

"Who in the world ever gave him that ridiculous nickname?" asked Mrs. Blythe.

"Why, the Lowbridge boys have called him that ever since I can remember, Mrs. Dr. dear.—I suppose because his face is so round and red, with that fringe of sandy whisker about it. It does not do for any one to call him that in his hearing, though, and that you may tie to. But worse than his whiskers, Mrs. Dr. dear, he is a very unreasonable man and has a great many queer ideas. He is an elder now and they say he is very religious; but *I* can well remember the time, Mrs. Dr. dear, twenty years ago, when he was caught pasturing his cow in the Lowbridge graveyard. Yes, indeed, I have not forgotten that, and I always think of it when he is praying in meeting. Well, that is all the notes and there is not much else in the paper of any importance. I never take much interest in foreign parts. Who is this Archduke man who has been murdered?"

"What does it matter to us?" asked Miss Cornelia, unaware of the hideous answer to her question which destiny was even then preparing. "Somebody is always murdering or being murdered in those Balkan States. It's their normal condition and I don't really think that our papers ought to print such shocking things. The *Enterprise* is getting far too sensational with its big headlines. Well, I must be getting home. No, Anne dearie, it's no use asking me to stay to supper. Marshall has got to thinking that if I'm not home for a meal it's not worth eating—just like a man. So off I go. Merciful goodness, Anne dearie, what is the matter with that cat? Is he having a fit?"—this, as Doc suddenly bounded to the rug at Miss

Cornelia's feet, laid back his ears, swore at her, and then disappeared with one fierce leap through the window.

"Oh, no. He's merely turning into Mr. Hyde—which means that we shall have rain or high wind before morning. Doc is as good as a barometer."

"Well, I am thankful he has gone on the rampage outside this time and not into my kitchen," said Susan. "And I am going out to see about supper. With such a crowd as we have at Ingleside now it behooves us to think about our meals betimes."

$\mathscr{D}$ew of Morning

Outside, the Ingleside lawn was full of golden pools of sunshine and plots of alluring shadows. Rilla Blythe was swinging in the hammock under the big Scotch pine, Gertrude Oliver sat at its roots beside her, and Walter was stretched at full length on the grass, lost in a romance of chivalry wherein old heroes and beauties of dead and gone centuries lived vividly again for him.

Rilla was the "baby" of the Blythe family and was in a chronic state of secret indignation because nobody believed she was grown up. She was so nearly fifteen that she called herself that, and she was quite as tall as Di and Nan; also, she was nearly as pretty as Susan believed her to be. She had great, dreamy, hazel eyes, a milky skin dappled with little golden freckles, and delicately arched eyebrows, giving her a demure, questioning look which made people, especially lads in their teens, want to answer it. Her hair was ripely, ruddily brown and a little dent in her upper lip looked as if some good fairy had pressed it in with her finger at Rilla's christening. Rilla, whose best friends could not deny her share of vanity, thought her face would do very well, but worried over her figure, and wished her mother could be prevailed upon to let her wear longer dresses. She, who had been so plump and roly-poly in the old Rainbow Valley days, was incredibly slim now, in the arms-and-legs period. Jem and Shirley harrowed her soul by calling her "Spider." Yet she somehow escaped awkwardness. There was something in her movements that made you think she never walked but always danced. She had been much petted and was a wee bit spoiled, but still the general opinion was that Rilla Blythe was a very sweet girl, even if she were not so clever as Nan and Di.

Miss Oliver, who was going home that night for vacation, had boarded for a year at Ingleside. The Blythes had taken her to please Rilla who was fathoms deep in love with her teacher and was even willing to share her room, since no other was available. Gertrude Oliver was twenty-eight and life had been a struggle for her. She was a striking-looking girl, with rather sad, almond-shaped brown eyes, a clever, rather mocking mouth, and enormous masses of black hair twisted about her head. She was not pretty but there was a certain charm of interest and mystery in her face, and Rilla found her fascinating. Even her occasional moods of gloom and cynicism had allurement for Rilla. These moods came only when Miss Oliver was tired. At all other times she was a stimulating companion, and the gay set at Ingleside never remembered that she was so much older than themselves. Walter and Rilla were her favourites and she was the confidante of the secret wishes and aspirations of both. She knew that Rilla longed to be "out"—to go to parties as Nan and Di did, and to have dainty evening dresses and—yes, there is no use mincing matters—*beaux*! In the plural, at that! As for Walter, Miss Oliver knew that he had written a sequence of sonnets "To Rosamond"—i.e. Faith Meredith—and that he aimed at a professorship of English literature in some big college. She knew his passionate love of beauty and his equally passionate hatred of ugliness; she knew his strength and his weakness.

Walter was, as ever, the handsomest of the Ingleside boys. Miss Oliver found pleasure in looking at him for his good looks—he was so exactly like what she would have liked her own son to be. Glossy black hair, brilliant dark grey eyes, faultless features. And a poet to his finger tips! That sonnet sequence was really a remarkable thing for a lad of twenty to write. Miss Oliver was no partial critic and she knew that Walter Blythe had a wonderful gift.

Rilla loved Walter with all her heart. He never teased her as Jem and Shirley did. He never called her "Spider." His pet name for her was "Rilla-my-Rilla"—a little pun on her real name, Marilla. She had been named after Aunt Marilla of Green Gables, but Aunt Marilla had died before Rilla was old enough to know her very well, and Rilla detested the name as being horribly old-fashioned and prim. Why couldn't they have called her by her first name, Bertha, which was beautiful and dignified, instead of that silly "Rilla"? She did not mind Walter's version, but nobody else was allowed to call her that, except Miss Oliver now and then. "Rilla-my-Rilla" in Walter's musical voice sounded very beautiful to her—like the lilt and ripple of some silvery brook. She would have *died* for Walter if it would have done him any good, so she told Miss Oliver. Rilla was as fond of italics as most girls of fifteen are—and the bitterest drop in her cup was her suspicion that he told Di more of his secrets than he told her.

"He thinks I'm not grown up enough to understand," she had once lamented rebelliously to Miss Oliver, "but I am! And I would *never* tell them to a single soul—not even to you, Miss Oliver. I tell *you* all my own—I just *couldn't* be happy if I had any secret from you, dearest—but I would never betray his. *I* tell *him* everything—I even show him my diary. And it hurts me *dreadfully* when he doesn't tell *me* things. He shows me all his poems, though—they are *marvellous*, Miss Oliver.

Oh, I just live in the hope that some day I shall be to Walter what Wordsworth's sister Dorothy was to him. Wordsworth never wrote *anything* like Walter's poems—nor Tennyson, either."

"I wouldn't say just that. Both of them wrote a great deal of trash," said Miss Oliver dryly. Then, repenting, as she saw a hurt look in Rilla's eye, she added hastily,

"But I believe Walter *will* be a great poet, too—some day—perhaps the first really great poet Canada has ever had—and you will have more of his confidence as you grow older."

"When Walter was in the hospital with typhoid last year I was almost crazy," sighed Rilla, a little importantly. "They never told me how ill he really was until it was all over—father wouldn't let them. I'm glad I didn't know—I *couldn't* have borne it. I cried myself to sleep every night as it was. But sometimes," concluded Rilla bitterly—she liked to speak bitterly now and then in imitation of Miss Oliver—"sometimes I think Walter cares more for Dog Monday than he does for me."

Dog Monday was the Ingleside dog, so called because he had come into the family on a Monday when Walter had been reading *Robinson Crusoe*. He really belonged to Jem but was much attached to Walter also. He was lying beside Walter now with nose snuggled against his arm, thumping his tail rapturously whenever Walter gave him an absent pat. Monday was not a collie or a setter or a hound or a New-foundland. He was just, as Jem said, "plain dog"—*very* plain dog, uncharitable people added. Certainly, Monday's looks were not his strong point. Black spots were scattered at random over his yellow carcass, one of them, apparently, blotting out an eye. His ears were in tatters, for Monday was never successful in affairs of honour. But he possessed one talisman. He knew that not all dogs could be handsome or eloquent or victorious, but that every dog could love. Inside his homely hide beat the most affectionate, loyal, faithful heart of any dog since dogs were; and something looked out of his brown eyes that was nearer akin to a soul than any theologian would allow. Everybody at Ingleside was fond of him, even Susan, although his one unfortunate propensity of sneaking into the spare room and going to sleep upon the bed tried her affection sorely.

On this particular afternoon Rilla had no quarrel on hand with existing conditions.

"Hasn't June been a delightful month?" she asked, looking dreamily afar at the little quiet silvery clouds hanging so peacefully over Rainbow Valley. "We've had such lovely times—and such lovely weather. It has just been perfect every way."

"I don't half like that," said Miss Oliver, with a sigh. "It's ominous—somehow. A perfect thing is a gift of the gods—a sort of compensation for what is coming afterwards. I've seen that so often that I don't care to hear people say they've had a perfect time. June *has* been delightful, though."

"Of course, it hasn't been very exciting," said Rilla. "The only exciting thing that has happened in the Glen for a year was old Miss Mead fainting in church. Sometimes I wish something *dramatic* would happen once in a while."

"Don't wish it. Dramatic things always have a bitterness for some one. What a nice summer all you gay creatures will have! And me moping at Lowbridge!"

"You'll be over often, won't you? I think there's going to be lots of fun this summer, though I'll just be on the fringe of things as usual, I suppose. Isn't it horrid when people keep thinking you're a little girl when you're not?"

"There's plenty of time for you to be grown up, Rilla. Don't wish your youth away. It goes too quickly. You'll begin to taste life soon enough."

"Taste life! I want to *eat* it," cried Rilla laughing. "I want everything—everything a girl can have. I'll be fifteen in another month, and *then* nobody can say I'm a child any longer. I heard some one say once that the years from fifteen to nineteen are the best years in a girl's life. I'm going to make them perfectly splendid—just fill them with fun."

"There's no use thinking about what you're going to do— you are tolerably sure not to do it."

"Oh, but you do get a lot of fun out of the thinking," cried Rilla.

"You think of nothing but fun, you monkey," said Miss Oliver indulgently, reflecting that Rilla's chin was really the last word in chins. "Well, what else is fifteen for? But have you any notion of going to college this fall?"

"No—nor any other fall. I don't want to. I never cared for all those ologies and isms Nan and Di are so crazy about. And there's five of us going to college already. Surely that's enough. There's bound to be one dunce in every family. I'm quite willing to be a dunce if I can be a pretty, popular, delightful one. I can't be clever. I have no talent at all, and you can't imagine how comfortable it is. Nobody expects me to do anything so I'm never pestered to do it. And I can't be a housewifely, cookly creature, either. I hate sewing and dusting, and when Susan couldn't teach me to make biscuits nobody could. Father says I toil not neither do I spin. Therefore, I must be a lily of the field," concluded Rilla, with another laugh.

"You are too young to give up your studies altogether, Rilla."

"Oh, mother will put me through a course of reading next winter. It will polish up her B.A. degree. Luckily I like reading. Don't look at me so sorrowfully and so disapprovingly, dearest. I can't be sober and serious—everything looks so rosy and rainbowy to me. Next month I'll be fifteen—and next year sixteen—and the year after that, seventeen. Could anything be more enchanting?"

"Rap wood," said Gertrude Oliver, half laughingly, half seriously. "Rap wood, Rilla-my-Rilla."

CHAPTER III

*M*oonlit Mirth

Rilla, who still buttoned up her eyes when she went to sleep so that she always looked as if she were laughing in her slumber, yawned, stretched, and smiled at Gertrude Oliver. The latter had come over from Lowbridge the previous evening and had been prevailed upon to remain for the dance at the Four Winds lighthouse the next night.

"The new day is knocking at the window. What will it bring us, I wonder."

Miss Oliver shivered a little. She never greeted the days with Rilla's enthusiasm. She had lived long enough to know that a day may bring a terrible thing.

"*I* think the nicest thing about days is their unexpectedness," went on Rilla. "It's jolly to wake up like this on a golden-fine morning and wonder what surprise packet the day will hand you. I always daydream for ten minutes before I get up, imagining the heaps of splendid things that *may* happen before night."

"I hope something very unexpected will happen today," said Gertrude. "I hope the mail will bring us news that war has been averted between Germany and France."

"Oh—yes," said Rilla vaguely. "It will be dreadful if it isn't, I suppose. But it won't really matter much to us, will it? I think a war would be so exciting. The Boer war was, they say, but I don't remember anything about it, of course. Miss Oliver, shall I wear my white dress tonight or my new green one? The green one is by far the prettier, of course, but I'm almost afraid to wear it to a shore dance for fear something will happen to it. And *will* you do my hair the new way? None of the other girls in the Glen wear it yet and it will make *such* a *sensation*."

"How did you induce your mother to let you go to the dance?"

"Oh, Walter coaxed her over. He knew I would be *heart-broken* if I didn't go. It's my first really-truly grown-up party, Miss Oliver, and I've just lain awake at nights for a week thinking it over. When I saw the sun shining this morning I wanted to whoop for joy. It would be simply *terrible* if it rained tonight. I think I'll wear the green dress and risk it. I want to look my nicest at my first party. Besides, it's an inch longer than my white one. And I'll wear my silver slippers too. Mrs. Ford sent them to me last Christmas and I've never had a chance to wear them yet. They're the dearest things. Oh, Miss Oliver, I do hope some of the boys will ask me to dance. I shall die of mortification—truly I will, if nobody does and I have to sit stuck up against the wall all the evening. Of course Carl and Jerry can't dance because they're the minister's sons, or else I could depend on them to save me from *utter* disgrace."

"You'll have plenty of partners—all the over-harbour boys are coming—there'll be far more boys than girls."

"I'm glad I'm not a minister's daughter," laughed Rilla. "Poor Faith is so furious because she won't dare to dance tonight. Una doesn't care, of course. She has never hankered after dancing. Somebody told Faith there would be a taffy-pull in the kitchen for those who didn't dance and you should have seen the face she made. She and Jem will sit out on the rocks most of the evening, I suppose. Did you know that we are all to walk down as far as that little creek below the old

House of Dreams and then sail to the lighthouse? Won't it just be absolutely divine?"

"When I was fifteen I talked in italics and superlatives too," said Miss Oliver sarcastically. "I think the party promises to be pleasant for young fry. *I* expect to be bored. None of those boys will bother dancing with an old maid like me. Jem and Walter will take me out once out of charity. There will be nobody for me even to talk to. So you can't expect me to look forward to it with your touching young rapture."

"Didn't you have a good time at *your* first party, though, Miss Oliver?"

"No. I had a hateful time. I was shabby and homely and nobody asked me to dance except one boy, homelier and shabbier than myself. He was so awkward I hated him—and even *he* didn't ask me again. I had no real girlhood, Rilla. It's a sad loss. That's why I want you to have a splendid, happy girlhood. And I hope your first party will be one you'll remember all your life with pleasure."

"I dreamed last night I was at the dance and right in the middle of things I discovered I was dressed in my kimono and bedroom shoes," sighed Rilla. "I woke up with a gasp of horror."

"Speaking of dreams—I had an odd one," said Miss Oliver absently. "It was one of those vivid dreams I sometimes have—they are not the vague jumble of ordinary dreams—they are as clear cut and real as life."

"What was your dream?"

"I was standing on the veranda steps, here at Ingleside, looking down over the fields of the Glen. All at once, far in the distance, I saw a long, silvery, glistening wave breaking over them. It came nearer and nearer—just a succession of little white waves like those that break on the sandshore sometimes. The Glen was being swallowed up. I thought, 'Surely the waves will not come near Ingleside'—but they came nearer and nearer—so rapidly—before I could move or call they were breaking right at my feet—and *everything* was gone—there was nothing but a waste of stormy water where the Glen had been. I tried to draw back—and I saw that the edge of my dress was wet *with blood*—and I woke— shivering. I don't like the dream. There was some sinister significance in it. That kind of vivid dream always 'comes true' with me."

"I hope it doesn't mean there's a storm coming up from the east to spoil the party," murmured Rilla anxiously.

"Incorrigible fifteen!" said Miss Oliver dryly. "No, Rilla- my-Rilla, I don't think there is any danger that it foretells anything so awful as *that*."

There had been an undercurrent of tension in the Ingleside existence for several days. Only Rilla, absorbed in her own budding life, was unaware of it. Dr. Blythe had taken to looking grave and saying little over the daily paper. Jem and Walter were keenly interested in the news it brought. Jem sought Walter out in excitement that evening.

"Oh, boy, Germany has declared war on France. This means that England will fight too, probably—and if she does—well, the Piper of your old fancy will have come at last."

"It wasn't a fancy," said Walter slowly. "It was a presenti- ment—a vision—Jem, I really *saw* him for a moment that evening long ago. Suppose England does fight?"

"Why, we'll all have to turn in and help her," cried Jem gaily. "We couldn't let the 'old grey mother of the northern sea' fight it out alone, could we? But you can't go—the typhoid has done you out of that. Sort of a shame, eh?"

Walter did not say whether it was a shame or not. He looked silently over the Glen to the dimpling blue harbour beyond.

"We're the cubs—we've got to pitch in tooth and claw if it comes to a family row," Jem went on cheerfully, rumpling up his red curls with a strong, lean, sensitive brown hand—the hand of the born surgeon, his father often thought. "What an adventure it would be! But I suppose Grey or some of those wary old chaps will patch matters up at the eleventh hour. It'll be a rotten shame if they leave France in the lurch, though. If they don't, we'll see some fun. Well, I suppose it's time to get ready for the spree at the light."

Jem departed whistling "Wi' a hundred pipers and a' and a'," and Walter stood for a long time where he was. There was a little frown on his forehead. This had all come up with the blackness and suddenness of a thundercloud. A few days ago nobody had even thought of such a thing. It was absurd to think of it now. Some way out would be found. War was a hellish, horrible, hideous thing—too horrible and hideous to happen in the twentieth century between civilized nations. The mere thought of it was hideous, and made Walter unhappy in its threat to the beauty of life. He would not think of it—he would resolutely put it out of his mind. How beautiful the old Glen was, in its August ripeness, with its chain of bowery old homesteads, tilled meadows and quiet gardens. The western sky was like a great golden pearl. Far down the harbour was frosted with a dawning moonlight. The air was full of exquisite sounds—sleepy robin whistles, wonderful, mournful, soft murmurs of wind in the twilit trees, rustle of aspen poplars talking in silvery whispers and shaking their dainty, heart-shaped leaves, lilting young laughter from the windows of rooms where the girls were making ready for the dance. The world was steeped in maddening loveliness of sound and colour. He would think only of these things and of the deep, subtle joy they gave him. "Anyhow, no one will expect me to go," he thought. "As Jem says, typhoid has seen to that."

Rilla was leaning out of her room window, dressed for the dance. A yellow pansy slipped from her hair and fell out over the sill like a falling star of gold. She caught at it vainly—but there were enough left. Miss Oliver had woven a little wreath of them for her pet's hair.

"It's so beautifully calm—isn't that splendid? We'll have a perfect night. Listen, Miss Oliver—I can hear those old bells in Rainbow Valley quite clearly. They've been hanging there for over ten years."

"Their wind chime always makes me think of the aerial, celestial music Adam and Eve heard in Milton's Eden," responded Miss Oliver.

"We used to have such fun in Rainbow Valley when we were children," said Rilla dreamily.

Nobody ever played in Rainbow Valley now. It was very silent on summer evenings. Walter liked to go there to read. Jem and Faith trysted there considerably; Jerry and Nan went there to pursue uninterruptedly the ceaseless wrangles and arguments on profound subjects that seemed to be their preferred method of sweethearting. And Rilla had a beloved little sylvan dell of her own there where she liked to sit and dream.

"I must run down to the kitchen before I go and show myself off to Susan. She would never forgive me if I didn't."

Rilla whirled into the shadowy kitchen at Ingleside, where Susan was prosaically darning socks, and lighted it up with her beauty. She wore her green dress with its little pink daisy garlands, her silk stockings and silver slippers. She had golden pansies in her hair and at her creamy throat. She was so pretty and young and glowing that even Cousin Sophia Crawford was compelled to admire her—and Cousin Sophia Crawford admired few transient earthly things. Cousin Sophia and Susan had made up, or ignored, their old feud since the former had come to live in the Glen, and Cousin Sophia often came across in the evenings to make a neighbourly call. Susan did not always welcome her rapturously for Cousin Sophia was not what could be called an exhilarating companion. "Some calls are visits and some are visitations, Mrs. Dr. dear," Susan said once, and left it to be inferred that Cousin Sophia's were the latter.

Cousin Sophia had a long, pale, wrinkled face, a long, thin nose, a long, thin mouth, and very long, thin, pale hands, generally folded resignedly on her black calico lap. Everything about her seemed long and thin and pale. She looked mournfully upon Rilla Blythe and said sadly,

"Is your hair all your own?"

"Of course it is," cried Rilla indignantly.

"Ah, well!" Cousin Sophia sighed. "It might be better for you if it wasn't! Such a lot of hair takes from a person's strength. It's a sign of consumption, I've heard, but I hope it won't turn out like that in your case. I s'pose you'll all be dancing tonight—even the minister's boys most likely. I s'pose his girls won't go that far. Ah, well, I never held with dancing. I knew a girl once who dropped dead while she was dancing. How any one could ever dance again after a judgment like that I cannot comprehend."

"*Did* she ever dance again?" asked Rilla pertly.

"I told you she dropped dead. Of course she never danced again, poor creature. She was a Kirke from Lowbridge. You ain't a-going off like that with nothing on your bare neck, are you?"

"It's a hot evening," protested Rilla. "But I'll put on a scarf when we go on the water."

"I knew of a boat load of young folks who went sailing on that harbour forty years ago just such a night as this—just *exactly* such a night as this," said Cousin Sophia lugubriously, "and they were upset and drowned—every last one of them. Ah, well, I hope nothing like that'll happen to you tonight. Do you ever try anything for the freckles? I used to find plaintain juice real good."

"You certainly should be a judge of freckles, Cousin Sophia," said Susan, rushing to Rilla's defence. "You were more speckled than any toad when you was a girl. Rilla's only come in summer but yours stayed put, season in and season out; and you had not a ground colour like hers behind them neither. You look real nice, Rilla, and that way of fixing your hair is becoming. But you are not going to walk to the harbour in those slippers, are you?"

"Oh, no. We'll all wear our old shoes to the harbour and carry our slippers. Do you like my dress, Susan?"

"It minds me of a dress I wore when I was a girl," sighed Cousin Sophia before Susan could reply. "It was green with pink posies in it, too, and it was flounced from the waist to the hem. We didn't wear the skimpy things girls wear nowadays. Ah me, times has changed and not for the better I'm afraid. I tore a big hole in it that night and some one spilled a cup of tea all over it. Ruined it completely. But I hope nothing will happen to your dress. It orter to be a bit longer I'm thinking—your legs are so terrible long and thin."

"Mrs. Dr. Blythe does not approve of little girls dressing like grown-up ones," said Susan stiffly, intending merely a snub to Cousin Sophia. But Rilla felt insulted. A little girl indeed! She whisked out of the kitchen in high dudgeon. Another time she wouldn't go down to show herself off to Susan—Susan, who thought nobody was grown up until she was sixty! And that horrid Cousin Sophia with her digs about freckles and legs! What business had an old—an old *beanpole* like that to talk of anybody else being long and thin? Rilla felt all her pleasure in herself and her evening clouded and spoiled. The very teeth of her soul were set on edge and she could have sat down and cried.

But later on her spirits rose again when she found herself one of the gay crowd bound for the Four Winds light.

The Blythes left Ingleside to the melancholy music of howls from Dog Monday, who was locked up in the barn lest he make an uninvited guest at the light. They picked up the Merediths in the village, and others joined them as they walked down the old harbour road. Mary Vance, resplendent in blue crepe, with lace overdress, came out of Miss Cornelia's gate and attached herself to Rilla and Miss Oliver who were walking together and who did not welcome her over-warmly. Rilla was not very fond of Mary Vance. She had never forgotten the humiliating day when Mary had chased her through the village with a dried codfish. Mary Vance, to tell the truth, was not exactly popular with any of her set. Still, they enjoyed her society—she had such a biting tongue that it was stimulating. "Mary Vance is a habit of ours—we can't do without her even when we are furious with her," Di Blythe had once said.

Most of the little crowd were paired off after a fashion. Jem walked with Faith Meredith, of course, and Jerry Meredith with Nan Blythe. Di and Walter were together, deep in confidential conversation which Rilla envied.

Carl Meredith was walking with Miranda Pryor, more to torment Joe Milgrave than for any other reason. Joe was known to have a strong hankering for the said Miranda, which shyness prevented him from indulging on all occasions. Joe might summon enough courage to amble up beside Miranda if the night were dark, but here, in this moonlit dusk, he simply could not do it. So he trailed along after the procession and thought things not lawful to be uttered of Carl Meredith. Miranda was the daughter of Whiskers-on-the-moon; she did not share her father's unpopularity but she was not much run after, being a pale, neutral little creature, somewhat addicted to nervous giggling. She had silvery blonde hair and her eyes were big china blue orbs that looked as if she had been badly frightened when she was little and had never got over it. She would much rather have walked with Joe than with Carl, with whom she did not feel in the least at home. Yet it was something of an honour, too, to have a college boy beside her, and a son of the manse at that.

Shirley Blythe was with Una Meredith and both were rather silent because such was their nature. Shirley was a lad of sixteen, sedate, sensible, thoughtful, full of a quiet humour. He was Susan's "little brown boy" yet, with his brown hair, brown eyes and clear brown skin. He liked to walk with Una Meredith because she never tried to make him talk or badgered him with chatter. Una was as sweet and shy as she had been in the Rainbow Valley days, and her large, dark-blue eyes were as dreamy and wistful. She had a secret, carefully-hidden fancy for Walter Blythe which nobody but Rilla ever suspected. Rilla sympathized with it and wished Walter would return it. She liked Una better than Faith, whose beauty and aplomb rather overshadowed other girls—and Rilla did not enjoy being overshadowed.

But just now she was very happy. It was so delightful to be tripping with her friends down that dark, gleaming road sprinkled with its little spruces and firs, whose balsam made all the air resinous around them. Meadows of sunset afterlight were behind the westering hills. Before them was the shining harbour. A bell was ringing in the little church over-harbour and the lingering dream-notes died around the dim, amethystine points. The gulf beyond was still silvery blue in the afterlight. Oh, it was all glorious—the clear air with its salt tang, the balsam of the firs, the laughter of her friends. Rilla loved life—its bloom and brilliance; she loved the ripple of music, the hum of merry conversation; she wanted to walk on forever over this road of silver and shadow. It was her first party and she was going to have a splendid time. There was nothing in the world to worry about—not even freckles and over-long legs—nothing except one little haunting fear that nobody would ask her to dance. It was beautiful and satisfying just to be alive—to be fifteen—to be pretty. Rilla drew a long breath of rapture—and caught it midway rather sharply. Jem was telling some story to Faith—something that had happened in the Balkan war.

"The doctor lost both his legs—they were smashed to pulp—and he was left on the field to die. And he crawled about from man to man, to all the wounded men around him, as long as he could, and did everything possible to relieve their sufferings—never thinking of himself—he was tying a bit of bandage around another man's leg when he went under. They found him there, the doctor's dead hands still held the bandage tight, the bleeding was stopped and the other man's life was saved. Some hero, wasn't he, Faith? I tell you when I read that—"

Jem and Faith moved on out of hearing. Gertrude Oliver suddenly shivered. Rilla pressed her arm sympathetically.

"Wasn't it dreadful, Miss Oliver? I don't wonder it made you shiver. I don't know why Jem tells such gruesome things at a time like this when we're all out for fun."

"Do you think it dreadful, Rilla? I thought it wonderful—beautiful. Such a story makes one ashamed of ever doubting human nature. That man's action was god-like. And how humanity responds to the ideal of self-sacrifice! As for my shiver, I don't know what caused it. The evening is certainly warm enough. Perhaps some one is walking over the dark, starshiny spot that is to be my grave. That is the explanation the old superstition would give. Well, I won't think of that on this lovely night. Do you know, Rilla, that when night-time comes I'm always glad I live in the country. We know the real charm of night here as town dwellers never do. Every night is beautiful in the country—even the stormy ones. I love a wild night storm on this old gulf shore. As for a night like this, it is almost *too* beautiful—it belongs to youth and dreamland and I'm half afraid of it."

"I feel as if I were part of it," said Rilla.

"Ah yes, you're young enough not to be afraid of perfect things. Well, here we are at the House of Dreams. It seems lonely this summer. The Fords didn't come?"

"No—at least Mr. and Mrs. Ford and Persis didn't. Kenneth did—but he stayed with his mother's people over-harbour. We haven't seen a great deal of him this summer. He's a little lame, so didn't go about very much."

"Lame? What happened to him?"

"He broke his ankle in a football game last fall and was laid up most of the winter. He has limped a little ever since but it is getting better all the time and he expects it will be all right before long. He has been up to Ingleside only twice."

"Ethel Reese is simply crazy about him," said Mary Vance.

"She hasn't got the sense she was born with where he is concerned. He walked home with her from the over-harbour church last prayer meeting night and the airs she has put on since would really make you weary of life. As if a Toronto boy like Ken Ford would ever really think of a country girl like Ethel!"

Rilla flushed. It did not matter to her if Kenneth Ford walked home with Ethel Reese a dozen times—it did *not*! *Nothing* that he did mattered to her. He was ages older than she was. He chummed with Nan and Di and Faith, and looked upon her, Rilla, as a child whom he never noticed except to tease. And she detested Ethel Reese and Ethel Reese hated her,—always had hated her since Walter had pummelled Dan so notoriously in Rainbow Valley days; but why need she be thought beneath Kenneth Ford's notice because she was a country girl, pray? As for Mary Vance, she was getting to be an out-and-out gossip and thought of nothing but who walked home with people!

There was a little pier on the harbour shore below the House of Dreams, and two boats were moored there. One boat was skippered by Jem Blythe, the other by Joe Milgrave, who knew all about boats and was nothing loth to let Miranda Pryor see it. They raced down the harbour and Joe's boat won. More boats were coming down from the Harbour Head and across the harbour from the western side. Everywhere there was laughter. The big white tower on Four Winds Point was overflowing with light, while its revolving beacon flashed overhead. A family from Charlottetown, relatives of the light's keeper, were summering at the light, and they were giving the party to which all the young people of Four Winds and Glen St. Mary and over-harbour had been invited. As Jem's boat swung in below the lighthouse Rilla desperately snatched off her shoes and donned her silver slippers behind Miss Oliver's screening back. A glance had told her that the rock-cut steps climbing up to the light were lined with boys, and lighted by Chinese lanterns, and she was determined she would *not* walk up those steps in the heavy shoes her mother had insisted on her wearing for the road. The slippers pinched abominably, but nobody would have suspected it as Rilla tripped smilingly up the steps, her soft dark eyes glowing and questioning, her colour deepening richly on her round, creamy cheeks. The very minute she reached the top of the steps an over-harbour boy asked her to dance and the next moment they were in the pavilion that had been built seaward of the lighthouse for dances. It was a delightful spot, roofed over with fir boughs and hung with lanterns. Beyond was the sea in a radiance that glowed and shimmered, to the left the moonlit crests and hollows of the sand dunes, to the right the rocky shore with its inky shadows and its crystalline coves. Rilla and her partner swung in among the dancers; she drew a long breath of delight; what witching music Ned Burr of the Upper Glen was coaxing from his fiddle—it was really like the magical pipes of the old tale which compelled all who heard them to dance. How cool and fresh the gulf breeze blew; how white and wonderful the moonlight was over everything! This was life—enchanting life. Rilla felt as if her feet and her soul both had wings.

CHAPTER IV

The Piper Pipes

Rilla's first party was a triumph—or so it seemed at first. She had so many partners that she had to split her dances. Her silver slippers seemed verily to dance of themselves and though they continued to pinch her toes and blister her heels that did not interfere with her enjoyment in the least. Ethel Reese gave her a bad ten minutes by beckoning her mysteriously out of the pavilion and whispering, with a Reese-like smirk, that her dress gaped behind and that there was a stain on the flounce. Rilla rushed miserably to the room in the lighthouse which was fitted up for a temporary ladies' dressing room, and discovered that the stain was merely a tiny grass smear and that the gap was equally tiny where a hook had pulled loose. Irene Howard fastened it up for her and gave her some over-sweet, condescending compliments. Rilla felt flattered by Irene's condescension. She was an Upper Glen girl of nineteen who seemed to like the society of the younger girls—spiteful friends said because she could queen it over them without rivalry. But Rilla thought Irene quite wonderful and loved her for her patronage. Irene was pretty and stylish; she sang *divinely* and spent every winter in Charlottetown taking music lessons. She had an aunt in Montreal who sent her wonderful things to wear; she was reported to have had a sad love affair—nobody knew just what, but its very mystery allured. Rilla felt that Irene's compliments crowned her evening. She ran gaily back to the pavilion and lingered for a moment in the glow of the lanterns at the entrance looking at the dancers. A momentary break in the whirling throng gave her a glimpse of Kenneth Ford standing at the other side.

Rilla's heart skipped a beat—or, if that be a physiological impossibility, she thought it did. So he was here, after all. She had concluded he was not coming—not that it mattered in the least. Would he see her? Would he take any notice of her? Of course, he wouldn't ask her to dance—*that* couldn't be hoped for. He thought her just a mere child. He had called her "Spider" not three weeks ago when he had been at Ingleside one evening. She had cried about it upstairs after-wards and hated him. But her heart skipped another beat when she saw that he was edging his way around the side of the pavilion towards her. Was he coming to her—was he?—was he?—yes, he was! He was looking for her—he was here beside her—he was gazing down at her with something in his dark grey eyes that Rilla had never seen in them. Oh, it was almost too much to bear! And everything was going on as before—the dancers were spinning around, the boys who couldn't get partners were hanging about the pavilion, canoodling couples were sitting out on the rocks—nobody seemed to realize what a stupendous thing had happened.

Kenneth was a tall lad, very good looking, with a certain careless grace of bearing that somehow made all the other boys seem stiff and awkward by contrast. He was reported to be awesomely clever, with the glamour of a faraway city and a big university hanging around him. He had also the reputa-tion of being a bit of a lady-killer. But that probably accrued to him from his possession of a laughing, velvety voice which no girl could hear without a heartbeat, and a dangerous way of listening as if she were saying something that he had longed all his life to hear.

"Is this Rilla-my-Rilla?" he asked in a low tone.

"Yeth," said Rilla, and immediately wished she could throw herself headlong down the lighthouse rock or otherwise vanish from a jeering world.

Rilla had lisped in early childhood; but she had grown out of it pretty thoroughly. Only on occasions of stress and strain did the tendency re-assert itself. She hadn't lisped for a year; and now at this very moment, when she was so especially desirous of appearing grown up and sophisticated, she must go and lisp like a baby! It was too mortifying; she felt as if tears were going to come into her eyes; the next minute she would be—blubbering—yes, just blubbering—she wished Kenneth would go away—she wished he had never come. The party was spoiled. Everything had turned to dust and ashes.

And he had called her "Rilla-my-Rilla"—not "Spider" or "Kid" or "Puss," as he had been used to call her when he took any notice whatever of her. She did not at all resent his using Walter's pet name for her; it sounded beautifully in his low caressing tones, with just the faintest suggestion of emphasis on the "my." It would have been so nice if she had not made a fool of herself. She dared not look up lest she should see laughter in his eyes. So she looked down; and as her lashes were very long and dark and her lids very thick and creamy, the effect was quite charming and provocative, and Kenneth reflected that Rilla Blythe was going to be the beauty of the Ingleside girls after all. He wanted to make her look up—to catch again that little, demure, questioning glance. She was the prettiest thing at the party, there was no doubt of that.

What was he saying? Rilla could hardly believe her ears.

"Can we have a dance?"

"Yes," said Rilla. She said it with such a fierce determination not to lisp that she fairly blurted the word out. Then she writhed in spirit again. It sounded so bold—so eager—as if she were fairly jumping at him! *What* would he think of her? Oh, why did dreadful things like this happen, just when a girl wanted to appear at her best?

Kenneth drew her in among the dancers.

"I think this game ankle of mine is good for one hop around, at least," he said.

"How *is* your ankle?" said Rilla. Oh, why couldn't she think of something else to say? She *knew* he was sick of inquiries about his ankle. She had heard him say so at Ingleside—heard him tell Di he was going to wear a placard on his breast announcing to all and sundry that the ankle was improving, etc., etc. And now she must go and ask this stale question again.

Kenneth *was* tired of inquiries about his ankle. But then he had not often been asked about it by lips with such an adorable kissable dent just above them. Perhaps that was why he answered very patiently that it was getting on well and didn't trouble him much, if he didn't walk or stand too long at a time.

"They tell me it will be as strong as ever in time, but I'll have to cut football out this fall."

They danced together and Rilla knew every girl in sight envied her. After the dance they went down the rock steps and Kenneth found a little flat and they rowed across the moonlit channel to the sandshore; they walked on the sand till Kenneth's ankle made protest and then they sat down among the dunes. Kenneth talked to her as he had talked to Nan and Di. Rilla, overcome with a shyness she did not understand, could not talk much, and thought he would think her frightfully stupid; but in spite of this it was all very wonderful—the exquisite moonlit night, the shining sea, the tiny little wavelets swishing on the sand, the cool and freakish wind of night crooning in the stiff grasses on the crest of the dunes, the music sounding faintly and sweetly over the channel.

"'A merry lilt o' moonlight for mermaiden revelry,'" quoted Kenneth softly from one of Walter's poems.

And just he and she alone together in the glamour of sound and sight! If only her slippers didn't bite so! And if only she could talk cleverly like Miss Oliver—nay, if she could only talk as she did herself to other boys! But words would not come, she could only listen and murmur little commonplace sentences now and again. But perhaps her dreamy eyes and her dented lip and her slender throat talked eloquently for her. At any rate Kenneth seemed in no hurry to suggest going back and when they did go back supper was in progress. He found a seat for her near the window of the lighthouse kitchen and sat on the sill beside her while she ate her ices and cake. Rilla looked about her and thought how lovely her first party had been. She would *never* forget it. The room re-echoed to laughter and jest. Beautiful young eyes sparkled and shone. From the pavilion outside came the lilt of the fiddle and the rhythmic steps of the dancers.

There was a little disturbance among a group of boys crowded about the door; a young fellow pushed through and halted on the threshold, looking about him rather sombrely. It was Jack Elliott from over-harbour—a McGill medical student, a quiet chap not much addicted to social doings. He had been invited to the party but had not been expected to come since he had to go to Charlottetown that day and could not be back until late. Yet here he was—and he carried a folded paper in his hand.

Gertrude Oliver looked at him from her corner and shivered again. She had enjoyed the party herself, after all, for she had foregathered with a Charlottetown acquaintance who, being a stranger and much older than most of the guests, felt himself rather out of it, and had been glad to fall in with this clever girl who could talk of world doings and outside events with the zest and vigour of a man. In the pleasure of his society she had forgotten some of her misgivings of the day. Now they suddenly returned to her. What news did Jack Elliott bring? Lines from an old poem flashed unbidden into her mind—"there was a sound of revelry by night"—"Hush! Hark! A deep sound strikes like a rising knell"—why should she think of that now? Why didn't Jack Elliott speak—if he had anything to tell? Why did he just stand there, glowering importantly?

"Ask him—ask him," she said feverishly to Allan Daly. But somebody else had already asked him. The room grew very silent all at once. Outside the fiddler had stopped for a rest and there was silence there too. Afar off they heard the low moan of the gulf—the presage of a storm already on its way up the Atlantic. A girl's laugh drifted up from the rocks and died away as if frightened out of existence by the sudden stillness.

"England declared war on Germany today," said Jack Elliott slowly. "The news came by wire just as I left town."

"God help us," whispered Gertrude Oliver under her breath. "My dream—my dream! The first wave has broken." She looked at Allan Daly and tried to smile.

"Is this Armageddon?" she asked.

"I'm afraid so," he said gravely.

A chorus of exclamations had arisen round them—light surprise and idle interest for the most part. Few there realized the import of the message—fewer still realized that it meant anything to them. Before long the dancing was on again and the hum of pleasure was as loud as ever. Gertrude and Allan

Daly talked the news over in low, troubled tones. Walter Blythe had turned pale and left the room. Outside he met Jem, hurrying up the rock steps.

"Have you heard the news, Jem?"

"Yes. The Piper has come. Hurrah! I knew England wouldn't leave France in the lurch. I've been trying to get Captain Josiah to hoist the flag but he says it isn't the proper caper till sunrise. Jack says they'll be calling for volunteers tomorrow."

"What a fuss to make over nothing," said Mary Vance disdainfully as Jem dashed off. She was sitting out with Miller Douglas on a lobster trap which was not only an unromantic but an uncomfortable seat. But Mary and Miller were both supremely happy on it, which was the main thing. Miller Douglas was a big, strapping, uncouth lad, who thought Mary Vance's tongue uncommonly gifted and Mary Vance's white eyes stars of the first magnitude; and neither of them had the least inkling why Jem Blythe wanted to hoist the lighthouse flag. "What does it matter if there's going to be a war over there in Europe? I'm sure it doesn't concern us."

Walter looked at her and had one of his odd visitations of prophecy.

"Before this war is over," he said—or something said through his lips—"every man and woman and child in Canada will feel it—you, Mary, will feel it—feel it to your heart's core. You will weep tears of blood over it. The Piper has come—and he will pipe until every corner of the world has heard his awful and irresistible music. It will be years before the dance of death is over—years, Mary. And in those years millions of hearts will break."

"Fancy now!" said Mary, who always said that when she couldn't think of anything else to say. She didn't know what

Walter meant but she felt uncomfortable. Walter Blythe was always saying odd things. That old Piper of his—she hadn't heard anything about him since their playdays in Rainbow Valley—and now here he was bobbing up again. She didn't like it, that was the long and short of it, and she wasn't going to listen to such nonsense.

"Aren't you painting it rather strong, Walter?" asked Harvey Crawford, coming up just then. "This war won't last for years—it'll be over in a month or two. England will just wipe Germany off the map in no time."

"Do you think a war for which Germany has been preparing for twenty years will be over in a few weeks?" said Walter passionately. "This isn't a paltry struggle in a Balkan corner, Harvey. It is a death grapple. Germany comes to conquer or to die. And do you know what will happen if she conquers? Canada will be a German colony."

"Well, I guess a few things will happen before *that*," said Harvey shrugging his shoulders. "The British navy would have to be licked for one; and for another, Miller here, now, and I, *we'd* raise a dust, wouldn't we, Miller? No Germans need apply for this old country, eh?"

Harvey ran down the steps laughing.

"I declare, I think all you boys talk the craziest stuff," said Mary Vance in disgust. She got up and dragged Miller off to the rock shore. It didn't happen often that they had a chance for a talk together; Mary was determined that this one shouldn't be spoiled by Walter Blythe's silly blather about Pipers and Germans and such like absurd things. They left Walter standing alone on the rock steps, looking out over the beauty of Four Winds with brooding eyes that saw it not.

The best of the evening was over for Rilla, too. Ever since Jack Elliott's announcement she had sensed that Kenneth was no longer thinking about her. She felt suddenly lonely and unhappy. It was worse than if he had never noticed her at all. Was life like this—something delightful happening and then, just as you were revelling in it, slipping away from you? Rilla told herself pathetically that she felt years older than when she had left home that evening. Perhaps she did—perhaps she was. Who knows? It does not do to laugh at the pangs of youth. They are very terrible because youth has not yet learned that "this, too, will pass away." Rilla sighed and wished she were home, in bed, crying into her pillow.

"Tired?" said Kenneth, gently but absently—oh, so absently. He really didn't care a bit whether she were tired or not, she thought.

"Kenneth," she ventured timidly, "you don't think this war will matter much to us in Canada, do you?"

"Matter? Of course it will matter to the lucky fellows who will be able to take a hand. I won't—thanks to this confounded ankle. Rotten luck, I call it."

"I don't see why we should fight England's battles," cried Rilla. "She's quite able to fight them herself."

"That isn't the point. We are part of the British Empire. It's a family affair. We've got to stand by each other. The worst of it is, it will all be over before I can be of any use."

"Do you mean that you would really volunteer to go if it wasn't for your ankle?" asked Rilla incredulously. The idea seemed so—so ridiculous.

"Sure I would. You see they'll go by thousands. Jem'll be off, I'll bet a cent—Walter won't be strong enough yet, I suppose. And Jerry Meredith—he'll go! Oh, boys! And I was worrying about being out of football this year!"

Rilla was too startled to say anything. Jem—and Jerry! Nonsense! Why father and Mr. Meredith wouldn't allow it.

They weren't through college. Oh, why hadn't Jack Elliott kept his horrid news to himself?

Mark Warren came up and asked her to dance. Rilla went, knowing Kenneth didn't care whether she went or stayed. An hour ago on the sandshore he had been looking at her as if she were the only being of any importance in the world. And now she was nobody. His thoughts were full of this Great Game which was to be played out on blood-stained fields with empires for stakes—a Game in which womenkind could have no part. Women, thought Rilla miserably, just had to sit and cry at home. But all this was foolishness. Kenneth couldn't go—he admitted that himself—and Walter couldn't—thank goodness for that—and Jem and Jerry would have more sense. She *wouldn't* worry—she *would* enjoy herself. But how awkward Mark Warren was! How he bungled his steps! Why, for mercy's sake, did boys try to dance who didn't know the first thing about dancing; and who had feet as big as boats? There, he had bumped her into somebody! She would *never* dance with him again.

But she danced with others, though the zest was gone out of the performance and she had begun to realize that her slippers hurt her badly. Kenneth seemed to have gone—at least nothing was to be seen of him. After all, her first party was spoiled, though it had seemed so beautiful at one time. Her head ached—her toes burned. And worse was yet to come. She had gone down with some over-harbour friends to the rock shore where they all lingered as dance after dance went on above them. It was cool and pleasant and they were tired. Rilla sat silent, taking no part in the gay conversation. She was glad when some one called down that the over-harbour boats were leaving. A laughing scramble up the lighthouse rock followed. A few couples still whirled about in the pavilion but the crowd had thinned out. Rilla looked about her for the Glen group. She could not see one of them. She ran into the lighthouse. Still, no sign of anybody. In dismay she ran to the rock steps, down which the over-harbour guests were hurrying. She could see the boats below—where was Jem's—where was Joe's?

"Why, Rilla Blythe, I thought you'd gone home long ago," said Mary Vance, who was waving her scarf at a boat skimming up the channel, skippered by Miller Douglas.

"Where are the rest?" gasped Rilla.

"Why, they're gone—Jem went an hour ago—Una had a headache. And the rest went with Joe about fifteen minutes ago. See—they're just going round Birch Point. I didn't go because it's getting rough and I knew I'd be seasick. I don't mind walking home from here. It's only a mile and a half. I s'posed you'd gone. Where were you?"

"Down on the rocks with Jen and Mollie Crawford. Oh, why didn't they look for me?"

"They did—but you couldn't be found. Then they concluded you must have gone in the other boat. Don't worry. You can stay all night with me and we'll 'phone up to Ingleside where you are."

Rilla realized that there was nothing else to do. Her lips trembled and tears came into her eyes. She blinked savagely— she would *not* let Mary Vance see her crying. But to be forgotten like this! To think nobody had thought it worth while to make sure where she was—not even Walter. Then she had a sudden dismayed recollection.

"My shoes," she exclaimed. "I left them in the boat."

"Well, I never," said Mary. "You're the most thoughtless kid *I* ever saw. You'll have to ask Hazel Lewison to lend you a pair of shoes."

"I won't," cried Rilla, who didn't like the said Hazel. "I'll go barefoot first."

Mary shrugged her shoulders.

"Just as you like. Pride must suffer pain. It'll teach you to be more careful. Well, let's hike."

Accordingly they hiked. But to "hike" along a deep-rutted, pebbly lane, in frail, silver-hued slippers with high French heels, is not an exhilarating performance. Rilla managed to limp and totter along until they reached the harbour road; but she could go no further in those detestable slippers. The pain simply could not be borne. She took them and her dear silk stockings off and started barefoot. That was not pleasant either; her feet were very tender and the pebbles and ruts of the road hurt them. Her blistered heels smarted. But physical pain was almost forgotten in the sting of her humiliation. This was a nice predicament! If Kenneth Ford could see her now, limping along like a little girl with a stone bruise! Oh, what a horrid way for her lovely party to end! She just *had* to cry—it was too terrible. Nobody cared for her—nobody bothered about her at all. Well, if she caught cold from walking home barefoot on a dew-wet road and went into a decline perhaps they would be sorry. She furtively wiped her tears away with her scarf—handkerchiefs seemed to have vanished like shoes!—but she could not help sniffling. Worse and worse!

"You've got a cold, I see," said Mary. "You ought to have known you would, sitting down in the wind on those rocks. Your mother won't let you out again in a hurry I can tell you. It's certainly been something of a party. The Lewisons know how to do things, I'll say that for them, though Hazel Lewison is no choice of mine. My, how black she looked when she saw you dancing with Ken Ford. And so did that little hussy of an Ethel Reese. What a flirt he is!"

"I don't think he's a flirt," said Rilla as defiantly as two desperate sniffs would let her.

"Oh well, you'll know more about men when you're as old as I am," said Mary patronizingly. "Mind you, it doesn't do to believe all they tell you. Don't let Ken Ford think that all he has to do to get you on the string is to drop his handkerchief. Have more spirit than that, child."

To be thus hectored and patronized by Mary Vance was unendurable! And it was unendurable to walk on stony roads with blistered heels and bare feet! And it was unendurable to be crying and have no handkerchief and not to be able to stop crying!

"I'm not thinking"—sniff—"about Kenneth"—sniff— "Ford"—two sniffs—"at *all*," cried tortured Rilla.

"There's no need to fly off the handle, child. You ought to be willing to take advice from older people. *I* saw how you slipped over to the sands with Ken and stayed there ever so long with him. Your mother wouldn't like it if she knew."

"I'll tell my mother all about it—and Miss Oliver—and Walter," Rilla gasped between sniffs. "*You* sat for *hours* with Miller Douglas on that lobster trap, Mary Vance! What would Mrs. Elliott say to *that* if *she* knew?"

"Oh, I'm not going to quarrel with you," said Mary, suddenly retreating to high and lofty ground. "All *I* say is, you should wait until you're grown up before you do things like that."

Rilla gave up trying to hide the fact that she was crying. *Everything* was spoiled—even that beautiful, dreamy, romantic, moonlit hour with Kenneth on the sands was vulgarized and cheapened. She loathed Mary Vance.

"Why, whatever's wrong?" cried mystified Mary. "What are you crying for?"

"My feet—hurt so—" sobbed Rilla, clinging to the last shred of her pride. It was less humiliating to admit crying because of your feet than because—because somebody had been amusing himself with you, and your friends had forgotten you, and other people patronized you.

"I daresay they are," said Mary, not unkindly. "Never mind. I know where there's a pot of goose grease in Cornelia's tidy pantry and it beats all the fancy cold creams in the world. I'll put some on your heels before you go to bed."

Goose grease on your heels! So this was what your first party and your first beau and your first moonlit romance ended in!

Rilla gave over crying in sheer disgust at the futility of tears and went to sleep in Mary Vance's bed in the calm of despair. Outside, the dawn came greyly in on wings of storm; Captain Josiah, true to his word, ran up the Union Jack at the Four Winds Light and it streamed on the fierce wind against the clouded sky like a gallant unquenchable beacon.

CHAPTER V

"*T*he Sound of a Going"

Rilla ran down through the sunlit glory of the maple grove behind Ingleside, to her favourite nook in Rainbow Valley. She sat down on a green-mossed stone among the fern, propped her chin on her hands and stared unseeingly at the dazzling blue sky of the August afternoon—so blue, so peaceful, so unchanged, just as it had arched over the valley in the mellow days of late summer ever since she could remember.

She wanted to be alone—to think things out—to adjust herself, if it were possible, to the new world into which she seemed to have been transplanted with a suddenness and completeness that left her half bewildered as to her own identity. Was she—could she be—the same Rilla Blythe who had danced at Four Winds Light six days ago—only six days ago? It seemed to Rilla that she had lived as much in those six days as in all her previous life—and if it be true that we should count time by heart-throbs she had. That evening, with its hopes and fears and triumphs and humiliations, seemed like ancient history now. Could she really ever have cried just because she had been forgotten and had to walk home with Mary Vance? Ah, thought Rilla sadly, how trivial and absurd such a cause of tears now appeared to her. She *could* cry *now* with a right good will—but she would *not*—she *must* not. What was it mother had said, looking, with her white lips and stricken eyes, as Rilla had never seen her mother look before,

*"'When our women fail in courage,
Shall our men be fearless still?'"*

Yes, that was it. She must be brave—like mother—and Nan—and Faith—Faith, who had cried with flashing eyes, "Oh, if I were only a man, to go too!" Only, when her eyes ached and her throat burned like this she had to hide herself in Rainbow Valley for a little, just to think things out and remember that she wasn't a child any longer—she was grown up and women had to face things like this. But it was—nice—to get away alone now and then, where nobody could see her and where she needn't feel that people thought her a little coward if some tears came in spite of her.

How sweet and woodsy the ferns smelled! How softly the great feathery boughs of the firs waved and murmured over her! How elfinly rang the bells on the "Tree Lovers"—just a tinkle now and then as the breeze swept by! How purple and elusive the haze where incense was being offered on many an altar of the hills! How the maple leaves whitened in the wind until the grove seemed covered with pale silvery blossoms! Everything was just the same as she had seen it hundreds of times; and yet the whole face of the world seemed changed.

"How wicked I was to wish that something dramatic would happen!" she thought. "Oh, if we could only have those dear, monotonous, pleasant days back again! I would never, *never* grumble about them again."

Rilla's world had tumbled to pieces the very day after the party. As they lingered around the dinner table at Ingleside, talking of the war, the telephone had rung. It was a long-distance call from Charlottetown for Jem. When he had finished talking he hung up the receiver and turned around, with a flushed face and glowing eyes. Before he had said a word his mother and Nan and Di had turned pale. As for Rilla, for the first time in her life she felt that everyone must hear her heart beating and that something had clutched at her throat.

"They are calling for volunteers in town, father," said Jem. "Scores have joined up already. I'm going in tonight to enlist."

"Oh—Little Jem," cried Mrs. Blythe brokenly. She had not called him that for many years—not since the day he had rebelled against it. "Oh—no—no—Little Jem."

"I must, mother. I'm right—am I not, father?" said Jem.

Dr. Blythe had risen. He was very pale, too, and his voice was husky. But he did not hesitate.

"Yes, Jem, yes—if you feel that way, yes—"

Mrs. Blythe covered her face. Walter stared moodily at his plate. Nan and Di clasped each other's hands. Shirley tried to look unconcerned. Susan sat as if paralyzed, her piece of pie half-eaten on her plate. Susan never did finish that piece of pie—a fact which bore eloquent testimony to the upheaval in her inner woman for Susan considered it a cardinal offence against civilized society to begin to eat anything and not finish it. That was wilful waste, hens to the contrary notwithstanding.

Jem turned to the 'phone again. "I must ring the manse. Jerry will want to go, too."

At this Nan had cried out "Oh!" as if a knife had been thrust into her, and rushed from the room. Di followed her. Rilla turned to Walter for comfort but Walter was lost to her in some reverie she could not share.

"All right," Jem was saying, as coolly as if he were arranging the details of a picnic. "I thought you would—yes, tonight—the seven o'clock—meet me at the station. So 'long."

"Mrs. Dr. dear," said poor Susan, pushing away her pie. "I wish you would wake me up. Am I dreaming—or am I awake?

Does that blessed boy realize what he is saying? Does he mean that he is going to enlist as a soldier? You do not mean to tell me that they want children like him! It is an outrage. Surely you and the doctor will not permit it."

"We can't stop him," said Mrs. Blythe, chokingly. "Oh, Gilbert!"

Dr. Blythe came up behind his wife and took her hand gently, looking down into the sweet grey eyes which he had only once before seen filled with such imploring anguish as now. They both thought of that other time—the day years ago in the House of Dreams when little Joyce had died.

"Would you have him stay, Anne—when the others are going—when he thinks it his duty—would you have him so selfish and small-souled?"

"No—no! But—oh—our first born son—he's only a lad—Gilbert—I'll try to be brave after awhile—just now I can't. It's all come so suddenly. Give me time."

The doctor and his wife went out of the room. Jem had gone—Walter had gone—Shirley got up to go. Rilla and Susan remained staring at each other across the deserted table. Rilla had not yet cried—she was too stunned for tears. Then she saw that Susan was crying—Susan, whom she had never seen shed a tear before.

"Oh, Susan, will he really go?" she asked.

"It—it—it is just ridiculous, that is what it is," said Susan. She wiped away her tears, gulped resolutely and got up.

"I am going to wash the dishes. That has to be done, even if everybody has gone crazy. There now, dearie, do not you cry. Jem will go, most likely—but the war will be over long before he gets anywhere near it. Let us take a brace and not worry your poor mother."

"In the *Enterprise* today it was reported that Lord Kitchener says the war will last three years," said Rilla dubiously.

"I am not acquainted with Lord Kitchener," said Susan, composedly, "but I daresay he makes mistakes as often as other people. Your father says it will be over in a few months and I have as much faith in *his* opinion as I have in Lord Anybody's. So just let us be calm and trust in the Almighty and get this place tidied up. I am done with crying which is a waste of time and discourages everybody."

Jem and Jerry went to Charlottetown that night and two days later they came back in khaki. The Glen hummed with excitement over it. Life at Ingleside had suddenly become a tense, strained, thrilling thing. Mrs. Blythe and Nan were brave and smiling and wonderful. Already Mrs. Blythe and Miss Cornelia were organizing a Red Cross. The Doctor and Mr. Meredith were rounding up the men for a Patriotic Society. Rilla, after the first shock, reacted to the romance of it all, in spite of her heartache. Jem certainly looked magnificent in his uniform. It *was* splendid to think of the lads of Canada answering so speedily and fearlessly and uncalculatingly to the call of their country. Rilla carried her head high among the girls whose brothers had not so responded. In her diary she wrote,

> "'He goes to do what I had done
> Had Douglas' daughter been his son,'"

and was sure she meant it. If she were a boy of course she would go, too! She hadn't the least doubt of that.

She wondered if it was very dreadful of her to feel glad that Walter hadn't got strong as soon as they had wished after the fever.

"I couldn't bear to have Walter go," she wrote. "I love Jem ever so much but Walter means more to me than any one in the world and I would *die* if he had to go. He seems so *changed* these days. He hardly ever talks to me. I suppose he wants to go, too, and feels badly because he can't. He doesn't go about with Jem and Jerry at all. I shall never forget Susan's face when Jem came home in his khaki. It worked and twisted as if she were going to cry, but all she said was, 'You look *almost* like a man in that, Jem.' Jem laughed. *He* never minds because Susan thinks him just a child still. Everybody seems busy but me. I wish there was something I could do but there doesn't seem to be anything. Mother and Nan and Di are busy all the time and I just wander about like a lonely ghost. What hurts me terribly, though, is that mother's smiles, and Nan's, just seem put on from the outside. Mother's *eyes* never laugh now. It makes me feel that I shouldn't laugh either—that it's wicked to feel *laughy*. And it's so hard for me to keep from laughing, even if Jem is going to be a soldier. But when I laugh I don't enjoy it either, as I used to do. There's something behind it all that keeps hurting me—especially when I wake up in the night. Then I cry because I am afraid that Kitchener of Khartoum is right and the war will last for years and Jem may be—but no, I won't write it. It would make me feel as if it were really going to happen. The other day Nan said, 'Nothing can ever be quite the same for any of us again.' It made me feel rebellious. Why shouldn't things be the same again—when everything is over and Jem and Jerry are back? We'll all be happy and jolly again and these days will seem just like a bad dream.

"The coming of the mail is the most exciting event of every day now. Father just snatches the paper—I never saw father snatch before—and the rest of us crowd around and look at the headlines over his shoulder. Susan vows she does not and will not believe a word the papers say but she always comes to the kitchen door, and listens and then goes back, shaking her head. She is terribly indignant all the time, but she cooks up all the things Jem likes especially, and she did not make a single bit of fuss when she found Monday asleep on the spare room bed yesterday right on top of Mrs. Rachel Lynde's apple-leaf spread. 'The Almighty only knows where your master will be having to sleep before long, you poor dumb beast,' she said as she put him quite gently out. But she never relents towards Doc. She says the minute he saw Jem in khaki he turned into Mr. Hyde then and there and she thinks that ought to be proof enough of what he really is. Susan is funny, but she is an old dear. Shirley says she is one half angel and the other half good cook. But then Shirley is the only one of us she never scolds.

"Faith Meredith is wonderful. I think she and Jem are really engaged now. She goes about with a shining light in her eyes, but her smiles are a little stiff and starched, just like mother's. I wonder if *I* could be as brave as she is if I had a lover and he was going to the war. It is bad enough when it is your brother. Bruce Meredith cried all night, Mrs. Meredith says, when he heard Jem and Jerry were going. And he wanted to know if the 'K. of K.' his father talked about was the King of Kings. He is the dearest kiddy. I just love him—though I don't really care much for children. I don't like babies one bit—though when I *say* so people look at me as if I had said something *perfectly shocking*. Well, I don't, and I've got to be honest about it. I don't mind *looking* at a nice clean baby if somebody else holds it—but I wouldn't *touch* it for *anything* and I don't feel a single real spark of interest in it. Gertrude Oliver says she just feels the same. (She is the most honest person I know. She *never* pretends anything.) She says babies bore her until they are old enough to talk and then she likes them—but still a good ways off. Mother and Nan and Di all adore babies and seem to think I'm unnatural because I don't.

"I haven't seen Kenneth since the night of the party. He was here one evening after Jem came back but I happened to be away. I don't think he mentioned me at all—at least nobody told me he did and I was *determined* I wouldn't *ask*—but I don't care in the least. All *that* matters *absolutely nothing* to me now. The only thing that does matter is that Jem has volunteered for active service and will be going to Valcartier in a few more days—my big, splendid brother Jem. Oh, I'm so proud of him!

"I suppose Kenneth would enlist too if it weren't for his ankle. I think that is quite Providential. He is his mother's *only* son and how dreadful she would feel if he went. Only sons should never think of going!"

Walter came wandering through the valley as Rilla sat there, with his head bent and his hands clasped behind him. When he saw Rilla he turned abruptly away; then as abruptly he turned and came back to her.

"Rilla-my-Rilla, what are you thinking of?"

"Everything is so changed, Walter," said Rilla wistfully. "Even you—you're changed. A week ago we were all so happy—and—and—now I just can't *find myself* at all. I'm lost."

Walter sat down on a neighbouring stone and took Rilla's little appealing hand.

"I'm afraid our old world has come to an end, Rilla. We've got to face that fact."

"It's so terrible to think of Jem," pleaded Rilla. "Sometimes I forget for a little while what it really means and feel excited and proud—and then it comes over me again like a cold wind."

"I envy Jem," said Walter moodily.

"Envy Jem! Oh, Walter, you—*you* don't want to go too."

"No," said Walter, gazing straight before him down the emerald vistas of the valley, "no, I *don't* want to go. That's just the trouble. Rilla, I'm *afraid* to go. I'm a coward."

"You're not!" Rilla burst out angrily. "Why, anybody would be afraid to go. You might be—why, you might be killed."

"I wouldn't mind *that* if it didn't hurt," muttered Walter. "I don't think I'm afraid of death itself—it's of the pain that might come before death—it wouldn't be so bad to die and have it over—but to keep on dying! Rilla, I've always been afraid of pain—you know that. I can't help it—I shudder when I think of the possibility of being mangled or—or *blinded*. Rilla, I *cannot* face *that* thought. To be blind—never to see the beauty of the world again—moonlight on Four Winds—the stars twinkling through the fir trees—mist on the gulf. I ought to go—I ought to *want* to go—but I don't—I hate the thought of it—and I'm ashamed—ashamed."

"But, Walter, you *couldn't* go anyhow," said Rilla piteously. She was sick with a new terror that Walter *would* go after all. "You're not strong enough."

"I *am*. I've felt as fit as ever I did this last month. I'd pass any examination—I know it. Everybody thinks I'm not strong yet—and I'm skulking behind that belief. I—I should have been a girl," Walter concluded in a burst of passionate bitterness.

"Even if you were strong enough, you oughtn't to go," sobbed Rilla. "What would mother do? She's breaking her heart over Jem. It would kill her to see you both go."

"Oh, I'm not going—don't worry. I tell you I'm afraid to go—*afraid*. I don't mince the matter to myself. It's a relief to own up even to you, Rilla. I wouldn't confess it to anybody else—Nan and Di would despise me. But I hate the whole thing—the horror, the pain, the ugliness. War isn't a khaki uniform or a drill parade—everything I've read in old histories haunts me. I lie awake at night and *see* things that have happened—see the blood and filth and misery of it all. And a bayonet charge! If I could face the other things I could *never* face that. It turns me sick to think of it—sicker even to think of giving it than receiving it—to think of thrusting a bayonet through another man." Walter writhed and shuddered. "I think of these things all the time—and it doesn't seem to me that Jem and Jerry *ever* think of them. They laugh and talk about 'potting Huns'! But it maddens me to see them in the khaki. And *they* think I'm grumpy because I'm not fit to go."

Walter laughed bitterly. It is not a nice thing to *feel* yourself a coward. But Rilla got her arms about him and cuddled her head on his shoulder. She was so glad he didn't want to go—for just one minute she had been horribly frightened. And it was so nice to have Walter confiding his troubles to her—to *her*, not Di. She didn't feel so lonely and superfluous any longer.

"Don't you despise me, Rilla-my-Rilla?" asked Walter wistfully. Somehow, it hurt him to think Rilla might despise him—hurt him as much as if it had been Di. He realized suddenly how very fond he was of this adoring kid sister with her appealing eyes and troubled, girlish face.

"No, I don't. Why, Walter, hundreds of people feel just as you do. You know what that verse of Shakespeare in the old Fifth Reader says—'the brave man is not he who feels no fear.'"

"No—but it is 'he whose noble soul its fear subdues.' I don't do that. We can't gloss it over, Rilla. I'm a coward."

"You're *not*. Think of how you fought Dan Reese long ago."

"One spurt of courage isn't enough for a lifetime."

"Walter, one time I heard father say that the trouble with you was a sensitive nature and a vivid imagination. I think I know now what he meant. You *feel* things before they really come—feel them all alone when there isn't anything to help you bear them—to *take away* from them. I don't express that very well—but I know that's the trouble. It isn't anything to be ashamed of. When you and Jem got your hands burned when the grass was fired on the sand hills two years ago Jem made twice the fuss over the pain that you did. As for this horrid old war, there'll be plenty to go without you. It won't last long."

"I wish I could believe it. Well, it's supper time, Rilla. You'd better run. I don't want anything."

"Neither do I. I couldn't eat a mouthful. Let me stay here with you, Walter. It's such a comfort to talk things over with some one. The rest all think that I'm too much of a baby to understand."

So they two sat there in the old valley until the evening star shone through a pale-grey, gauzy cloud over the maple grove, and a fragrant dewy darkness filled their little sylvan dell. It was one of the evenings Rilla was to treasure in remembrance all her life—the first one on which Walter had ever talked to her as if she were a woman and not a child. They comforted and strengthened each other. Walter felt, for the time being at least, that it was not such a despicable thing after all to dread the horror of war; and Rilla was glad to be made the confidante of his struggles—to sympathize with and encourage him. She was of importance to somebody.

When they went back to Ingleside they found callers sitting on the veranda. Mr. and Mrs. Meredith had come over from the manse, and Mr. and Mrs. Norman Douglas had come up from the farm. Cousin Sophia was there also, sitting with Susan in the shadowy background. Mrs. Blythe and Nan and Di were away, but Dr. Blythe was home and so was Dr. Jekyll, sitting in golden majesty on the top step. And of course they were all talking of the war, except Dr. Jekyll who kept his own counsel and looked contempt as only a cat can. When two people foregathered in those days they talked of the war; and old Highland Sandy of the Harbour Head talked of it when he was alone and hurled anathemas at the Kaiser across all the acres of his farm. Walter slipped away, not caring to see or be seen, but Rilla sat down on the steps, where the garden mint was dewy and pungent. It was a very calm evening with a dim, golden afterlight irradiating the glen. She felt happier than at any time in the dreadful week that had passed. She was no longer haunted by the fear that Walter would go.

"I'd go myself if I was twenty years younger," Norman Douglas was shouting. Norman always shouted when he was excited. "*I'd* show the Kaiser a thing or two! Did I ever say there wasn't a hell? Of course there's a hell—dozens of hells— hundreds of hells—where the Kaiser and all his brood are bound for."

"*I* knew this war was coming," said Mrs. Norman triumphantly. "*I* saw it coming right along. *I* could have told all those stupid Englishmen what was ahead of them. I told *you*, John Meredith, years ago what the Kaiser was up to but you wouldn't believe it. You said he would never plunge the world in war. Who was right about the Kaiser, John? You—or I? Tell me that."

"You were, I admit," said Mr. Meredith.

"It's too late to admit it now," said Mrs. Norman, shaking her head, as if to intimate that if John Meredith *had* admitted it sooner there might have been no war.

"Thank God, England's navy is ready," said the doctor.

"Amen to that," nodded Mrs. Norman. "Bat-blind as most of them were somebody had foresight enough to see to *that*."

"Maybe England'll manage not to get into trouble over it," said Cousin Sophia plaintively. "*I* dunno. But I'm much afraid."

"One would suppose England was in trouble over it already, up to her neck, Sophia Crawford," said Susan. "But your ways of thinking are beyond me and always were. It is my opinion that the British navy will settle Germany in a jiffy and that we are all getting worked up over nothing."

Susan spat out the words as if she wanted to convince herself more than anybody else. She had her little store of homely philosophies to guide her through life, but she had nothing to buckler her against the thunderbolts of the week that had just passed. What had an honest, hard-working, Presbyterian old maid of Glen St. Mary to do with a war thousands of miles away? Susan felt that it was indecent that she should have to be disturbed by it.

"The British *army* will settle Germany," shouted Norman. "Just wait till *it* gets into line and the Kaiser will find that real war is a different thing from parading round Berlin with your moustaches cocked up."

"Britain hasn't got an army," said Mrs. Norman emphatically. "You needn't glare at *me*, Norman. Glaring won't make soldiers out of timothy stalks. A hundred thousand men will just be a mouthful for Germany's millions."

"There'll be some tough chewing in the mouthful, I reckon," persisted Norman valiantly. "Germany'll break her teeth on it. Don't you tell me one Britisher isn't a match for ten foreigners. I could polish off a dozen of 'em myself with both hands tied behind my back!"

"I am told," said Susan, "that old Mr. Pryor does not believe in this war. I am told that he says England went into it just because she was jealous of Germany and that she did not really care in the least what happened to Belgium."

"I believe he's been talking some such rot," said Norman. "*I* haven't heard him. When I do, Whiskers-on-the-moon won't know what happened to him. That precious relative of mine, Kitty Alec, holds forth to the same effect, I understand. Not before *me*, though—somehow, folks don't indulge in that kind of conversation in my presence. Lord love you, they've a kind of presentiment, so to speak, that it wouldn't be healthy for their complaint."

"I am much afraid that this war has been sent as a punishment for our sins," said Cousin Sophia, unclasping her pale hands from her lap and re-clasping them solemnly over her stomach. "'The world is very evil—the times are waxing late.'"

"Parson here's got something of the same idea," chuckled Norman. "Haven't you, Parson? That's why you preached 'tother night on the text 'Without shedding of blood there is no remission of sins.' I didn't agree with you—wanted to get up in the pew and shout out that there wasn't a word of sense in what you were saying, but Ellen, here, she held me down. I never have any fun sassing parsons since I got married."

"Without shedding of blood there is no *anything*," said Mr. Meredith, in the gently dreamy way which had an unexpected trick of convincing his hearers. "*Everything*, it seems to me, has to be purchased by self-sacrifice. Our race has marked every step of its painful ascent with blood. And now torrents of it must flow again. No, Mrs. Crawford, I don't think the war has been sent as a punishment for sin. I think it is the price humanity must pay for some blessing—some advance great enough to be worth the price—which *we* may not live to see but which our children's children will inherit."

"If Jerry is killed will you feel so fine about it?" demanded Norman, who had been saying things like that all his life and never could be made to see any reason why he shouldn't. "Now, never mind kicking me in the shins, Ellen. I want to see if Parson meant what he said or if it was just a pulpit frill."

Mr. Meredith's face quivered. He had had a terrible hour alone in his study on the night Jem and Jerry had gone to town. But he answered quietly.

"Whatever I felt, it could not alter my belief—my *assurance* that a country whose sons are ready to lay down their lives in her defence will win a new vision because of their sacrifice."

"You *do* mean it, Parson. I can always tell when people mean what they say. It's a gift that was born in me. Makes me a terror to most parsons, that! But I've never caught you yet saying anything you didn't mean. I'm always hoping I will—that's what reconciles me to going to church. It'd be such a comfort to me—such a weapon to batter Ellen here with when she tries to civilize me. Well, I'm off over the road to see Ab. Crawford a minute. The gods be good to you all."

"The old pagan!" muttered Susan, as Norman strode away. She did not care if Ellen Douglas did hear her. Susan could never understand why fire did not descend from heaven upon Norman Douglas when he insulted ministers the way he did. But the astonishing thing was Mr. Meredith seemed really to like his brother-in-law.

Rilla wished they would talk of something besides war. She had heard nothing else for a week and she was really a little tired of it. Now that she was relieved from her haunting fear that Walter would want to go it made her quite impatient. But she supposed—with a sigh—that there would be three or four months of it yet.

CHAPTER VI

$\mathcal{S}$usan, Rilla, and Dog Monday Make a Resolution

The big living room at Ingleside was snowed over with drifts of white cotton. Word had come from Red Cross headquarters that sheets and bandages would be required. Nan and Di and Rilla were hard at work. Mrs. Blythe and Susan were upstairs in the boys' room, engaged in a more personal task. With dry, anguished eyes they were packing up Jem's belongings. He must leave for Valcartier the next morning. They had been expecting the word but it was none the less dreadful when it came.

Rilla was basting the hem of a sheet for the first time in her life. When the word had come that Jem must go she had her cry out among the pines in Rainbow Valley and then she had gone to her mother.

"Mother, I want to do something. I'm only a girl—I can't do anything to win the war—but I must do something to help at home."

"The cotton has come up for the sheets," said Mrs. Blythe. "You can help Nan and Di make them up. And, Rilla, don't you think you could organize a Junior Red Cross among the young girls? I think they would like it better and do better work by themselves than if mixed up with the older people."

"But, mother—I've never done anything like that."

"We will all have to do a great many things in the months ahead of us that we have never done before, Rilla."

"Well"—Rilla took the plunge—"I'll try, mother—if you'll tell me how to begin. I have been thinking it all over and I

have decided that I must be as *brave* and *heroic* and *unselfish* as
I can possibly be."

Mrs. Blythe did not smile at Rilla's italics. Perhaps she did
not feel like smiling or perhaps she detected a real grain of
serious purpose behind Rilla's romantic pose. So here was
Rilla hemming sheets and organizing a Junior Red Cross in
her thoughts as she hemmed; moreover, she was enjoying it—
the organizing that is, not the hemming. It was interesting
and Rilla discovered a certain aptitude in herself for it that
surprised her. Who would be president? Not she. The older
girls would not like that. Irene Howard? No, somehow Irene
was not quite as popular as she deserved to be. Marjorie
Drew? No, Marjorie hadn't enough backbone. She was too
prone to agree with the last speaker. Betty Mead—calm,
capable, tactful Betty—the very one! And Una Meredith for
treasurer; and, if they were *very* insistent, they might make
her, Rilla, secretary. As for the various committees, they must
be chosen after the Juniors were organized, but Rilla knew
just who should be put on which. They would meet around—
and there must be no eats—Rilla knew she would have a
pitched battle with Olive Kirk over that—and everything
should be strictly business-like and constitutional. Her
minute book should be covered in white with a Red Cross on
the cover—and wouldn't it be nice to have some kind of
uniform which they could all wear at the concerts they would
have to get up to raise money—something simple but smart?

"You have basted the top hem of that sheet on one side and
the bottom hem on the other," said Di.

Rilla picked out her stitches and reflected that she
hated sewing. Running the Junior Reds would be much more
interesting.

Mrs. Blythe was saying upstairs,

"Susan, do you remember that first day Jem lifted up his little arms to me and called me 'mo'er'—the very first word he ever tried to say?"

"You could not mention anything about that blessed baby that I do not and will not remember till my dying day," said Susan drearily.

"Susan, I keep thinking today of one night when he cried for me in the night. He was just a few months old. Gilbert didn't want me to go to him—he said the child was well and warm and that it would be fostering bad habits in him. But I went—and took him up—I can feel that tight clinging of his little arms round my neck yet. Susan, if I *hadn't* gone that night, twenty-one years ago, and taken my baby up when he cried for me I *couldn't* face tomorrow morning."

"I do not know how we are going to face it anyhow, Mrs. Dr. dear. But do not tell me that it will be the final farewell. He will be back on leave before he goes overseas, will he not?"

"We hope so but we are not very sure. I am making up my mind that he will not, so that there will be no disappointment to bear. Susan, I am determined that I will send my boy off tomorrow with a smile. He shall not carry away with him the remembrance of a weak mother who had not the courage to send when he had the courage to go. I hope none of us will cry."

"*I* am not going to cry, Mrs. Dr. dear, and that you may tie to, but whether I shall manage to smile or not will be as Providence ordains and as the pit of my stomach feels. Have you room there for this fruit cake? And the short-bread? And the mince pie? That blessed boy shall not starve, whether they have anything to eat in that Quebec place or not. Everything seems to be changing all at once, does it not?

Even the old cat at the manse has passed away. He breathed his last at a quarter to ten last night and Bruce is quite heart-broken, they tell me."

"It's time that pussy went where good cats go. He must be at least fifteen years old. He has seemed so lonely since Aunt Martha died."

"I should not have lamented, Mrs. Dr. dear, if that Hyde-beast had died also. He has been Mr. Hyde most of the time since Jem came home in khaki, and *that* has a meaning I will maintain. I do not know what Monday will do when Jem is gone. The creature just goes about with a human look in his eyes that takes all the good out of me when I see it. Ellen West used to be always railing at the Kaiser and we thought her crazy, but now I see that there was a method in her madness. This tray is packed, Mrs. Dr. dear, and I will go down and put in my best licks preparing supper. I wish I knew when I would cook another supper for Jem but such things are hidden from our eyes."

Jem Blythe and Jerry Meredith left next morning. It was a dull day, threatening rain, and the clouds lay in heavy grey rolls over the sky; but almost everybody in the Glen and Four Winds and Harbour Head and Upper Glen and over-harbour—except Whiskers-on-the-moon—was there to see them off. The Blythe family and the Meredith family were all smiling. Even Susan, as Providence did ordain, wore a smile, though the effect was somewhat more painful than tears would have been. Faith and Nan were very pale and very gallant. Rilla thought she would get on very well if something in her throat didn't choke her, and if her lips didn't take such spells of trembling. Dog Monday was there, too. Jem had tried to say good-bye to him at Ingleside, but Monday implored so eloquently that Jem relented, and let him go to the station. He kept close to Jem's legs, and watched every movement of his beloved master.

"I can't bear that dog's eyes," said Mrs. Meredith.

"The beast has more sense than most humans," said Mary Vance. "Well, did we any of us ever think we'd live to see this day? I bawled all night to think of Jem and Jerry going like this. *I* think they're plumb deranged. Miller got a maggot in his head about going but I soon talked him out of it—likewise his aunt said a few touching things. For once in our lives Kitty Alec and I agree. It's a miracle that isn't likely to happen again. There's Ken, Rilla."

Rilla knew Kenneth was there. She had been acutely conscious of it from the moment he had sprung from Leo West's buggy. Now he came up to her smiling.

"Doing the brave-smiling-sister-stunt, I see. What a crowd for the Glen to muster! Well, I'm off home in a few days myself."

A queer little wind of desolation that even Jem's going had not caused, blew over Rilla's spirit.

"Why? You have another month of vacation."

"Yes—but I can't hang round Four Winds and enjoy myself when the world's on fire like this. It's me for little old Toronto where I'll find some way of helping in spite of this bally ankle. I'm not looking at Jem and Jerry—makes me too sick with envy. You girls are great—no crying, no grim endurance. The boys'll go off with a good taste in their mouths. I hope Persis and mother will be as game when my turn comes."

"Oh, Kenneth—the war will be over before your turn cometh."

There! She had lisped again. Another great moment of life spoiled! Well, it was her fate. And anyhow, nothing mattered. Kenneth was off already—he was talking to Ethel Reese, who was dressed, at seven in the morning, in the gown she had worn to the dance, and was crying. What on earth had Ethel to cry about? None of the Reeses were in khaki. Rilla wanted to cry, too—but she would *not*. What was that horrid old Mrs. Drew saying to mother, in that melancholy whine of hers? "I don't see how you can stand this, Mrs. Blythe. *I* couldn't if it was *my* pore boy." And mother—oh, mother could always be depended on! How her grey eyes flashed in her pale face. "It might have been worse, Mrs. Drew. I might have had to urge him to go." Mrs. Drew did not understand but Rilla did. She flung up her head. Her brother did not have to be urged to go.

Rilla found herself standing alone and listening to discon-nected scraps of talk as people walked up and down past her.

"I told Mark to wait and see if they asked for a second lot of men. If they did I'd let him go—but they won't," said Mrs. Palmer Burr.

"I think I'll have it made with a crush girdle of velvet," said Bessie Clow.

"I'm frightened to look at my husband's face for fear I'll see in it that he wants to go too," said a little over-harbour bride.

"I'm scared stiff," said whimsical Mrs. Jim Howard. "I'm scared Jim will enlist—and I'm scared he won't."

"The war will be over by Christmas," said Joe Vickers.

"Let them Europeen nations fight it out between them," said Abner Reese.

"When he was a boy I gave him many a good trouncing," shouted Norman Douglas, who seemed to be referring to some one high in military circles in Charlottetown. "Yes, sir, I walloped him well, big gun as he is now."

"The existence of the British Empire is at stake," said the Methodist minister.

"There's certainly *something* about uniforms," sighed Irene Howard.

"It's a commercial war when all is said and done and not worth one drop of good Canadian blood," said a stranger from the shore hotel.

"The Blythe family are taking it easy," said Kate Drew.

"Them young fools are just going for adventure," growled Nathan Crawford.

"I have absolute confidence in Kitchener," said the over-harbour doctor.

"'It's a long, long way to Tipperary,'" hummed Rick MacAllister.

In these ten minutes Rilla passed through a dizzying succession of anger, laughter, contempt, depression and inspiration. Oh, people were—funny! How little they understood. "Taking it easy," indeed—when even Susan hadn't slept a wink all night! Kate Drew always was a minx.

Rilla felt as if she were in some fantastic nightmare. Were these the people who, three weeks ago, were talking of crops and prices and local gossip?

There—the train was coming—mother was holding Jem's hand—Dog Monday was licking it—everybody was saying good-bye—the train was in! Jem kissed Faith before everybody—old Mrs. Drew whooped hysterically—the men, led by Kenneth, cheered—Rilla felt Jem seize her hand— "Good-bye, Spider"—somebody kissed her cheek—she believed it was Jerry but never was sure—they were off—the train was pulling out—Jem and Jerry were waving to everybody—everybody was waving back—mother and Nan were smiling still, but as if they had just forgotten to take the smile off—Monday was howling dismally and being forcibly restrained by the Methodist minister from tearing after the train—Susan was waving her best bonnet and hurrahing like a man—*had* she gone crazy?—the train rounded a curve. They had gone.

Rilla came to herself with a gasp. There was a sudden quiet. Nothing to do now but to go home—and wait. The doctor and Mrs. Blythe walked off together—so did Nan and Faith—so did John Meredith and Rosemary. Walter and Una and Shirley and Di and Carl and Rilla went in a group. Susan had put her bonnet back on her head, hindside foremost, and stalked grimly off alone. Nobody missed Dog Monday at first. When they did Shirley went back for him. He found Dog Monday curled up in one of the shipping sheds near the station and tried to coax him home. Dog Monday would not move. He wagged his tail to show he had no hard feelings but no blandishments availed to budge him.

"Guess Monday has made up his mind to wait there till Jem comes back," said Shirley, trying to laugh as he rejoined the rest.

Which was exactly what Dog Monday had done. His dear master had gone—he, Monday, had been deliberately and of malice aforethought prevented from going with him by a demon disguised in the garb of a Methodist minister. Wherefore, he, Monday, would wait there until the smoking, snorting monster, which had carried his hero off, carried him back.

Ay, wait there, little faithful dog with the soft, wistful, puzzled eyes. But it will be many a long bitter day before your boyish comrade comes back to you.

The doctor was away on a case that night and Susan stalked into Mrs. Blythe's room on her way to bed to see if her adored Mrs. Dr. dear were "comfortable and composed." She paused solemnly at the foot of the bed and solemnly declared,

"Mrs. Dr. dear, I have made up my mind to be a heroine."

"Mrs. Dr. dear" found herself violently inclined to laugh—which was manifestly unfair, since she had not laughed when Rilla had announced a similar heroic determination. To be sure, Rilla was a slim, white-robed thing, with a flower-like face and starry young eyes aglow with feeling; whereas Susan was arrayed in a grey flannel nightgown of strait simplicity, and had a strip of red woolen worsted tied around her grey hair as a charm against neuralgia. But that should not make any vital difference. Was it not the spirit that counted? Yet Mrs. Blythe was hard put to it not to laugh.

"I am not," proceeded Susan firmly, "going to lament or whine or question the wisdom of the Almighty any more as I have been doing lately. Whining and shirking and blaming Providence do not get us anywhere. We have just got to grapple with whatever we have to do whether it is weeding the onion patch, or running the Government. *I* shall grapple. Those blessed boys have gone to war; and *we women*, Mrs. Dr. dear, must tarry by the stuff and keep a stiff upper lip."

CHAPTER VII

A War Baby and a Soup Tureen

"Liége and Namur—and now Brussels!" The doctor shook his head. "I don't like it—I don't like it."

"Do not you lose heart, Dr. dear; they were just defended by foreigners," said Susan superbly. "Wait you till the Germans come against the British; there will be a very different story to tell and that you may tie to."

The doctor shook his head again, but a little less gravely; perhaps they all shared subconsciously in Susan's belief that "the thin grey line" was unbreakable, even by the victorious rush of Germany's ready millions. At any rate, when the terrible day came—the first of many terrible days—with the news that the British army was driven back they stared at each other in blank dismay.

"It—it can't be true," gasped Nan, taking a brief refuge in temporary incredulity.

"I felt that there was to be bad news today," said Susan, "for that cat-creature turned into Mr. Hyde this morning without rhyme or reason for it, and *that* was no good omen."

"'A broken, a beaten, but not a demoralized, army,'" muttered the doctor, from a London dispatch. "Can it be England's army of which such a thing is said?"

"It will be a long time now before the war is ended," said Mrs. Blythe despairingly.

Susan's faith, which had for a moment been temporarily submerged, now reappeared triumphantly.

"Remember, Mrs. Dr. dear, that the British army is not the

British navy. Never forget *that*. And the Russians are on their way, too, though Russians are people I do not know much about and consequently will not tie to."

"The Russians will not be in time to save Paris," said Walter gloomily. "Paris is the heart of France—and the road to it is open. Oh, I wish"—he stopped abruptly and went out.

After a paralyzed day the Ingleside folk found it was possible to "carry on" even in the face of ever-darkening bad news. Susan worked fiercely in her kitchen, the doctor went out on his round of visits, Nan and Di returned to their Red Cross activities; Mrs. Blythe went to Charlottetown to attend a Red Cross Convention; Rilla after relieving her feelings by a stormy fit of tears in Rainbow Valley and an outburst in her diary, remembered that she had elected to be brave and heroic. And, she thought, it really was heroic to volunteer to drive about the Glen and Four Winds one day, collecting promised Red Cross supplies with Abner Crawford's old grey horse. One of the Ingleside horses was lame and the doctor needed the other, so there was nothing for it but the Crawford nag, a placid, unhasting, thick-skinned creature with an amiable habit of stopping every few yards to kick a fly off one leg with the foot of the other. Rilla felt that this, coupled with the fact that the Germans were only fifty miles from Paris, was hardly to be endured. But she started off gallantly on an errand fraught with amazing results.

Late in the afternoon she found herself, with a buggy full of parcels, at the entrance to a grassy, deep-rutted lane leading to the harbour shore, wondering whether it was worth while to call down at the Anderson house. The Andersons were desperately poor and it was not likely Mrs. Anderson had anything to give. On the other hand, her husband, who was an Englishman by birth and who had been working in Kingsport when the war broke out, had promptly sailed for England to enlist there, without, it may be said, coming home or sending much hard cash to represent him. So possibly Mrs. Anderson might feel hurt if she were overlooked. Rilla decided to call. There were times afterwards when she wished she hadn't, but in the long run she was very thankful that she did.

The Anderson house was a small and tumble-down affair, crouching in a grove of battered spruces near the shore as if rather ashamed of itself and anxious to hide. Rilla tied her grey nag to the rickety fence and went to the door. It was open; and the sight she saw bereft her temporarily of the power of speech or motion.

Through the open door of the small bedroom opposite her, Rilla saw Mrs. Anderson lying on the untidy bed; *and Mrs. Anderson was dead*. There was no doubt of that; neither was there any doubt that the big, frowzy, red-headed, red-faced, over-fat woman sitting near the doorway, smoking a pipe quite comfortably, was very much alive. She rocked idly back and forth amid her surroundings of squalid disorder, and paid no attention whatever to the piercing wails proceeding from a cradle in the middle of the room.

Rilla knew the woman by sight and reputation. Her name was Mrs. Conover; she lived down at the fishing village; she was a great aunt of Mrs. Anderson's; and she drank as well as smoked.

Rilla's first impulse was to turn and flee. But that would not do. Perhaps this woman, repulsive as she was, needed help—though she certainly did not look as if she were worrying over the lack of it.

"Come in," said Mrs. Conover, removing her pipe and staring at Rilla with her little, rat-like eyes.

"Is—is Mrs. Anderson really dead?" asked Rilla timidly, as she stepped over the sill.

"Dead as a door nail," responded Mrs. Conover cheerfully. "Kicked the bucket half an hour ago. I've sent Jen Conover to 'phone for the undertaker and get some help up from the shore. You're the doctor's miss, ain't ye? Have a cheer?"

Rilla did not see any chair which was not cluttered with something. She remained standing.

"Wasn't it—very sudden?"

"Well, she's been a-pining ever since that worthless Jim lit out for England—which I say it's a pity as he ever left. It's my belief she was took for death when she heard the news. That young un there was born a fortnight ago and since then she's just gone down and today she up and died, without a soul expecting it."

"Is there anything I can do to—to help?" hesitated Rilla.

"Bless yez, no—unless ye've a knack with kids. *I* haven't. That young un there never lets up squalling, day or night. I've just got that I take no notice of it."

Rilla tiptoed gingerly over to the cradle and more gingerly still pulled down the dirty blanket. She had no intention of touching the baby—*she* had no "knack with kids" either. She saw an ugly midget with a red, distorted little face, rolled up in a piece of dingy old flannel. She had never seen an uglier baby. Yet a feeling of pity for the desolate, orphaned mite which had "come out of the everywhere" into such a dubious "here," took sudden possession of her.

"What is going to become of the baby?" she asked.

"Lord knows," said Mrs. Conover candidly. "Min worried awful over that before she died. She kept on a-saying 'Oh, what will become of my pore baby' till it really got on my nerves. *I* ain't a-going to trouble myself with it, I can tell yez.

I brung up a boy that my sister left and he skinned out as soon as he got to be some good and won't give me a mite o' help in my old age, ungrateful whelp as he is. I told Min it'd have to be sent to an orphan asylum till we'd see if Jim ever came back to look after it. Would yez believe it, she didn't relish the idee. But that's the long and short of it."

"But who will look after it until it can be taken to the asylum?" persisted Rilla. Somehow the baby's fate worried her.

"'S'pose I'll have to," grunted Mrs. Conover. She put away her pipe and took an unblushing swig from a black bottle she produced from a shelf near her. "It's my opinion the kid won't live long. It's sickly. Min never had no gimp and I guess it hain't either. Likely it won't trouble any one long and good riddance, sez I."

Rilla drew the blanket down a little further.

"Why, the baby isn't dressed!" she exclaimed, in a shocked tone.

"Who was to dress him I'd like to know," demanded Mrs. Conover truculently. "*I* hadn't time—took me all the time there was looking after Min. 'Sides, as I told yez, I don't know nothing about kids. Old Mrs. Billy Crawford, she was here when it was born and she washed it and rolled it up in that flannel, and Jen she's tended it a bit since. The critter is warm enough. This weather would melt a brass monkey."

Rilla was silent, looking down at the crying baby. She had never encountered any of the tragedies of life before and this one smote her to the core of her heart. The thought of the poor mother going down into the valley of the shadow alone, fretting about her baby, with no one near but this abominable old woman, hurt her terribly. If she had only come a little sooner! Yet what could she have done—what could she do now? She didn't know, but she must do *something*. She hated babies—but she simply could *not* go away and leave that poor little creature with Mrs. Conover—who was applying herself again to her black bottle and would probably be helplessly drunk before anybody came.

"*I* can't stay," thought Rilla. "Mr. Crawford said I *must* be home by supper time because he wanted the pony this evening himself. Oh, what can I do?"

She made a sudden, desperate, impulsive resolution.

"I'll take the baby home with me," she said. "Can I?"

"Sure, if yez wants to," said Mrs. Conover amiably. "I hain't any objection. Take it and welcome."

"I—I can't carry it," said Rilla. "I have to drive the horse and I'd be afraid I'd drop it. Is there a—a basket anywhere that I could put it in?"

"Not as I knows on. There ain't much here of *anything*, I kin tell yez. Min was pore and as shiftless as Jim. Ef yez opens that drawer over there yez'll find a few baby clo'es. Best take them along."

Rilla got the clothes—the cheap, sleazy garments the poor mother had made ready as best she could. But this did not solve the pressing problem of the baby's transportation. Rilla looked helplessly round. Oh, for mother—or Susan! Her eyes fell on an enormous blue soup tureen at the back of the dresser.

"Can I have this to—to lay him in?" she asked.

"Well, 'tain't mine but I guess yez kin take it. Don't smash it if yez can help—Jim might make a fuss about it if he comes back alive,—which he sure will, seein' he ain't any good. He brung that old tureen out from England with him—said it'd always been in the family. Him and Min never used it—never had enough soup to put in it—but Jim thought the world of

83

it. He was mighty perticuler about some things but it didn't worry him none that there weren't much in the way o' eatables to put in the dishes."

For the first time in her life Rilla Blythe touched a baby—lifted it—rolled it in a blanket, trembling with nervousness lest she drop it or—or—break it. Then she put it in the soup tureen.

"Is there any fear of it smothering?" she asked anxiously.

"Not much odds if it do," said Mrs. Conover.

Horrified Rilla loosened the blanket around the baby's face a little. The mite had stopped crying and was blinking up at her. It had big dark eyes in its ugly little face.

"Better not let the wind blow on it," admonished Mrs. Conover. "Take its breath if it do."

Rilla wrapped the tattered little quilt around the soup tureen.

"Will you hand this to me after I get into the buggy, please?"

"Sure I will," said Mrs. Conover, getting up with a grunt.

And so it was that Rilla Blythe, who had driven to the Anderson house a self-confessed hater of babies, drove away from it carrying one in a soup tureen on her lap!

Rilla thought she would never get to Ingleside. That miserable pony fairly crawled. In the soup tureen there was an uncanny silence. In one way she was thankful the baby did not cry but she wished it would give an occasional squeak to prove that it was alive. Suppose it were smothered! Rilla dared not unwrap it to see, lest the wind, which was now blowing a hurricane, should "take its breath," whatever dreadful thing that might be. She was a thankful girl when at last she reached harbour at Ingleside.

Rilla carried the soup tureen to the kitchen, set it on the table under Susan's eyes and removed the quilt. Susan looked into the tureen and for once in her life was so completely floored that she had not a word to say.

"What in the world is this?" asked the doctor, coming in.

Rilla poured out her story. "I just *had* to bring it, father," she concluded. "I couldn't leave it there."

"What are you going to do with it?" asked the doctor coolly.

Rilla hadn't exactly expected this kind of question.

"We—we can keep it here for awhile—can't we—until something can be arranged?" she stammered confusedly.

Dr. Blythe walked up and down the kitchen for a moment or two while the baby stared at the white walls of the soup tureen and Susan showed signs of returning animation.

Presently the doctor confronted Rilla.

"A young baby means a great deal of additional work and trouble in a household, Rilla. Nan and Di are leaving for Redmond next week and neither your mother nor Susan is able to assume so much extra care under present conditions. If you want to keep that baby here you must attend to it yourself."

"Me!" Rilla was dismayed into being ungrammatical. "Why—father—I—I couldn't!"

"Younger girls than you have had to look after babies. My advice and Susan's is at your disposal. If you cannot, then the baby must go back to Meg Conover. Its lease of life will be short if it does for it is evident that it is a delicate child, and requires particular care. I doubt if it would survive even if sent to an orphan's home. But I cannot have your mother and Susan over-taxed."

The doctor walked out of the kitchen, looking very stern and immovable. In his heart he knew quite well that the small inhabitant of the big soup tureen would remain at Ingleside, but he meant to see if Rilla could not be induced to rise to the occasion.

Rilla sat looking blankly at the baby. It was absurd to think *she* could take care of it. But—that poor little, frail, dead mother who had worried about it—that dreadful old Meg Conover.

"Susan, what must be done for a baby?" she asked dolefully.

"You must keep it warm and dry and wash it every day, and be sure the water is neither too hot nor too cold, and feed it every two hours. If it has colic, you put hot things on its stomach," said Susan, rather feebly and flatly for her.

The baby began to cry again.

"It must be hungry—it has to be fed anyhow," said Rilla desperately. "Tell me what to get for it, Susan, and I'll get it."

Under Susan's directions a ration of milk and water was prepared, and a bottle obtained from the doctor's office. Then Rilla lifted the baby out of the soup tureen and fed it. She brought down the old basket of her own infancy from the attic and lay the now sleeping baby in it. She put the soup tureen away in the pantry. Then she sat down to think things over.

The result of her thinking things over was that she went to Susan when the baby woke.

"I'm going to see what I can do, Susan. I can't let that poor little thing go back to Mrs. Conover. Tell me how to wash and dress it."

Under Susan's supervision Rilla bathed the baby. Susan dared not help, other than by suggestion, for the doctor was in the living room and might pop in at any moment. Susan had learned by experience that when Dr. Blythe put his foot down and said a thing must be, that thing was. Rilla set her teeth and went ahead. In the name of goodness, how many wrinkles and kinks did a baby have? Why, there wasn't enough of it to take hold of. Oh, suppose she let it slip into the water—it was *so* wobbly! If it would only *stop* howling like that! How could such a tiny morsel make such an enormous noise. Its shrieks could be heard over Ingleside from cellar to attic.

"Am I really hurting it much, Susan, do you suppose?" she asked piteously.

"No dearie. Most new babies hate like poison to be washed. You are real knacky for a beginner. Keep your hand under its back, whatever you do, and keep cool."

Keep cool! Rilla was oozing perspiration at every pore. When the baby was dried and dressed and temporarily quieted with another bottle she was as limp as a rag.

"What must I do with it tonight, Susan?"

A baby by day was dreadful enough; a baby by night was unthinkable.

"Set the basket on a chair by your bed and keep it covered. You will have to feed it once or twice in the night, so you would better take the oil heater upstairs. If you cannot manage it call me and I will go, doctor or no doctor."

"But, Susan, if it cries?"

The baby, however, did not cry. It was surprisingly good—perhaps because its poor little stomach was filled with proper food. It slept most of the night but Rilla did not. She was afraid to go to sleep for fear something would happen to the baby. She prepared its three o'clock ration with a grim determination that she would *not* call Susan. Oh, was she dreaming? Was it really she, Rilla Blythe, who had got into this absurd predicament? She did not care if the Germans were near Paris—she did not care if they were *in* Paris—if only the baby wouldn't cry or choke or smother or have convulsions. Babies *did* have convulsions, didn't they? Oh, why had she forgotten to ask Susan what she must do if the baby had convulsions? She reflected rather bitterly that father was very considerate of mother's and Susan's health, but what about hers? Did he think she could continue to exist if she never got any sleep? But she was not going to back down now—not she. She would look after this detestable little animal if it killed her. She would get a book on baby hygiene and be beholden to nobody. She would *never* go to father for advice— she wouldn't bother mother—and she would only condescend to Susan in dire extremity. They would all see!

Thus it came about that Mrs. Blythe, when she returned home two nights later and asked Susan where Rilla was, was electrified by Susan's composed reply.

"She's upstairs, Mrs. Dr. dear, putting her baby to bed."

$\mathscr{R}$illa Decides

Families and individuals alike soon become used to new conditions and accept them unquestioningly. By the time a week had elapsed it seemed as if the Anderson baby had always been at Ingleside; it was simply part of the routine of daily life. After the first three distracted nights Rilla began to sleep again, waking automatically to attend to her charge on schedule time. She bathed and fed and dressed it as skilfully as if she had been doing it all her life. She liked neither her job nor the baby any the better; she still handled it as gingerly as if it were some kind of a small lizard, and a breakable lizard at that; but she did her work thoroughly and there was not a cleaner, better-cared-for infant in Glen St. Mary. She even took to weighing the creature every day and jotting the result down in her diary; but sometimes she asked herself pathetically why unkind destiny had ever led her down the Anderson lane on that fatal day. Shirley, Nan and Di did not tease her as much as she had expected. They all seemed rather stunned by the mere fact of Rilla adopting a war baby; perhaps, too, the doctor had issued instructions. Walter, of course, never had teased her over anything; one day he told her she was a brick.

"It took more courage for you to tackle that five pounds of new infant, Rilla-my-Rilla, than it would be for Jem to face a mile of Germans. I wish I had half your pluck," he said ruefully.

Rilla was very proud of Walter's approval; nevertheless, she wrote gloomily in her diary that night:—

"I wish I could *like* the baby a little bit. It would make things easier. But I don't. I've heard people say that when you took care of a baby you got fond of it—but you don't—*I* don't, anyway. And it's a *nuisance*—it interferes with everything. It just ties me down—and now of all times when I'm trying to get the Junior Reds started. And I couldn't go to Alice Clow's party last night and I was just dying to. Of course father isn't really unreasonable and I can always get an hour or two off in the evening when it's necessary; but I knew he wouldn't stand for my being out half the night and leaving Susan or mother to see to the baby. I suppose it was just as well, because the thing did take colic—or something—about one o'clock. It didn't kick or stiffen out, so I knew that, according to Morgan, it wasn't crying for temper; and it wasn't hungry and no pins were sticking in it. It screamed till it was black in the face; I got up and heated water and put the hot water bottle on its stomach, and it howled worse than ever and drew up its poor wee thin legs. I was afraid I had burnt it but I don't believe I did. Then I walked the floor with it although 'Morgan on Infants' says that should *never* be done. I walked miles, and oh, I was so tired and discouraged and *mad*—yes, I was. I could have shaken the creature if it had been big enough to shake, but it wasn't. Father was out on a case, and mother had had a headache and Susan is squiffy because when she and Morgan differ I insist upon going by what Morgan says, so I was determined I wouldn't call her unless I had to.

"Finally, Miss Oliver came in. She rooms with Nan now, not me, all because of the baby, and I am broken-hearted about it. I miss our long talks after we went to bed, so much. It was the only time I ever had her to myself. I hated to think the baby's yells had wakened her up, for she has so much to bear now. Mr. Grant is at Valcartier, too, and Miss Oliver feels it *dreadfully*, though she is splendid about it. She thinks he will never come back and her eyes just break my heart,—they are so *tragic*. She said it wasn't the baby that woke her—she hadn't been able to sleep because the Germans are so near Paris; she took the little wretch and laid it flat on its stomach across her knee and thumped its back gently a few times, and it stopped shrieking and went right off to sleep and slept like a lamb the rest of the night. *I* didn't—I was too worn out. I have just felt all day like something the cats had brought in, as Susan says.

"I'm having a *perfectly dreadful* time getting the Junior Reds started. I succeeded in getting Betty Mead as president, and I am secretary, but they put Jen Vickers in as treasurer and I *despise* her. She is the sort of girl who calls any clever or handsome or distinguished people she knows slightly by their first names—*behind their backs*. And she is sly and two-faced. Una doesn't mind, of course. She is willing to do anything that comes to hand and never minds whether she has an office or not. She is just a perfect angel, while I am only angelic in spots and demonic in other spots. I wish Walter would take a fancy to her, but he never seems to think about her in that way, although I heard him say once she was like a tea rose. She *is*, too. And she gets imposed upon, just because she is so sweet and willing; but *I* don't allow people to impose on Rilla Blythe and 'that you may tie to,' as Susan says.

"Just as I expected, Olive was determined we should have lunch served at our meetings. We had a battle royal over it. The majority was against eats and now the minority is sulking. Irene Howard was on the eats side and she has been very cool to me ever since and it makes me feel miserable. I wonder if Mother and Mrs. Elliott have problems in the Senior Society too. I suppose they have, but they just go on calmly in spite of everything. *I* go on—but *not* calmly—I rage and cry—but I do it all in private and blow off steam in this diary; and when it's over I vow I'll show them. I *never* sulk. I detest people who sulk. Anyhow, we've got the society started and we're to meet once a week, and we're all going to learn to knit. So much is accomplished.

"Shirley and I went down to the station again to try to induce Dog Monday to come home but we failed. All the family have tried and failed. Three days after Jem had gone Walter went down and brought Monday home by main force in the buggy and shut him up for three days. Then Monday went on a hunger strike and howled like a Banshee night and day. We *had* to let him out or he would have starved to death.

"So we have decided to let him alone and father has arranged with the butcher near the station to feed him with bones and scraps. Besides, one of us goes down nearly every day to take him something. He just lies curled up in the shipping shed, and every time a train comes in he will rush over to the platform, wagging his tail expectantly, and tear around to everyone who comes off the train. And then, when the train goes and he realizes that Jem has not come, he creeps dejectedly back to his shed, with his disappointed eyes, and lies down patiently to wait for the next train. Mr. Gray, the station master, says there are times when he can hardly help crying from sheer sympathy. One day some boys threw stones at Monday and old Johnny Mead, who never was known to take notice of anything before, snatched up a meat axe in the butcher's shop and chased them through the village. Nobody has molested Monday since.

"Kenneth Ford has gone back to Toronto. He came up two evenings ago to say good-bye. I wasn't home—some clothes had to be made for the baby and Mrs. Meredith offered to help me, so I was over at the manse, and I didn't see Kenneth.

Not that it matters; he told Nan to say good-bye to Spider for him and tell me not to forget him wholly in my absorbing maternal duties. If he could leave such a frivolous, insulting message as that for me it shows plainly that our beautiful hour on the sandshore meant *nothing* to him and I am not going to think about him or it again.

"Fred Arnold was at the manse and walked home with me. He is the new Methodist minister's son and very nice and clever, and would be quite handsome if it were not for his nose. It is a really dreadful nose. When he talks of common-place things it does not matter so much, but when he talks of poetry and ideals the contrast between his nose and his conversation is too much for me and I want to shriek with laughter. It is really not fair, because everything he said was perfectly charming and if somebody like Kenneth had said it I would have been *enraptured*. When I listened to him with my eyes cast down I was quite fascinated; but as soon as I looked up and saw his nose the spell was broken. He wants to enlist, too, but can't because he is only seventeen. Mrs. Elliott met us as we were walking through the village and could not have looked more horrified if she had caught me walking with the Kaiser himself. Mrs. Elliott detests the Methodists and all their works. Father says it is an obsession with her."

About the first of September there was an exodus from Ingleside and the manse. Faith, Nan, Di and Walter left for Redmond; Carl betook himself to his Harbour Head school and Shirley was off to Queen's. Rilla was left alone at Ingleside and would have been very lonely if she had had time to be. She missed Walter keenly; since their talk in Rainbow Valley they had grown very near together and Rilla discussed problems with Walter which she never mentioned to others. But she was so busy with the Junior Reds and her baby that there was rarely a spare minute for loneliness; sometimes, for a brief space after she went to bed she cried a little in her pillow over Walter's absence and Jem at Valcartier and Kenneth's unromantic farewell message, but she was generally asleep before the tears got fairly started.

"Shall I make arrangements to have the baby sent to Hopetown?" the doctor asked one day two weeks after the baby's arrival at Ingleside.

For a moment Rilla was tempted to say "yes." The baby could be sent to Hopetown—it would be decently looked after—she could have her free days and untrammelled nights back again. But—but—that poor young mother who hadn't wanted it to go to the asylum! Rilla couldn't get that out of her thoughts. *And* that very morning she discovered that the baby had gained eight ounces since its coming to Ingleside. Rilla had felt such a thrill of pride over this.

"You—you said it mightn't live if it went to Hopetown," she said.

"It mightn't. Somehow, institutional care, no matter how good it may be, doesn't always succeed with delicate babies. But you know what it means if you want it kept here, Rilla."

"I've taken care of it for a fortnight—and it has gained half a pound," cried Rilla. "I think we'd better wait until we hear from its father anyhow. *He* mightn't want to have it sent to an orphan asylum, when he is fighting the battles of his country."

The doctor and Mrs. Blythe exchanged amused, satisfied smiles behind Rilla's back; and nothing more was said about Hopetown.

Then the smile faded from the doctor's face; the Germans were twenty miles from Paris. Horrible tales were beginning to appear in the papers of deeds done in martyred Belgium. Life was very tense at Ingleside for the older people.

"We *eat* up the war news," Gertrude Oliver told Mrs. Meredith, trying to laugh and failing. "We study the maps and nip the whole Hun army in a few well-directed strategic moves. But Papa Joffre hasn't the benefit of our advice—and so Paris—must—fall."

"Will they reach it—will not some mighty hand yet intervene?" murmured John Meredith.

"I teach school like one in a dream," continued Gertrude; "then I come home and shut myself in my room and walk the floor. I am wearing a path right across Nan's carpet. We are so horribly *near* this war. It means so much to us all."

"Them German men are at Sen*lis*. Nothing nor nobody can save Paris now," wailed Cousin Sophia. Cousin Sophia had taken to reading the newspapers and had learned more about the geography of Northern France, if not about the pronunciation of French names, in her seventy-first year than she had ever known in her schooldays.

"I have not such a poor opinion of the Almighty, or of Kitchener," said Susan stubbornly. "I see there is a Bernstoff man in the States who says that the war is over and Germany has won,—and they tell me Whiskers-on-the-moon says the same thing and is quite pleased about it, but *I* could tell them both that it is chancy work counting chickens even the day before they are hatched, and bears have been known to live long after their skins were sold."

"Why ain't the British navy doing more?" persisted Cousin Sophia.

"Even the British navy cannot sail on dry land, Sophia Crawford. I have not given up hope, and I shall not, Tomascow and Mobbage and all such barbarous names to the contrary notwithstanding. Mrs. Dr. dear, can you tell me if R-h-e-i-m-s is Rimes or Reems or Rames or Rems?"

"I believe it's really more like 'Rhangs,' Susan."

"Oh, those French names," groaned Susan.

"They tell me the Germans has about ruined the church there," sighed Cousin Sophia. "I always thought the Germans was Christians."

"A church is bad enough but their doings in Belgium are far worse," said Susan grimly. "When I heard the doctor reading about them bayonetting the babies, Mrs. Dr. dear, I just thought, 'Oh, what if it were our Little Jem!' I was stirring the soup at the time, as you know, when that thought came to me and I just felt that if I could have lifted that saucepan full of that boiling soup and thrown it at the Kaiser I would not have lived in vain."

"Tomorrow—tomorrow—will bring the news that the Germans are in Paris," said Gertrude Oliver, through her tense lips. She had one of those souls that are always tied to the stake, burning in the suffering of the world around them. Apart from her own personal interest in the war, she was racked by the thought of Paris falling into the ruthless hands of the hordes who had burned Louvain and ruined the wonder of Rheims.

But on the morrow and the next morrow came the news of the miracle of the Marne. Rilla rushed madly home from the office waving the *Enterprise* with its big red headlines. Susan ran out with trembling hands to hoist the flag. The doctor stalked about muttering "Thank God." Mrs. Blythe cried and laughed and cried again.

"God just put out His hand and touched them—'thus far—no further,'" said Mr. Meredith that evening.

Rilla was singing upstairs as she put the baby to bed. Paris was saved—the war *was* over—Germany had lost—there would soon be an end now—Jem and Jerry would be back. The black clouds had rolled by.

"Don't you dare have colic this joyful night," she told the baby. "If you do I'll clap you back into your soup tureen and ship you off to Hopetown—by freight—on the early train. You *have* got beautiful eyes—and you're not quite as red and wrinkled as you were—but you haven't a speck of hair—and your hands are like little claws—and I don't like you a bit better than I ever did. But I hope your poor little white mother *knows* that you're tucked in a soft basket with a bottle of milk as rich as Morgan allows instead of perishing by inches with old Meg Conover. And I hope she *doesn't* know that I nearly drowned you that first morning when Susan wasn't there and I let you slip right out of my hands into the water. Why *will* you be so slippery? No, I don't like you and I never will but for all that I'm going to make a decent, upstanding infant of you. You are going to get as fat as a self-respecting child should be, for one thing. I am *not* going to have people saying 'what a puny little thing that baby of Rilla Blythe's is,' as old Mrs. Drew said at the senior Red Cross yesterday. If I can't love you I mean to be proud of you at least."

CHAPTER IX

$\mathscr{D}$oc Has a Misadventure

"The war will not be over before next spring now," said Dr. Blythe, when it became apparent that the long battle of the Aisne had resulted in stalemate.

Rilla was murmuring "knit four, purl one" under her breath, and rocking the baby's cradle with one foot. Morgan disapproved of cradles for babies but Susan did not, and it was worth while to make some slight sacrifice of principle to keep Susan in good humour. So a cradle had been substituted for Rilla's old basket. She laid down her knitting for a moment and said, "Oh, *how* can we bear it so long?"—then picked up her sock and went on. The Rilla of two months before would have rushed off to Rainbow Valley and cried.

Miss Oliver sighed and Mrs. Blythe clasped her hands for a moment. Then Susan said briskly, "Well, we must just gird up our loins and pitch in. Business as usual is England's motto, they tell me, Mrs. Dr. dear, and I have taken it for mine, not thinking I could easily find a better. I shall make the same kind of pudding today I always made on Saturday. It is a good deal of trouble to make, and that is well, for it will employ my thoughts. I will remember that Kitchener is at the helm and Joffer is doing very well for a Frenchman. I shall get that box of cake off to Little Jem and finish that pair of socks today likewise. A sock a day is my allowance. Old Mrs. Albert Mead of Harbour Head manages a pair and a half a day but she has nothing to do but knit. You know, Mrs. Dr. dear, she has been bedrid for years and she has been worrying terrible because she was no good to anybody and a dreadful expense, and yet could not die and be out of the way. And now they tell me she is quite chirked up and resigned to living because there is something she can do, and she knits for the soldiers from daylight until dark. Even Cousin Sophia has taken to knitting, Mrs. Dr. dear, and it is a good thing, for she cannot think of quite so many doleful speeches to make when her hands are busy with her needles instead of being folded on her stomach. She thinks we will all be Germans this time next year but I tell her it will take more than a year to make a German out of *me*. Do you know that Rick MacAllister has enlisted, Mrs. Dr. dear? And they say Joe Milgrave would too, only he is afraid that if he does that Whiskers-on-the-moon will not let him have Miranda. Whiskers says that he will believe the stories of German atrocities when he sees them, and that it is a good thing that Rangs Cathedral has been destroyed because it was a Roman Catholic church. Now, I am not a Roman Catholic, Mrs. Dr. dear, being born and bred a good Presbyterian and meaning to live and die one, but I maintain that the Catholics have as good a right to their churches as we have to ours and that the Huns had no kind of business to destroy them. Just think, Mrs. Dr. dear," concluded Susan pathetically, "how *we* would feel if a German shell knocked down the spire of *our* church here in the Glen, and I am sure it is every bit as bad to think of Rangs Cathedral being hammered to pieces."

And, meanwhile, everywhere, the lads of the world rich and poor, low and high, white and brown, were following the Piper's call.

"Even Billy Andrews' boy is going—and Jane's only son— and Diana's little Jack," said Mrs. Blythe. "Priscilla's son has gone from Japan and Stella's from Vancouver—and both the

Rev. Jo's boys. Philippa writes that her boys 'went right away, not being afflicted with her indecision.'"

"Jem says that he thinks they will be leaving very soon now, and that he will not be able to get leave to come so far before they go, as they will have to start at a few hours' notice," said the doctor, passing the letter to his wife.

"That is not fair," said Susan indignantly. "Has Sir Sam Hughes no regard for our feelings? The idea of whisking that blessed boy away to Europe without letting us even have a last glimpse of him! If I were you, doctor dear, I would write to the papers about it, that I would."

"Perhaps it is as well," said the disappointed mother. "I don't believe I could bear another parting from him—now that I know the war will not be over as soon as we hoped when he left first. Oh, if only—but no, I won't say it! Like Susan and Rilla," concluded Mrs. Blythe, achieving a laugh, "I am determined to be a heroine."

"You're all good stuff," said the doctor, "I'm proud of my women folks. Even Rilla here, my 'lily of the field,' is running a Red Cross Society full blast and saving a little life for Canada. That's a good piece of work. Rilla, daughter of Anne, what are you going to call your war baby?"

"I'm waiting to hear from Jim Anderson," said Rilla. "He may want to name his own child."

But as the autumn weeks went by no word came from Jim Anderson, who had never been heard from since he sailed from Halifax, and to whom the fate of wife and child seemed a matter of indifference. Eventually Rilla decided to call the baby James, and Susan opined that Kitchener should be added thereto. So James Kitchener Anderson became the possessor of a name somewhat more imposing than himself. The Ingleside family promptly shortened it to "Jims," but

Susan obstinately called him "Little Kitchener" and nothing else.

"Jims is no name for a Christian child, Mrs. Dr. dear," she said disapprovingly. "Cousin Sophia says it is too flippant, and for once I consider she utters sense, though I would not please her by openly agreeing with her. As for the child, he is beginning to look something like a baby, and I must admit that Rilla is wonderful with him, though I would not pamper pride by saying so to her face. Mrs. Dr. dear, I shall never, no never, forget the first sight I had of that infant, lying in that big soup tureen, rolled up in dirty flannel. It is not often that Susan Baker is flabbergasted, but flabbergasted I was then, and that you may tie to. For one awful moment I thought my mind had given way and that I was seeing visions. Then thinks I, 'No, I never heard of any one having a vision of a soup tureen, so *it* must be real at least,' and I plucked up confidence. When I heard the Doctor tell Rilla that she must take care of the baby I thought he was joking, for I did not believe for a minute she would or could do it. But you see what has happened and it is making a woman of her. When we *have* to do a thing, Mrs. Dr. dear, we *can* do it."

Susan added another proof to this concluding dictum of hers one day in October. The doctor and his wife were away. Rilla was presiding over Jims' afternoon siesta upstairs, purling four and knitting one with ceaseless vim. Susan was seated on the back veranda, shelling beans, and Cousin Sophia was helping her. Peace and tranquillity brooded over the Glen; the sky was fleeced over with silvery, shining clouds. Rainbow Valley lay in a soft, autumnal haze of fairy purple. The maple grove was a burning bush of colour and the hedge of sweet-briar around the kitchen yard was a thing of wonder in its subtle tintings. It did not seem that strife could be in the world, and Susan's faithful heart was lulled into a brief forgetfulness, although she had lain awake most of the preceding night thinking of Little Jem far out on the Atlantic, where the great fleet was carrying Canada's first army across the ocean. Even Cousin Sophia looked less melancholy than usual and admitted that there was not much fault to be found in the day, although there was no doubt it was a weather-breeder and there would be an awful storm on its heels.

"Things is too calm to last," she said.

As if in confirmation of her assertion, a most unearthly din suddenly arose behind them. It was quite impossible to describe the confused medley of bangs and rattles and muffled shrieks and yowls that proceeded from the kitchen, accompanied by occasional crashes. Susan and Cousin Sophia stared at each other in dismay.

"What upon airth has bruk loose in there?" gasped Cousin Sophia.

"It must be that Hyde-cat gone clean mad at last," muttered Susan. "I have always expected it."

Rilla came flying out of the side door of the living room.

"What has happened?" she demanded.

"It is beyond me to say, but that possessed beast of yours is evidently at the bottom of it," said Susan. "Do not go near him, at least. I will open the door and peep in. There goes some more of the crockery. I have always said that the devil was in him and that I will tie to."

"It is my opinion that the cat has hydrophobia," said Cousin Sophia solemnly. "I once heard of a cat that went mad and bit three people—and they all died a most terrible death, and turned as black as ink."

Undismayed by this, Susan opened the door and looked in. The floor was littered with fragments of broken dishes, for it seemed that the fatal tragedy had taken place on the long dresser where Susan's array of cooking bowls had been marshalled in shining state. Around and around the kitchen tore a frantic cat, with his head wedged tightly in an old salmon can. Blindly he careened about with shrieks and profanity commingled, now banging the can madly against anything he encountered, now trying vainly to wrench it off with his paws.

The sight was so funny that Rilla doubled up with laughter. Susan looked at her reproachfully.

"I see nothing to laugh at. That beast has broken your ma's big blue mixing bowl that she brought from Green Gables when she was married. That is no small calamity, in my opinion. But the thing to consider now is how to get that can off Hyde's head."

"Don't you dast go touching it," exclaimed Cousin Sophia, galvanized into animation. "It might be your death. Shut the kitchen up and send for Albert."

"I am not in the habit of sending for Albert during family difficulties," said Susan loftily. "That beast is in torment, and whatever my opinion of him may be, I cannot endure to see him suffering pain. He is not mad—at least not any madder than he frequently is. But you keep away, Rilla, for little Kitchener's sake, and I will see what I can do."

Susan stalked undauntedly into the kitchen, seized an old storm coat of the doctor's and after a wild pursuit and several fruitless dashes and pounces, managed to throw it over the cat and can. Then she proceeded to saw the can loose with a can opener, while Rilla held the squirming animal, rolled in the coat. Anything like Doc's shrieks while the process was going on was never heard at Ingleside. Susan was in mortal dread that the Albert Crawfords would hear it and conclude she was torturing the creature to death. Doc was a wrathful and indignant cat when he was freed. Evidently he thought the whole thing was a put up job to bring him low. He gave Susan a baleful glance by way of gratitude and rushed out of the kitchen to take sanctuary in the jungle of the sweet-briar hedge, where he sulked for the rest of the day. Susan swept up her broken dishes grimly.

"The Huns themselves couldn't have worked more havoc here," she said bitterly. "But when people *will* keep a Satanic animal like that, in spite of all warnings, they cannot complain when their wedding bowls get broken. Things have come to a pretty pass when an honest woman cannot leave her kitchen for a few minutes without a fiend of a cat rampaging through it with his head in a salmon can."

$\mathscr{T}$he Troubles of Rilla

October passed out and the dreary days of November and December dragged by. The world shook with the thunder of contending armies; Antwerp fell—Turkey declared war— gallant little Serbia gathered herself together and struck a deadly blow at her oppressor; and in quiet, hill-girdled Glen St. Mary, thousands of miles away, hearts beat with hope and fear over the varying dispatches from day to day.

"A few months ago," said Miss Oliver, "we thought and talked in terms of Glen St. Mary. Now, we think and talk in terms of military tactics and diplomatic intrigue."

There was just one great event every day—the coming of the mail. Even Susan admitted, that from the time the mail- courier's buggy rumbled over the little bridge between the station and the village until the papers were brought home and read, she could not work properly.

"I must take up my knitting then and knit hard till the papers come, Mrs. Dr. dear. Knitting is something you can do, even when your heart is going like a trip-hammer and the pit of your stomach feels all gone and your thoughts are catawampus. Then when I see the headlines, be they good or be they bad, I calm down and am able to go about my business again. It is an unfortunate thing that the mail comes in just when our dinner rush is on, and I think the Government could arrange things better. But the drive on Calais has failed, as I felt perfectly sure it would, and the Kaiser will not eat his Christmas dinner in London *this* year. Do you know, Mrs.

Dr. dear"—Susan's voice lowered as a token that she was going to impart a very shocking piece of information,—"I have been told on good authority—or else you may be sure I would not be repeating it when it concerns a minister—that the Rev. Mr. Arnold goes to Charlottetown every week and takes a Turkish bath for his rheumatism. The idea of him doing that when we are at war with Turkey? One of his own deacons has always insisted that Mr. Arnold's theology was not sound and I am beginning to believe that there is some reason to fear it. Well, I must bestir myself this afternoon and get Little Jem's Christmas cake packed up for him. He will enjoy it, if the blessed boy is not drowned in mud before that time."

Jem was in camp on Salisbury Plain and was writing gay, cheery letters home in spite of the mud. Walter was at Redmond and his letters to Rilla were anything but cheerful. She never opened one without a dread tugging at her heart that it would tell her he had enlisted. His unhappiness made her unhappy. She wanted to put her arm around him and comfort him, as she had done that day in Rainbow Valley. She hated everybody who was responsible for Walter's unhappiness.

"He will go yet," she murmured miserably to herself one afternoon, as she sat alone in Rainbow Valley, reading a letter from him, "he will go yet—and if he does I just can't bear it."

Walter wrote that some one had sent him an envelope containing a white feather.

"I deserved it, Rilla. I felt that I ought to put it on and wear it—proclaiming myself to all Redmond the coward I know I am. The boys of my year are going—going. Every day two or three of them join up. Some days I *almost* make up my mind to do it—and then I see myself thrusting a bayonet through another man—some woman's husband or sweetheart or son—perhaps the father of little children—I see myself lying alone torn and mangled, burning with thirst on a cold, wet field, surrounded by dead and dying men—and I know I *never* can. I can't face even the thought of it. How could I face the reality? There are times when I wish I had never been born. Life has always seemed such a beautiful thing to me—I wanted to make it more beautiful—and now it is a hideous thing. Rilla-my-Rilla, if it weren't for your letters—your dear, bright, merry, funny, comical, *believing* letters—I think I'd give up. And Una's! Una is really a little brick, isn't she? There's a wonderful fineness and firmness under all that shy, wistful, girlishness of her. She hasn't your knack of writing laugh-provoking epistles, but there's something in her letters—I don't know what—that makes me feel at least while I'm reading them, that I could even go to the front. Not that she ever says a word about my going—or hints that I ought to go—she isn't that kind. It's just the *spirit* of them—the personality that is in them. Well, I can't go. You have a brother and Una has a friend who is a *coward*."

"Oh, I wish Walter wouldn't write such things," sighed Rilla. "It *hurts* me. He isn't a coward—he isn't—he isn't!"

She looked wistfully about her—at the little woodland valley and the grey, lonely fallows beyond. How everything reminded her of Walter! The red leaves still clung to the wild sweet-briars that overhung a curve of the brook; their stems were gemmed with the pearls of the gentle rain that had fallen a little while before. Walter had once written a poem describing them. The wind was sighing and rustling among the frosted brown bracken ferns, then lessening sorrowfully away down the brook. Walter had said once that he loved the melancholy of the autumn wind on a November day. The old

Tree Lovers still clasped each other in a faithful embrace, and the White Lady, now a great white-branched tree, stood out beautifully fine, against the grey velvet sky. Walter had named them long ago; and last November, when he had walked with her and Miss Oliver in the Valley, he had said, looking at the leafless Lady, with a young silver moon hanging over her, "A white birch is a beautiful Pagan maiden who has never lost the Eden secret of being naked and unashamed." Miss Oliver had said, "Put that into a poem, Walter," and he had done so, and read it to them the next day—just a short thing with goblin imagination in every line of it. Oh, how happy they had been then!

Well—Rilla scrambled to her feet—time was up. Jims would soon be awake—his lunch had to be prepared—his little slips had to be ironed—there was a committee meeting of the Junior Reds that night—there was her new knitting bag to finish—it would be the handsomest bag in the Junior Society—handsomer even than Irene Howard's—she must get home and get to work. She was busy these days from morning till night. That little monkey of a Jims took so much time. But he was growing—he was certainly growing. And there were times when Rilla felt sure that it was not merely a pious hope but an absolute fact that he was getting decidedly better looking. Sometimes she felt quite proud of him; and sometimes she yearned to spank him. But she never kissed him or wanted to kiss him.

"The Germans captured Lodz today," said Miss Oliver, one December evening, when she, Mrs. Blythe and Susan were busy sewing or knitting in the cosy living room. "This war is at least extending my knowledge of geography. Schoolma'am though I am, three months ago I didn't know there was such a place in the world as Lodz. Had I heard it mentioned I would have known nothing about it and cared as little. I know all about it now—its size, its standing, its military significance. Yesterday the news that the Germans have captured it in their second rush to Warsaw made my heart sink into my boots. I woke up in the night and worried over it. I don't wonder babies always cry when they wake up in the night. Everything presses on my soul then and no cloud has a silver lining."

"When *I* wake up in the night and cannot go to sleep again," remarked Susan, who was knitting and reading at the same time, "I pass the moments by torturing the Kaiser to death. Last night I fried him in boiling oil and a great comfort it was to me, remembering those Belgian babies."

"If the Kaiser were here and had a pain in his shoulder you'd be the first to run for the liniment bottle to rub him down," laughed Miss Oliver.

"Would I?" cried outraged Susan. "Would I, Miss Oliver? I would rub him down with coal oil, Miss Oliver—and leave it to blister. *That* is what I would do and that you may tie to. A pain in his shoulder, indeed! He will have pains all over him before he is through with what he has started."

"We are told to love our enemies, Susan," said the doctor solemnly.

"Yes, *our* enemies, but not King George's enemies, doctor dear," retorted Susan crushingly. She was so well pleased with herself over this flattening out of the doctor completely that she even smiled as she polished her glasses. Susan had never given in to glasses before, but she had done so at last in order to be able to read the war news—and not a dispatch got by her. "Can you tell me, Miss Oliver, how to pronounce M-l-a-w-a and B-z-u-r-a and P-r-z-e-m-y-s-l?"

"That last is a conundrum which nobody seems to have solved yet, Susan. And I can make only a guess at the others."

"These foreign names are far from being decent, in my opinion," said disgusted Susan.

"I daresay the Austrians and Russians would think Saskatchewan and Musquodoboit about as bad, Susan," said Miss Oliver. "The Serbians have done wonderfully of late. They have captured Belgrade."

"And sent the Austrian creatures packing across the Danube with a flea in their ear," said Susan with a relish, as she settled down to examine a map of Eastern Europe, prodding each locality with her knitting needle to brand it on her memory. "Cousin Sophia said awhile ago that Serbia was done for, but I told her there was still such a thing as an over-ruling Providence, doubt it who might. It says here that the slaughter was terrible. For all they were foreigners it is awful to think of so many men being killed, Mrs. Dr. dear—for they are scarce enough as it is."

Rilla was upstairs relieving her over-charged feelings by writing in her diary.

"Things have all 'gone catawampus,' as Susan says, with me this week. Part of it was my own fault and part of it wasn't, and I seem to be equally unhappy over both parts.

"I went to town the other day to buy a new winter hat. It was the first time nobody insisted on coming with me to help me select it, and I felt that mother had really given up thinking of me as a child. And I found the dearest hat—it was simply bewitching. It was a velvet hat, of the very shade of rich green that was *made* for me. It just goes with my hair and complexion beautifully, bringing out the red-brown shades and what Miss Oliver calls my 'creaminess' so well. Only once before in my life have I come across that precise shade of green. When I was twelve I had a little beaver hat of it, and all the girls in school were wild over it. Well, as soon as I saw this hat I felt that I simply must have it—and have it I did. The price was dreadful. I will not put it down here because I don't want my descendants to know I was guilty of paying so much for a hat in war time, too, when everybody is—or should be—trying to be economical.

"When I got home and tried on the hat again in my room I was assailed by qualms. Of course, it was very becoming; but somehow it seemed too elaborate and fussy for church going and our quiet little doings in the Glen—too conspicuous, in short. It hadn't seemed so at the milliner's but here in my little white room it did. And that dreadful price tag! *And* the starving Belgians! When mother saw the hat and the tag she just *looked* at me. Mother is some expert at looking. Father says she looked him into love with her years ago in Avonlea school and I can well believe it—though I *have* heard a weird tale of her banging him over the head with a slate at the very beginning of their acquaintance. Mother was a limb when she was a little girl, I understand, and even up to the time when Jem went away she was full of ginger. But let me return to my mutton—that is to say, my new green velvet hat.

"'Do you think, Rilla,' mother said quietly—far too quietly—'that it was right to spend so much for a hat, especially just now when the need of the world is so great?'

"'I paid for it out of my own allowance, mother,' I exclaimed.

"'That is not the point. Your allowance is based on the principle of a reasonable amount for each thing you need. If you pay too much for one thing you must cut off somewhere else and that is not satisfactory. But if you think you did right, Rilla, I have no more to say. I leave it to your conscience.'

"I *wish* mother would not leave things to my conscience! And anyway, what was I to do? I couldn't take that hat back—

I had worn it to a concert in town—I had to keep it! I was so uncomfortable that I flew into a temper—a cold, calm, deadly temper.

"'Mother,' I said haughtily, 'I am sorry you disapprove of my hat—'

"'Not of the hat exactly,' said mother, 'though I consider it in doubtful taste for so young a girl—but of the price you paid for it.'

"Being interrupted didn't improve my temper, so I went on, colder and calmer and deadlier than ever, just as if mother had not spoken,

"'—but I have to keep it now. However, I promise you that I will not get another hat for three years or for the duration of the war, if it lasts longer than that. Even *you*'—oh, the sarcasm I put into the 'you'—'cannot say that what I paid was too much when spread over at least three years.'

"'You will be very tired of that hat before three years, Rilla,' said mother, with a provoking grin, which, being interpreted, meant that I wouldn't stick it out.

"'Tired or not, I will wear it that long,' I said: and then I marched upstairs and cried to think that I had been sarcastic to mother.

"I hate that hat already. But three years or the duration of the war, I said, and three years or the duration of the war it shall be. I vowed and I shall keep my vow, cost what it will.

"That is one of the 'catawampus' things. The other is that I have quarrelled with Irene Howard—or she quarrelled with me—or, no, we *both* quarrelled.

"The Junior Red Cross met here yesterday. The hour of meeting was half past two but Irene came at half past one, because she got the chance of a drive down from the Upper Glen. Irene hasn't been a bit nice to me since the fuss about the eats; and besides I feel sure she resents not being president. But I have been determined that things should go smoothly, so I have never taken any notice, and when she came yesterday she seemed so nice and sweet again that I hoped she had got over her huffiness and we could be the chums we used to be.

"But as soon as we sat down Irene began to rub me the wrong way. I saw her cast a look at my knitting bag. All the girls have always said Irene was jealous-minded and I would never believe them before. But now I feel that perhaps she is.

"The first thing she did was to pounce on Jims—Irene pretends to adore babies—pick him out of his cradle and kiss him *all over his face*. Now, Irene knows perfectly well that I don't like to have Jims kissed like that. It is not hygienic. After she had worried him till he began to fuss, she looked at me and gave quite a nasty little laugh but she said, oh, so sweetly,

"'Why, Rilla, *darling*, you look as if you thought I was poisoning the baby.'

"'Oh, no, I don't, Irene,' I said—*every bit* as sweetly, 'but you know Morgan says that the only place a baby should be kissed is on its forehead, for fear of germs, and that is my rule with Jims.'

"'Dear me, am I so full of germs?' said Irene plaintively. I knew she was making fun of me and I began to boil inside—but outside no sign of a simmer. I was determined I would *not* scrap with Irene.

"Then she began to *bounce* Jims. Now, Morgan says bouncing is almost the worst thing that can be done to a baby. I *never* allow Jims to be bounced. But Irene bounced him and that exasperating child liked it. He smiled—for the very first time. He is four months old and he has never smiled once before. Not even mother or Susan have been able to coax that thing to smile, try as they would. And here he was smiling because Irene Howard bounced him! Talk of gratitude!

"I admit that smile made a big difference in him. Two of the dearest dimples came out in his cheeks and his big brown eyes seemed full of laughter. The way Irene raved over those dimples was silly, I consider. You would have supposed she thought she had really brought them into existence. But I sewed steadily and did not enthuse, and soon Irene got tired of bouncing Jims and put him back in his cradle. He did not like that after being played with, and he began to cry and was fussy the rest of the afternoon, whereas if Irene had only left him alone he would not have been a bit of trouble. Irene looked at him and said,

"'Does he often cry like that?'—as if she had never heard a baby crying before.

"I explained patiently that children *have* to cry so many minutes per day in order to expand their lungs. Morgan says so.

"'If Jims didn't cry at all I'd have to *make* him cry for at *least* twenty minutes,' I said.

"'Oh, *indeed*!' said Irene, laughing as if she didn't believe me. 'Morgan on the Care of Infants' was upstairs or I would soon have convinced her. Then she said Jims didn't have much hair—she had never seen a four months' old baby so bald.

"Of course, I knew Jims hadn't much hair—yet; but Irene said it in a tone that seemed to imply it was my fault that he hadn't any hair. I said I had seen *dozens* of babies every bit as bald as Jims, and Irene said, Oh, very well, she hadn't meant to offend me—when I *wasn't* offended.

"It went on like that the rest of the hour—Irene kept giving me little digs all the time. The girls have always said she was revengeful like that if she were peeved about anything; but I never believed it before; I used to think Irene just perfect, and it hurt me dreadfully to find she could stoop to this. But I corked up my feelings and sewed away for dear life on a Belgian child's nightgown.

"Then Irene told me the meanest, most contemptible thing that some one had said about *Walter*. I won't write it down—I can't. Of course, *she* said it made *her* furious to hear it and all that—but there was no need for her to tell me such a thing even if she *did* hear it. She simply did it to hurt me.

"I just exploded.

"'How dare you come here and repeat such a thing to me about my brother, Irene Howard?' I exclaimed. 'I shall never forgive you—never. *Your* brother hasn't enlisted—hasn't any idea of enlisting.'

"'Why Rilla, *dear*, *I* didn't say it,' said Irene. 'I told you it was Mrs. George Burr. And *I* told *her*—'

"'I don't want to hear what you told her. Don't you *ever* speak to me again, Irene Howard.'

"Of course, I shouldn't have said that. But it just seemed to say itself. Then the other girls all came in a bunch and I had to calm down and act the hostess' part as well as I could. Irene paired off with Olive Kirk all the rest of the afternoon and went away without so much as a look. So I suppose she means to take me at my word and I don't care, for I do not want to be friends with a girl who could repeat such a falsehood about Walter. But I feel unhappy over it for all that. We've always been such good chums and until lately Irene *was* lovely to me; and now another illusion has been stripped from my eyes and I feel as if there wasn't such a thing as real true friendship in the world.

"Father got old Joe Mead to build a little kennel for Dog Monday in the corner of the shipping shed today. We thought perhaps Monday would come home when the cold weather came but he wouldn't. No earthly influence can coax Monday away from that shed even for a few minutes. There he stays and meets every train. So we had to do something to make him comfortable. Joe built the kennel so that Monday could lie in it and still see the platform, so we hope he will occupy it.

"Monday has become quite famous. A reporter of the *Enterprise* came out from town and photographed him and wrote up the whole story of his faithful vigil. It was published in the *Enterprise* and copied all over Canada. But that doesn't matter to poor little Monday, Jem has gone away—Monday doesn't know where or why—but he will wait until he comes back. Somehow it comforts me: it's foolish, I suppose, but it gives me a feeling that Jem *will* come back or else Monday wouldn't keep on waiting for him.

"Jims is snoring beside me in his cradle. It is just a cold that makes him snore—not adenoids. Irene had a cold yesterday and I *know* she gave it to him, kissing him. He is not quite such a nuisance as he was; he has got some backbone and can sit up quite nicely, and he loves his bath now and splashes unsmilingly in the water instead of twisting and shrieking. Oh, shall I *ever* forget those first two months! I don't know how I lived through them. But here I am and here is Jims and we are both going to 'carry on.' I tickled him a little bit tonight when I undressed him—I wouldn't bounce him but Morgan doesn't mention tickling—just to see if he would smile for *me* as well as for Irene. And he *did*—and out popped the dimples. What a pity his mother couldn't have seen them!

"I finished my sixth pair of socks today. With the first three I got Susan to set the heel for me. Then I thought that was a bit of shirking, so I learned to do it myself. I hate it—

but I have done so many things I hate since the fourth of August that one more or less doesn't matter. I just think of Jem joking about the mud on Salisbury Plain and I go at them."

CHAPTER XI

$\mathcal{D}$ark and Bright

At Christmas the college boys and girls came home and for a little while Ingleside was gay again. But all were not there—for the first time one was missing from the circle around the Christmas table. Jem, of the steady lips and fearless eyes, was far away, and Rilla felt that the sight of his vacant chair was more than she could endure. Susan had taken a stubborn freak and insisted on setting out Jem's place for him as usual, with the twisted little napkin ring he had always had since a boy, and the odd, high Green Gables goblet which Aunt Marilla had once given him and from which he always insisted on drinking.

"That blessed boy shall have his place, Mrs. Dr. dear," said Susan firmly, "and do not you feel over it, for you may be sure he is here in spirit and next Christmas he will be here in the body. Wait you till the Big Push comes in the spring and the war will be over in a jiffy."

They tried to think so, but a shadow stalked in the background of their determined merrymaking. Walter, too, was quiet and dull, all through the holidays. He showed Rilla a cruel, anonymous letter he had received at Redmond—a letter far more conspicuous for malice than for patriotic indignation.

"Nevertheless, all it says is true, Rilla."

Rilla had caught it from him and thrown it into the fire.

"There isn't one word of truth in it," she declared hotly. "Walter, you've got morbid—as Miss Oliver says she gets when she broods too long over one thing."

"I can't get away from it at Redmond, Rilla. The whole college is aflame over the war. A perfectly fit fellow, of military age, who doesn't join up is looked upon as a shirker and treated accordingly. Dr. Milne, the English professor, who has always made a special pet of me, has two sons in khaki; and I can feel the change in his manner towards me."

"It's not fair—you're not fit."

"Physically I am. Sound as a bell. The unfitness is in the soul and it's a taint and a disgrace. There, don't cry, Rilla. I'm not going if that's what you're afraid of. The Piper's music rings in my ears day and night—but I cannot follow."

"You would break mother's heart and mine if you did," sobbed Rilla. "Oh, Walter, one is enough for any family."

The holidays were an unhappy time for her. Still, having Nan and Di and Walter and Shirley home helped in the enduring of things. A letter and book came for her from Kenneth Ford, too; some sentences in the letter made her cheeks burn and her heart beat—until the last paragraph, which sent an icy chill over everything.

"My ankle is about as good as new. I'll be fit to join up in a couple of months more, Rilla-my-Rilla. It will be some feeling to get into khaki all right. Little Ken will be able to look the whole world in the face then and owe not any man. It's been rotten lately, since I've been able to walk without limping. People who don't know look at me as much as to say 'Slacker!' Well, they won't have the chance to look it much longer."

"I hate this war," said Rilla bitterly, as she gazed out into the maple grove that was a chill glory of pink and gold in the winter sunset.

"Nineteen-fourteen has gone," said Dr. Blythe on New Year's Day. "Its sun, which rose fairly, has set in blood. What will nineteen-fifteen bring?"

"Victory!" said Susan, for once laconic.

"Do you really believe we'll win the war, Susan?" said Miss Oliver drearily. She had come over from Lowbridge to spend the day and see Walter and the girls before they went back to Redmond. She was in a rather blue and cynical mood and inclined to look on the dark side.

"'Believe' we'll win the war!" exclaimed Susan. "No, Miss Oliver, dear, I do not *believe*—I *know*. *That* does not worry me. What *does* worry me is the trouble and expense of it all. But then you cannot make omelets without breaking eggs, so we must just trust in God and make big guns."

"Sometimes I think the big guns are better to trust in than God," said Miss Oliver defiantly.

"No, no, dear, you do not. The Germans had the big guns at the Marne, had they not? But Providence settled *them*. Do not ever forget *that*. Just hold on to that when you feel inclined to doubt. Clutch hold of the sides of your chair and sit tight and keep saying, 'Big guns are good but the Almighty is better, and *He* is on our side, no matter what the Kaiser says about it.' I would have gone crazy many a day lately, Miss Oliver, dear, if I had not sat tight and repeated that to myself. My cousin Sophia is, like you, somewhat inclined to despond. 'Oh, dear me, what will we do if the Germans ever get here,' she wailed to me yesterday. 'Bury them,' said I, just as off-hand as that. 'There is plenty of room for the graves.' Cousin Sophia said that I was flippant but I was not flippant, Miss Oliver, dear, only calm and confident in the British navy and our Canadian boys. I am like old Mr. William Pollock of the Harbour Head. He is very old and has been ill for a long time, and one night last week he was so low that his daughter-in-law whispered to some one that she thought he was dead. 'Darn it, I ain't,' he called right out—only, Miss Oliver, dear, he did not use so mild a word as 'darn'—'darn it, I ain't, and I don't mean to die until the Kaiser is well licked.' Now, *that*, Miss Oliver, dear," concluded Susan, "is the kind of spirit I admire."

"I admire it but I can't emulate it," sighed Gertrude. "Before this, I have always been able to escape from the hard things of life for a little while by going into dreamland, and coming back like a giant refreshed. But I can't escape from *this*."

"Nor I," said Mrs. Blythe. "I hate going to bed now. All my life I've liked going to bed, to have a gay, mad, splendid half hour of imagining things before sleeping. Now I imagine them still. But such different things."

"*I* am rather glad when the time comes to go to bed," said Miss Oliver. "I like the darkness because I can be *myself* in it—I needn't smile or talk bravely. But sometimes my imagination gets out of hand, too, and I see what you do—terrible things—terrible years to come."

"I am very thankful that I never had any imagination to speak of," said Susan. "I have been spared *that*. I see by this paper that the Crown Prince is killed again. Do you suppose there is any hope of his staying dead this time? And I also see that Woodrow Wilson is going to write another note. I wonder," concluded Susan, with the bitter irony she had of late begun to use when referring to the poor president, "if that man's schoolmaster is alive."

In January Jims was five months old and Rilla celebrated the anniversary by shortening him.

"He weighs fourteen pounds," she announced jubilantly.

"Just exactly what he should weigh at five months, according to Morgan."

There was no longer any doubt in anybody's mind that Jims was getting positively pretty. His little cheeks were round and firm and faintly pink, his eyes were big and bright, his tiny paws had dimples at the root of every finger. He had even begun to grow hair, much to Rilla's unspoken relief. There was a pale golden fuzz all over his head which was distinctly visible in some lights. He was a good infant, generally sleeping and digesting as Morgan decreed. Occasionally he smiled but he had never laughed, in spite of all efforts to make him. This worried Rilla also, because Morgan said that babies usually laughed aloud from the third to the fifth month. Jims was five and had no notion of laughing. Why hadn't he? Wasn't he normal?

One night Rilla came home late from a recruiting meeting at the Glen where she had been giving patriotic recitations. Rilla had never been willing to recite in public before. She was afraid of her tendency to lisp, which had a habit of reviving if she were doing anything that made her nervous. When she had first been asked to recite at the Upper Glen meeting she had refused. Then she began to worry over her refusal. Was it cowardly? What would Jem think if he knew? After two days of worry Rilla 'phoned to the president of the Patriotic Society that she would recite. She did, and lisped several times, and lay awake most of the night in an agony of wounded vanity. Then two nights after she recited again at Harbour Head. She had been at Lowbridge and over-harbour since then and had become resigned to an occasional lisp. Nobody except herself seemed to mind it. And she was so earnest and appealing and shining-eyed! More than one recruit joined up because Rilla's eyes seemed to look right at *him* when she passionately demanded how could men die better than fighting for the ashes of their fathers and the temples of their gods, or assured her audience with thrilling intensity that one crowded hour of glorious life was worth an age without a name. Even stolid Miller Douglas was so fired one night that it took Mary Vance a good hour to talk him back to sense. Mary Vance said bitterly that if Rilla Blythe felt as bad as she had pretended to feel over Jem's going to the front she wouldn't be urging other girls' brothers and friends to go.

On this particular night Rilla was tired and cold and very thankful to creep into her warm nest and cuddle down between her blankets, though as usual with a sorrowful wonder how Jem and Jerry were faring. She was just getting warm and drowsy when Jims suddenly began to cry—and kept on crying.

Rilla curled herself up in her bed and determined she would let him cry. She had Morgan behind her for justification. Jims was warm, physically comfortable—his cry wasn't the cry of pain—and had his little tummy as full as was good for him. Under such circumstances it would be simply spoiling him to fuss over him, and she wasn't going to do it. He could cry until he got good and tired and ready to go to sleep again.

Then Rilla's imagination began to torment her. Suppose, she thought, I was a tiny, helpless creature only five months old, with my father somewhere in France and my poor little mother, who had been so worried about me, in the graveyard. Suppose I was lying in a basket in a big, black room, without one speck of light, and nobody within miles of me, for all I could see or know. Suppose there wasn't a human being anywhere who loved me—for a father who had never seen me couldn't love me very much, especially when he had never written a word to or about me. Wouldn't I cry, too? Wouldn't I feel just so lonely and forsaken and frightened that I'd *have* to cry?

Rilla hopped out. She picked Jims out of his basket and took him into her own bed. His hands *were* cold, poor mite. But he had promptly ceased to cry. And then, as she held him close to her in the darkness, suddenly Jims laughed—a real, gurgly, chuckly, delighted, delightful laugh.

"Oh, you dear little thing!" exclaimed Rilla. "Are you so pleased at finding you're not all alone, lost in a huge, big, black room?" Then she knew she wanted to kiss him and she did. She kissed his silky, scented little head, she kissed his chubby little cheek, she kissed his little cold hands. She wanted to squeeze him—to cuddle him, just as she used to squeeze and cuddle her kittens. Something delightful and yearning and brooding seemed to have taken possession of her. She had never felt like this before.

In a few minutes Jims was sound asleep; and, as Rilla listened to his soft, regular breathing and felt the little body warm and contented against her, she realized that—at last—she loved her war baby.

"He has got to be—such—a—darling," she thought drowsily, as she drifted off to slumberland herself.

In February Jem and Jerry and Robert Grant were in the trenches and a little more tension and dread was added to the Ingleside life. In March "Yiprez" as Susan called it, had come to have a bitter significance. The daily list of casualties had begun to appear in the papers and no one at Ingleside ever answered the telephone without a horrible cold shrinking— for it *might* be the station master 'phoning up to say a telegram had come from overseas. No one at Ingleside ever got up in the morning without a sudden piercing wonder over what the day might bring.

"And I used to welcome the mornings so," thought Rilla.

Yet the round of life and duty went steadily on and every week or so some one else went into khaki from the Glen lads who had just the other day been rollicking schoolboys.

"It is bitter cold out tonight, Mrs. Dr. dear," said Susan, coming in out of the clear starlit crispness of the Canadian winter twilight. "I wonder if the boys in the trenches are warm."

"How *everything* comes back to this war," cried Gertrude Oliver. "We can't get away from it—not even when we talk of the weather. I never go out these dark cold nights myself without thinking of the men in the trenches—not only *our* men but *everybody's* men. I would feel the same if there were nobody I knew at the front. When I snuggle down in my comfortable bed I am ashamed of being comfortable. It seems as if it were wicked of me to be so when many are not."

"I saw Mrs. Meredith down at the store," said Susan, "and she tells me that they are really troubled over Bruce, he takes things so much to heart. He has cried himself to sleep for a week over the starving Belgians. 'Oh, mother,' he will say to her, so beseeching-like, 'surely the babies are never hungry— oh, not the *babies*, mother! Just say the *babies* are not hungry, mother.' And she cannot say it because it would not be true, and she is at her wits' end. They try to keep such things from him but he finds them out and then they cannot comfort him. It breaks my heart to read about them myself, Mrs. Dr. dear, and I cannot console myself with the thought that the tales are not true. When I read a novel that makes me want to weep I just say severely to myself, 'Now, Susan Baker, you know that is all a pack of lies.' But we must carry on. Jack

Crawford says he is going to the war because he is tired of farming. I hope he will find it a pleasant change. And Mrs. Richard Elliott over-harbour is worrying herself sick because she used to be always scolding her husband about smoking up the parlour curtains. Now that he has enlisted she wishes she had never said a word to him. You know Josiah Cooper and William Daley, Mrs. Dr. dear. They used to be fast friends but they quarrelled twenty years ago and have never spoken since. Well, the other day Josiah went to William and said right out, 'Let us be friends. 'Tain't any time to be holding grudges.' William was real glad and held out his hand, and they sat down for a good talk. And in less than half an hour they had quarrelled again, over how the war ought to be fought, Josiah holding that the Dardanelles expedition was rank folly and William maintaining that it was the one sensible thing the Allies had done. And now they are madder at each other than ever and William says Josiah is as bad a pro-German as Whiskers-on-the-moon. Whiskers vows he is no pro-German but calls himself a pacifist, whatever that may be, Mrs. Dr. dear. It is nothing proper or Whiskers would not be it and that you may tie to. He says that the big British victory at New Chapelle cost more than it was worth and he has forbid Joe Milgrave to come near the house because Joe ran up his father's flag when the news came. Have you noticed, Mrs. Dr. dear, that the Czar has changed that Prish name to Premysl, which proves that the man had good sense, Russian though he is? Joe Vickers told me in the store that he saw a very queer looking thing in the sky tonight over Lowbridge way. Do you suppose it could have been a Zeppelin, Mrs. Dr. dear?"

"I do not think it very likely, Susan."

"Well, I would feel easier about it if Whiskers-on-the-moon were not living in the Glen. They say he was seen going through strange manœuvres with a lantern in his back yard one night lately. Some people think he was signalling."

"To whom—or what?"

"Ah, *that* is the mystery, Mrs. Dr. dear. In my opinion the Government would do well to keep an eye on that man if it does not want us to be all murdered in our beds some night. Now I shall just look over the papers a minute before going to write a letter to Little Jem. Two things I never did, Mrs. Dr. dear, were write letters and read politics. Yet here I am doing both regular and I find there is something in politics after all. Whatever Woodrow Wilson means I cannot fathom but I am hoping I will puzzle it out yet."

Susan, in her pursuit of Wilson and politics, presently came upon something that disturbed her and exclaimed in a tone of bitter disappointment,

"That devilish Kaiser has only a boil after all."

"Don't swear, Susan," said Dr. Blythe, pulling a long face.

"'Devilish' is not swearing, doctor, dear. I have always understood that swearing was taking the name of the Almighty in vain?"

"Well, it isn't—ahem—refined," said the doctor, winking at Miss Oliver.

"No, doctor, dear, the devil and the Kaiser—if so be that they are really two different people—are *not* refined. And you cannot refer to them in a refined way. So I abide by what I said, although you may notice that I am careful not to use such expressions when young Rilla is about. And I maintain that the papers have no right to say that the Kaiser has pneumonia and raise people's hopes, and then come out and say he has nothing but a boil. A boil, indeed! I wish he was covered with them."

Whereupon Susan stalked out to the kitchen and settled down to write to Jem; deeming him in need of home comfort from certain passages in his letter that day.

"We're in an old wine cellar tonight, dad," he wrote, "in water to our knees. Rats everywhere—no fire—a drizzling rain coming down—rather dismal. But it might be worse. I got Susan's box today and everything was in tip-top order and we had a feast. Jerry is up the line somewhere and he says the rations are rather worse than Aunt Martha's ditto used to be. But here they're not bad—only monotonous. Tell Susan I'd give a year's pay for a good batch of her monkey-faces; but don't let that inspire her to send any for they wouldn't keep.

"We have been under fire since the last week in February. One boy—he was a Nova Scotian—was killed right beside me yesterday. A shell burst near us and when the muss cleared away he was lying dead—not mangled at all—he just looked a little startled. It was the first time I'd been close to anything like that and it was a nasty sensation, but one soon gets used to horrors here. We're in an absolutely different world. The only things that are the same are the stars—and they are never in their right places, somehow.

"Tell mother not to worry—I'm all right—fit as a fiddle—and glad I came. There's something across from us here that has got to be wiped out of the world, that's all—an emanation of evil that would otherwise poison life forever. It's got to be done, dad, however long it takes, and whatever it costs, and you tell the Glen people this for me. They don't realize yet what it is that has broken loose—I didn't when I first joined up. I thought it was fun. Well, it isn't! But I'm in the right place all right—make no mistake about that. When I saw what had been done here to homes and gardens and people— well, dad, I seemed to see a gang of Huns marching through

Rainbow Valley and the Glen, and the garden at Ingleside. There were gardens over here—beautiful gardens with the beauty of centuries—and what are they now? Mangled, desecrated things! We are fighting to make those dear old places where we had played as children, safe for other boys and girls—fighting for the preservation and safety of all sweet, wholesome things.

"Whenever any of you go to the station be sure to give Dog Monday a double pat for me. Fancy the faithful little beggar waiting there for me like that! Honestly, dad, on some of these dark cold nights in the trenches, it heartens and braces me up to no end to think that thousands of miles away at the old Glen station there is a small spotted dog sharing my vigil.

"Tell Rilla I'm glad her war baby is turning out so well, and tell Susan that I'm fighting a good fight against both Huns and cooties."

"Mrs. Dr. dear," whispered Susan solemnly, "what are cooties?"

Mrs. Blythe whispered back and then said in reply to Susan's horrified ejaculations, "It's always like that in the trenches, Susan."

Susan shook her head and went away in grim silence to re-open a parcel she had sewed up for Jem and slip in a fine tooth comb.

CHAPTER XII

In the Days of Langemarck

"How can spring come and be beautiful in such a horror," wrote Rilla in her diary. "When the sun shines and the fluffy yellow catkins are coming out on the willow trees down by the brook, and the garden is beginning to be beautiful I can't realize that such *dreadful* things are happening in Flanders. But they *are*!

"This past week has been terrible for us all, since the news came of the fighting around Ypres and the battles of Langemarck and St. Julien. Our Canadian boys have done splendidly—General French says they 'saved the situation,' when the Germans had all but broken through. But I can't feel pride or exultation or anything but a gnawing anxiety over Jem and Jerry and Mr. Grant. The casualty lists are coming out in the papers every day—oh, there are so many of them. I can't bear to read them for fear I'd find Jem's name—for there *have* been cases where people have seen their boys' names in the casualty lists *before* the official telegram came. As for the telephone, for a day or two I just refused to answer it, because I thought I could not endure the horrible moment that came between saying 'Hello' and hearing the response. That moment seemed a hundred years long, for I was always dreading to hear 'There is a telegram for Dr. Blythe.' Then, when I had shirked for awhile, I was ashamed of leaving it all for mother or Susan, and now I *make* myself go. But it never gets any easier. Gertrude teaches school and reads compositions and sets examination papers just as she always has done, but I know her thoughts are over in Flanders all the time. Her eyes *haunt* me.

"And Kenneth is in khaki now, too. He has got a lieutenant's commission and expects to go overseas in midsummer, so he wrote me. There wasn't much else in the letter—he seemed to be thinking of nothing *but* going overseas. I shall not see him again before he goes—perhaps I will *never* see him again. Sometimes I ask myself if that evening at Four Winds was all a dream. It might as well be—it seems as if it happened in another life lived years ago—and everybody has forgotten it but me.

"Walter and Nan and Di came home last night from Redmond. When Walter stepped off the train Dog Monday rushed to meet him, frantic with joy. I suppose he thought Jem would be there, too. After the first moment, he paid no attention to Walter and his pats, but just stood there, wagging his tail nervously and looking past Walter at the other people coming out, with eyes that made me choke up, for I couldn't help thinking that, for all we knew, Monday might never see Jem come off that train again. Then, when all the people were out, Monday looked up at Walter, gave his hand a little lick as if to say, 'I know it isn't your fault he didn't come—excuse me for feeling disappointed,' and then he trotted back to his shed, with that funny little sidelong waggle of his which always makes it seem that his hind legs are travelling directly away from the point at which his forelegs are aiming.

"We tried to coax him home with us—Di even got down and kissed him between the eyes and said, 'Monday, old duck, *won't* you come up with us just for the evening?' And Monday said—he *did*!—'I am very sorry but I can't. I've got a date to meet Jem here, you know, and there's a train goes through at eight.'

"It's lovely to have Walter back again though he seems quiet and sad, just as he was at Christmas. But I'm going to love him *hard* and cheer him up and *make* him laugh as he used to. It seems to me that every day of my life Walter means more to me.

"The other evening Susan happened to say that the mayflowers were out in Rainbow Valley. I chanced to be looking at mother when Susan spoke. Her face changed and she gave a queer little choked cry. Most of the time mother is so spunky and gay you would never guess what she feels inside; but now and then some little thing is too much for her and we see under the surface. 'Mayflowers!' she said. 'Jem brought me mayflowers last year!' and she got up and went out of the room. I would have rushed off to Rainbow Valley and brought her an armful of mayflowers, but I knew that wasn't what she wanted. And after Walter got home last night he slipped away to the valley and brought mother home all the mayflowers he could find. Nobody had said a word to him about it—he just remembered himself that Jem used to bring mother the first mayflowers and so he brought them in Jem's place. It shows how tender and thoughtful he is. And yet there are people who send him cruel letters!

"It seems strange that we can go on with ordinary life just as if nothing were happening overseas that concerned us, just as if any day might not bring us awful news. But we can and do. Susan is putting in the garden, and mother and she are housecleaning, and we Junior Reds are getting up a concert in aid of the Belgians. We have been practising for a month and having no end of trouble and bother with cranky people. Miranda Pryor promised to help with a dialogue and when she had her part all learned her father put his foot down and refused to allow her to help at all. I am not blaming Miranda exactly, but I do think she might have a little more spunk sometimes. If *she* put her foot down once in a while she might bring her father to terms, for she is all the housekeeper he has and what would he do if she 'struck'? If *I* were in Miranda's shoes I'd find some way of managing Whiskers-on-the-moon—yea, verily, I would horsewhip him—or *bite* him, if nothing else would serve. But Miranda is a meek and obedient daughter whose days should be long in the land.

"I couldn't get any one else to take the part, because nobody liked it, so I finally had to take it myself. Olive Kirk is on the concert committee and goes against me in every single thing. But I got my way in asking Mrs. Channing to come out from town and sing for us, anyhow. She is a beautiful singer and will draw such a crowd that we will make more than we will have to pay her. Olive Kirk thought our 'local talent' good enough and Minnie Clow won't sing at all now in the choruses because she would be 'so nervous' before Mrs. Channing. And Minnie is the only good alto we have! There are times when I am so exasperated that I feel tempted to wash my hands of the whole affair; but after I dance around my room a few times in sheer rage I cool down and have another whack at it. Just at present I am racked with worry for fear the Isaac Reeses are taking whooping cough. They have all got a dreadful cold and there are five of them who have important parts in the program and if they go and develop whooping cough what shall I do? Dick Reese's violin solo is to be one of our titbits and Kit Reese is in every tableau and the three small girls have the cutest flag drill. I've been toiling for weeks to train them in it, and now it seems likely that all my trouble will go for nothing.

"Jims cut his first tooth today. I am very glad, for he is nearly nine months old and Mary Vance has been insinuating that he is awfully backward about cutting his teeth. He has begun to creep but he doesn't crawl as most babies do. He trots about on all fours and carries things in his mouth like a little dog. Nobody can say he isn't up to schedule time in the matter of creeping anyway—away ahead of it indeed, since ten months is Morgan's average for creeping. He is so cute, it will be a shame if his dad never sees him. His hair is coming on nicely too, and I am not without hope that it will be curly.

"Just for a few minutes, while I've been writing of Jims and the concert, I've forgotten Ypres and the poison gas and the casualty lists. Now it all rushes back, worse than ever. Oh, if we could just know that Jem is all right! I used to be so furious with Jem when he called me 'Spider.' And now, if he would just come whistling through the hall and call out, 'Hello, Spider,' as he used to do, I would think it the loveliest name in the world."

Rilla put away her diary and went out to the garden. The spring evening was very lovely. The long, green, seaward-looking Glen was filled with dusk, and beyond it were meadows of sunset. The harbour was radiant, purple here, azure there, opal elsewhere. The maple grove was beginning to be misty green. Rilla looked about her with wistful eyes. Who said that spring was the joy of the year? It was the heart-break of the year. And all the pale-purply mornings and the daffodil stars and the wind in the old pine were so many separate pangs of the heart-break. Would life *ever* be free from dread again?

"It's good to see a P.E.I. twilight once more," said Walter, joining her. "I didn't really remember that the sea was so blue and the roads so red and the wood nooks so wild and fairy haunted. Yes, the fairies still abide here. I vow I could find scores of them under the violets in Rainbow Valley."

Rilla was momentarily happy. This sounded like the Walter of yore. She hoped he was forgetting certain things that had troubled him.

"And isn't the sky blue over Rainbow Valley?" she said, responding to his mood. "Blue—blue—you'd have to say 'blue' a hundred times before you could express how blue it is."

Susan wandered by, her head tied up with a shawl, her hands full of garden implements. Doc, stealthy and wild-eyed, was shadowing her steps among the spirea bushes.

"The sky may be blue," said Susan, "but that cat has been Hyde all day so we will likely have rain tonight and by the same token I have rheumatism in my shoulder."

"It may rain—but don't think rheumatism, Susan—think violets," said Walter gaily—rather too gaily, Rilla thought.

Susan considered him unsympathetic.

"Indeed, Walter dear, I do not know what you mean by thinking violets," she responded stiffly, "and rheumatism is not a thing to be joked about, as you may some day realize for yourself. I hope I am not of the kind that is always complaining of their aches and pains, especially now when the news is so terrible. Rheumatism is bad enough but I realize, and none better, that it is not to be compared to being gassed by the Huns."

"Oh, my God, no!" exclaimed Walter passionately. He turned and went back to the house.

Susan shook her head. She disapproved entirely of such ejaculations. "I hope he will not let his mother hear him talking like that," she thought as she stacked her hoes and rakes away.

Rilla was standing among the budding daffodils with tear-filled eyes. Her evening was spoiled; she detested Susan, who had somehow hurt Walter; and Jem—had Jem been gassed? Had he died in torture?

"I can't endure this suspense any longer," said Rilla desperately.

But she endured it as the others did for another week. Then a letter came from Jem. He was all right.

"I've come through without a scratch, dad. Don't know how I or any of us did it. You'll have seen all about it in the papers—I can't write of it. But the Huns haven't got through—they won't get through. Jerry was knocked stiff by a shell one time, but it was only the shock. He was all right in a few days. Grant is safe, too."

Nan had a letter from Jerry Meredith. "I came back to consciousness at dawn," he wrote. "Couldn't tell what had happened to me but thought I was done for. I was all alone and *afraid*—terribly afraid. Dead men were all around me, lying on the horrible grey, slimy fields. I was woefully thirsty—and I thought of David and the Bethlehem water—and of the old spring in Rainbow Valley under the maples. I seemed to see it just before me—and you standing laughing on the other side of it—and I thought it was all over with me. And I didn't care. Honestly, I didn't care. I just felt a dreadful childish fear of the *loneliness* and of all those dead men around me, and a sort of wonder how this could have happened to *me*. Then they found me and carted me off and before long I discovered that there wasn't really anything wrong with me. I'm going back to the trenches tomorrow. Every man is needed there that can be got."

"Laughter is gone out of the world," said Faith Meredith, who had come over to report on her letters. "I remember telling old Mrs. Taylor long ago that the world was a world of laughter. But it isn't so any longer."

"It's a shriek of anguish," said Gertrude Oliver.

"We must keep a little laughter, girls," said Mrs. Blythe. "A good laugh is as good as a prayer sometimes—only sometimes," she added under her breath. She had found it very hard to laugh during the three weeks she had just lived through—she, Anne Blythe, to whom laughter had always come so easily and freshly. And what hurt most was that Rilla's laughter had grown so rare—Rilla whom she used to think laughed over-much. Was all the child's girlhood to be so clouded? Yet how strong and clever and womanly she was growing! How patiently she knit and sewed and manipulated those uncertain Junior Reds! And how wonderful she was with Jims.

"She really could not do better for that child than if she had raised a baker's dozen, Mrs. Dr. dear," Susan had avowed solemnly. "Little did I ever expect it of her on the day she landed in here with that soup tureen."

$\mathcal{A}$ Slice of Humble Pie

"I am very much afraid, Mrs. Dr. dear," said Susan, who had been on a pilgrimage to the station with some choice bones for Dog Monday, "that something terrible has happened. Whiskers-on-the-moon came off the train from Charlotte-town and he was *looking pleased*. I do not remember that I ever saw him with a smile on in public before. Of course he may have just been getting the better of somebody in a cattle deal but I have an awful presentiment that the Huns have broken through somewhere."

Perhaps Susan was unjust in connecting Mr. Pryor's smile with the sinking of the *Lusitania*, news of which circulated an hour later when the mail was distributed. But the Glen boys turned out that night in a body and broke all his windows in a fine frenzy of indignation over the Kaiser's doings.

"I do not say they did right and I do not say they did wrong," said Susan, when she heard of it. "But I will say that I would not have minded throwing a few stones myself. One thing is certain—Whiskers-on-the-moon said in the post office the day the news came, in the presence of witnesses, that folks who could not stay home after they had been warned deserved no better fate. That man, Mrs. Dr. dear, may be and is a member of our session, but I know one thing. If I was dead and he came to my funeral I would rise up and order him out. Norman Douglas is fairly foaming at the mouth over it all. 'If the devil doesn't get those men who sunk the *Lusitania* then there is no use in there being a devil,' he was shouting in

Carter's store last night. Norman Douglas always has believed that anybody who opposed *him* was on the side of the devil, but a man like that is bound to be right once in a while. Bruce Meredith is worrying over the babies who were drowned. And it seems he prayed for something very special last Friday night and didn't get it, and was feeling quite disgruntled over it. But when he heard about the *Lusitania* he told his mother that he understood now why God didn't answer his prayer— He was too busy attending to the souls of all the people who went down on the *Lusitania*. That child's brain is a hundred years older than his body, Mrs. Dr. dear. As for the *Lusitania*, it is an awful occurrence, whatever way you look at it. But Woodrow Wilson is going to write a note about it, so why worry? A pretty president!" and Susan banged her pots about wrathfully. President Wilson was rapidly becoming anathema in Susan's kitchen.

Mary Vance dropped in one evening to tell the Ingleside folks that she had withdrawn all opposition to Miller Douglas' enlisting.

"This *Lusitania* business was too much for me," said Mary brusquely. "When the Kaiser takes to drowning innocent babies it's high time somebody told him where he gets off at. This thing must be fought to a finish. It's been soaking into my mind slow but I'm on now. So I up and told Miller he could go as far as I was concerned. Old Kitty Alec won't be converted though. If every ship in the world was submarined and every baby drowned, Kitty wouldn't turn a hair. But I flatter myself that it was *me* kept Miller back all along and not the fair Kitty. I may have deceived myself—but we shall see."

They did see. The next Sunday Miller Douglas walked into the Glen church beside Mary Vance in khaki. And Mary was so proud of him that her white eyes fairly blazed. Joe

Milgrave, back under the gallery, looked at Miller and Mary and then at Miranda Pryor, and sighed so heavily that everyone within a radius of three pews heard him and knew what his trouble was. Walter Blythe did not sigh. But Rilla, scanning his face anxiously, saw a look that cut her to the heart. It haunted her for the next week and made an undercurrent of soreness in her soul, which was externally being harrowed up by the near approach of the Red Cross concert and the worries connected therewith. The Reese cold had not developed into whooping cough, so that tangle was straightened out. But other things were hanging in the balance; and on the very day before the concert came a regretful letter from Mrs. Channing saying that she could not come to sing. Her son, who was in Kingsport with his regiment, was seriously ill with pneumonia, and she must go to him at once.

The members of the concert committee looked at each other in blank dismay. What was to be done?

"This comes of depending on outside help," said Olive Kirk, disagreeably.

"We must do something," said Rilla, too desperate to care for Olive's manner. "We've advertised the concert everywhere—and crowds are coming—there's even a big party coming out from town—and we were short enough of music as it was. We *must* get some one to sing in Mrs. Channing's place."

"I don't know who you can get at this late date," said Olive. "Irene Howard could do it; but it is not likely she will after the way she was insulted by our society."

"How did our society insult her?" asked Rilla, in what she called her "cold, pale tone." Its coldness and pallor did not daunt Olive.

"You insulted her," she answered sharply. "Irene told me all about it—she was literally *heart-broken*. You told her never to speak to you again—and Irene told me she simply could not imagine what she had said or done to deserve such treatment. That was why she never came to our meetings again but joined in with the Lowbridge Red Cross. I do not blame her in the least, and I, for one, will not ask her to *lower herself* by helping us out of this scrape."

"You don't expect *me* to ask her?" giggled Amy MacAllister, the other member of the committee. "Irene and I haven't spoken for a hundred years. Irene is always getting 'insulted' by somebody. But she *is* a lovely singer, I'll admit that, and people would just as soon hear her as Mrs. Channing."

"It wouldn't do any good if *you* did ask her," said Olive significantly. "Soon after we began planning this concert, back in April, I met Irene in town one day and asked her if she wouldn't help us out. She said she'd love to but she really didn't see how she could when Rilla Blythe was running the program, after the strange way Rilla had behaved to her. So there it is and here we are, and a nice failure our concert will be."

Rilla went home and shut herself up in her room, her soul in a turmoil. She would not humiliate herself by apologizing to Irene Howard! Irene had been as much in the wrong as she had been; and she had told such mean, distorted versions of their quarrel everywhere, posing as a puzzled, injured martyr. Rilla could never bring herself to tell *her* side of it. The fact that a slur at Walter was mixed up in it tied her tongue. So most people believed that Irene had been badly used, except a few girls who had never liked her and sided with Rilla. Rilla, however, did not get much comfort out of their sympathy for it was barbed by subtle reminders of other days when she had fought Irene's battles with these very girls and snubbed them because they did not idolize her. And yet—the concert over which she had worked so hard was going to be a failure. Mrs. Channing's four solos were the feature of the whole program.

"Miss Oliver, what do you think about it?" she asked in desperation.

"I think Irene is the one who should apologize," said Miss Oliver. "But unfortunately my opinion will not fill the blanks in your program."

"If I went and apologized meekly to Irene she would sing, I am sure," sighed Rilla. "She really loves to sing in public. But I know she'll be nasty about it—I feel I'd rather do *anything* than go. I suppose I *should* go—if Jem and Jerry can face the Huns surely I can face Irene Howard, and swallow my pride to ask a favour of her for the good of the Belgians. Just at present I feel that I *cannot* do it but for all that I have a pre-sentiment that after supper you'll see me meekly trotting through Rainbow Valley on my way to the Upper Glen Road."

Rilla's presentiment proved correct. After supper she dressed herself carefully in her blue, beaded crepe—for vanity is harder to quell than pride and Irene always saw any flaw or shortcoming in another girl's appearance. Besides, as Rilla had told her mother one day when she was nine years old, "it is easier to behave nicely when you have your good clothes on." It *was* easier: it kept up the morale of the army.

Rilla did her hair very becomingly and donned a long raincoat for fear of a shower. But all the while her thoughts were concerned with the coming distasteful interview, and she kept rehearsing mentally her part in it. She wished it were over—she wished she had never tried to get up a Belgian Relief concert—she wished she had not quarrelled with Irene.

After all, disdainful silence would have been much more effective in meeting the slur upon Walter. It was foolish and childish to fly out as she had done—well, she would be wiser in future, but meanwhile a large and very unpalatable slice of humble pie had to be eaten, and Rilla Blythe was no fonder of that wholesome article of diet than the rest of us.

By sunset she was at the door of the Howard house—a pretentious abode, with white scroll-work around the eaves and an eruption of bay windows on all its sides. Mrs. Howard, a plump, voluble dame, met Rilla gushingly and left her in the parlour while she went to call Irene. Rilla threw off her raincoat and looked at herself critically in the mirror over the mantel. Hair, hat and dress were satisfactory—nothing there for Miss Irene to make fun of. Rilla remembered how clever and amusing she used to think Irene's biting little comments about other girls. Well, it had come home to her now.

Presently, Irene skimmed down, elegantly gowned, with her pale, straw-coloured hair done in the latest and most extreme fashion, and an over-luscious atmosphere of perfume enveloping her.

"Why, how do you do, Miss Blythe?" she said sweetly. "This is a very unexpected pleasure."

Rilla had risen to take Irene's chilly finger tips and now, as she sat down again, she saw something that temporarily stunned her. Irene saw it too, as *she* sat down, and a little amused, impertinent smile appeared on her lips and hovered there during the rest of the interview.

On one of Rilla's feet was a smart little steel-buckled shoe and filmy blue silk stocking. The other was clad in a stout and rather shabby boot and black lisle!

Poor Rilla! She had changed, or begun to change her boots and stockings after she had put on her dress. *This* was the result of doing one thing with your hands and another with your brain. Oh, what a ridiculous position to be in—and before Irene Howard of all people—Irene, who was staring at Rilla's feet as if she had never seen feet before! And once she had thought Irene's manner perfection! Everything that Rilla had prepared to say vanished from her memory. Vainly trying to tuck her unlucky foot under her chair, she blurted out a blunt statement.

"I have come to athk a favour of you, Irene."

There—lisping! Oh, she had been prepared for humiliation but not to this extent! Really, there were limits!

"Yes?" said Irene in a cool, questioning tone, lifting her shallowly-set, insolent eyes to Rilla's crimson face for a moment and then dropping them again as if she really could not tear them from their fascinated gaze at the shabby boot and the gallant shoe.

Rilla gathered herself together. She would *not* lisp—she *would* be calm and composed.

"Mrs. Channing cannot come because her son is ill in Kingsport, and I have come on behalf of the committee to ask you if you will be so kind as to sing for us in her place." Rilla enunciated every word so precisely and carefully that she seemed to be reciting a lesson.

"It's something of a fiddler's invitation, isn't it?" said Irene, with one of her disagreeable smiles.

"Olive Kirk asked you to help when we first thought of the concert and you refused," said Rilla.

"Why, I could hardly help—then—could I?" asked Irene plaintively. "After you had ordered me never to speak to you again? It would have been very awkward for us both, don't you think?"

Now for the humble pie.

"I want to apologize to you for saying that, Irene," said Rilla steadily. "I should not have said it and I have been very sorry ever since. Will you forgive me?"

"And sing at your concert?" said Irene sweetly and insultingly.

"If you mean," said Rilla miserably, "that I would *not* be apologizing to you if it were not for the concert perhaps that is true. But it is also true that I have felt ever since it happened that I should not have said what I did and that I have been sorry for it all winter. That is all I can say. If you feel you can't forgive me I suppose there is nothing more to be said."

"Oh, Rilla dear, don't snap me up like that," pleaded Irene. "Of course I'll forgive you—though I did feel awfully about it—how awfully I hope you'll never know. I cried for *weeks* over it. And when I hadn't said or done a thing!"

Rilla choked back a retort. After all, there was no use in arguing with Irene and the Belgians were starving.

"Don't you think you can help us with the concert," she forced herself to say. Oh, if only Irene would stop looking at that boot! Rilla could just *hear* her giving Olive Kirk an account of it.

"I don't see how I really can at the last moment like this," protested Irene. "There isn't time to learn anything new."

"Oh, you have lots of lovely songs that nobody in the Glen ever heard before," said Rilla, who knew Irene had been going to town all winter for lessons and that this was only a pretext. "They will all be new down there."

"But I have no accompanist," protested Irene.

"Una Meredith can accompany you," said Rilla.

"Oh, I couldn't ask *her*," sighed Irene. "We haven't spoken since last fall. She was so hateful to me the time of our Sunday School concert that I simply had to give her up."

Dear, dear, was Irene at feud with everybody? As for Una Meredith being hateful to anybody, the idea was so farcical that Rilla had much ado to keep from laughing in Irene's very face.

"Miss Oliver is a beautiful pianist and can play any accompaniment at sight," said Rilla desperately. "She will play for you and you could run over your songs easily tomorrow evening at Ingleside before the concert."

"But I haven't anything to wear. My new evening dress isn't home from Charlottetown yet, and I simply cannot wear my old one at such a big affair. It is too shabby and old-fashioned."

"Our concert," said Rilla slowly, "is in aid of Belgian children who are starving to death. Don't you think you could wear a shabby dress once for their sake, Irene?"

"Oh, don't you think those accounts we get of the conditions of the Belgians are very much exaggerated?" said Irene. "I'm sure they can't be actually *starving*, you know, in the twentieth century. The newspapers always colour things so highly."

Rilla concluded that she had humiliated herself enough. There was such a thing as self-respect. No more coaxing, concert or no concert. She got up, boot and all.

"I am sorry you can't help us, Irene, but since you cannot we must do the best we can."

Now this did not suit Irene at all. She desired exceedingly to sing at that concert, and all her hesitations were merely by way of enhancing the boon of her final consent. Besides, she really wanted to be friends with Rilla again. Rilla's wholehearted, ungrudging adoration had been very sweet incense to her. *And* Ingleside was a very charming house to visit, especially when a handsome college student like Walter was home. She stopped looking at Rilla's feet.

"Rilla, darling, don't be *so* abrupt. I really want to help you, if I can manage it. Just sit down and let's talk it over."

"I'm sorry but I can't. I have to be home soon—Jims has to be settled for the night, you know."

"Oh, yes—the baby you are bringing up by book. It's perfectly sweet of you to do it when you hate children so. How cross you were just because I kissed him! But we'll forget all that and be chums again, won't we? Now, about the concert—I daresay I can run into town on the morning train after my dress, and out again on the afternoon one in plenty of time for the concert, if you'll ask Miss Oliver to play for me. *I* couldn't—she's so dreadfully haughty and supercilious that she simply paralyzes poor little me."

Rilla did not waste time or breath defending Miss Oliver. She coolly thanked Irene, who had suddenly become very amiable and gushing, and got away. She was very thankful the interview was over. But she knew now that she and Irene could never be the friends they had been. Friendly, yes—but *friends*, no. Nor did she wish it. All winter she had felt under her other and more serious worries, a little feeling of regret for her lost chum. Now it was suddenly gone. Irene was not as Mrs. Elliott would say, of the race that knew Joseph. Rilla did not say or think that she had outgrown Irene. Had the thought occurred to her she would have considered it absurd when she was not yet seventeen and Irene was twenty. But it was the truth. Irene was just what she had been a year ago— just what she would always be. Rilla Blythe's nature in that year had changed and matured and deepened. She found herself seeing through Irene with a disconcerting clearness— discerning under all her superficial sweetness her pettiness, her vindictiveness, her insincerity, her essential cheapness. Irene had lost forever her faithful worshipper.

But not until Rilla had traversed the Upper Glen Road and found herself in the moon-dappled solitude of Rainbow Valley did she fully recover her composure of spirit. Then she stopped under a tall wild plum that was ghostly white and fair in its misty spring-bloom and laughed.

"There is only one thing of importance just now—and that is that the Allies win the war," she said aloud. "*Therefore*, it follows without dispute that the fact that I went to see Irene Howard with odd shoes and stockings on is of *no* importance whatever. Nevertheless, I Bertha Marilla Blythe, swear solemnly with the moon as witness"—Rilla lifted her hand dramatically to the said moon,—"that I will never leave my room again without looking carefully at *both* my feet."

CHAPTER XIV

The Valley of Decision

Susan kept the flag flying at Ingleside all the next day, in honour of Italy's declaration of war.

"And not before it was time, Mrs. Dr. dear, considering the way things have begun to go on the Russian front. Say what you will, those Russians are kittle cattle, the Grand Duke Nicholas to the contrary notwithstanding. It is a fortunate thing for Italy that she has come in on the right side, but whether it is as fortunate for the Allies I will not predict until I know more about Italians than I do now. However, she will give that old reprobate of a Francis Joseph something to think about. A pretty emperor indeed,—with one foot in the grave and yet plotting wholesale murder"—and Susan thumped and kneaded her bread with as much vicious energy as she could have expended in punching Francis Joseph himself if he had been so unlucky as to fall into her clutches.

Walter had gone to town on the early train, and Nan offered to look after Jims for the day and so set Rilla free. Rilla was wildly busy all day, helping to decorate the Glen hall and seeing to a hundred last things. The evening was beautiful, in spite of the fact that Mr. Pryor was reported to have said that he "hoped it would rain pitchforks points down," and to have wantonly kicked Miranda's dog as he said it. Rilla, rushing home from the hall, dressed hurriedly. Everything had gone surprisingly well at the last; Irene was even then downstairs practising her songs with Miss Oliver; Rilla was excited and happy, forgetful even of the western front for the moment. It gave her a sense of achievement and victory to have brought her efforts of weeks to such a successful conclusion. She knew that there had not lacked people who thought and hinted that Rilla Blythe had not the tact or patience to engineer a concert program. She had shown them! Little snatches of song bubbled up from her lips as she dressed. She thought she was looking very well. Excitement brought a faint, becoming pink into her round creamy cheeks, quite drowning out her few freckles, and her hair gleamed with red-brown lustre. Should she wear crab-apple blossoms in it, or her little fillet of pearls? After some agonized wavering she decided on the crab-apple blossoms and tucked the white waxen cluster behind her left ear. Now for a final look at her feet. Yes, both slippers were on. She gave the sleeping Jims a kiss—what a dear little warm, rosy, satin face he had—and hurried down the hill to the hall. Already it was filling—soon it was crowded. Her concert was going to be a brilliant success.

The first three numbers were successfully over. Rilla was in the little dressing room behind the platform, looking out on the moonlit harbour and rehearsing her own recitations. She was alone, the rest of the performers being in the larger room on the other side. Suddenly she felt two soft bare arms slipping round her waist; then Irene Howard dropped a light kiss on her cheek.

"Rilla, you sweet thing, you're looking *simply angelic* tonight. You *have* spunk—I thought you would feel so badly over Walter's enlisting that you'd hardly be able to bear up at all, and here you are as cool as a cucumber. I wish I had *half* your nerve."

Rilla stood perfectly still. She felt no emotion whatever— she felt *nothing*. The world of feeling had just *gone blank*.

"Walter—enlisting"—she heard herself saying—then she heard Irene's affected little laugh.

"Why, didn't you know? I thought you did of course, or I wouldn't have mentioned it. I am always putting my foot in it, amn't I? Yes, that is what he went to town for today—he told me coming out on the train tonight. *I* was the first person he told. He isn't in khaki yet—they were out of uniforms—but he will be in a day or two. I *always* said Walter had as much pluck as anybody. I assure you I felt *proud* of him, Rilla, when he told me what he'd done. Oh, there's an end of Rick MacAllister's reading. I must fly. I promised I'd play for the next chorus—Alice Clow has such a headache."

She was gone—oh, thank God, she was gone! Rilla was alone again, staring out at the unchanged, dream-like beauty of moonlit Four Winds. Feeling was coming back to her—a pang of agony so acute as to be almost physical seemed to rend her apart.

"I *cannot* bear it," she said. And then came the awful thought that perhaps she *could* bear it and that there might be years of this hideous suffering before her.

She must get away—she must rush home—she must be alone. She could not go out there and play for drills and give readings and take part in dialogues now. It would spoil half the concert—but that did not matter—nothing mattered. Was this she, Rilla Blythe—this tortured thing who had been quite happy a few minutes ago? Outside, a quartette was singing "We'll never let the old flag fall"—the music seemed to be coming from some remote distance. Why couldn't she cry, as she had cried when Jem told them he must go? If she could cry perhaps this horrible something that seemed to have seized on her very life might let go. But no tears came!

Where was her scarf and coat? She must get away and hide herself like an animal hurt to the death.

Was it a coward's part to run away like this? The question came to her suddenly as if some one else had asked it. She thought of the shambles of the Flanders front—she thought of her brother and her playmate helping to hold those fire-swept trenches. What would they think of her if she shirked her little duty here—the humble duty of carrying the program through for her Red Cross? But she couldn't stay—she couldn't—yet what was it mother had said when Jem went— "when our women fail in courage shall our men be fearless still?" But this—this was *unbearable*.

Still, she stopped half way to the door and went back to the window. Irene was singing now; her beautiful voice—the only real thing about her—soared clear and sweet through the building. Rilla knew that the girls' Fairy Drill came next. Could she go out there and play for it? Her head was aching now—her throat was burning. Oh, why had Irene told her just then, when telling could do no good? Irene had been very cruel. Rilla remembered now that more than once that day she had caught her mother looking at her with an odd expression. She had been too busy to wonder what it meant. She understood now. Mother had known why Walter went to town but wouldn't tell her until the concert was over. What spirit and endurance mother had!

"I must stay here and see things through," said Rilla, clasping her cold hands together.

The rest of the evening always seemed like a fevered dream to her. Her body was crowded by people but her soul was alone in a torture chamber of its own. Yet she played steadily for the drills and gave her readings without faltering. She even put on a grotesque old Irish woman's costume and acted the part in the dialogue which Miranda Pryor had not taken. But she did not give her "brogue" the inimitable twist she had given it in the practices, and her readings lacked their usual fire and appeal. As she stood before the audience she saw one face only—that of the handsome, dark-haired lad sitting beside her mother—and she saw that same face in the trenches—saw it lying cold and dead under the stars—saw it pining in prison—saw the light of his eyes blotted out—saw a hundred horrible things as she stood there on the beflagged platform of the Glen hall with her own face whiter than the milky crab blossoms in her hair. Between her numbers she walked restlessly up and down the little dressing room. Would the concert *never* end!

It ended at last. Olive Kirk rushed up and told her exultantly that they had made a hundred dollars. "That's good," Rilla said mechanically. Then she was away from them all—oh, thank God, she was away from them all—Walter was waiting for her at the door. He put his arm through hers silently and they went together down the moonlit road. The frogs were singing in the marshes, the dim, ensilvered fields of home lay all around them. The spring night was lovely and appealing. Rilla felt that its beauty was an insult to her pain. She would *hate* moonlight forever.

"You know?" said Walter.

"Yes. Irene told me," answered Rilla chokingly.

"We didn't want you to know till the evening was over. I knew when you came out for the drill that you had heard. Little sister, I had to do it. I couldn't live any longer on such terms with myself as I have been since the *Lusitania* was sunk. When I pictured those dead women and children floating about in that pitiless, ice-cold water—well, at first I just felt a sort of nausea with life. I wanted to get out of the world where such a thing could happen—shake its accursed dust from my feet forever. Then I knew I had to go."

"There are—plenty—without you."

"That isn't the point, Rilla-my-Rilla. I'm going for my own sake—to save my soul alive. It will shrink to something small and mean and lifeless if I don't go. That would be worse than blindness or mutilation or any of the things I've feared."

"You may—be—killed." Rilla hated herself for saying it— she knew it was a weak and cowardly thing to say—but she had rather gone to pieces after the tension of the evening.

"'Comes he slow or comes he fast
It is but death who comes at last,'"

quoted Walter. "It's not death I fear—I told you that long ago. One can pay too high a price for mere life, little sister. There's so much *hideousness* in this war—I've got to go and help wipe it out of the world. I'm going to fight for the *beauty* of life, Rilla-my-Rilla—that is *my* duty. There may be a higher duty, perhaps—but that is mine. I owe life and Canada *that*, and I've got to pay it. Rilla, tonight for the first time since Jem left I've got back my self-respect. I could write poetry," Walter laughed. "I've never been able to write a line since last August. Tonight I'm full of it. Little sister, be brave—you were so plucky when Jem went."

"This—is—different." Rilla had to stop after every word to fight down a wild outburst of sobs. "I loved—Jem—of course—but—when—he went—away—we thought—the war—would soon—be over—and you are—*everything* to me, Walter."

"You must be brave to help *me*, Rilla-my-Rilla. I'm exalted tonight—drunk with the excitement of victory over myself—

but there will be other times when it won't be like this—I'll need your help then."

"When—do—you—go?" She must know the worst at once.

"Not for a week—then we go to Kingsport for training. I suppose we'll go overseas about the middle of July—we don't know."

One week—only one week more with Walter! The eyes of youth did not see how she was to go on living.

When they turned in at the Ingleside gate Walter stopped in the shadows of the old pines and drew Rilla close to him.

"Rilla-my-Rilla, there were girls as sweet and pure as you in Belgium and Flanders. You—even you—know what their fate was. We must make it impossible for such things to happen again while the world lasts. You'll help me, won't you?"

"I'll try, Walter," she said. "Oh, I *will* try."

As she clung to him with her face pressed against his shoulder she knew that it had to be. She accepted the fact then and there. He must go—her beautiful Walter with his beautiful soul and dreams and ideals. And she had known all along that it would come sooner or later. She had seen it coming to her—coming—coming—as one sees the shadow of a cloud drawing near over a sunny field, swiftly and inescapably. Amid all her pain she was conscious of an odd feeling of relief in some hidden part of her soul, where a little dull, unacknowledged soreness had been lurking all winter. No one—*no one* could ever call Walter a slacker now.

Rilla did not sleep that night. Perhaps no one at Ingleside did except Jims. The body grows slowly and steadily but the soul grows by leaps and bounds. It may come to its full stature in an hour. From that night Rilla Blythe's soul was the soul of a woman in its capacity for suffering, for strength, for endurance.

When the bitter dawn came she rose and went to her window. Below her was a big apple tree, a great swelling cone of rosy blossom. Walter had planted it years ago when he was a little boy. Beyond Rainbow Valley there was a cloudy shore of morning with little ripples of sunrise breaking over it. The far, cold beauty of a lingering star shone above it. Why, in this world of springtime loveliness, must hearts break?

Rilla felt arms go about her lovingly, protectingly. It was mother—pale, large-eyed mother.

"Oh, mother, how can you bear it?" she cried wildly.

"Rilla, dear, I've known for several days that Walter meant to go. I've had time to—to rebel and grow reconciled. We must give him up. There is a Call greater and more insistent than the call of our love—he has listened to it. We must not add to the bitterness of his sacrifice."

"*Our* sacrifice is greater than *his*," cried Rilla passionately. "Our boys give only *themselves*. *We* give them."

Before Mrs. Blythe could reply Susan stuck her head in at the door, never troubling over such frills of etiquette as knocking. Her eyes were suspiciously red but all she said was,

"Will I bring up your breakfast, Mrs. Dr. dear."

"No, no, Susan. We will all be down presently. Do you know—that Walter has joined up."

"Yes, Mrs. Dr. dear. The doctor told me last night. I suppose the Almighty has His own reasons for allowing such things. We must submit and endeavour to look on the bright side. It may cure him of being a poet, at least"—Susan still persisted in thinking that poets and tramps were tarred with the same brush—"and that would be something. But thank God," she muttered in a lower tone, "that Shirley is not old enough to go."

"Isn't that the same thing as thanking Him that some other woman's son has to go in Shirley's place?" asked the doctor, pausing on the threshold.

"No, it is not, Dr. dear," said Susan defiantly, as she picked up Jims, who was opening his big dark eyes and stretching up his dimpled paws. "Do not you put words in my mouth that I would never dream of uttering. I am a plain woman and cannot argue with you, but I do not thank God that anybody has to go. I only know that it seems they do have to go, unless we all want to be Kaiserized—for I can assure you the Monroe doctrine, whatever it is, is nothing to tie to, with Woodrow Wilson behind it. The Huns, Dr. dear, will never be brought to book by notes. And now," concluded Susan, tucking Jims in the crook of her gaunt arms and marching downstairs, "having cried my cry and said my say I shall take a brace, and if I cannot look pleasant I will look as pleasant as I can."

$\mathcal{U}$ntil the Day Break

"The Germans have recaptured Premysl," said Susan despairingly, looking up from her newspaper, "and now I suppose we will have to begin calling it by that uncivilized name again. Cousin Sophia was in when the mail came and when she heard the news she hove a sigh up from the depths of her stomach, Mrs. Dr. dear, and said, 'Ah yes, and they will get Petrograd next I have no doubt.' *I* said to her, 'My knowledge of geography is not so profound as I wish it was but I have an idea that it is quite a walk from Premysl to Petrograd.' Cousin Sophia sighed again and said, 'The Grand Duke Nicholas is not the man I took him to be.' 'Do not let him know that,' said I. 'It might hurt his feelings and he has likely enough to worry him as it is.' But you cannot cheer Cousin Sophia up, no matter how sarcastic you are, Mrs. Dr. dear. She sighed for the third time and groaned out, 'But the Russians are retreating fast,' and *I* said, 'Well, what of it? They have plenty of room for retreating, have they not?' But all the same, Mrs. Dr. dear, though I would never admit it to Cousin Sophia, I do *not* like the situation on the eastern front."

Nobody else liked it either; but all summer the Russian retreat went on—a long-drawn-out agony.

"I wonder if I shall ever again be able to await the coming of the mail with feelings of composure—never to speak of pleasure," said Gertrude Oliver. "The thought that haunts me night and day is—will the Germans smash Russia completely and then hurl their eastern army, flushed with victory, against the western front?"

"They will not, Miss Oliver dear," said Susan, assuming the role of prophetess. "In the first place, the Almighty will not allow it, in the second, Grand Duke Nicholas, though he may have been a disappointment to us in some respects, knows how to run away decently and in order, and that is a very useful knowledge when Germans are chasing you. Norman Douglas declares he is just luring them on and killing ten of them to one he loses. But I am of the opinion he cannot help himself and is just doing the best he can under the circumstances, the same as the rest of us. So do not go so far afield to borrow trouble, Miss Oliver dear, when there is plenty of it already camping on our very doorstep."

Walter had gone to Kingsport the first of June. Nan, Di and Faith had gone also to do Red Cross work in their vacation. In mid-July Walter came home for a week's leave before going overseas. Rilla had lived through the days of his absence on the hope of that week, and now that it had come she drank every minute of it thirstily, hating even the hours she had to spend in sleep, they seemed such a waste of precious moments. In spite of its sadness, it was a beautiful week, full of poignant, unforgettable hours, when she and Walter had long walks and talks and silences together. He was all her own and she knew that he found strength and comfort in her sympathy and understanding. It was very wonderful to know she meant so much to him—the knowledge helped her through moments that would otherwise have been unendurable, and gave her power to smile—and even to laugh a little by times. When Walter had gone she might indulge in the comfort of tears, but not while he was here. She would not even let herself cry at night, lest her eyes should betray her to him in the morning.

On his last evening at home they went together to Rainbow Valley and sat down on the bank of the brook, under the White Lady, where the gay revels of olden days had been held in the cloudless years. Rainbow Valley was roofed over with a sunset of unusual splendour that night; a wonderful grey dusk just touched with starlight followed it; and then came moonshine, hinting, hiding, revealing, lighting up little dells and hollows here, leaving others in dark, velvet shadow.

"When I am 'somewhere in France,'" said Walter looking around him with eager eyes on all the beauty his soul loved, "I shall remember these still, dewy, moon-drenched places. The balsam of the fir trees—the peace of those white pools of moonshine—the 'strength of the hills'—what a beautiful old Biblical phrase that is. Rilla! Look at those old hills around us—the hills we looked up at as children, wondering what lay for us in the great world beyond them. How calm and strong they are—how patient and changeless—like the heart of a good woman. Rilla-my-Rilla, do you know what you have been to me the past year? I want to tell you before I go. I could not have lived through it if it had not been for you, little loving, *believing* heart."

Rilla dared not try to speak. She slipped her hand into Walter's and pressed it hard.

"And when I'm over there, Rilla, in that hell upon earth which men who have forgotten God have made, it will be the thought of you that will help me most. I know you'll be as plucky and patient as you have shown yourself to be this past year—I'm not afraid for you. I know that no matter what happens, you'll be Rilla-*my*-Rilla—*no matter* what happens."

Rilla repressed tear and sigh, but she could not repress a little shiver, and Walter knew that he had said enough. After a moment of silence, in which each made an unworded promise to each other, he said,

"Now we won't be sober any more. We'll look beyond the years—to the time when the war will be over and Jem and Jerry and I will come marching home and we'll all be happy again."

"We won't be—happy—in the same way," said Rilla.

"No, not in the same way. Nobody whom this war has touched will ever be happy again in quite the same way. But it will be a better happiness, I think, little sister—a happiness we've *earned*. We *were* very happy before the war, weren't we? With a home like Ingleside, and a father and mother like ours we couldn't help being happy. But that happiness was a gift from life and love; it wasn't really ours—life could take it back at any time. It can never take away the happiness we win for ourselves in the way of duty. I've realized that since I went into khaki. In spite of my occasional funks, when I fall to living over things beforehand, I've been happy since that night in May. Rilla, be awfully good to mother while I'm away. It must be a horrible thing to be a mother in this war—the mothers and sisters and wives and sweethearts have the hardest times. Rilla, you beautiful little thing, are *you* anybody's sweetheart? If you are, tell me before I go."

"No," said Rilla. Then, impelled by a wish to be absolutely frank with Walter in this talk that *might* be the last they would ever have, she added, blushing wildly in the moonlight, "but if—Kenneth Ford—*wanted* me to be—"

"I see," said Walter. "And Ken's in khaki, too. Poor little girlie, it's a bit hard for you all round. Well, I'm not leaving any girl to break her heart about me—thank God for that."

Rilla glanced up at the manse on the hill. She could see a light in Una Meredith's window. She felt tempted to say something—then she knew she must not. It was not *her* secret: and, anyway, she did not *know*—she only suspected.

Walter looked about him lingeringly and lovingly. This spot had always been so dear to him. What fun they all had had here lang syne. Phantoms of memory seemed to pace the dappled paths and peep merrily through the swinging boughs—Jem and Jerry, bare-legged, sunburned schoolboys, fishing in the brook and frying trout over the old stone fireplace, Nan and Di and Faith, in their dimpled, fresh-eyed childish beauty, Una the sweet and shy, Carl, poring over ants and bugs, little slangy, sharp-tongued, good-hearted Mary Vance—the old Walter that had been himself lying on the grass reading poetry or wandering through palaces of fancy. They were all there around him—he could see them almost as plainly as he saw Rilla—as plainly as he had once seen the Pied Piper piping down the valley in a vanished twilight. And they said to him, those gay little ghosts of other days, "*We* were the children of yesterday, Walter—fight a good fight for the children of today and tomorrow."

"Where are you, Walter," cried Rilla, laughing a little. "Come back—come back."

Walter came back with a long breath. He stood up and looked about him at the beautiful valley of moonlight, as if to impress on his mind and heart every charm it possessed—the great dark plumes of the firs against the silvery sky, the stately White Lady, the old magic of the dancing brook, the faithful Tree Lovers, the beckoning, tricksy paths.

"I shall see it so in my dreams," he said, as he turned away.

They went back to Ingleside. Mr. and Mrs. Meredith were there, with Gertrude Oliver who had come from Lowbridge to say good-bye. Everybody was quite cheerful and bright, but nobody said much about the war being soon over, as they had said when Jem went away. They did not talk about the war at all—and they thought of nothing else. At last they gathered around the piano and sang the grand old hymn,

> *"Oh God, our help in ages past*
> *Our hope for years to come.*
> *Our shelter from the stormy blast*
> *And our eternal home."*

"We all come back to God in these days of soul-sifting," said Gertrude to John Meredith. "There have been many days in the past when I didn't believe in God—not *as* God—only as the impersonal Great First Cause of the scientists. I believe in Him now—I *have* to—there's nothing else to fall back on but God—humbly, starkly, unconditionally."

"'Our help in ages past'—'the same yesterday, today and forever,'" said the minister gently. "When we forget God—He remembers us."

There was no crowd at the Glen station the next morning to see Walter off. It was becoming a commonplace for a khaki clad boy to board that early morning train after his last leave. Besides his own, only the manse folk were there, and Mary Vance. Mary had sent her Miller off the week before, with a determined grin, and now considered herself entitled to give expert opinion on how such partings should be conducted.

"The main thing is to smile and act as if nothing was happening," she informed the Ingleside group. "The boys all hate the sob act like poison. Miller told me I wasn't to come near the station if I couldn't keep from bawling. So I got through with my crying beforehand and at the last I said to him, 'Good luck, Miller, and if you come back you'll find I haven't changed any, and if you don't come back I'll always be proud you went, and in any case don't fall in love with a French girl.' Miller swore he wouldn't, but you never can tell about those fascinating foreign hussies. Anyhow, the last sight he had of *me* I was smiling to my limit. Gee, all the rest of the day my face felt as if it had been starched and ironed into a smile."

In spite of Mary's advice and example Mrs. Blythe, who had sent Jem off with a smile, could not quite manage one for Walter. But at least no one cried. Dog Monday came out of his lair in the shipping shed and sat down close to Walter, thumping his tail vigorously on the boards of the platform whenever Walter spoke to him, and looking up with confident eyes, as if to say, "I know you'll find Jem and bring him back to me."

"So long, old fellow," said Carl Meredith cheerfully, when the good-byes had to be said. "Tell them over there to keep their spirits up—*I* am coming along presently."

"Me, too," said Shirley laconically, proffering a brown paw. Susan heard him and her face turned very grey.

Una shook hands quietly, looking at him with wistful, sorrowful, dark-blue eyes. But then Una's eyes had always been wistful. Walter bent his handsome black head in his khaki cap and kissed her with the warm, comradely kiss of a brother. He had never kissed her before, and for a fleeting moment Una's face betrayed her, if any one had noticed. But nobody did; the conductor was shouting "all aboard"; everybody was trying to look very cheerful. Walter turned to Rilla; she held his hands and looked up at him. She would not see him again until the day broke and the shadows vanished—

and she knew not if that daybreak would be on this side of the grave or beyond it.

"Good-bye," she said.

On her lips it lost all the bitterness it had won through the ages of parting and bore instead all the sweetness of the old loves of all the women who had ever loved and prayed for the beloved.

"Write me often and bring Jims up faithfully, according to the gospel of Morgan," Walter said lightly, having said all his serious things the night before in Rainbow Valley. But at the last moment he took her face between his hands and looked deep into her gallant eyes. "God bless you, Rilla-*my*-Rilla," he said softly and tenderly. After all it was not a hard thing to fight for a land that bore daughters like this.

He stood on the rear platform and waved to them as the train pulled out. Rilla was standing by herself but Una Meredith came to her and the two girls who loved him most stood together and held each other's cold hands as the train rounded the curve of the wooded hill.

Rilla spent an hour in Rainbow Valley that morning about which she never said a word to any one; she did not even write in her diary about it; when it was over she went home and made rompers for Jims during the rest of the day; in the evening she went to a Junior Red Cross committee meeting and was severely business-like.

"You would never suppose," said Irene Howard to Olive Kirk afterwards, "that Walter had left for the front only this morning. But some people really have no depth of feeling. I suppose it is much the best thing for them. I often wish *I* could take things as lightly as Rilla Blythe."

CHAPTER XVI

ℛealism and Romance

"Warsaw has fallen," said Dr. Blythe with a resigned air, as he brought the mail in one warm August day.

Gertrude and Mrs. Blythe looked dismally at each other, and Rilla, who was feeding Jims a Morganized diet from a carefully sterilized spoon, laid the said spoon down on his tray, utterly regardless of germs, and said, "Oh, dear me," in as tragic a tone as if the news had come as a thunderbolt instead of being a foregone conclusion from the preceding week's dispatches. They had thought they were quite resigned to Warsaw's fall but now they knew they had, as always, hoped against hope.

"Now, let us take a brace," said Susan. "It is not the terrible thing we have been thinking. I read a dispatch three columns long in the Montreal *Herald* yesterday which proved that Warsaw was not important from a military point of view at all. So let us take the military point of view, Dr. dear."

"I read that dispatch, too, and it has encouraged me immensely," said Gertrude. "I knew then and I know now that it was a lie from beginning to end. But I am in that state of mind where even a lie is a comfort, providing it is a cheerful lie."

"In that case, Miss Oliver dear, the German official reports ought to be all you need," said Susan sarcastically. "I never read them now because they make me so mad I cannot put my thoughts properly on my work after a dose of them. Even this news about Warsaw has taken the edge off my afternoon's plans. Misfortunes never come singly. I spoiled my baking of bread today—and now Warsaw has fallen—and here is little Kitchener bent on choking himself to death."

Jims was evidently trying to swallow his spoon, germs and all. Rilla rescued him mechanically and was about to resume the operation of feeding him when a casual remark of her father's sent such a shock and thrill over her that for the second time she dropped that doomed spoon.

"Kenneth Ford is down at Martin West's over-harbour," the doctor was saying. "His regiment was on its way to the front but was held up in Kingsport for some reason, and Ken got leave of absence to come over to the Island."

"I hope he will come up to see us," exclaimed Mrs. Blythe.

"He only has a day or two off, I believe," said the doctor absently.

Nobody noticed Rilla's flushed face and trembling hands. Even the most thoughtful and watchful of parents do not see everything that goes on under their very noses. Rilla made a third attempt to give the long-suffering Jims his dinner but all she could think of was the question—Would Ken come to see her before he went away? She had not heard from him for a long while. Had he forgotten her completely? If he did not come she would know that he had. Perhaps there was even— some other girl back there in Toronto. Of course there was. She was a little fool to be thinking about him at all. She would *not* think about him. If he came, well and good. It would only be courteous of him to make a farewell call at Ingleside where he had often been a guest. If he did not come—well and good, too. It did not matter very much. Nobody was going to fret. That was all settled comfortably—she was quite indifferent— but meanwhile Jims was being fed with a haste and reckless- ness that would have filled the soul of Morgan with horror.

Jims himself didn't like it, being a methodical baby, accustomed to swallowing spoonfuls with a decent interval for breath between each. He protested, but his protests availed him nothing. Rilla, as far as the care and feeding of infants was concerned, was utterly demoralized.

Then the telephone bell rang. There was nothing unusual about the telephone ringing. It rang on an average every ten minutes at Ingleside. But Rilla dropped Jims' spoon again—on the carpet this time—and flew to the 'phone as if life depended on her getting there before anybody else. Jims, his patience exhausted, lifted up his voice and wept.

"Hello, is that Ingleside?"

"Yes."

"That you, Rilla?"

"Yeth—yeth"—oh, why couldn't Jims stop howling for just one little minute? *Why* didn't *somebody* come in and choke him?

"Know who's speaking?"

Oh, didn't she know! Wouldn't she know that voice anywhere—at any time?

"It's Ken—isn't it?"

"Sure thing. I'm here for a look-in. Can I come up to Ingleside tonight and see you?"

"Of courthe."

Had he used "you" in the singular or plural sense? Presently she would wring Jims' neck—oh, *what* was Ken saying?

"See here, Rilla, can you arrange that there won't be more than a few dozen people around? Understand? I can't make my meaning clearer over this bally rural line. There are a dozen receivers down."

Did she understand! Yes, she understood.

"I'll try," she said tremulously.

"I'll be up about eight then. By-by."

Rilla hung up the 'phone and flew to Jims. But she did not wring that injured infant's neck. Instead she snatched him bodily out of his chair, crushed him against her face, kissed him rapturously on his milky mouth, and danced wildly around the room with him in her arms. After this Jims was relieved to find that she returned to sanity, gave him the rest of his dinner properly, and tucked him away for his afternoon nap with the little lullaby he loved best of all. She sewed at Red Cross shirts for the rest of the afternoon and built a crystal castle of dreams, all a-quiver with rainbows. Ken wanted to see *her*—to see her *alone*. That could be easily managed. Shirley wouldn't bother them, father and mother were going to the manse, Miss Oliver never played goose-berry, and Jims always slept the clock round from seven to seven. She would entertain Ken on the veranda—it would be moonlight—she would wear her white Georgette dress and do her hair *up*—yes, she would—at least in a low knot at the nape of her neck. Mother couldn't object to *that*, surely. Oh, how wonderful and romantic it would be! Would Ken say *anything*—he must mean to say *something* or why should he be so particular about seeing her alone? What if it rained—Susan had been complaining about Mr. Hyde that morning! What if some officious Junior Red called to discuss Belgians and shirts? Or, worst of all, what if Fred Arnold dropped in? He did occasionally.

The evening came at last and was all that could be desired in an evening. The doctor and his wife went to the manse, Shirley and Miss Oliver went they alone knew where, Susan went to the store for household supplies, and Jims went to Dreamland. Rilla put on her Georgette gown, knotted up her hair and bound a little double string of pearls around it. Then she tucked a cluster of pale pink baby roses at her belt. Would

Ken ask her for a rose for a keepsake? She knew that Jem had carried to the trenches in Flanders a faded rose that Faith Meredith had kissed and given him the night before he left.

Rilla looked very sweet when she met Ken in the mingled moonlight and vine shadows of the big veranda. The hand she gave him was cold and she was so desperately anxious not to lisp that her greeting was prim and precise. How handsome and tall Kenneth looked in his lieutenant's uniform! It made him seem older, too—so much so that Rilla felt rather foolish. Hadn't it been the height of absurdity for her to suppose that this splendid young officer had anything special to say to *her*, little Rilla Blythe of Glen St. Mary? Likely she hadn't understood him after all—he had only meant that he didn't want a mob of folks around making a fuss over him and trying to lionize him, as they had probably done over-harbour. Yes, of course, that was all he meant—and she, little idiot, had gone and vainly imagined that he didn't want anybody but her. And he would think she had manœuvred everybody away so that they could be alone together, and he would laugh to himself at her.

"This is better luck than I hoped for," said Ken, leaning back in his chair and looking at her with very unconcealed admiration in his eloquent eyes. "I was sure some one would be hanging about and it was just *you* I wanted to see, Rilla-my-Rilla."

Rilla's dream castle flashed into the landscape again. *This* was unmistakable enough certainly—not much doubt as to his meaning *here*.

"There aren't—so many of us—to poke around as there used to be," she said softly.

"No, that's so," said Ken gently. "Jem and Walter and the girls away—it makes a big blank, doesn't it? But"—he leaned forward until his dark curls almost brushed her hair—"doesn't Fred Arnold try to fill the blank occasionally? I've been told so."

At this moment, before Rilla could make any reply, Jims began to cry at the top of his voice in the room whose open window was just above them—Jims, who hardly *ever* cried in the evening. Moreover, he was crying, as Rilla knew from experience, with a vim and energy that betokened that he had been already whimpering softly unheard for some time and was thoroughly exasperated. When Jims started in crying like that he made a thorough job of it. Rilla knew that there was no use to sit still and pretend to ignore him. He wouldn't stop; and conversation of any kind was out of the question when such shrieks and howls were floating over your head. Besides, she was afraid Kenneth would think she was utterly unfeeling if she sat still and let a baby cry like that. He was not likely acquainted with Morgan's invaluable volume.

She got up. "Jims has had a nightmare, I think. He sometimes has one and he is always badly frightened by it. Excuse me for a moment."

Rilla flew upstairs, wishing quite frankly that soup tureens had never been invented. But when Jims, at sight of her, lifted his little arms entreatingly and swallowed several sobs, with tears rolling down his cheeks, resentment went out of her heart. After all, the poor darling was frightened. She picked him up gently and rocked him soothingly until his sobs ceased and his eyes closed. Then she essayed to lay him down in his crib. Jims opened his eyes and shrieked a protest. This performance was repeated twice. Rilla grew desperate. She couldn't leave Ken down there alone any longer—she had been away nearly half an hour already. With a resigned air she marched downstairs, carrying Jims, and sat down on the veranda. It was, no doubt, a ridiculous thing to sit and cuddle a contrary war baby when your best young man was making his farewell call but there was nothing else to be done.

Jims was supremely happy. He kicked his little pink-soled feet rapturously out under his white nighty and gave one of his rare laughs. He was beginning to be a very pretty baby; his golden hair curled in silken ringlets all over his little round head and his eyes were beautiful.

"He's a decorative kiddy all right, isn't he?" said Ken.

"His looks are very well," said Rilla, bitterly, as if to imply that they were much the best of him. Jims, being an astute infant, sensed trouble in the atmosphere and realized that it was up to him to clear it away. He turned his face up to Rilla, smiled adorably and said, clearly and beguilingly, "Will—Will."

It was the very first time he had spoken a word or tried to speak. Rilla was so delighted that she forgot her grudge against him. She forgave him with a hug and kiss. Jims, understanding that he was restored to favour, cuddled down against her just where a gleam of light from the lamp in the living room struck across his hair and turned it into a halo of gold against her breast.

Kenneth sat very still and silent, looking at Rilla—at the delicate, girlish silhouette of her, her long lashes, her dented lip, her adorable chin. In the dim moonlight, as she sat with her head bent a little over Jims, the lamplight glinting on her pearls until they glistened like a slender nimbus, he thought she looked exactly like the Madonna that hung over his mother's desk at home. He carried that picture of her in his heart to the horror of the battlefields of France. He had had a strong fancy for Rilla Blythe ever since the night of the Four Winds dance; but it was when he saw her there, with little

Jims in her arms, that he loved her and realized it. And all the while, poor Rilla was sitting, disappointed and humiliated, feeling that her last evening with Ken was spoiled and wondering why things always had to go so contrarily outside of books. She felt too absurd to try to talk. Evidently Ken was completely disgusted, too, since he was sitting there in such stony silence.

Hope revived momentarily when Jims went so thoroughly asleep that she thought it would be safe to lay him down on the couch in the living room. But when she came out again Susan was sitting on the veranda, loosening her bonnet strings with the air of one who meant to stay where she was for some time.

"Have you got your baby to sleep?" she asked kindly.

Your baby! Really, Susan might have more tact. "Yes," said Miss Rilla shortly.

Susan laid her parcels on the reed table, as one determined to do her duty. She was very tired but she must help Rilla out. Here was Kenneth Ford who had come to call on the family and they were all unfortunately out and "the poor child" had had to entertain him alone. But Susan had come to her rescue—Susan would do her part no matter how tired she was.

"Dear me, how you have grown up," she said, looking at Ken's six feet of khaki uniform without the least awe. Susan had grown used to khaki now and at sixty-four even a lieutenant's uniform is just clothes and nothing else. "It is an amazing thing how fast children do grow up. Rilla here, now, is almost fifteen."

"I'm going on seventeen, Susan," cried Rilla almost passionately. She was a whole month past sixteen. It was intolerable of Susan.

"It seems just the other day that you were all babies," said Susan, ignoring Rilla's protest. "You were really the prettiest baby I ever saw, Ken, though your mother had an awful time trying to cure you of sucking your thumb. Do you remember the day I spanked you?"

"No," said Ken.

"Oh well, I suppose you would be too young—you were only about four and you were here with your mother and you insisted on teasing Nan until she cried. I had tried several ways of stopping you but none availed and I saw that a spanking was the only thing that would serve. So I picked you up and laid you across my knee and lambasted you well. You howled at the top of your voice but you left Nan alone after that."

Rilla was writhing. Hadn't Susan *any* realization that she was addressing an officer of the Canadian Army? Apparently she had not. Oh, what would Ken think?

"I suppose you do not remember the time your mother spanked you either," continued Susan, who seemed to be bent on reviving tender reminiscences that evening. "I shall never, no, never forget it. She was up here one night with you when you were about three and you and Walter were playing out in the kitchen yard with a kitten. I had a big puncheon of rainwater by the spout which I was reserving for making soap. And you and Walter began quarrelling over the kitten. Walter was at one side of the puncheon standing on a chair, holding the kitten, and you were standing on a chair at the other side. You leaned across that puncheon and grabbed the kitten and pulled. You were always a great hand for taking what you wanted without too much ceremony. Walter held on tight and the poor kitten yelled but you dragged Walter and the kitten half over and then you both lost your balance and tumbled into that puncheon, kitten and all. If I had not been on the spot you would both have been drowned. I flew to the rescue and hauled you all three out before much harm was done, and your mother, who had seen it all from the upstairs window, came down and picked you up, dripping as you were, and gave you a beautiful spanking. Ah," said Susan with a sigh, "those were happy old days at Ingleside."

"Must have been," said Ken. His tone sounded queer and stiff. Rilla supposed he was hopelessly enraged. The truth was he dared not trust his voice lest it betray his frantic desire to laugh.

"Rilla here, now," said Susan, looking affectionately at that unhappy damsel, "never was much spanked. She was a real well-behaved child for the most part. But her father did spank her once. She got two bottles of pills out of his office and dared Alice Clow to see which of them could swallow all the pills first, and if her father had not happened in in the nick of time those two children would have been corpses by night. As it was, they were both sick enough shortly after. But the doctor spanked Rilla then and there and he made such a thorough job of it that she never meddled with anything in his office afterwards. We hear a great deal nowadays of something that is called 'moral persuasion' but in my opinion a good spanking and no nagging afterwards is a much better thing."

Rilla wondered viciously whether Susan meant to relate *all* the family spankings. But Susan had finished with the subject and branched off to another cheerful one.

"I remember little Tod MacAllister over-harbour killed himself that very way, eating up a whole box of fruitatives because he thought they were candy. It was a very sad affair. He was," said Susan earnestly, "the very cutest little corpse I ever laid my eyes on. It was very careless of his mother to leave the fruitatives where he could get them, but she was well-known to be a heedless creature. One day she found a nest of five eggs as she was going across the fields to church with a brand-new blue silk dress on. So she put them in the pocket of her petticoat and when she got to church she forgot all about them and sat down on them and her dress was ruined, not to speak of the petticoat. Let me see—would not Tod be some relation of yours? Your great grandmother West was a MacAllister. Her brother Amos was a Mac-donaldite in religion. I am told he used to take the jerks something fearful. But you look more like your great grand-father West than the MacAllisters. *He* died of a paralytic stroke quite early in life."

"Did you see anybody at the store?" asked Rilla desperately, in the faint hope of directing Susan's conversation into more agreeable channels.

"Nobody except Mary Vance," said Susan, "and she was stepping round as brisk as the Irishman's flea."

What terrible similes Susan used! Would Kenneth think she acquired them from the family!

"To hear Mary talk about Miller Douglas you would think he was the only Glen boy who had enlisted," Susan went on. "But of course she always did brag and she has some good qualities I am willing to admit, though I did not think so that time she chased Rilla here through the village with a dried codfish till the poor child fell, heels over head, into the puddle before Carter Flagg's store."

Rilla went cold all over with wrath and shame. Were there any more disgraceful scenes in her past that Susan could rake up? As for Ken, he could have howled over Susan's speeches, but he would not so insult the duenna of his lady, so he sat with a preternaturally solemn face which seemed to poor Rilla a haughty and offended one.

"I paid eleven cents for a bottle of ink tonight," complained Susan. "Ink is twice as high as it was last year. Perhaps it is because Woodrow Wilson has been writing so many notes. It must cost him considerable. My cousin Sophia says Woodrow Wilson is not the man she expected him to be—but then no man ever was. Being an old maid, I do not know much about men and have never pretended to, but my cousin Sophia is very hard on them, although she married two of them, which you might think was a fair share. Albert Crawford's chimney blew down in that big gale we had last week, and when Sophia heard the bricks clattering on the roof she thought it was a Zeppelin raid and went into hysterics. And Mrs. Albert Crawford says that of the two things she would have preferred the Zeppelin raid."

Rilla sat limply in her chair like one hypnotized. She knew Susan would stop talking when she was ready to stop and that no earthly power could make her stop any sooner. As a rule, she was very fond of Susan but just now she hated her with a deadly hatred. It was ten o'clock. Ken would soon have to go—the others would soon be home—and she had not even had a chance to explain to Ken that Fred Arnold filled no blank in her life nor ever could. Her rainbow castle lay in ruins round her.

Kenneth got up at last. He realized that Susan was there to stay as long as he did and it was a three mile walk to Martin West's, over-harbour. He wondered if Rilla had put Susan up to this, not wanting to be left alone with him, lest he say something Fred Arnold's sweetheart did not want to hear. Rilla got up, too, and walked silently the length of the veranda with him. They stood there for a moment, Ken on the lower step. The step was half sunk into the earth and mint grew thickly about and over its edge. Often crushed by so many passing feet it gave out its essence freely, and the spicy odour hung around them like a soundless, invisible benediction. Ken looked up at Rilla, whose hair was shining in the moonlight and whose eyes were pools of allurement. All at once he felt sure there was nothing in that gossip about Fred Arnold.

"Rilla," he said in a sudden, intense whisper, "you are the sweetest thing."

Rilla flushed and looked at Susan. Ken looked, too, and saw that Susan's back was turned. He put his arm about Rilla and kissed her. It was the first time Rilla had ever been kissed. She thought perhaps she ought to resent it but she didn't. Instead, she glanced timidly into Kenneth's seeking eyes and her glance was a kiss.

"Rilla-my-Rilla," said Ken, "will you promise that you won't let any one else kiss you until I come back?"

"Yes," said Rilla, trembling and thrilling.

Susan was turning round. Ken loosened his hold and stepped to the walk.

"Good-bye," he said casually. Rilla heard herself saying it just as casually. She stood and watched him down the walk, out of the gate, and down the road. When the fir wood hid him from her sight she suddenly said "Oh," in a choked way and ran down to the gate, sweet blossomy things catching at her skirts as she ran. Leaning over the gate she saw Kenneth walking briskly down the road, over the bars of tree shadows and moonlight, his tall, erect figure grey in the white radiance. As he reached the turn he stopped and looked back and saw her standing amid the tall white lilies by the gate. He waved his hand—she waved hers—he was gone around the turn.

Rilla stood there for a little while, gazing across the fields of mist and silver. She had heard her mother say that she loved turns in roads—they were so provocative and alluring. Rilla thought she hated them. She had seen Jem and Jerry vanish from her around a bend in the road—then Walter—and now Ken. Brothers and playmate and sweetheart—they were all gone, never, it might be, to return. Yet still the Piper piped and the dance of death went on.

When Rilla walked slowly back to the house Susan was still sitting by the veranda table and Susan was sniffing suspiciously.

"I have been thinking, Rilla dear, of the old days in the House of Dreams when Kenneth's mother and father were courting and Jem was a little baby and you were not born or thought of. It was a very romantic affair and she and your mother were such chums. To think I should have lived to see her son going to the front. As if she had not had enough trouble in her early life without this coming upon her! But we must take a brace and see it through."

All Rilla's anger against Susan had evaporated. With Ken's kiss still burning on her lips, and the wonderful significance of the promise he had asked thrilling heart and soul, she could not be angry with any one. She put her slim white hand into Susan's brown, work-hardened one and gave it a squeeze. Susan was a faithful old dear and would lay down her life for any one of them.

"You are tired, Rilla dear, and had better go to bed," Susan said, patting her hand. "I noticed you were too tired to talk tonight. I am glad I came home in time to help you out. It is very tiresome trying to entertain young men when you are not accustomed to it."

Rilla carried Jims upstairs and went to bed but not before

she had sat for a long time at her window reconstructing her rainbow castle, with several added domes and turrets.

"I wonder," she said to herself, "if I am, or am not engaged to Kenneth Ford."

CHAPTER XVII

The Weeks Wear By

Rilla read her first love letter in her Rainbow Valley fir-shadowed nook, and a girl's first love letter, whatever blasé, older people may think of it, is an event of tremendous importance in the teens. After Kenneth's regiment had left Kingsport there came a fortnight of dully-aching anxiety and when the congregation sang in church on Sunday evenings,

"Oh, hear us when we cry to Thee
For those in peril on the sea,"

Rilla's voice always failed her, for with the words came a horribly vivid mind picture of a submarined ship sinking beneath pitiless waves amid the struggles and cries of drowning men. Then word came that Kenneth's regiment had arrived safely in England; and now, at last, here was his letter. It began with something that made Rilla supremely happy for the moment and ended with a paragraph that crimsoned her cheeks with the wonder and thrill and delight of it. Between beginning and ending the letter was just such a jolly, newsy epistle as Ken might have written to any one; but for the sake of that beginning and ending Rilla slept with the letter under her pillow for weeks, sometimes waking in the night to slip her fingers under and just touch it, and looked with secret pity on other girls whose sweethearts could never have written them anything half so wonderful and exquisite. Kenneth was not the son of a famous novelist for nothing. He "had a way" of expressing things in a few poignant, significant words which seemed to suggest far more than they uttered, and never grew stale or flat or foolish with ever so many scores of readings. Rilla went home from Rainbow Valley as if she flew rather than walked.

But such moments of uplift were rare that autumn. To be sure, there was one day in September when great news came of a big Allied victory in the west and Susan ran out to hoist the flag—the first time she had hoisted it since the Russian line broke and the last time she was to hoist it for many dismal moons.

"Likely the Big Push has begun at last, Mrs. Dr. dear," she exclaimed, "and we will soon see the finish of the Huns. Our boys will be home by Christmas now. Hurrah!"

Susan was ashamed of herself for hurrahing the minute she had done it, and apologized meekly for such an outburst of juvenility. "But indeed, Mrs. Dr. dear, this good news has gone to my head after this awful summer of Russian slumps and Gallipoli setbacks."

"Good news!" said Miss Oliver bitterly. "I wonder if the women whose men have been killed for it will call it good news. Just because our own men are not on that part of the front we are rejoicing as if the victory had cost no lives."

"Now, Miss Oliver dear, do not take that view of it," deprecated Susan. "We have not had much to rejoice over of late and yet men were being killed just the same. Do not let yourself slump like poor Cousin Sophia. *She* said, when this word came, 'Ah, it is nothing but a rift in the clouds. We are up this week but we will be down the next.' 'Well, Sophia Crawford,' said I—for I never will give in to her, Mrs. Dr. dear—'God Himself cannot make two hills without a hollow between them, as I have heard it said, but that is no reason why we should not take the good of the hills when we are on them.' But Cousin Sophia moaned on. 'Here is the Galli*polly* expedition a failure and the Grand Duke Nicholas sent off, and everyone knows the Czar of Rooshia is a pro-German and the Allies have no ammunition and Bulgaria is going against us. And the end is not yet, for England and France must be punished for their deadly sins until they repent in sackcloth and ashes.' 'I think myself,' I said, 'that they will do *their* repenting in khaki and trench mud, and it also seems to me that the Huns should have a few sins to repent of also.' 'They are instruments in the hand of the Almighty, to purge the garner,' said Sophia. And then I got mad, Mrs. Dr. dear, and told her I did not and never would believe that the Almighty ever took such dirty instruments in hand for any purpose whatever, and that I did not consider it decent for her to be using the words of Holy Writ as glibly as she was doing in ordinary conversation. She was not, I told her, a minister or even an elder. And for the time being I squelched her, Mrs. Dr. dear. Cousin Sophia has no spirit. She is very different from her niece, Mrs. Dean Crawford over-harbour. You know the Dean Crawfords had five boys and now the new baby is another boy. All the connection and especially Dean Crawford were much disappointed because their hearts had been set on a girl; but Mrs. Dean just laughed and said, 'Everywhere I went this summer I saw the sign "MEN WANTED" staring me in the face. Do you think I could go and have a girl under such circumstances?' *There* is a spirit for you, Mrs. Dr. dear. But Cousin Sophia would say the child was just so much more cannon fodder."

Cousin Sophia had full range for her pessimism that gloomy autumn, and even Susan, incorrigible old optimist as she was, was hard put to it for cheer. When Bulgaria lined up with Germany Susan only remarked scornfully, "One more nation anxious for a licking," but the Greek tangle worried her beyond her powers of philosophy to endure calmly.

"Constantine of Greece has a German wife, Mrs. Dr. dear, and that fact squelches hope. To think that I should have lived to care what kind of a wife Constantine of Greece had! The miserable creature is under his wife's thumb and that is a bad place for any man to be. I am an old maid and an old maid has to be independent or she will be squashed out. But if I had been a married woman, Mrs. Dr. dear, I would have been meek and humble. It is my opinion that this Sophia of Greece is a minx."

Susan was furious when the news came that Venizelos had met with defeat.

"I could spank Constantine and skin him alive afterwards, that I could," she exclaimed bitterly.

"Oh, Susan, I'm surprised at you," said the doctor, pulling a long face. "Have you no regard for the proprieties? Skin him alive by all means but omit the spanking."

"If he had been well spanked in his younger days he might have more sense now," retorted Susan. "But I suppose princes are never spanked, more is the pity. I see the Allies have sent him an ultimatum. I could tell them that it will take more than ultimatums to skin a snake like Constantine. Perhaps the Allied blockade will hammer sense into his head; but that will take some time I am thinking, and in the meantime what is to become of poor Serbia?"

They saw what became of Serbia, and during the process Susan was hardly to be lived with. In her exasperation she abused everything and everybody except Kitchener, and she fell upon poor President Wilson tooth and claw.

"If he had done his duty and gone into the war long ago we should not have seen this mess in Serbia," she avowed.

"It would be a serious thing to plunge a great country like the United States, with its mixed population, into the war, Susan," said the doctor, who sometimes came to the defence of the president, not because he thought Wilson needed it especially, but from an unholy love of baiting Susan.

"Maybe, Dr. dear,—maybe! But that makes me think of the old story of the girl who told her grandmother she was going to be married. 'It is a solemn thing to be married,' said the old lady. 'Yes, but it is a solemner thing not to be,' said the girl. And I can testify to *that* out of my own experience, Dr. dear. And *I* think it is a solemner thing for the Yankees that they have kept out of the war than it would have been if they had gone into it. However, though I do not know much about them, I am of the opinion that we will see them starting something yet, Woodrow Wilson or no Woodrow Wilson, when they get it into their heads that this war is not a correspondence school. They will not," said Susan, energetically waving a saucepan with one hand and a soup ladle with the other, "be too proud to fight then."

On a pale-yellow, windy evening in October Carl Meredith went away. He had enlisted on his eighteenth birthday. John Meredith saw him off with a set face. His two boys were gone—there was only little Bruce left now. He loved Bruce and Bruce's mother dearly; but Jerry and Carl were the sons of the bride of his youth and Carl was the only one of all his children who had Cecilia's very eyes. As they looked lovingly out at him above Carl's uniform the pale minister suddenly remembered the day when for the first and last time he had tried to whip Carl for his prank with the eel. That was the first time he had realized how much Carl's eyes were like Cecilia's. Now he realized it again once more. Would he ever again see his dead wife's eyes looking at him from his son's face? What a bonny, clean, handsome lad he was! It was—hard—to see him go. John Meredith seemed to be looking at a torn plain strewn with the bodies of "able-bodied men between the ages of eighteen and forty-five." Only the other day Carl had been a little scrap of a boy, hunting bugs in Rainbow Valley, taking lizards to bed with him, and scandalizing the Glen by carrying frogs to Sunday School. It seemed hardly—right—somehow that he should be an "able-bodied" man in khaki. Yet John Meredith had said no word to dissuade him when Carl had told him he must go.

Rilla felt Carl's going keenly. They had always been cronies and playmates. He was only a little older than she was and they had been children in Rainbow Valley together. She recalled all their old pranks and escapades as she walked slowly home alone. The full moon peeped through the scudding clouds with sudden floods of weird illumination, the telephone wires sang a shrill song in the wind, and the tall spikes of withered, grey-headed golden rod in the fence corners swayed and beckoned wildly to her like groups of old witches weaving unholy spells. On such a night as this, long ago, Carl would come over to Ingleside and whisper her out to the gate. "Let's go on a moon-spree, Rilla," he would say, and the two of them would scamper off to Rainbow Valley. Rilla had never been afraid of his beetles and bugs, though she drew a hard and fast line at snakes. They used to talk together of almost everything and were teased about each other at school; but one evening when they were about ten years of age they had solemnly promised, by the old spring in Rainbow Valley, that they would never marry each other. Alice Clow had "crossed out" their names on her slate in school that day and it came out that "both married." They did not like the idea at all, hence the mutual vow in Rainbow Valley. There was nothing like an ounce of prevention. Rilla laughed over the old memory—and then sighed. That very day a dispatch from some London paper had contained the cheerful announcement that "the present moment is the darkest since the war began." It was dark enough, and Rilla wished desperately that she could do something besides waiting and serving at home, as day after day the Glen boys she had known went away. If she were only a boy, speeding in khaki by Carl's side to the western front! She had wished that in a burst of romance when Jem had gone, without, perhaps, really meaning it. She meant it now. There were moments when waiting at home, in safety and comfort, seemed an unendurable thing.

The moon burst triumphantly through an especially dark cloud and shadow and silver chased each other in waves over the Glen. Rilla remembered one moonlit evening of childhood when she had said to her mother, "The moon just looks like a *sorry, sorry* face." She thought it looked like that still—an agonized, careworn face, as though it looked down on dreadful sights. What did it see on the western front? In broken Serbia? On shell-swept Gallipoli?

"I am tired," Miss Oliver had said that day, in a rare outburst of impatience, "of this horrible rack of strained emotions, when every day brings a new horror or the dread of it. No, don't look reproachfully at me, Mrs. Blythe. There's nothing heroic about me today. I've slumped. I wish England had left Belgium to her fate—I wish Canada had never sent a man—I wish we'd tied our boys to our apron strings and not let one of them go. Oh—I shall be ashamed of myself in half an hour—but at this very minute I mean every word of it. Will the Allies *never* strike?"

"Patience is a tired mare but she jogs on," said Susan.

"While the steeds of Armageddon thunder, trampling over our hearts," retorted Miss Oliver. "Serbia is being throttled and the Allies on the western front seem able to do nothing but purchase a few paltry yards of trenches a day. Susan, tell me—don't you ever—didn't you ever—take spells of feeling that you *must scream*—or swear—or smash something—just because your torture reaches a point when it becomes unbearable?"

"I have never sworn or desired to swear, Miss Oliver dear, but I will admit," said Susan, with the air of one determined to make a clean breast of it once for all, "that I have experienced occasions when it was a relief to do considerable banging."

"Don't you think that is a kind of swearing, Susan? What is the difference between slamming a door viciously and saying d—"

"Miss Oliver dear," interrupted Susan, desperately determined to save Gertrude from herself, if human power could do it, "you are all tired out and unstrung—and no wonder, teaching those obstreperous youngsters all day and coming home to bad war news. But just you go upstairs and lie down and I will bring you up a cup of hot tea and a bite of toast and very soon you will not want to slam doors or swear."

"Susan, you're a good soul—a very pearl of Susans! But, Susan, it *would* be such a relief—to say just one soft, low, little tiny d—"

"I will bring you a hot water bottle for the soles of your feet, also," interposed Susan resolutely, "and it would *not* be any relief to say that word you are thinking of, Miss Oliver, and that you may tie to."

"Well, I'll try the hot water bottle first," said Miss Oliver, repenting herself of teasing Susan and vanishing upstairs, to Susan's intense relief. Susan shook her head ominously as she filled the hot water bottle. The war was certainly relaxing the standards of behaviour woefully. Here was Miss Oliver admittedly on the point of profanity.

"We must draw the blood from her brain," said Susan, "and if this bottle is not effective I will see what can be done with a mustard plaster."

Gertrude rallied and carried on. Lord Kitchener went to Greece, whereat Susan foretold that Constantine would soon experience a change of heart. Lloyd George began to heckle the Allies regarding equipment and guns and Susan said you would hear more of Lloyd George yet. The gallant Anzacs withdrew from Gallipoli and Susan approved the step, with reservations. The siege of Kut-El-Amara began and Susan pored over maps of Mesopotamia and abused the Turks. Henry Ford started for Europe and Susan flayed him with sarcasm. Sir John French was superseded by Sir Douglas Haig and Susan dubiously opined that it was poor policy to swap horses crossing a stream, "though, to be sure, Haig was a good name and French had a foreign sound, say what you might." Not a move on the great chess board of king or bishop or pawn escaped Susan, who had once read only Glen St. Mary notes. "There was a time," she said sorrowfully, "when I did not care what happened outside of P.E. Island, and now a king cannot have a toothache in Russia or China but it worries me. It may be broadening to the mind, as the doctor said, but it is very painful to the feelings."

When Christmas came again Susan did not set any vacant places at the festive board. Two empty chairs were too much even for Susan who had thought in September that there would not be one.

"This is the first Christmas that Walter was not home," Rilla wrote in her diary that night. "Jem used to be away for Christmases up in Avonlea, but Walter never was. I had letters from Ken and him today. They are still in England but expect to be in the trenches very soon. And *then*—but I suppose we'll be able to endure it somehow. To me, the strangest of all the strange things since 1914 is how we have all learned to accept things we never thought we could—to go on with life as a matter of course. I know that Jem and Jerry are in the trenches—that Ken and Walter will be soon—that if one of them does not come back my heart will break—yet I go on and work and plan—yes, and even enjoy life by times. There are moments when we have real fun because, just for the moment, we don't think about things and then—we remember—and the remembering is worse than thinking of it all the time would have been.

"Today was dark and cloudy and tonight is wild enough, as Gertrude says, to please any novelist in search of suitable matter for a murder or elopement. The raindrops streaming over the panes look like tears running down a face, and the wind is shrieking through the maple grove.

"This hasn't been a nice Christmas day in any way. Nan had toothache and Susan had red eyes, and assumed a weird and gruesome flippancy of manner to deceive us into thinking she hadn't; and Jims had a bad cold all day and I'm afraid of croup. He has had croup twice since October. The first time I was nearly frightened to death, for father and mother were both away—father always *is* away, it seems to me, when any of this household get sick. But Susan was cool as a fish and knew just what to do, and by morning Jims was all right. That child is a cross between a duck and an imp. He's a year and four months old, trots about everywhere, and says quite a few words. He has the cutest little way of calling me "Willa-will." It always brings back that dreadful, ridiculous, delightful night when Ken came to say good-bye, and I was so furious and happy. Jims is pink and white and big-eyed and curly-haired and every now and then I discover a new dimple in him. I can never quite believe he is really the same creature as that scrawny, yellow, ugly little changeling I brought home in the soup tureen. Nobody has ever heard a word from Jim Anderson. If he never comes back I shall keep Jims always. Everybody here worships and spoils him—or would spoil him if Morgan and I didn't stand remorselessly in the way. Susan says Jims is the cleverest child she ever saw and can recognize Old Nick when he sees him—this because Jims threw poor Doc out of an upstairs window one day. Doc turned into Mr. Hyde on his way down and landed in a currant bush, spitting and swearing. I tried to console his inner cat with a saucer of milk but he would have none of it, and remained Mr. Hyde the rest of the day. Jims' latest exploit was to paint the cushion of the big arm chair in the sun parlour with molasses; and before anybody found it out Mrs. Fred Clow came in on Red Cross business and sat down on it. Her new silk dress was ruined and nobody could blame her for being vexed. But she went into one of her tempers and said nasty things and gave me such slams about 'spoiling' Jims that I nearly boiled over, too. But I kept the lid on till she had waddled away and then I exploded.

"'The fat, clumsy, horrid old thing,' I said—and oh, what a satisfaction it was to say it.

"'She has three sons at the front,' mother said rebukingly.

"'I suppose that covers all her shortcomings in manners,' I retorted. But I was ashamed—for it is true that all her boys have gone and she was very plucky and loyal about it too; and she is a perfect tower of strength in the Red Cross. It's a little hard to remember all the heroines. Just the same, it was her second new silk dress in one year and that when everybody is—or should be—trying to 'save and serve.'

"I had to bring out my green velvet hat again lately and begin wearing it. I hung on to my blue straw sailor as long as I could. How I hate the green velvet hat! It is so elaborate and conspicuous. I don't see how I could ever have liked it. But I vowed to wear it and wear it I will.

"Shirley and I went down to the station this morning to take Little Dog Monday a bang-up Christmas dinner. Dog Monday waits and watches there still, with just as much hope and confidence as ever. Sometimes he hangs around the station house and talks to people and the rest of his time he sits at his little kennel door and watches the track unwinkingly. We never try to coax him home now: we know it is of no use. When Jem comes back Monday will come home with him; and if Jem—never comes back—Monday will wait there for him as long as his dear dog heart goes on beating.

"Fred Arnold was here last night. He was eighteen in November and is going to enlist just as soon as his mother is over an operation she has to have. He has been coming here very often lately and though I like him so much it makes me uncomfortable, because I am afraid he is thinking that perhaps I could care something for him. I can't tell him about Ken—because, after all, what is there to tell? And yet I don't like to behave coldly and distantly when he will be going away so soon. It is very perplexing. I remember I used to think it would be such fun to have *dozens* of beaux—and now I'm worried to death because two are too many.

"I am learning to cook. Susan is teaching me. I tried to learn long ago—but no, let me be honest—Susan tried to teach me, which is a very different thing. I never seemed to succeed with anything and I got discouraged. But since the boys have gone away I wanted to be able to make cake and things for them myself and so I started in again and this time I'm getting on surprisingly well. Susan says it is all in the way I hold my mouth and father says my subconscious mind is desirous of learning now, and I daresay they're both right. Anyhow, I can make dandy short-bread and fruit cake. I got ambitious last week and attempted cream puffs, but made an awful failure of them. They came out of the oven flat as flukes. I thought maybe the cream would fill them up again and make them plump but it didn't. I think Susan was secretly pleased. She is past mistress in the art of making cream puffs and it would break her heart if any one else here could make them as well. I wonder if Susan tampered—but no, I won't suspect her of such a thing.

"Miranda Pryor spent an afternoon here a few days ago, helping me cut out certain Red Cross garments known by the charming name of 'vermin shirts.' Susan thinks that name is not quite decent, so I suggested she call them 'cootie sarks,' which is old Highland Sandy's version of it. But she shook her head and I heard her telling mother later on that, in her opinion, 'cooties' and 'sarks' were not proper subjects for young girls to talk about. She was especially horrified when Jem wrote in his last letter to mother, 'Tell Susan I had a fine cootie hunt this morning and caught fifty-three!' Susan positively turned pea-green. 'Mrs. Dr. dear,' she said, 'when I was young, if decent people were so unfortunate as to get—those insects—they kept it a secret if possible. I do not want to be narrow-minded, Mrs. Dr. dear, but I still think it is better not to mention such things.'

"Miranda grew confidential over our vermin shirts and told me all her troubles. She is desperately unhappy. She is engaged to Joe Milgrave and Joe joined up in October and has been training in Charlottetown ever since. Her father was furious when he joined and forbade Miranda ever to have any dealings or communication with him again. Poor Joe expects to go overseas any day and wants Miranda to marry him before he goes, which shows that there have been 'communications' in spite of Whiskers-on-the-moon. Miranda wants to marry him but cannot, and she declares it will break her heart.

"'Why don't you run away and marry him?' I said. It didn't go against my conscience in the least to give her such advice. Joe Milgrave is a splendid fellow and Mr. Pryor fairly beamed on him until the war broke out and I knew Mr. Pryor would forgive Miranda very quickly, once it was over and he wanted his housekeeper back. But Miranda shook her silvery head dolefully.

"'Joe wants me to but I can't. Mother's last words to me, as she lay on her dying bed, were, "never, never run away, Miranda," and I promised.'

"Miranda's mother died two years ago, and it seems, according to Miranda, that her mother and father actually ran away to be married themselves. To picture Whiskers-on-the-moon as the hero of an elopement is beyond my power. But such was the case and Mrs. Pryor at least lived to repent it. She had a hard life of it with Mr. Pryor, and she thought it was a punishment on her for running away. So she made Miranda promise *she* would never, for any reason whatever, do it.

"Of course, you cannot urge a girl to break a promise made to a dying mother, so I did not see what Miranda could do unless she got Joe to come to the house when her father was away and marry her there. But Miranda said that couldn't be managed. Her father seemed to suspect she might be up to something of the sort and he never went away for long at a time, and, of course, Joe couldn't get leave of absence at an hour's notice.

"'No, I shall just have to let Joe go, and he will be killed—I know he will be killed—and my heart will break,' said Miranda, her tears running down and copiously bedewing the vermin shirts!

"I am not writing like this for lack of any real sympathy with poor Miranda. I've just got into the habit of giving things a comical twist if I can, when I'm writing to Jem and Walter and Ken, to make them laugh. I really felt sorry for Miranda who is as much in love with Joe as a china-blue girl can be with any one and who is dreadfully ashamed of her father's pro-German sentiments. I think she understood that I did, for she said she had wanted to tell me all about her worries because I had grown so sympathetic this past year. I wonder if I have. I know I used to be a selfish, thoughtless creature—how selfish and thoughtless I am ashamed to remember now, so I can't be quite so bad as I was.

"I wish I could help Miranda. It would be very romantic to contrive a war wedding and I should dearly love to get the better of Whiskers-on-the-moon. But at present the oracle has not spoken."

CHAPTER XVIII

A War Wedding

"I can tell you this Dr. dear," said Susan, pale with wrath, "that Germany is getting to be perfectly ridiculous."

They were all in the big Ingleside kitchen. Susan was mixing biscuits for supper. Mrs. Blythe was making short-bread for Jem and Rilla was compounding candy for Ken and Walter—it had once been "Walter and Ken" in her thoughts but somehow, quite unconsciously, this had changed until Ken's name came naturally first. Cousin Sophia was also there, knitting. All the boys were going to be killed in the long run, so Cousin Sophia felt in her bones, but they might better die with warm feet than cold ones, so Cousin Sophia knitted faithfully and gloomily.

Into this peaceful scene erupted the doctor, wrathful and excited over the burning of the Parliament buildings in Ottawa. And Susan became automatically quite as wrathful and excited.

"What will those Huns do next?" she demanded. "Coming over here and burning *our* Parliament buildings! Did any one ever *hear* of such an outrage?"

"We don't know that the Germans are responsible for this," said the doctor—much as if he felt quite sure they were, though. "Fires *do* start without their agency sometimes. And Uncle Mark MacAllister's barn was burned last week. You can hardly accuse the Germans of that, Susan."

"Indeed, Dr. dear, I do not know," Susan nodded slowly and portentously. "Whiskers-on-the-moon was there that very day. The fire broke out half an hour after he was gone. So much is a fact—but *I* shall not accuse a Presbyterian elder of burning anybody's barn until I have proof. However, everybody knows, Dr. dear, that both Uncle Mark's boys have enlisted, and that Uncle Mark himself makes speeches at all the recruiting meetings. So no doubt Germany is anxious to get square with him."

"*I* could never speak at a recruiting meeting," said Cousin Sophia solemnly. "*I* could never reconcile it to *my* conscience to ask another woman's son to go, to murder and be murdered."

"Could you not?" said Susan. "Well, Sophia Crawford, *I* felt as if I could ask any one to go when I read last night that there were no children under eight years of age left alive in Poland. Think of that, Sophia Crawford"—Susan shook a floury finger at Sophia—"not—one—child—under—eight—years—of—age!"

"I suppose the Germans has et 'em all," sighed Cousin Sophia.

"Well, no-o-o," said Susan reluctantly, as if she hated to admit that there was any crime the Huns couldn't be accused of. "The Germans have not turned cannibal yet—*as far as I know*. They have died of starvation and exposure, the poor little creatures. There is murdering for you, Cousin Sophia Crawford. The thought of it poisons every bite and sup I take."

"I see that Fred Carson of Lowbridge has been awarded a Distinguished Conduct Medal," remarked the doctor, over his local paper.

"I heard that last week," said Susan. "He is a battalion runner and he did something extra brave and daring. His letter, telling his folks about it, came when his old

Grandmother Carson was on her dying bed. She had only a few minutes more to live and the Episcopal minister, who was there, asked her if she would not like him to pray. 'Oh, yes, yes, you can pray,' she said impatient-like—she was a Dean, Dr. dear, and the Deans were always high-spirited—'you can pray, but for pity's sake pray low and don't disturb me. I want to think over this splendid news and I have not much time left to do it.' That was Almira Carson all over. Fred was the apple of her eye. She was seventy-five years of age and had not a grey hair in her head, they tell me."

"By the way, that reminds me—*I* found a grey hair this morning—my very first," said Mrs. Blythe.

"I have noticed that grey hair for some time, Mrs. Dr. dear, but I did not speak of it. Thought I to myself, 'She has enough to bear.' But now that you have discovered it let me remind you that grey hairs are honourable."

"I must be getting old, Gilbert," Mrs. Blythe laughed a trifle ruefully. "People are beginning to tell me I *look so young*. They never tell you that when you are young. But I shall not worry over my silver thread. I never liked red hair. Gilbert, did I ever tell you of that time, years ago at Green Gables, when I dyed my hair? Nobody but Marilla and I knew about it."

"Was that the reason you came out once with your hair shingled to the bone?"

"Yes. I bought a bottle of dye from a German Jew pedlar. I fondly expected it would turn my hair black—and it turned it green. So it had to be cut off."

"You had a narrow escape, Mrs. Dr. dear," exclaimed Susan. "Of course you were too young then to know what a German was. It was a special mercy of Providence that it was only green dye and not poison."

"It seems hundreds of years since those Green Gable days," sighed Mrs. Blythe. "They belonged to another world altogether. Life has been cut in two by the chasm of the war. What is ahead I don't know—but it can't be a bit like the past. I wonder if those of us who have lived half our lives in the old world will ever feel wholly at home in the new."

"Have you noticed," asked Miss Oliver, glancing up from her book, "how everything written before the war seems so far away now, too? One feels as if one was reading something as ancient as the Iliad. This poem of Wordsworth's—the Senior class have it in their entrance work—I've been glancing over it. Its classic calm and repose and the beauty of the lines seem to belong to another planet, and to have as little to do with the present world-welter as the evening star."

"The only thing that I find much comfort in reading nowadays is the Bible," remarked Susan, whisking her biscuits into the oven. "There are so many passages in it that seem to me exactly descriptive of the Huns. Old Highland Sandy declares that there is no doubt that the Kaiser is the Anti-Christ spoken of in Revelations, but I do not go as far as that. It would, in my humble opinion, Mrs. Dr. dear, be too great an honour for him."

Early one morning, several days later, Miranda Pryor slipped up to Ingleside, ostensibly to get some Red Cross sewing, but in reality to talk over with sympathetic Rilla troubles that were past bearing alone. She brought her dog with her—an over-fed, bandy-legged little animal very dear to her heart because Joe Milgrave had given it to her when it was a puppy. Mr. Pryor regarded all dogs with disfavour; but in those days he had looked kindly upon Joe as a suitor for Miranda's hand and so he had allowed her to keep the puppy. Miranda was so grateful that she endeavoured to please her father by naming her dog after his political idol, the great Liberal chieftain, Sir Wilfrid Laurier—though this title was soon abbreviated to Wilfy. Sir Wilfrid grew and flourished and waxed fat; but Miranda spoiled him absurdly and nobody else liked him. Rilla especially hated him because of what she thought his detestable trick of lying flat on his back and entreating you with waving paws to tickle his sleek stomach. When she saw that Miranda's pale eyes bore unmistakable testimony to her having cried all night, Rilla asked her to come up to her room, knowing that Miranda had a tale of woe to tell, but she ordered Sir Wilfrid to remain below.

"Oh, can't he come, too?" said Miranda wistfully. "Poor Wilfy won't be any bother—and I wiped his paws *so* carefully before I brought him in. He is always so lonesome in a strange place without me—and very soon he'll be—all—I'll have left—to remind me—of Joe."

Rilla yielded, and Sir Wilfrid, with his tail curled at a saucy angle over his brindled back, trotted triumphantly up the stairs before them.

"Oh, Rilla," sobbed Miranda, when they had reached sanctuary. "I'm *so* unhappy. I can't begin to tell you how unhappy I am. Truly, my heart is breaking."

Rilla sat down on the lounge beside her. Sir Wilfrid squatted on his haunches before them, with his impertinent pink tongue stuck out, and listened.

"What is the trouble, Miranda?"

"Joe is coming home tonight on his last leave. I had a letter from him Saturday—he sends my letters in care of Bob Crawford, you know, because of father—and, oh, Rilla, he will only have four days—he has to go away Friday morning—and I may never see him again."

"Does he still want you to marry him?" asked Rilla.

"Oh, yes. He *implored* me in his letter to run away and be married. But I cannot do that, Rilla, not even for Joe. My only comfort is that I will be able to see him for a little while tomorrow afternoon. Father has to go to Charlottetown on business. At least we will have one good farewell talk. But oh—afterwards—why, Rilla, I know father won't even let me go to the station Friday morning to see Joe off."

"Why in the world don't you and Joe get married tomorrow afternoon at home?" demanded Rilla.

Miranda swallowed a sob in such amazement that she almost choked.

"Why—why—that is impossible, Rilla."

"Why?" briefly demanded the organizer of the Junior Red Cross and the transporter of babies in soup tureens.

"Why—why—we never thought of such a thing—Joe hasn't a license—I have no dress—I couldn't be married in *black*—I—I—we—you—you—"

Miranda lost herself altogether and Sir Wilfrid, seeing that she was in dire distress, threw back his head and emitted a melancholy yelp.

Rilla Blythe thought hard and rapidly for a few minutes. Then she said,

"Miranda, if you will put yourself into my hands I'll have you married to Joe before four o'clock tomorrow afternoon."

"Oh, you couldn't."

"I can and I will. But you'll have to do exactly as I tell you."

"Oh—I—don't think—oh, father will kill me—"

"Nonsense. He'll be very angry I suppose. But are you more afraid of your father's anger than you are of Joe's never coming back to you?"

"No," said Miranda, with sudden firmness, "I'm not."

"Will you do as I tell you then?"

"Yes, I will."

"Then get Joe on the long-distance at once and tell him to bring out a license and ring tonight."

"Oh, I couldn't," wailed the aghast Miranda, "it—it would be so—so *indelicate*."

Rilla shut her little white teeth together with a snap. "Heaven grant me patience," she said under her breath. "I'll do it then," she said aloud, "and meanwhile, you go home and make what preparations you can. When I 'phone down to you to come up and help me sew come at once."

As soon as Miranda, pallid, scared, but desperately resolved, had gone, Rilla flew to the telephone and put in a long-distance call for Charlottetown. She got through with such surprising quickness that she was convinced Providence approved of her undertaking, but it was a good hour before she could get into touch with Joe Milgrave at his camp. Meanwhile, she paced impatiently about, and prayed that when she did get Joe there would be no listeners on the line to carry news to Whiskers-on-the-moon.

"Is that you, Joe? Rilla Blythe is speaking—Rilla—Rilla—oh, never mind. Listen to this. Before you come home tonight get a marriage license—a marriage license—yes, a marriage license—and a wedding ring. Did you get that? And will you do it? Very well, be sure you do it—it is your only chance."

Flushed with triumph—for her only fear was that she might not be able to locate Joe in time—Rilla rang the Pryor ring. This time she had not such good luck for she drew Whiskers-on-the-moon.

"Is that Miranda? *Oh*—Mr. Pryor! Well, Mr. Pryor, will you kindly ask Miranda if she can come up this afternoon and help me with some sewing. It is *very* important, or I would not trouble her. Oh—*thank* you."

Mr. Pryor had consented somewhat grumpily, but he *had* consented—he did not want to offend Dr. Blythe, and he knew that if he refused to allow Miranda to do any Red Cross work public opinion would make the Glen too hot for comfort. Rilla went out to the kitchen, shut all the doors with a mysterious expression which alarmed Susan, and then said solemnly,

"Susan, can you make a wedding cake this afternoon?"

"A wedding cake!" Susan stared. Rilla had, without any warning, brought her a war baby once upon a time. Was she now, with equal suddenness, going to produce a husband?

"Yes, a wedding cake—a scrumptious wedding cake, Susan,—a beautiful, plummy, eggy, citron-peely wedding cake. And we must make other things too. I'll help you in the morning. But I can't help you this afternoon for I have to make a wedding dress and time is the essence of the contract, Susan."

Susan felt that she was really too old to be subjected to such shocks.

"Who are you going to marry, Rilla?" she asked feebly.

"Susan, darling, *I* am not the happy bride. Miranda Pryor is going to marry Joe Milgrave tomorrow afternoon while her father is away in town. A war wedding, Susan—isn't that thrilling and romantic? I never was so excited in my life."

The excitement soon spread over Ingleside, infecting even Mrs. Blythe and Susan.

"I'll go to work on that cake at once," vowed Susan, with a glance at the clock. "Mrs. Dr. dear, will you pick over the fruit and beat up the eggs? If you will, I can have that cake ready for the oven by the evening. Tomorrow morning we can make salads and other things. I will work all night if necessary to get the better of Whiskers-on-the-moon."

Miranda arrived, tearful and breathless.

"We must fix over my white dress for you to wear," said Rilla. "It will fit you very nicely with a little alteration."

To work went the two girls, ripping, fitting, basting, sewing, for dear life. By dint of unceasing effort they got the dress done by seven o'clock and Miranda tried it on in Rilla's room.

"It's very pretty—but oh, if I could just have a veil," sighed Miranda. "I've always dreamed of being married in a lovely white veil."

Some good fairy evidently waits on the wishes of war brides. The door opened and Mrs. Blythe came in, her arms full of a filmy burden.

"Miranda dear," she said, "I want you to wear my wedding veil tomorrow. It is twenty-four years since I was a bride at old Green Gables—the happiest bride that ever was—and the wedding veil of a happy bride brings good luck, they say."

"Oh, how sweet of you, Mrs. Blythe," said Miranda, the ready tears starting to her eyes.

The veil was tried on and draped. Susan dropped in to approve but dared not linger.

"I've got that cake in the oven," she said, "and I am pursuing a policy of watchful waiting. The evening news is that the Grand Duke has captured Erzerum. That is a pill for the Turks. I wish I had a chance to tell the Czar just what a mistake he made when he turned Nicholas down."

Susan disappeared downstairs to the kitchen, whence a dreadful thud and a piercing shriek presently sounded. Everybody rushed to the kitchen—the doctor and Miss Oliver, Mrs. Blythe, Rilla, Miranda in her wedding veil. Susan was sitting flatly in the middle of the kitchen floor with a dazed, bewildered look on her face, while "Doc," evidently in his Hyde incarnation, was standing on the dresser, with his back up, his eyes blazing, and his tail the size of three tails.

"Susan, what has happened?" cried Mrs. Blythe in alarm. "Did you fall? Are you hurt?"

Susan picked herself up.

"No," she said grimly, "I am not hurt, though I am jarred all over. Do not be alarmed. As for what has happened—I tried to kick that darned cat with both feet, that is what has happened."

Everybody shrieked with laughter. The doctor was quite helpless.

"Oh, Susan, Susan," he gasped. "That I should live to hear *you* swear."

"I am sorry," said Susan in real distress, "that I used such an expression before two young girls. But I said that beast was darned and darned it is. It belongs to the Old Nick."

"Do you expect it will vanish some of these days with a bang and the odour of brimstone, Susan?"

"It will go to its own place in due time and that you may tie to," said Susan dourly, shaking out her raddled bones and going to her oven. "I suppose my plunking down like that has shaken my cake so that it will be as heavy as lead."

But the cake was not heavy. It was all a bride's cake should be, and Susan iced it beautifully. Next day she and Rilla worked all the forenoon, making delicacies for the wedding feast, and as soon as Miranda 'phoned up that her father was safely off everything was packed in a big hamper and taken down to the Pryor house. Joe soon arrived in his uniform and a state of violent excitement, accompanied by his best man, Sergeant Malcolm Crawford. There were quite a few guests, for all the Manse and Ingleside folk were there, and a dozen or so of Joe's relatives, including his mother, "Mrs. Dead

Angus Milgrave," so called, cheerfully, to distinguish her from another lady whose Angus was living. Mrs. Dead Angus wore a rather disapproving expression, not caring overmuch for this alliance with the house of Whiskers-on-the-moon.

So Miranda Pryor was married to Pte. Joseph Milgrave on his last leave. It should have been a romantic wedding but it was not. There were too many factors working against romance, as even Rilla had to admit. In the first place, Miranda, in spite of her dress and veil, was such a flat-faced, commonplace, uninteresting little bride. In the second place, Joe cried bitterly all through the ceremony, and this vexed Miranda unreasonably. Long afterwards she told Rilla: "I just felt like saying to him then and there, 'If you feel so bad over having to marry me you *don't* have to.' But it was just because he was thinking all the time of how soon he would have to leave me."

In the third place, Jims, who was usually so well-behaved in public, took a fit of shyness and contrariness combined, and began to cry at the top of his voice for "Willa." Nobody wanted to take him out, because everybody wanted to see the marriage, so Rilla who was bridesmaid, had to take him and hold him during the ceremony.

In the fourth place, Sir Wilfrid Laurier took a fit.

Sir Wilfrid was entrenched in a corner of the room behind Miranda's piano. During his seizure he made the weirdest, most unearthly noises. He would begin with a series of choking, spasmodic sounds, continuing into a gruesome gurgle, and ending up with a strangled howl. Nobody could hear a word Mr. Meredith was saying, except now and then, when Sir Wilfrid stopped for breath. Nobody looked at the bride except Susan, who never dragged her fascinated eyes from Miranda's face—all the others were gazing at the dog.

Miranda had been trembling with nervousness but as soon as Sir Wilfrid began his performance she forgot it. All that she could think of was that her dear dog was dying and she could not go to him. She never remembered a word of the ceremony.

Rilla, who in spite of Jims, had been trying her best to look rapt and romantic, as beseemed a war bridesmaid, gave up the hopeless attempt, and devoted her energies to choking down untimely merriment. She dared not look at anybody in the room, especially Mrs. Dead Angus, for fear all her suppressed mirth should suddenly explode in a most un-young-ladylike yell of laughter.

But married they were, and then they had a wedding supper in the dining room which was so lavish and bountiful that you would have thought it was the product of a month's labour. Everybody had brought something. Mrs. Dead Angus had brought a large apple pie, which she placed on a chair in the dining room and then absently sat down on it. Neither her temper nor her black silk wedding garment was improved thereby, but the pie was never missed at the gay bridal feast. Mrs. Dead Angus eventually took it home with her again. Whiskers-on-the-moon's pacifist pig should not get it, anyhow.

That evening Mr. and Mrs. Joe, accompanied by the recovered Sir Wilfrid, departed for the Four Winds lighthouse, which was kept by Joe's uncle and in which they meant to spend their brief honeymoon. Una Meredith and Rilla and Susan washed the dishes, tidied up, left a cold supper and Miranda's pitiful little note on the table for Mr. Pryor, and walked home, while the mystic veil of dreamy, haunted winter twilight wrapped itself over the Glen.

"I would really not have minded being a war bride myself," remarked Susan sentimentally.

But Rilla felt rather flat—perhaps as a reaction to all the excitement and rush of the past thirty-six hours. She was disappointed somehow—the whole affair had been so ludicrous, and Miranda and Joe so lachrymose and commonplace.

"If Miranda hadn't given that wretched dog such an enormous dinner he wouldn't have had that fit," she said crossly. "I warned her—but she said she couldn't starve the poor dog—he would soon be all she had left, etc. I could have shaken her."

"The best man was more excited than Joe was," said Susan. "He wished Miranda many happy returns of the day. She did not look very happy, but perhaps you could not expect that under the circumstances."

"Anyhow," thought Rilla, "I can write a perfectly killing account of it all to the boys. How Jem will howl over Sir Wilfrid's part in it!"

But if Rilla was rather disappointed in the war wedding she found nothing lacking on Friday morning when Miranda said good-bye to her bridegroom at the Glen station. The dawn was white as a pearl, clear as a diamond. Behind the station the balsamy copse of young firs was frost-misted. The cold moon of dawn hung over the westering snow fields but the golden fleeces of sunrise shone above the maples up at Ingleside. Joe took his pale little bride in his arms and she lifted her face to his. Rilla choked suddenly. It did not matter that Miranda was insignificant and commonplace and flat-featured. It did not matter that she was the daughter of Whiskers-on-the-moon. All that mattered was that rapt, sacrificial look in her eyes—that ever-burning, sacred fire of devotion and loyalty and fine courage that she was mutely promising Joe she and thousands of other women would keep alive at home while their men held the western front.

Rilla walked away, realizing that she must not spy on such a moment. She went down to the end of the platform where Sir Wilfrid and Dog Monday were sitting, looking at each other.

Sir Wilfrid remarked condescendingly,

"Why do you haunt this old shed when you might lie on the hearthrug at Ingleside and live on the fat of the land? Is it a pose? Or a fixed idea?"

Whereat Dog Monday, laconically:—

"I have a tryst to keep."

When the train had gone Rilla rejoined the little trembling Miranda.

"Well, he's gone," said Miranda, "and he may never come back—but I'm his wife, and I'm going to be worthy of him. I'm going home."

"Don't you think you had better come with me now?" asked Rilla doubtfully. Nobody knew yet how Mr. Pryor had taken the matter.

"No. If Joe can face the Huns I guess I can face father," said Miranda daringly. "A soldier's wife can't be a coward. Come on, Wilfy. I'll go straight home and meet the worst."

There was nothing very dreadful to face, however. Perhaps Mr. Pryor had reflected that housekeepers were hard to get and that there were many Milgrave homes open to Miranda—also, that there was such a thing as a separation allowance. At all events, though he told her grumpily that she had made a nice fool of herself, and would live to regret it, he said nothing worse and Mrs. Joe put on her apron and went to work as usual, while Sir Wilfrid Laurier, who had a poor opinion of lighthouses for winter residences, went to sleep in his pet nook behind the woodbox, a thankful dog that he was done with war weddings.

CHAPTER XIX

"They Shall Not Pass"

One cold grey morning in February, Gertrude Oliver wakened with a shiver, slipped into Rilla's room, and crept in beside her.

"Rilla—I'm frightened—frightened as a baby—I've had another of my strange dreams. Something terrible is before us—I *know*."

"What was it?" asked Rilla.

"I was standing again on the veranda steps—just as I stood in that dream on the night before the lighthouse dance, and in the sky a huge black, menacing thundercloud rolled up from the east. I could see its shadow racing before it and when it enveloped me I shivered with icy cold. Then the storm broke—and it was a dreadful storm—blinding flash after flash and deafening peal after peal, driving torrents of rain. I turned in panic and tried to run for shelter, and as I did so a man—a soldier in the uniform of a French army officer—dashed up the steps and stood beside me on the threshold of the door. His clothes were soaked with blood from a wound in his breast, he seemed spent and exhausted; but his white face was set and his eyes blazed in his hollow face. 'They shall not pass,' he said, in low, passionate tones which I heard distinctly amid all the turmoil of the storm. Then I awakened. Rilla, I'm frightened—the spring will not bring the Big Push we've all been hoping for—instead it is going to bring some dreadful blow to France. I am sure of it. The Germans will try to smash through somewhere."

"But he told you that they would not pass," said Rilla, seriously. She never laughed at Gertrude's dreams as the doctor did.

"I do not know if that was prophecy or desperation. Rilla, the horror of that dream holds me yet in an icy grip. We shall need all our courage before long."

Dr. Blythe *did* laugh at the breakfast table—but he never laughed at Miss Oliver's dreams again; for that day brought news of the opening of the Verdun offensive, and thereafter through all the beautiful weeks of spring the Ingleside family, one and all, lived in a trance of dread. There were days when they waited in despair for the end as foot by foot the Germans crept nearer and nearer to the grim barrier of desperate France.

Susan's deeds were in her spotless kitchen at Ingleside, but her thoughts were on the hills around Verdun. "Mrs. Dr. dear," she would stick her head in at Mrs. Blythe's door the last thing at night to remark, "I do hope the French have hung on to the Crow's Wood today," and she woke at dawn to wonder if Dead Man's Hill—surely so named by some prophet—was still held by the "poyloos." Susan could have drawn a map of the country around Verdun that would have satisfied a chief of staff.

"If the Germans capture Verdun the spirit of France will be broken," Miss Oliver said bitterly.

"But they will not capture it," staunchly said Susan, who could not eat her dinner that day for fear lest they do that very thing. "In the first place, you dreamed they would not—you dreamed the very thing the French are saying before they ever said it—'they shall not pass.' I declare to you, Miss Oliver, dear, when I read that in the paper, and remembered your dream, I went cold all over with awe. It seemed to me like Biblical times when people dreamed things like that quite frequently."

"I know—I know," said Gertrude, walking restlessly about. "I cling to a persistent faith in my dream, too—but every time bad news comes it fails me. Then I tell myself 'mere coincidence'—'subconscious memory' and so forth."

"I do not see how any memory could remember a thing before it was ever said at all," persisted Susan, "though of course *I* am not educated like you and the doctor. I would rather *not* be, if it makes anything as simple as that so hard to believe. But in any case we need not worry over Verdun, even if the Huns get it. Joffer says it has no military significance."

"That old sop of comfort has been served up too often already when reverses came," retorted Gertrude. "It has lost its power to charm."

"Was there ever a battle like this in the world before?" said Mr. Meredith, one evening in mid-April.

"It's such a titanic thing we can't grasp it," said the doctor. "What were the scraps of a few Homeric handfuls compared to this? The whole Trojan war might be fought around a Verdun fort and a newspaper correspondent would give it no more than a sentence. I am not in the confidence of the occult powers"—the doctor threw Gertrude a twinkle—"but I have a hunch that the fate of the whole war hangs on the issue of Verdun. As Susan and Joffre say, it has no real military significance; but it has the tremendous significance of an Idea. If Germany wins there she will win the war. If she loses, the tide will set against her."

"Lose she will," said Mr. Meredith emphatically. "The *Idea* cannot be conquered. France is certainly very wonderful. It seems to me that in her I see the white form of civilization making a determined stand against the black powers of barbarism. I think our whole world realizes this and that is why we all await the issue so breathlessly. It isn't merely the question of a few forts changing hands or a few miles of blood-soaked ground lost and won."

"I wonder," said Gertrude dreamily, "if some great blessing, great enough for the price, will be the meed of all our pain? Is the agony in which the world is shuddering the birth-pang of some wondrous new era? Or is it merely a futile

'struggle of ants
In the gleam of a million million of suns'?

We think very lightly, Mr. Meredith, of a calamity which destroys an ant-hill and half its inhabitants. Does the Power that runs the universe think *us* of more importance than we think ants?"

"You forget," said Mr. Meredith, with a flash of his dark eyes, "that an infinite Power must be infinitely little as well as infinitely great. *We* are neither, therefore there are things too little as well as too great for us to apprehend. To the infinitely little an ant is of as much importance as a mastodon. We are witnessing the birth-pangs of a new era—but it will be born a feeble, wailing life like everything else. I am not one of those who expect a new heaven and a new earth as the immediate result of this war. That is not the way God works. But work He does, Miss Oliver, and in the end His purpose will be fulfilled."

"Sound and orthodox—sound and orthodox," muttered Susan approvingly in the kitchen. Susan liked to see Miss Oliver sat upon by the minister now and then. Susan was very fond of her but she thought Miss Oliver liked saying heretical things to ministers far too well, and deserved an occasional reminder that these matters were quite beyond her province.

In May Walter wrote home that he had been awarded a D.C. Medal. He did not say what for, but the other boys took care that the Glen should know the brave thing Walter had done. "In any war but this," wrote Jerry Meredith, "it would have meant a V.C. But they can't make V.C.'s as common as the brave things done every day here."

"He should have had the V.C.," said Susan, and was very indignant over it. She was not quite sure who was to blame for his not getting it but if it were General Haig she began for the first time to entertain serious doubts as to his fitness for being Commander-in-Chief.

Rilla was beside herself with delight. It was her dear Walter who had done this thing—Walter, to whom some one had sent a white feather at Redmond—it was Walter who had dashed back from the safety of the trench to drag in a wounded comrade who had fallen on No-man's-land. Oh, she could see his white beautiful face and wonderful eyes as he did it! What a thing to be the sister of such a hero! And he hadn't thought it worth while writing about. His letter was full of other things—little intimate things that they two had known and loved together in the dear old cloudless days of a century ago.

"I've been thinking of the daffodils in the garden at Ingleside," he wrote. "By the time you get this they will be out, blowing there under that lovely rosy sky. Are they really as bright and golden as ever, Rilla? It seems to me that they must be dyed red with blood—like our poppies here. And every whisper of spring will be falling as a violet in Rainbow Valley.

"There is a young moon tonight—a slender, silver, lovely thing hanging over these pits of torment. Will you see it tonight over the maple grove?

"I'm enclosing a little scrap of verse, Rilla. I wrote it one evening in my trench dug-out by the light of a bit of candle—or rather it *came* to me there—I didn't feel as if I were writing it—something seemed to use me as an instrument. I've had that feeling once or twice before but very rarely and never so strongly as this time. That was why I sent it over to the London *Spectator*. It printed it and the copy came today. I hope you'll like it. It's the only poem I've written since I came overseas."

The poem was a short, poignant little thing. In a month it had carried Walter's name to every corner of the globe. Everywhere it was copied—in metropolitan dailies and little village weeklies, in profound reviews and "agony columns," in Red Cross appeals and Government recruiting propaganda. Mothers and sisters wept over it, young lads thrilled to it, the whole great heart of humanity caught it up as an epitome of all the pain and hope and pity and purpose of the mighty conflict, crystallized in three brief immortal verses. A Canadian lad in the Flanders trenches had written the one great poem of the war. "The Piper," by Pte. Walter Blythe, was a classic from its first printing.

Rilla copied it in her diary at the beginning of an entry in which she poured out the story of the hard week that had just passed.

"It has been such a dreadful week," she wrote, "and even though it is over and we know that it was all a mistake that does not seem to do away with the bruises left by it. And yet it has in some ways been a very wonderful week and I have had some glimpses of things I never realized before—of how fine and brave people can be even in the midst of horrible suffering. I am sure I could never be as splendid as Miss Oliver was.

"Just a week ago today she had a letter from Mr. Grant's mother in Charlottetown. And it told her that a cable had just come saying that Major Robert Grant had been killed in action a few days before.

"Oh, poor Gertrude! At first she was crushed. Then after just a day she pulled herself together and went back to her school. She did not cry—I never saw her shed a tear—but oh, her face and her eyes!

"'I must go on with my work,' she said. 'That is my duty just now.'

"*I* could never have risen to such a height.

"She never spoke bitterly except once, when Susan said something about spring being here at last, and Gertrude said,

"'Can the spring really come this year?'

"Then she laughed—such a dreadful little laugh, just as one might laugh in the face of death, I think, and said,

"'Observe my egotism. Because *I*, Gertrude Oliver, have lost a friend, it is incredible that the spring can come as usual. The spring does not fail because of the million agonies of others—but for *mine*—oh, can the universe go on?'

"'Don't feel bitter with yourself, dear,' mother said gently. 'It is a very natural thing to feel as if things *couldn't* go on just the same when some great blow has changed the world for us. We all feel like that.'

"Then that horrid old Cousin Sophia of Susan's piped up. She was sitting there, knitting and croaking like an old 'raven of bode and woe' as Walter used to call her.

"'You ain't as bad off as some, Miss Oliver,' she said, 'and you shouldn't take it so hard. There's some as has lost their husbands; that's a hard blow; and there's some as has lost their sons. You haven't lost either husband or son.'

"'No,' said Gertrude, more bitterly still. 'It's true I haven't lost a husband—I have only lost the man who would have been my husband. I have lost no son—only the sons and daughters who might have been born to me—who will never be born to me now.'

"'It isn't ladylike to talk like that,' said Cousin Sophia in a shocked tone; and then Gertrude laughed right out, so wildly that Cousin Sophia was really frightened. And when poor tortured Gertrude, unable to endure it any longer, hurried out of the room, Cousin Sophia asked mother if the blow hadn't affected Miss Oliver's mind.

"'I suffered the loss of two good kind partners,' she said, 'but it did not affect me like that.'

"I should think it wouldn't! Those poor men must have been thankful to die.

"I heard Gertrude walking up and down her room most of the night. She walked like that every night. But never so long as that night. And once I heard her give a dreadful sudden little cry as if she had been stabbed. I couldn't sleep for suffering with her; and I couldn't help her. I thought the night would never end. But it did; and then 'joy came in the morning' as the Bible says. Only it didn't come exactly in the morning but well along in the afternoon. The telephone rang and I answered it. It was old Mrs. Grant speaking from Charlottetown, and her news was that it was all a mistake—Robert wasn't killed at all; he had only been slightly wounded in the arm and was safe in the hospital out of harm's way for a time anyhow. They hadn't learned yet how the mistake had happened but supposed there must have been another Robert Grant.

"I hung up the telephone and flew to Rainbow Valley. I'm sure I *did* fly—I can't remember my feet ever touching the ground. I met Gertrude on her way home from school in the glade of spruces where we used to play, and I just gasped out the news to her. I ought to have had more sense, of course. A doctor's daughter to do such a thing! But I was so crazy with joy and excitement that I never stopped to think. Gertrude just dropped there among the golden young ferns as if she had been shot. The fright it gave me ought to make me sensible—in this respect at least—for the rest of my life. I thought I had killed her—I remembered that her mother had died very suddenly from heart failure when quite a young woman. It seemed years to me before I discovered that her heart was still beating. A pretty time I had! I never saw anybody faint before and I knew there was nobody up at the house to help, because everybody else had gone to the station to meet Di and Nan coming home from Redmond. But I knew—theoretically—how people in a faint should be treated, and now I know it practically. Luckily the brook was handy and after I had worked frantically over her for awhile Gertrude came back to life. She never said one word about my news and I didn't dare to refer to it again. I helped her walk up through the maple grove and up to her room, and then she said, 'Rob—is—living,' as if the words were torn out of her, and flung herself on her bed and cried and cried and cried. I never saw any one cry so before. All the tears that she *hadn't* shed all that week came then. She cried most of last night, I think, but her face this morning looked as if she had seen a vision of some kind, and we were all so happy that we were almost afraid.

"Di and Nan are home for a couple of weeks. Then they go back to Red Cross work in the training camp at Kingsport. I envy them. Father says I'm doing just as good work here, with Jims and my Junior Reds. But it lacks the *romance* theirs must have.

"Kut has fallen. It was almost a relief when it *did* fall, we had been dreading it so long. It crushed us flat for a day and then we picked up and put it behind us. Cousin Sophia was as gloomy as usual and came over and groaned that the British were losing everywhere.

"'They're good losers,' said Susan grimly. 'When they lose a thing they keep on looking till they find it again! Anyhow, my king and country need me now to cut potato sets for the back garden, so get you a knife and help me, Sophia Crawford. It will divert your thoughts and keep you from worrying over a campaign that you are not called upon to run.'

"Susan is an old brick and the way she flattens out poor Cousin Sophia is beautiful to behold.

"As for Verdun, the battle goes on and on, and we seesaw between hope and fear. But I *know* that strange dream of Miss Oliver's foretold the victory of France. 'They shall not pass.'"

CHAPTER XX

*N*orman Douglas Speaks Out in Meeting

"Where are you wandering, Anne o' mine?" asked the doctor, who even yet, after twenty-four years of marriage, occasionally addressed his wife thus when nobody was about. Anne was sitting on the veranda steps, gazing absently over the wonderful bridal world of spring blossom. Beyond the white orchard was a copse of dark young firs and creamy wild cherries, where the robins were whistling madly; for it was evening and the fire of early stars was burning over the maple grove.

Anne came back with a little sigh.

"I was just taking relief from intolerable realities in a dream, Gilbert—a dream that all our children were home again—and all small again—playing in Rainbow Valley. It is always so silent now—but I was imagining I heard clear voices and gay, childish sounds coming up as I used to. I could hear Jem's whistle and Walter's yodel, and the twins' laughter, and for just a few blessed minutes I forgot about the guns on the western front, and had a little false, sweet happiness."

The doctor did not answer. Sometimes his work tricked him into forgetting for a few moments the western front, but not often. There was a good deal of grey now in his still thick curls that had not been there two years ago. Yet he smiled down into the starry eyes he loved—the eyes that had once been so full of laughter, and now seemed always full of unshed tears.

Susan wandered by with a hoe in her hand and her second best bonnet on her head.

"I have just finished reading a piece in the *Enterprise* which told of a couple being married in an aeroplane. Do you think it would be legal, Dr. dear?" she inquired anxiously.

"I think so," said the doctor gravely.

"Well," said Susan dubiously, "it seems to me that a wedding is too solemn for anything so giddy as an aeroplane. But nothing is the same as it used to be. Well, it is half an hour yet before prayer-meeting time, so I am going around to the kitchen garden to have a little evening hate with the weeds. But all the time I am strafing them I will be thinking about this new worry in the Trentino. I do *not* like this Austrian caper, Mrs. Dr. dear."

"Nor I," said Mrs. Blythe ruefully. "All the forenoon I preserved rhubarb with my hands and waited for the war news with my soul. When it came I shrivelled. Well, I suppose I must go and get ready for the prayer-meeting, too."

Every village has its own little unwritten history, handed down from lip to lip through the generations, of tragic, comic and dramatic events. They are told at weddings and festivals, and rehearsed around winter firesides. And in these oral annals of Glen St. Mary the tale of the union prayer-meeting held that night in the Methodist church was destined to fill an imperishable place.

The union prayer-meeting was Mr. Arnold's idea. The county battalion, which had been training all winter in Charlottetown, was to leave shortly for overseas. The Four Winds Harbour boys belonging to it from the Glen and over-harbour and Harbour Head and Upper Glen were all home on their last leave and Mr. Arnold thought, properly enough, that it would be a fitting thing to hold a union prayer-meeting for them before they went away. Mr. Meredith having agreed, the meeting was announced to be held in the Methodist church. Glen prayer-meetings were not apt to be too well attended but on this particular evening the Methodist church was crowded. Everybody who could go was there. Even Miss Cornelia came—and it was the first time in her life that Miss Cornelia had ever set foot inside a Methodist church. It took no less than a world conflict to bring that about.

"I used to hate Methodists," said Miss Cornelia calmly, when her husband expressed surprise over her going, "but I don't hate them now. There is no sense in hating Methodists when there is a Kaiser or a Hindenburg in the world."

So Miss Cornelia went. Norman Douglas and his wife went too. And Whiskers-on-the-moon strutted up the aisle to a front pew, as if he fully realized what a distinction he conferred upon the building. People were somewhat surprised that he should be there, since he usually avoided all assemblages connected in any way with the war. But Mr. Meredith had said that he hoped his session would be well represented, and Mr. Pryor had evidently taken the request to heart. He wore his best black suit and white tie, his thick, tight, iron-grey curls were neatly arranged, and his broad, red, round face looked, as Susan most uncharitably thought, more "sanctimonious" than ever.

"The minute I saw that man coming into the church, looking like that, I felt that mischief was brewing, Mrs. Dr. dear," she said afterwards. "What form it would take I could not tell, but I knew from the face of him that he had come there for no good."

The prayer-meeting opened conventionally and continued quietly. Mr. Meredith spoke first with his usual eloquence and feeling. Mr. Arnold followed with an address which even Miss Cornelia had to confess was irreproachable in taste and subject-matter.

And then Mr. Arnold asked Mr. Pryor to lead in prayer.

Miss Cornelia had always averred that Mr. Arnold had no gumption. Miss Cornelia was not apt to err on the side of charity in her judgment of Methodist ministers, but in this case she did not greatly over-shoot the mark. The Rev. Mr. Arnold certainly did not have much of that desirable, indefinable quality known as gumption, or he would never have asked Whiskers-on-the-moon to lead in prayer at a khaki prayer-meeting. He thought he was returning the compliment to Mr. Meredith, who, at the conclusion of *his* address, had asked a Methodist deacon to lead.

Some people expected Mr. Pryor to refuse grumpily—and *that* would have made enough scandal. But Mr. Pryor bounded briskly to his feet, unctuously said, "Let us pray" and forthwith prayed. In a sonorous voice which penetrated to every corner of the crowded building Mr. Pryor poured forth a flood of fluent words, and was well on in his prayer before his dazed and horrified audience awakened to the fact that they were listening to a pacifist appeal of the rankest sort. Mr. Pryor had at least the courage of his convictions; or perhaps, as people afterwards said, he thought he was safe in a church and that it was an excellent chance to air certain opinions he dared not voice elsewhere, for fear of being mobbed. He prayed that the unholy war might cease—that the deluded armies being driven to slaughter on the western front might have their eyes opened to their iniquity and repent while yet there was time—that the poor young men present in khaki who had been hounded into a path of murder and militarism, should yet be rescued—

Mr. Pryor had got this far without let or hindrance; and so paralyzed were his hearers, and so deeply imbued with their born-and-bred conviction that no disturbance must ever be made in a church, no matter what the provocation, that it seemed likely that he would continue unchecked to the end. But one man at least in that audience was not hampered by inherited or acquired reverence for the sacred edifice. Norman Douglas was, as Susan had often vowed crisply, nothing more or less than a "pagan." But he was a rampantly patriotic pagan, and when the significance of what Mr. Pryor was saying fully dawned on him, Norman Douglas suddenly went berserk. With a positive roar he bounded to his feet in his side pew, facing the audience, and shouted in tones of thunder,

"Stop—*stop*—STOP that abominable prayer! *What* an abominable prayer!"

Every head in the church flew up. A boy in khaki at the back gave a faint cheer. Mr. Meredith raised a deprecating hand, but Norman was past caring for anything like that. Eluding his wife's restraining grasp, he gave one mad spring over the front of the pew and caught the unfortunate Whiskers-on-the-moon by his coat collar. Mr. Pryor had not "stopped" when so bidden, but he stopped now, perforce, for Norman, his long red beard literally bristling with fury, was shaking him until his bones fairly rattled, and punctuating his shakes with a lurid assortment of abusive epithets.

"You blatant beast!"—shake—"You malignant carrion"—shake—"You pig-headed varmint!"—shake—"you putrid pup,"—shake—"you pestilential parasite"—shake—"you—Hunnish scum"—shake—"you indecent reptile,—you—you—"

Norman choked for a moment. Everybody believed that the next thing he would say, church or no church, would be something that would have to be spelled with asterisks; but at that moment Norman encountered his wife's eye and he fell back with a thud on Holy Writ. "You whited sepulchre!" he bellowed, with a final shake, and cast Whiskers-on-the-moon from him with a vigour which impelled that unhappy pacifist to the very verge of the choir entrance door. Mr. Pryor's once ruddy face was ashen. But he turned at bay. "I'll have the law on you for this," he gasped.

"Do—do," roared Norman, making another rush. But Mr. Pryor was gone. He had no desire to fall a second time into the hands of an avenging militarist. Norman turned to the platform for one graceless, triumphant moment.

"Don't look so flabbergasted, parsons," he boomed. "*You* couldn't do it—nobody would expect it of the cloth—but somebody had to do it. You know you're glad I threw him out,—he couldn't be let go on yammering and yodelling and yawping sedition and treason. Sedition and treason— somebody had to deal with it. I was born for this hour—I've had my innings in church at last. I can sit quiet for another sixty years now! Go ahead with your meeting, parsons. I reckon you won't be troubled with any more pacifist prayers."

But the spirit of devotion and reverence had fled. Both ministers realized it and realized that the only thing to do was to close the meeting quietly and let the excited people go. Mr. Meredith addressed a few earnest words to the boys in khaki—which probably saved Mr. Pryor's windows from a second onslaught—and Mr. Arnold pronounced an incongru- ous benediction—at least, he felt it was incongruous, for he could not at once banish from his memory the sight of gigantic Norman Douglas shaking the fat, pompous little Whiskers-on-the-moon as a huge mastiff might shake an overgrown puppy. And he knew that the same picture was in everybody's mind. Altogether the union prayer-meeting could hardly be called an unqualified success. But it was remembered in Glen St. Mary when scores of orthodox and undisturbed assemblies were totally forgotten.

"You will never, no, never, Mrs. Dr. dear, hear me call Norman Douglas a pagan again," said Susan when she reached home. "If Ellen Douglas is not a proud woman this night she should be."

"Norman Douglas did a wholly indefensible thing," said the doctor. "Pryor should have been let severely alone until the meeting was over. Then later on, his own minister and session should deal with him. That would have been the proper procedure. Norman's performance was utterly improper and scandalous and outrageous; but, by George,"— the doctor threw back his head and chuckled, "by George, Anne-girl, it was *satisfying*."

CHAPTER XXI

"Love Affairs Are Horrible"

"INGLESIDE,
"June 20th, 1916

"We have been so busy, and day after day has brought such exciting news, good and bad, that I haven't had time and composure to write in my diary for weeks. I like to keep it up regularly, for father says a diary of the years of the war should be a very interesting thing to hand down to one's children. The trouble is, I like to write a few personal things in this blessed old book that might not be exactly what I'd want my children to read. I feel that I shall be a far greater stickler for propriety in regard to them than I am for myself!

"The first week in June was another dreadful one. The Austrians seemed just on the point of overrunning Italy: and then came the first awful news of the Battle of Jutland, which the Germans claimed as a great victory. I shall never forget that day. We just gave up completely. If the British Navy had failed us what was there to trust to? 'I feel as if I had received a staggering blow in the face from a trusted friend,' said Miss Oliver, and I think we all had just the same sensation. Susan was the only one who carried on. 'You need never tell *me* that the Kaiser has defeated the British Navy,' she said, with a contemptuous sniff. 'It is all a German lie and that you may tie to.' And when a couple of days later we found out that she was right and that it had been a British victory instead of a British defeat, we had to put up with a great many 'I told you so's,' but we endured them very comfortably.

"It took Kitchener's death to finish Susan. For the first time I saw her down and out. We all felt the shock of it but Susan plumbed the deeps of despair. The news came at night by 'phone but Susan wouldn't believe it until she saw the *Enterprise* headline the next day. She did not cry or faint or go into hysterics; but she forgot to put salt in the soup and that is something Susan never did in my recollection. Mother and Miss Oliver and I cried but Susan looked at us in stony sarcasm and said,

"'The Kaiser and his six sons are all alive and thriving. So the world is not left wholly desolate. Why cry, Mrs. Dr. dear?' Susan continued in this stony, hopeless condition for twenty-four hours, and then Cousin Sophia appeared and began to condole with her.

"'This is terrible news, ain't it, Susan? We might as well prepare for the worst for it is bound to come. You said once—and well do I remember the words, Susan Baker—that you had complete confidence in God and Kitchener. Ah well, Susan Baker, there is only God left now.'

"Whereat Cousin Sophia put her handkerchief to her eyes pathetically as if the world were indeed in terrible straits.

"As for Susan, Cousin Sophia was the salvation of her. She came to life with a jerk.

"'Sophia Crawford, hold your peace!' she said sternly. 'You may be an idiot but you need not be an irreverent idiot. It is no more than decent to be weeping and wailing because the Almighty is the sole stay of the Allies now. As for Kitchener, his death is a great loss and I do not dispute it. But the outcome of this war does not depend on one man's life and now that the Russians are coming on again you will soon see a change for the better.'

"Susan said this so energetically that she convinced herself and cheered up immediately. But Cousin Sophia shook her head.

"'Albert's wife wants to call the baby after Brusiloff,' she said, 'but I told her to wait and see what becomes of him first. Them Russians has such a habit of petering out.'

"The Russians are doing splendidly, however, and they have saved Italy. But even when the daily news of their sweeping advance comes we don't feel like running up the flag as we used to do. As Gertrude says, Verdun has slain all exultation. We would all feel more like rejoicing if the victories were on the western front. 'When will the British strike?' Gertrude sighed this morning. 'We have waited so long—so long.'

"Our greatest local event in recent weeks was the route march the county battalion made through the county before it left for overseas. They marched from Charlottetown to Lowbridge, then round the Harbour Head and through the Upper Glen and so down to the St. Mary station. Everybody turned out to see them, except old Aunt Fannie Clow, who is bedridden and Mr. Pryor, who hadn't been seen out even in church since the night of the Union Prayer Meeting the previous week.

"It was wonderful and heart-breaking to see that battalion marching past. There were young men and middle-aged men in it. There was Laurie MacAllister from over-harbour who is only sixteen but swore he was eighteen, so that he could enlist; and there was Angus Mackenzie, from the Upper Glen who is fifty-five if he is a day and swore he was forty-four. There were two South African veterans from Lowbridge, and the three eighteen-year-old Baxter triplets from Harbour Head. Everybody cheered as they went by, and they cheered Foster Booth, who is forty, walking side by side with his son Charley who is twenty. Charley's mother died when he was born, and when Charley enlisted Foster said he'd never yet let Charley go anywhere he daren't go himself, and he didn't mean to begin with the Flanders trenches. At the station Dog Monday nearly went out of his head. He tore about and sent messages to Jem by them all. Mr. Meredith read an address and Reta Crawford recited 'The Piper.' The soldiers cheered her like mad and cried 'We'll follow—we'll follow—we won't break faith,' and I felt so proud to think that it was my dear brother who had written such a wonderful, heart-stirring thing. And then I looked at the khaki ranks and wondered if those tall fellows in uniform *could* be the boys I've laughed with and played with and danced with and teased all my life. Something seems to have touched them and set them apart. They have heard the Piper's call.

"Fred Arnold was in the battalion and I felt dreadfully about *him*, for I realized that it was because of me that he was going away with such a sorrowful expression. I couldn't help it but I felt as badly as if I could.

"The last evening of his leave Fred came up to Ingleside and told me he loved me and asked me if I would promise to marry him some day, if he ever came back. He was desperately in earnest and I felt more wretched than I ever did in my life. I *couldn't* promise him that—why, even if there was no question of Ken, I don't care for Fred that way and never could—but it seemed so cruel and heartless to send him away to the front without *any* hope or comfort. I cried like a baby; and yet—oh, I am afraid that there must be something incurably frivolous about me, because, right in the middle of it all, with me crying and Fred looking so wild and tragic, the thought popped into my head that it would be an unendurable thing to see that nose across from me at the breakfast table every morning of my life. There, that is one of the entries I wouldn't want my descendants to read in this journal. But it is the humiliating truth; and perhaps it's just as well that thought did come or I might have been tricked by pity and remorse into giving him some rash assurance. If Fred's nose were as handsome as his eyes and mouth some such thing might have happened. And *then* what an unthinkable predicament I should have been in!

"When poor Fred became convinced that I couldn't promise him, he behaved beautifully—though *that* rather made things worse. If he *had* been nasty about it I wouldn't have felt so heart-broken and remorseful—though why I should feel remorseful I don't know, for I *never* encouraged Fred to think I cared a bit about him. Yet feel remorseful I did—and do. If Fred Arnold never comes back from overseas, this will haunt me all my life.

"Then Fred said if he couldn't take my love with him to the trenches at least he wanted to feel that he had my friendship, and would I kiss him just once in good-bye before he went—perhaps forever?

"I don't know how I could ever have imagined that love affairs were delightful, interesting things. They are *horrible*. I couldn't even give poor heart-broken Fred one little kiss, because of my promise to Ken. It seemed *brutal*. I *had* to tell Fred that of course he would have my friendship, but that I couldn't kiss him because I had promised somebody else I wouldn't.

"He said, 'Is it—is it—Ken Ford?'

"I nodded. It seemed dreadful to have to tell it—it was such a sacred little secret just between me and Ken.

"When Fred went away I came up here to my room and cried so long and so bitterly that mother came up and insisted on knowing what was the matter. I told her. She listened to my tale with an expression that clearly said, 'Can it be possible that any one has been wanting to marry this baby?' But she was so nice and understanding and sympathetic, oh, just so *race-of-Josephy*—that I felt indescribably comforted. Mothers are the dearest things.

"'But oh, mother,' I sobbed, 'he wanted me to kiss him good-bye—and I couldn't—and that hurt me worse than all the rest.'

"'Well, why didn't you kiss him?' asked mother coolly. 'Considering the circumstances, I think you might have.'

"'But I couldn't, mother—I promised Ken when he went away that I wouldn't kiss *anybody* else until he came back.'

"This was another high explosive for poor mother. She exclaimed, with the queerest little catch in her voice,

"'Rilla, are you engaged to Kenneth Ford?'

"'I—don't—know,' I sobbed.

"'You—don't—know?' repeated mother.

"Then I had to tell *her* the whole story, too; and every time I tell it it seems sillier and sillier to imagine that Ken meant anything serious. I felt idiotic and ashamed by the time I got through.

"Mother sat a little while in silence. Then she came over, sat down beside me, and took me in her arms.

"'Don't cry, dear little Rilla-my-Rilla. You have nothing to reproach yourself with in regard to Fred; and if Leslie West's son asked you to keep your lips for him, I think you may consider yourself engaged to him. But—oh, my baby—my last little baby—I have lost you—the war has made a woman of you too soon.'

"I shall never be too much of a woman to find comfort in mother's hugs. Nevertheless, when I saw Fred marching by two days later in the parade, my heart ached unbearably.

"But I'm glad mother thinks I'm really engaged to Ken!"

CHAPTER XXII

*L*ittle Dog Monday Knows

"It is two years tonight since the dance at the light, when Jack Elliott brought us news of the war. Do you remember, Miss Oliver?"

Cousin Sophia answered for Miss Oliver.

"Oh, indeed, Rilla, I remember that evening only too well, and you a-prancing down here to show off your party clothes. Didn't I warn you that we could not tell what was before us? Little did you think that night what was before *you*."

"Little did any of us think that," said Susan sharply, "not being gifted with the power of prophecy. It does *not* require any great foresight, Sophia Crawford, to tell a body that she will have some trouble before her life is over. I could do as much myself."

"We all thought the war would be over in a few months then," said Rilla wistfully. "When I look back it seems so ridiculous that we ever could have supposed it."

"And now, two years later, it is no nearer the end than it was then," said Miss Oliver gloomily.

Susan clicked her knitting needles briskly.

"Now, Miss Oliver, dear, you know that is not a reasonable remark. You know we are just two years nearer the end, whenever the end is appointed to be."

"Albert read in a Montreal paper today that a war expert gives it as his opinion that it will last five years more," was Cousin Sophia's cheerful contribution.

"It can't," cried Rilla; then she added with a sigh, "Two

years ago we would have said 'It can't last two years.' But five more years of *this*!"

"If Roumania comes in, as I have strong hopes now of her doing, you will see the end in five months instead of five years," said Susan.

"I've no faith in furriners," sighed Cousin Sophia.

"The French are foreigners," retorted Susan, "and look at Verdun. One of your precious war experts says 'there is not the slightest doubt now that Verdun is saved.' Not the slightest doubt, Sophia Crawford. And think of all the Somme victories this blessed summer. The Big Push is on and the Russians are still going well. Why, General Haig says that the German officers he has captured admit that they have lost the war."

"You can't believe a word the Germans say," protested Cousin Sophia. "There is no sense in believing a thing just because you'd *like* to believe it, Susan Baker. The British have lost millions of men at the Somme and how far have they got? Look facts in the face, Susan Baker, look facts in the face."

"They are wearing the Germans out and so long as that happens it does not matter whether it is done a few miles east or a few miles west. I am not," admitted Susan in tremendous humility, "I am not a military expert, Sophia Crawford, but even *I* can see that, and so could you if you were not determined to take a gloomy view of everything. The Huns have not got all the cleverness in the world. Have you not heard the story of Alistair MacCallum's son Roderick, from the Upper Glen? He is a prisoner in Germany and his mother got a letter from him last week. He wrote that he was being very kindly treated and that all the prisoners had plenty of food and so on, till you would have supposed everything was lovely. But when he signed his name, right in between Roderick and MacCallum, he wrote two Gaelic words that meant 'all lies,' and the German censor did not understand Gaelic and thought it was all part of Roddy's name. So he let it pass, never dreaming how he was diddled. Well, I am going to leave the war to Haig for the rest of the day and make a frosting for my chocolate cake. And when it is made I shall put it on the top shelf. The last one I made I left it on the lower shelf and little Kitchener sneaked in and clawed all the icing off and ate it. We had company for tea that night and when I went to get my cake what a sight did I behold!"

"Has that pore orphan's father never been heerd from yet?" asked Cousin Sophia.

"Yes, I had a letter from him in July," said Rilla. "He said that when he got word of his wife's death and of my taking the baby,—Mr. Meredith wrote him, you know,—he wrote right away, but as he never got any answer he had begun to think his letter must have been lost."

"It took him two years to begin to think it," said Susan scornfully. "Some people think very slow. Jim Anderson has not got a scratch, for all he has been two years in the trenches. A fool for luck, as the old proverb says."

"He wrote very nicely about Jims and said he'd like to see him," said Rilla. "So I wrote and told him all about the wee man, and sent him snapshots. Jims will be two years old next week and he is a perfect duck."

"You didn't used to be very fond of babies," said Cousin Sophia.

"I'm not a bit fonder of babies in the abstract than ever I was," said Rilla, frankly. "But I do love Jims, and I'm afraid I wasn't really half as glad as I should have been when Jim Anderson's letter proved that he was safe and sound."

"You wasn't hoping the man would be killed!" cried Cousin Sophia in horrified accents.

"No—no—no! I just hoped he would go on forgetting about Jims, Mrs. Crawford."

"And then your pa would have the expense of raising him," said Cousin Sophia reprovingly. "You young creeturs are terrible thoughtless."

Jims himself ran in at this juncture, so rosy and curly and kissable, that he extorted a qualified compliment even from Cousin Sophia.

"He's a reel healthy looking child now, though mebbee his colour is a mite too high—sorter consumptive looking, as you might say. I never thought you'd raise him when I saw him the day after you brung him home. I reely did not think it was in you and I told Albert's wife so when I got home. Albert's wife says, says she, 'There's more in Rilla Blythe than you'd think for, Aunt Sophia.' Them was her very words. 'More in Rilla Blythe than you'd think for.' Albert's wife always had a good opinion of you."

Cousin Sophia sighed, as if to imply that Albert's wife stood alone in this against the world. But Cousin Sophia really did not mean that. She was quite fond of Rilla in her own melancholy way; but young creeturs had to be kept down. If they were not kept down society would be demoralized.

"Do you remember your walk home from the light two years ago tonight?" whispered Gertrude Oliver to Rilla, teasingly.

"I should think I do," smiled Rilla; and then her smile grew dreamy and absent; she was remembering something else— that hour with Kenneth on the sandshore. *Where would Ken be tonight?* And Jem and Jerry and Walter and all the other boys who had danced and moonlighted on the old Four Winds

Point that evening of mirth and laughter—their last joyous unclouded evening. In the filthy trenches of the Somme front, with the roar of the guns and the groans of stricken men for the music of Ned Burr's violin, and the flash of star shells for the silver sparkles on the old blue gulf. Two of them were sleeping under the Flanders poppies—Alec Burr from the Upper Glen, and Clark Manley of Lowbridge. Others were wounded in the hospitals. But so far nothing had touched the manse and the Ingleside boys. They seemed to bear charmed lives. Yet the suspense never grew any easier to bear as the weeks and months of war went by.

"It isn't as if it were some sort of fever to which you might conclude they were immune when they hadn't taken it for two years," sighed Rilla. "The danger is just as great and just as real as it was the first day they went into the trenches. I know this, and it tortures me every day. And yet I *can't* help hoping that since they've come this far unhurt they'll come through. Oh, Miss Oliver, what would it be like *not* to wake up in the morning feeling afraid of the news the day would bring? I can't picture such a state of things somehow. And two years ago this morning I woke wondering what delightful gift the new day would give me. These are the two years I thought would be filled with fun."

"Would you exchange them—now—for two years filled with fun?"

"No," said Rilla slowly, "I wouldn't. It's strange—isn't it?— They have been two terrible years—and yet I have a queer feeling of thankfulness for them—as if they had brought me something very precious, with all their pain. I wouldn't *want* to go back and be the girl I was two years ago, not even if I could. Not that I think I've made any wonderful progress— but I'm *not* quite the selfish, frivolous little doll I was then. I suppose I had a soul then, Miss Oliver—but I didn't know it. I know it now—and that is worth a great deal—worth all the suffering of the past two years. And still"—Rilla gave a little apologetic laugh, "I don't *want* to suffer any more—not even for the sake of more soul growth. At the end of two more years I might look back and be thankful for the development they had brought me, too; but I don't want it now."

"We never do," said Miss Oliver. "That is why we are not left to choose our own means and measure of development, I suppose. No matter how much we value what our lessons have brought us we don't want to go on with the bitter schooling. Well, let us hope for the best, as Susan says; things are really going well now and if Roumania lines up, the end may come with a suddenness that will surprise us all."

Roumania did come in—and Susan remarked approvingly that its king and queen were the finest looking royal couple she had seen pictures of. So the summer passed away. Early in September word came that the Canadians had been shifted to the Somme front and anxiety grew tenser and deeper. For the first time Mrs. Blythe's spirit failed her a little, and as the days of suspense wore on the doctor began to look gravely at her, and veto this or that special effort in Red Cross work.

"Oh, let me work—let me work, Gilbert," she entreated feverishly. "While I'm working I don't *think* so much. If I'm idle I imagine everything—rest is only torture for me. My two boys are on the frightful Somme front—and Shirley pores day and night over aviation literature and *says* nothing. But I see the purpose growing in his eyes. No, I cannot rest—don't ask it of me, Gilbert."

But the doctor was inexorable.

"I can't let you kill yourself, Anne-girl," he said. "When the boys come back I want a mother here to welcome them. Why, you're getting transparent. It won't do—ask Susan there if it will do."

"Oh, if Susan and you are both banded together against me!" said Anne helplessly.

One day the glorious news came that the Canadians had taken Courcelette and Martenpuich, with many prisoners and guns. Susan ran up the flag and said it was plain to be seen that Haig knew what soldiers to pick for a hard job. The others dared not feel exultant. Who knew what price had been paid?

Rilla woke that morning when the dawn was beginning to break and went to her window to look out, her thick creamy eyelids heavy with sleep. Just at dawn the world looks as it never looks at any other time. The air was cold with dew and the orchard and grove and Rainbow Valley were full of mystery and wonder. Over the eastern hill were golden deeps and silvery-pink shallows. There was no wind, and Rilla heard distinctly a dog howling in a melancholy way down in the direction of the station. Was it Dog Monday? And if it were, why was he howling like that? Rilla shivered; the sound had something boding and grievous in it. She remembered that Miss Oliver said once, when they were coming home in the darkness and heard a dog howl, "When a dog cries like that the Angel of Death is passing." Rilla listened with a curdling fear at her heart. It *was* Dog Monday—she felt sure of it. Whose dirge was he howling—to whose spirit was he sending that anguished greeting and farewell?

Rilla went back to bed but she could not sleep. All day she watched and waited in a dread of which she did not speak to any one. She went down to see Dog Monday and the station master said,

"That dog of yours howled from midnight to sunrise

something weird. I dunno what got into him. He kept the wife awake and I got up once and went out and hollered at him but he paid no 'tention to me. He was sitting all alone in the moonlight out there at the end of the platform, and every few minutes the poor lonely little beggar'd lift his nose and howl as if his heart was breaking. He never did it afore— always slept in his kennel real quiet and canny from train to train. But he sure had something on his mind last night."

Dog Monday was lying in his kennel. He wagged his tail and licked Rilla's hand. But he would not touch the food she brought for him.

"I'm afraid he's sick," she said anxiously. She hated to go away and leave him. But no bad news came that day—nor the next—nor the next. Rilla's fear lifted. Dog Monday howled no more and resumed his routine of train meeting and watching. When five days had passed the Ingleside people began to feel that they might be cheerful again. Rilla dashed about the kitchen helping Susan with the breakfast and singing so sweetly and clearly that Cousin Sophia across the road heard her and croaked out to Mrs. Albert,

"'Sing before eating, cry before sleeping,' I've always heard."

But Rilla shed no tears before the nightfall. When her father, his face grey and drawn and old, came to her that afternoon and told her that Walter had been killed in action at Courcelette she crumpled up in a pitiful little heap of merciful unconsciousness in his arms. Nor did she waken to her pain for many hours.

CHAPTER XXIII

"And So, Goodnight"

The fierce flame of agony had burned itself out and the grey dust of its ashes was over all the world. Rilla's younger life recovered physically sooner than her mother. For weeks Mrs. Blythe lay ill from grief and shock. Rilla found it was possible to go on with existence, since existence had still to be reckoned with. There was work to be done, for Susan could not do all. For her mother's sake she had to put on calmness and endurance as a garment in the day; but night after night she lay in her bed, weeping the bitter rebellious tears of youth until at last tears were all wept out and the little patient ache that was to be in her heart until she died took their place.

She clung to Miss Oliver, who knew what to say and what not to say. So few people did. Kind, well-meaning callers and comforters gave Rilla some terrible moments.

"You'll get over it in time," Mrs. William Reese said, cheerfully. Mrs. Reese had three stalwart sons, not one of whom had gone to the front.

"It's such a blessing it was Walter who was taken and not Jem," said Miss Sarah Clow. "Walter was a member of the church, and Jem wasn't. I've told Mr. Meredith many a time that he should have spoken seriously to Jem about it before he went away."

"Pore, pore, Walter," sighed Mrs. Reese.

"Do not you come here calling him poor Walter," said Susan indignantly, appearing in the kitchen door, much to the relief of Rilla, who felt that she could endure no more just then. "He was *not* poor. He was richer than any of you. It is you who stay at home and will not let your sons go who are poor—poor and naked and mean and small—pisen poor, and so are your sons, with all their prosperous farms and fat cattle and their souls no bigger than a flea's—if as big."

"I came here to comfort the afflicted and not to be insulted," said Mrs. Reese, taking her departure, unregretted by any one. Then the fire went out of Susan and she retreated to her kitchen, laid her faithful old head on the table and wept bitterly for a time. Then she went to work and ironed Jims' little rompers. Rilla scolded her gently for it when she herself came in to do it.

"I am not going to have you kill yourself working for any war baby," Susan said obstinately.

"Oh, I wish I could just keep on working *all* the time, Susan," cried poor Rilla. "And I wish I didn't have to go to sleep. It is hideous to go to sleep and forget it for a little while, and wake up and have it all rush over me anew the next morning. Do people *ever* get used to things like this, Susan? And oh, Susan, I can't get away from what Mrs. Reese said. *Did* Walter suffer much—he was always so sensitive to pain. Oh, Susan, if I knew that he didn't, I think I could gather up a little courage and strength."

This merciful knowledge was given to Rilla. A letter came from Walter's commanding officer, telling them that he had been killed instantly by a bullet during a charge at Courcelette. The same day there was a letter for Rilla from Walter himself.

Rilla carried it unopened to Rainbow Valley and read it there, in the spot where she had had her last talk with him. It is a strange thing to read a letter after the writer is dead—a bittersweet thing, in which pain and comfort are strangely mingled. For the first time since the blow had fallen Rilla *felt*—a different thing from tremulous hope and faith—that Walter, of the glorious gift and the splendid ideals, *still lived*, with just the same gift and just the same ideals. *That* could not be destroyed—*these* could suffer no eclipse. The personality that had expressed itself in that last letter, written on the eve of Courcelette, could not be snuffed out by a German bullet. It must carry on, though the earthly link with things of earth were broken.

"We're going over the top tomorrow, Rilla-my-Rilla," wrote Walter. "I wrote mother and Di yesterday, but somehow I feel as if I *must* write *you* tonight. I hadn't intended to do any writing tonight—but I've got to. Do you remember old Mrs. Tom Crawford over-harbour, who was always saying that it was 'laid on her' to do such and such a thing? Well, that is just how I feel. It's 'laid on me' to write you tonight—*you*, sister and chum of mine. There are some things I want to say before—well, before tomorrow.

"You and Ingleside seem strangely *near* me tonight. It's the first time I've felt this since I came. Always home has seemed so far away,—so *hopelessly* far away from this hideous welter of filth and blood. But tonight it is quite close to me—it seems to me I can almost *see* you—hear you speak. And I can see the moonlight shining white and still on the old hills of home. It has seemed to me ever since I came here that it was impossible that there could be calm gentle nights and unshattered moonlight anywhere in the world. But tonight somehow, all the beautiful things I have always loved seem to have become possible again—and this is good, and makes me feel a deep, certain, exquisite happiness. It must be autumn at home now—the harbour is a-dream and the old Glen hills blue with haze, and Rainbow Valley a haunt of delight with wild asters blowing all over it,—our old 'farewell-summers.' I always liked that name so much better than 'aster'—it was a poem in itself.

"Rilla, you know I've always had premonitions. You remember the Pied Piper—but no, of course you wouldn't—you were too young. One evening long ago when Nan and Di and Jem and the Merediths and I were together in Rainbow Valley I had a queer vision or presentiment—whatever you like to call it. Rilla, I saw the Piper coming down the Valley with a shadowy host behind him. The others thought I was only pretending—but I *saw* him for just one moment. And, Rilla, last night I saw him again. I was doing sentry-go and I saw him marching across No-man's-land from our trenches to the German trenches—the same tall shadowy form, piping weirdly,—and behind him followed boys in khaki. Rilla, I tell you I *saw* him—it was no fancy—no illusion. I *heard* his music, and then—he was *gone*. But I *had* seen him—and I knew what it meant—I knew that I was among those who followed him.

"Rilla, the Piper will pipe me 'west' tomorrow. I feel sure of this. And Rilla, I'm not afraid. When you hear the news, remember that. I've won my own freedom here—freedom from all fear. I shall never be afraid of anything again—not of death—nor of life, if, after all, I am to go on living. And life, I think, would be the harder of the two to face,—for it could never be beautiful for me again. There would always be such horrible things to remember—things that would make life ugly and painful always for me. I could never forget them. But whether it's life or death, I'm not afraid, Rilla-my-Rilla, and I am not sorry that I came. I'm *satisfied*. I'll never write the poems I once dreamed of writing—but I've helped to make Canada safe for the poets of the future—for the workers of the future—ay, and the dreamers, too—for if no man dreams, there will be nothing for the workers to fulfil,—the future, not of Canada only but of the world—when the 'red rain' of Langemarck and Verdun shall have brought forth a golden harvest—not in a year or two, as some foolishly think, but a generation later, when the seed sown now shall have had time to germinate and grow. Yes, I'm glad I came, Rilla. It isn't only the fate of the little sea-born island I love that is in the balance—nor of Canada—nor of England. It's the fate of mankind. That is what we're fighting for. And we shall win— never for a moment doubt that, Rilla. For it isn't only the *living* who are fighting—the *dead* are fighting too. Such an army *cannot* be defeated.

"Is there laughter in your face yet, Rilla? I hope so. The world will need laughter and courage more than ever in the years that will come next. I don't want to preach—this isn't any time for it. But I just want to say something that may help you over the worst when you hear that I've 'gone west.' I've a pre-monition about you, Rilla, as well as about myself. I think Ken will go back to you—and that there are long years of happiness for you by-and-by. And you will tell your children of the *Idea* we fought and died for—teach them it must be *lived for* as well as died for, else the price paid for it will have been given for naught. This will be part of *your* work, Rilla. And if you—all you girls back in the homeland—do it, then we who don't come back will know that you have not 'broken faith' with us.

"I meant to write Una tonight, too, but I won't have time now. Read this letter to her and tell her it's really meant for you both—you two dear, fine loyal girls. Tomorrow, when we go over the top, I'll think of you both—of your laughter, Rilla-my-Rilla, and the *steadfastness* in Una's blue eyes—somehow I see those eyes very plainly tonight, too. Yes, you'll both keep faith—I'm sure of that—you and Una. And so—goodnight. We go over the top at dawn."

Rilla read her letter over many times. There was a new light on her pale young face when she finally stood up, amid the asters Walter had loved, with the sunshine of autumn around her. For the moment at least, she was lifted above pain and loneliness.

"I will keep faith, Walter," she said steadily. "I will work—and teach—and learn—and laugh, yes, I will even *laugh*—through all my years, because of you and because of what you gave when you followed the call."

Rilla meant to keep Walter's letter as a sacred treasure. But, seeing the look on Una Meredith's face when Una had read it and held it back to her, she thought of something. Could she do it? Oh, no, she could not give up Walter's letter—his last letter. Surely it was not selfishness to keep it. A copy would be such a soulless thing. But Una—Una had so little—and her eyes were the eyes of a woman stricken to the heart, who yet must not cry out or ask for sympathy.

"Una, would you like to have this letter—to keep?" she asked slowly.

"Yes—if you can give it to me," Una said dully.

"Then—you may have it," said Rilla hurriedly.

"Thank you," said Una. It was all she said, but there was something in her voice which repaid Rilla for her bit of sacrifice.

Una took the letter and when Rilla had gone she pressed it against her lonely lips. Una knew that love would never come into her life now—it was buried forever under the blood-stained soil "Somewhere in France." No one but herself—and perhaps Rilla—knew it—would ever know it. She had no right in the eyes of her world to grieve. She must hide and bear her long pain as best she could—alone. But she, too, would keep faith.

$\mathcal{M}$ary Is Just in Time

The autumn of 1916 was a bitter season for Ingleside. Mrs. Blythe's return to health was slow, and sorrow and loneliness were in all hearts. Everyone tried to hide it from the others and "carry on" cheerfully. Rilla laughed a good deal. Nobody at Ingleside was deceived by her laughter; it came from her lips only, never from her heart. But outsiders said some people got over trouble very easily, and Irene Howard remarked that she was surprised to find how shallow Rilla Blythe really was. "Why, after all her pose of being so devoted to Walter, she doesn't seem to mind his death at all. Nobody has even seen her shed a tear or heard her mention his name. She has evidently quite forgotten him. Poor fellow,—you'd really think his family *would* feel it more. I spoke of him to Rilla at the last Junior Red meeting—of how fine and brave and splendid he was—and I said life could never be just the same to *me* again, now that Walter had gone—we were *such* friends, you know—why *I* was the *very first person* he told about having enlisted—and Rilla answered, as coolly and indifferently as if she were speaking of an entire stranger, 'He was just one of many fine and splendid boys who have given everything for their country.' Well, I wish *I* could take things as calmly,—but I'm not made like that. I'm *so* sensitive— things hurt *me* terribly—I really *never* get over them. I asked Rilla right out why she didn't put on mourning for Walter. She said her mother didn't wish it. But everyone is talking about it."

"Rilla doesn't wear colours—nothing but white," protested Betty Mead.

"White becomes her better than anything else," said Irene significantly. "And we all know black doesn't suit her complexion at all. But of course I'm not saying *that* is the reason she doesn't wear it. Only, it's funny. If *my* brother had died I'd have gone into *deep* mourning. I wouldn't have had the *heart* for anything else. I confess I'm disappointed in Rilla Blythe."

"*I* am not, then," cried Betty Mead, loyally, "I think Rilla is just a wonderful girl. A few years ago I admit I *did* think she was rather too vain and gigglesome, but now she is nothing of the sort. I don't think there is a girl in the Glen who is so unselfish and plucky as Rilla, or who has 'done her bit' as thoroughly and patiently. Our Junior Red Cross would have gone on the rocks a dozen times if it hadn't been for her tact and perseverance and enthusiasm—you know that perfectly well, Irene."

"Why, *I* am not running Rilla down," said Irene, opening her eyes widely. "It was only her lack of feeling I was criticizing. I suppose she can't help it. Of course, she's a born manager—everyone knows that. She's very fond of managing, too—and people like that are very necessary I admit. So don't look at me as if I'd said something perfectly dreadful, Betty, please. I'm quite willing to agree that Rilla Blythe is the embodiment of *all* the virtues, if that will please you. And no doubt it is a virtue to be quite unmoved by things that would *crush* most people."

Some of Irene's remarks were reported to Rilla; but they did not hurt her as they would once have done. They didn't matter, that was all. Life was too big to leave room for pettiness. She had a pact to keep and a work to do; and through the long hard days and weeks of that disastrous autumn she was faithful to her task. The war news was consistently bad, for Germany marched from victory to victory over poor Roumania. "Foreigners—foreigners," Susan muttered dubiously. "Russians or Roumanians or whatever they may be, they are foreigners and you cannot tie to them. But after Verdun I shall not give up hope. And can you tell me, Mrs. Dr. dear, if the Dobruja is a river or a mountain range, or a condition of the atmosphere?"

The Presidential election in the United States came off in November, and Susan was red-hot over that—and quite apologetic for her excitement.

"I never thought I would live to see the day when I would be interested in a Yankee election, Mrs. Dr. dear. It only goes to show we can never know what we will come to in this world and therefore we should not be proud."

Susan stayed up late the evening of the seventh, ostensibly to finish a pair of socks. But she 'phoned down to Carter Flagg's store at intervals, and when the first report came through that Hughes had been elected she stalked solemnly upstairs to Mrs. Blythe's room and announced it in a thrilling whisper from the foot of the bed.

"I thought if you were not asleep you would be interested in knowing it. I believe it is for the best. Perhaps he will just fall to writing notes, too, Mrs. Dr. dear, but I hope for better things. I never was very partial to whiskers but one cannot have everything."

When news came in the morning that after all Wilson was re-elected, Susan tacked to catch another breeze of optimism.

"Well, better a fool you know than a fool you do not know, as the old proverb has it," she remarked cheerfully. "Not that I hold Woodrow to be a fool by any means, though by times you would not think he had the sense he was born with. But he is a good letter writer at least, and we do not know if the Hughes man is even that. All things being considered I commend the Yankees. They have shown good sense and I do not mind admitting it. Cousin Sophia wanted them to elect Roosevelt and is much disgruntled because they would not give him a chance. I had a hankering for him myself but we must believe that Providence overrules these matters and be satisfied,—though what the Almighty means in this affair of Roumania I cannot fathom—saying it with all reverence."

Susan fathomed it—or thought she did—when the Asquith ministry went down and Lloyd George became Premier.

"Mrs. Dr. dear, Lloyd George is at the helm at last. I have been praying for this for many a day. *Now* we shall soon see a blessed change. It took the Roumanian disaster to bring it about, no less, and that is the meaning of *it*, though I could not see it before. There will be no more shilly-shallying. I consider that the war is as good as won, and that I shall tie to, whether Bucharest falls or not."

Bucharest did fall—and Germany proposed peace negotiations. Whereat Susan scornfully turned a deaf ear and absolutely refused to listen to such proposals. When President Wilson sent his famous December peace note Susan waxed violently sarcastic.

"Woodrow Wilson is going to make peace, I understand. First Henry Ford had a try at it and now comes Wilson. But peace is not made with ink, Woodrow, and that you may tie to," said Susan, apostrophizing the unlucky president out of the kitchen window nearest the United States. "Lloyd George's speech will tell the Kaiser what is what, and you may keep your peace screeds at home and save postage."

"What a pity President Wilson can't hear you, Susan," said Rilla slyly.

"Indeed, Rilla dear, it *is* a pity that he has no one near him to give him good advice, as it is clear he has not, in all those Democrats and Republicans," retorted Susan. "*I* do not know the difference between them, for the politics of the Yankees is a puzzle I cannot solve, study it as I may. But as far as seeing through a grindstone goes, I am afraid—" Susan shook her head dubiously, "that they are all tarred with the same brush."

"I am thankful Christmas is over," Rilla wrote in her diary during the last week of a stormy December. "We had dreaded it so—the first Christmas since Courcelette. But we had all the Merediths down for dinner and nobody *tried* to be gay or cheerful. We were all just quiet and friendly, and *that* helped. Then, too, I was so thankful that Jims had got better—so thankful that I almost felt glad—*almost* but not quite. I wonder if I shall ever feel *really* glad over anything again. It seems as if gladness were killed in me—shot down by the same bullet that pierced Walter's heart. Perhaps some day a new kind of gladness will be born in my soul—but the old kind will never live again.

"Winter set in awfully early this year. Ten days before Christmas we had a big snowstorm—at least we thought it big at the time. As it happened, it was only a prelude to the real performance. It was fine the next day and Ingleside and Rainbow Valley were wonderful, with the trees all covered with snow, and big drifts everywhere, carved into the most fantastic shapes by the chisel of the northeast wind. Father and mother went up to Avonlea. Father thought the change would do mother good and they wanted to see poor Aunt Diana, whose son Jack had been seriously wounded a short time before. They left Susan and me to keep house and father expected to be back the next day. But he never got back for a week. That night it began to storm again, and it stormed unbrokenly for four days. It was the worst and longest storm that Prince Edward Island has known for years. Everything was disorganized—the roads were completely choked up, the trains blockaded, and the telephone wires put entirely out of commission.

"*And* then Jims took ill.

"He had a little cold when father and mother went away and he kept getting worse for a couple of days, but it didn't occur to me that there was danger of anything serious. I never even took his temperature and I can't forgive myself, because it was sheer carelessness. The truth is I had *slumped* just then. Mother was away, so I let myself go. All at once I was tired of keeping up and pretending to be brave and cheerful, and I just gave up for a few days and spent most of the time lying on my face on my bed, crying. I neglected Jims—that is the hateful truth—I was cowardly and false to what I promised Walter—and if Jims had died I could never have forgiven myself.

"Then, the third night after father and mother went away, Jims suddenly got worse—oh, so much worse—all at once. Susan and I were all alone. Gertrude had been at Lowbridge when the storm began and had never got back. At first we were not much alarmed. Jims has had several bouts of croup and Susan and Morgan and I have always brought him through without much trouble. But it wasn't very long before we were dreadfully alarmed.

"'I never saw croup like this before,' said Susan.

"As for me, I knew, when it was too late, what kind of croup it was. I knew it was not the ordinary croup—'false croup' as doctors call it,—but the 'true' croup—and I knew that it was a deadly and dangerous thing. And father was away and there was no doctor nearer than Lowbridge—and we could not 'phone—and neither horse nor man could get through the drifts that night.

"Gallant little Jims put up a good fight for his life,—Susan and I tried every remedy we could think of or find in father's books, but he continued to grow worse. It was heart-rending to see and hear him. He gasped so horribly for breath—the poor little soul—and his face turned a dreadful bluish colour and had such an agonized expression, and he kept struggling with his little hands,—as if he were appealing to us to help him somehow. I found myself thinking that the boys who had been gassed at the front must have looked like that, and the thought haunted me amid all my dread and misery over Jims. And all the time the fatal membrane in his wee throat grew and thickened and he couldn't get it up.

"Oh, I was just wild! I never realized how dear Jims was to me until that moment. And I felt so utterly helpless. It was just as if we were fighting a relentless foe without any real weapons,—just like those poor Russian soldiers who had only their bare hands to oppose to German machine guns.

"And then Susan gave up.

"'We cannot save him—oh, if your father was here—look at him, the poor little fellow! I know not what to do.'

"I looked at Jims and I thought he was dying. Susan was holding him up in his crib to give him a better chance for breath, but it didn't seem as if he could breathe at all. My little war baby, with his dear ways and sweet roguish face, was choking to death before my very eyes, and I couldn't help him. I threw down the hot poultice I had ready in despair. Of what use was it? Jims was dying—and it was my fault—I hadn't been careful enough!

"Just then—at eleven o'clock at night—the door bell rang. Such a ring—it pealed all over the house above the roar of the storm. Susan couldn't go—she dared not lay Jims down,—so I rushed downstairs. In the hall I paused just a minute—I was suddenly overcome by an absurd dread. I thought of a weird story Gertrude had told me once. An aunt of hers was alone in a house one night with her sick husband. She heard a knock at the door. And when she went and opened it—there was *nothing* there—nothing that could be *seen*, at least. But when she opened the door a deadly cold wind blew in and seemed to sweep past her right up the stairs, although it was a calm, warm summer night outside. Immediately she heard a cry— she ran upstairs—and her husband was dead. And she always believed, so Gertrude said, that when she opened that door she *let Death in*.

"It was ridiculous of me to feel so frightened. But I was distracted and worn out—and I simply felt for a moment that I *dared* not open the door—that death was waiting outside. Then I remembered that I had no time to waste—must not be so foolish—I sprang forward and opened the door.

"Certainly a cold wind did blow in and filled the hall with a whirl of snow. But there on the threshold stood a form of flesh and blood—Mary Vance, coated from head to foot with snow—and she brought Life, not Death, with her, though I didn't know *that* then. I just stared at her.

"'I haven't been turned out,' grinned Mary, as she stepped in and shut the door. 'I came up to Carter Flagg's two days ago and I've been storm-stayed there ever since. But old Abbie Flagg got on my nerves at last, and tonight I just made up my mind to come up here. I thought I could wade this far but I can tell you it was as much as a bargain. Once I thought I was stuck for keeps. Ain't it an awful night?'

"I came to myself and knew I must hurry upstairs. I explained as quickly as I could to Mary, and left her trying to brush the snow off. Upstairs I found that Jims was over that paroxysm, but almost as soon as I got back to the room he was in the grip of another. I hung over him and wrung my hands. I was completely 'no good'—I couldn't do anything but moan and cry—oh, how ashamed I am when I think of it; and yet what *could* I do—we had tried everything we knew—and then all at once I heard Mary Vance saying loudly behind me,

"'Why, that child is dying!'

"I whirled around. Didn't I know he was dying—my little Jims! I could have thrown Mary Vance out of the door or the window—anywhere—at that moment. There she stood, cool and composed, looking down at my baby, with those weird white eyes of hers, as she might look at a choking kitten. I had always disliked Mary Vance—and just then I *hated* her.

"'We have tried everything,' said poor Susan dully. 'It is not ordinary croup.'

"'No, it's the dipthery croup,' said Mary briskly, snatching up an apron. 'And there's mighty little time to lose—but *I* know what to do. When I lived over-harbour with Mrs. Wiley years ago Will Crawford's kid died of dipthery croup, in spite of two doctors. And when old Aunt Christina MacAllister heard of it,—*she* was the one brought *me* round when I died of pneumonia you know—she was a wonder—no doctor was a patch on *her*—they don't hatch *her* breed of cats nowadays, let me tell you—she said she could have saved him with her grandmother's remedy if she'd been there. She told Mrs. Wiley what it was and I've never forgot it. I've the greatest memory ever—a thing just lies in the back of my head till the time comes to use it. Got any sulphur in the house, Susan?'

"Yes, we had sulphur. Susan went down with Mary to get it and I held Jims. I hadn't any hope—not the least. Mary Vance might brag as she liked—she was always bragging—but I didn't believe any grandmother's remedy could save Jims now. Presently Mary came back. She had tied a piece of thick flannel over her mouth and nose and she carried Susan's old tin chip pan, half full of burning coals.

"'You watch *me*,' she said boastfully. 'I've never done this, but I know how it's done. It's kill or cure—but that child is dying anyway.'

"She sprinkled a spoonful of sulphur over the coals; and then she picked up Jims, turned him over, and held him face downward, right over those choking, blinding fumes. I don't know why I didn't spring forward and snatch him away. Susan says it was because it was foreordained that I shouldn't, and I think she is right, because it did really seem that I was powerless to move. Susan herself seemed transfixed, watching Mary from the doorway. Jims writhed in those big, firm, capable hands of Mary—oh yes, she is capable all right,—and choked and wheezed—and choked and wheezed—and I felt that he was being tortured to death—and then all at once, after what seemed to me an hour, though it really wasn't long, he coughed up the membrane that was killing him. Mary turned him over and laid him back on his bed. He was white as marble and the tears were pouring out of his brown eyes—but that awful livid look was gone from his face and he could breathe quite easily.

"'Wasn't that some trick?' said Mary gaily. 'I hadn't any idea how it would work, but I just took a chance. I'll smoke his throat out again once or twice before morning, just to kill all the germs, but you'll see he'll be all right now.'

"Jims went right to sleep—real sleep, not coma, as I feared at first. Mary 'smoked him,' as she called it, twice through the night, and at daylight his throat was perfectly clear and his temperature was almost normal. When I made sure of that I turned and looked at Mary Vance. She was sitting on the lounge laying down the law to Susan on some subject about which Susan must have known forty times as much as she did. But I didn't mind how much law she laid down or how much she bragged. She had a *right* to brag—she had dared to do what I would never have dared and had saved Jims from a horrible death. It didn't matter any more that she had once chased me through the Glen with a codfish—it didn't matter that she had smeared goose grease all over my dream of romance the night of the lighthouse dance—it didn't matter that she thought she knew more than anybody else and always rubbed it in,—I would never dislike Mary Vance again. I went over to her and kissed her.

"'What's up now?' she said.

"'Nothing—only I'm so grateful to you, Mary.'

"'Well, I think you ought to be, that's a fact. You two would have let that baby die on your hands if I hadn't happened along,' said Mary, just beaming with complacency. She got Susan and me a tip-top breakfast and made us eat it, and 'bossed the life out of us,' as Susan says, for two days, until the roads were opened so that she could get home. Jims was almost well by that time and father turned up. He heard our tale without saying much. Father is rather scornful generally about what he calls 'old wives' remedies.' He laughed a little and said, 'After this, Mary Vance will expect me to call her in for consultation in all my serious cases.'

"So Christmas was not so hard as I expected it to be; and now the New Year is coming—and we are still hoping for the

'Big Push' that will end the war—and Little Dog Monday is getting stiff and rheumatic from his cold vigils, but still he 'carries on,' and Shirley continues to read the exploits of the aces. Oh, nineteen-seventeen, what will you bring?"

CHAPTER XXV

*S*hirley Goes

"No, Woodrow, there will be no peace without victory," said Susan, sticking her knitting needle viciously through President Wilson's name in the newspaper column. "*We* Canadians mean to have peace *and* victory, too. You, if it pleases you, Woodrow, can have the peace *without* the victory,"—and Susan stalked off to bed with the comfortable consciousness of having got the better of the argument with the president. But a few days later she rushed to Mrs. Blythe in red-hot excitement.

"Mrs. Dr. dear, what do you think? A 'phone message has just come through from Charlottetown that Woodrow Wilson has sent that German ambassador man to the right about at last. They tell me that means war. So I begin to think that Woodrow's heart is in the right place after all, wherever his head may be, and I am going to commandeer a little sugar and celebrate the occasion with some fudge, despite the howls of the Food Board. I thought that submarine business would bring things to a crisis. I told Cousin Sophia so when she said it was the beginning of the end for the Allies."

"Don't let the doctor hear of the fudge, Susan," said Anne, with a smile. "You know he has laid down very strict rules for us along the lines of economy the government has asked for."

"Yes, Mrs. Dr. dear, and a man should be master in his own household and his women folk should bow to his decrees. I flatter myself that I am becoming quite efficient in economizing,"—Susan had taken to using certain German terms with killing effect,—"but one can exercise a little gumption on the quiet now and then. Shirley was wishing for some of my fudge the other day—the Susan brand, as he called it— and I said 'The first victory there is to celebrate I shall make you some.' I consider this news quite equal to a victory and what the doctor does not know will never grieve him. *I* take the whole responsibility, Mrs. Dr. dear, so do not you vex your conscience."

Susan spoiled Shirley shamelessly that winter. He came home from Queen's every week-end and Susan had all his favourite dishes for him, in so far as she could evade or wheedle the doctor, and waited on him hand and foot. Though she talked war constantly to everyone else she never mentioned it to him or before him; but she watched him like a cat watching a mouse; and when the German retreat from the Bapaume salient began and continued Susan's exultation was linked up with something deeper than anything she expressed. Surely the end was in sight—would come now before—any one else—could go.

"Things are coming our way at last," she told Cousin Sophia triumphantly. "The United States has declared war at last, as I always believed they would, in spite of Woodrow's gift for letter writing, and you will see they will go into it with a vim since I understand that is their habit, when they do start. And we have got the Germans on the run, too."

"The States mean well," moaned Cousin Sophia, "but all the vim in the world cannot put them on the fighting line this spring and the Allies will be finished before that. The Germans are just luring them on. That man Simonds says their retreat has put the Allies in a hold."

"That man Simonds has said more than he will ever live to make good," retorted Susan. "I do not worry myself about his opinion as long as Lloyd George is Premier of England. He will not be bamboozled, and that you may tie to. Things look good to me. The U.S. is in the war, and we have got Kut and Bagdad back—and I would not be surprised to see the Allies in Berlin by June—and the Russians, too, since they have got rid of the Czar. That in my opinion was a good piece of work."

"Time will show if it is," said Cousin Sophia, who would have been very indignant if any one had told her that she would rather see Susan put to shame as a seer than a successful overthrow of tyranny, or even the march of the Allies down Unter den Linden. But then the woes of the Russian people were quite unknown to Cousin Sophia, while this aggravating, optimistic Susan was an ever-present thorn in her side.

Just at that moment Shirley was sitting on the edge of the table in the living room, swinging his legs—a brown, ruddy, wholesome lad, from top to toe, every inch of him—and saying coolly,

"Mother and dad, I was eighteen last Monday. Don't you think it's about time I joined up?"

The pale mother looked at him.

"Two of my sons have gone and one will never return. Must I give you too, Shirley?"

The age-old cry—"Joseph is not and Simeon is not; and ye will take Benjamin away." How the mothers of the Great War echoed the old Patriarch's moan of so many centuries agone!

"You wouldn't have me a slacker, mother? I can get into the flying corps. What say, dad?"

The doctor's hands were not quite steady as he folded up the powders he was concocting for Abbie Flagg's rheumatism. He had known this moment was coming, yet he was not altogether prepared for it. He answered slowly,

"I won't try to hold you back from what you believe to be your duty. But you must not go unless your mother says you may."

Shirley said nothing more. He was not a lad of many words. Anne did not say anything more just then, either. She was thinking of little Joyce's grave in the old burying-ground over-harbour,—little Joyce who would have been a woman now, had she lived—of the white cross in France and the splendid grey eyes of the little boy who had been taught his first lessons of duty and loyalty at her knee—of Jem in the terrible trenches—of Nan and Di and Rilla, waiting—waiting—*waiting*, while the golden years of youth passed by—and she wondered if she could bear any more. She thought not; surely she had given enough.

Yet that night she told Shirley that he might go.

They did not tell Susan right away. She did not know it until, a few days later, Shirley presented himself in her kitchen in his aviation uniform. Susan didn't make half the fuss she had made when Jem and Walter had gone. She said stonily,

"So they're going to take you, too."

"*Take* me? No. I'm *going*, Susan—got to."

Susan sat down by the table, folded her knotted old hands, that had grown warped and twisted working for the Ingleside children, to still their shaking, and said,

"Yes, you must go. I did not see once why such things must be but I can see now."

"You're a brick, Susan," said Shirley. He was relieved that she took it so coolly—he had been a little afraid, with a boy's horror of "a scene." He went out whistling gaily; but half an hour later, when pale Anne Blythe came in, Susan was still sitting there, with unwashed dishes around her.

"Mrs. Dr. dear," said Susan, making an admission she

would once have died rather than make, "I feel very old. Jem and Walter were yours but Shirley is *mine*. And I *cannot* bear to think of him flying—and his machine crashing down—the life crushed out of his body—the dear little body I nursed and cuddled when he was a wee baby."

"Susan—*don't*," cried Anne.

"Oh, Mrs. Dr. dear, I beg your pardon. I ought not to have said anything like that out loud. I sometimes forget that I resolved to be a heroine. This—this has shaken me a little. But I will not forget myself again. Only if things do not go as smoothly as usual in the kitchen for a few days I hope you will make due allowance for me. At least," said poor Susan, forcing a grim smile in a desperate effort to recover lost standing, "at least flying is a *clean* job. He will not get so dirty and messed up as he would in the trenches, and that is well for he has always been a tidy child."

So Shirley went—not radiantly, as to a high adventure, like Jem, not in a white flame of sacrifice, like Walter, but in a cool, business-like mood, as of one doing something, rather dirty and disagreeable, that had just got to be done. He kissed Susan for the first time since he was five years old, and said "Good-bye, Susan,—*mother* Susan."

"My little brown boy—my little brown boy," said Susan. "I wonder," she thought bitterly, as she looked at the doctor's sorrowful face, "if you remember how you spanked him once when he was a baby. I am thankful I have nothing like *that* on my conscience now."

The doctor did not remember the old discipline. But before he put on his hat to go out on his round of calls he stood for a moment in the great silent living room that had once been full of children's laughter.

"Our last son—our last son," he said aloud. "A good, sturdy, sensible lad, too. Always reminded me of my father. I suppose I ought to be proud that he wanted to go—I was proud when Jem went,—even when Walter went—but 'our house is left us desolate.'"

"I have been thinking, doctor," old Sandy of the Upper Glen said to him that afternoon, "that your house will be seeming very big the day."

Highland Sandy's quaint phrase struck the doctor as perfectly expressive. Ingleside did seem very big and empty that night. Yet Shirley had been away all winter except for week-ends and had always been a quiet fellow even when home. Was it because he had been the only one left that his going seemed to leave such a huge blank—that every room seemed vacant and deserted—that the very trees on the lawn seemed to be trying to comfort each other with caresses of freshly-budding boughs for the loss of the last of the little lads who had romped under them in childhood?

Susan worked very hard all day and late into the night. When she had wound the kitchen clock and put Dr. Jekyll out, none too gently, she stood for a little while on the doorstep, looking down the Glen, which lay tranced in faint, silvery light from a sinking young moon. But Susan did not see the familiar hills and harbour. She was looking at the aviation camp in Kingsport where Shirley was that night.

"He called me 'Mother Susan,'" she was thinking. "Well, all our men folk have gone now—Jem and Walter and Shirley and Jerry and Carl. And none of them had to be driven to it. So we have a right to be proud. But pride—" Susan sighed bitterly,—"pride is cold company and that there is no gainsaying."

The moon sank lower into a black cloud in the west, the Glen went out in an eclipse of sudden shadow,—and thousands of miles away the Canadian boys in khaki—the living and the dead—were in possession of Vimy Ridge.

Vimy Ridge is a name written in crimson and gold on the Canadian annals of the Great War. "The British couldn't take it and the French couldn't take it," said a German prisoner to his captors, "but you Canadians are such fools that you don't know when a place can't be taken!"

So the "fools" took it—and paid the price.

Jerry Meredith was seriously wounded at Vimy Ridge—shot in the back the telegram said.

"Poor Nan," said Mrs. Blythe, when the news came. She thought of her own happy girlhood at old Green Gables. There had been no tragedy like this in it. How the girls of today had to suffer! When Nan came home from Redmond two weeks later her face showed what those weeks had meant to her. John Meredith, too, seemed to have grown old suddenly in them. Faith did not come home; she was on her way across the Atlantic as a V.A.D. Di had tried to wring from her father consent to her going also but had been told that for her mother's sake it could not be given. So Di, after a flying visit home, went back to her Red Cross work in Kingsport.

The mayflowers bloomed in the secret nooks of Rainbow Valley. Rilla was watching for them. Jem had once taken his mother the earliest mayflowers; Walter brought them to her when Jem was gone; last spring Shirley had sought them out for her; now, Rilla thought, she must take the boys' place in this. But before she had discovered any, Bruce Meredith came to Ingleside one twilight with his hands full of delicate pink sprays. He stalked up the steps of the veranda and laid them on Mrs. Blythe's lap.

"Because Shirley isn't here to bring them," he said in his funny, shy, blunt way.

"And you thought of this, you darling," said Anne, her lips quivering, as she looked at the stocky, black-browed little chap, standing before her, with his hands thrust into his pockets.

"I wrote Jem today and told him not to worry 'bout you not getting your mayflowers," said Bruce seriously, "'cause I'd see to that. And I told him I would be ten pretty soon now, so it won't be very long before I'll be eighteen and then I'll go to help him fight, and maybe let him come home for a rest while I took his place. I wrote Jerry, too. Jerry's getting better, you know."

"Is he? Have you had any good news about him?"

"Yes. Mother had a letter today, and it said he was out of danger."

"Oh, thank God," murmured Mrs. Blythe, in a half-whisper.

Bruce looked at her curiously.

"That is what father said when mother told him. But when *I* said it the other day when I found out Mr. Mead's dog hadn't hurt my kitten,—I thought he had shooken it to death, you know—father looked awful solemn and said I must never say that again about a kitten. But I couldn't understand why, Mrs. Blythe. I felt *awful* thankful, and it *must* have been God that saved Stripey, because that Mead dog had 'normous jaws and oh, how it shook poor Stripey. And so why couldn't I thank Him? 'Course," added Bruce reminiscently, "maybe I said it *too loud*— 'cause I was awful glad and excited when I found Stripey was all right. I 'most shouted it, Mrs. Blythe. Maybe if I'd said it sort of whispery like you and father it would have been all right. Do you know, Mrs. Blythe,"—Bruce dropped to a "whispery" tone, edging a little nearer to Anne—"what I would like to do to the Kaiser if I could?"

"What would you like to do, laddie?"

"Norman Reese said in school today that he would like to tie the Kaiser to a tree and set cross dogs to worrying him," said Bruce gravely. "And Emily Flagg said she would like to put him in a cage and poke sharp things into him. And they all said things like that. But Mrs. Blythe"—Bruce took a little square paw out of his pocket and put it earnestly on Anne's knee,—"I would like to turn the Kaiser into a good man—a *very* good man—all at once if I could. That is what *I* would do. Don't you think, Mrs. Blythe, *that* would be the very worstest punishment of all?"

"Bless the child," said Susan, "how do you make out that would be any kind of a punishment for that wicked fiend?"

"Don't you see," said Bruce, looking levelly at Susan, out of his blackly-blue eyes, "if he was turned into a good man he would understand how dreadful the things he has done are and he would feel so terrible about it that he would be more unhappy and miserable than he could ever be in any other way. He would feel *just awful*—and he would go on feeling like that *forever*. Yes"—Bruce clenched his hands and nodded his head emphatically, "yes, *I* would make the Kaiser a good man—that is what *I* would do—it would serve him 'zackly right."

CHAPTER XXVI

*S*usan Has a Proposal of Marriage

An aeroplane was flying over Glen St. Mary, like a great bird poised against the western sky,—a sky so clear and of such a pale, silvery yellow, that it gave an impression of a vast, wind-freshened space of freedom. The little group on the Ingleside lawn looked up at it with fascinated eyes, although it was by no means an unusual thing to see an occasional hovering plane that summer. Susan was always intensely excited. Who knew but that it might be Shirley away up there in the clouds, flying over to the Island from Kingsport? But Shirley had gone overseas now, so Susan was not so keenly interested in this particular aeroplane and its pilot. Nevertheless, she looked at it with awe.

"I wonder, Mrs. Dr. dear," she said solemnly, "what the old folks down there in the graveyard would think if they could rise out of their graves for one moment and behold that sight. I am sure my father would disapprove of it, for he was a man who did not believe in new-fangled ideas of any sort. He always cut his grain with a reaping hook to the day of his death. A mower he would not have. What was good enough for *his* father was good enough for *him*, he used to say. I hope it is not unfilial to say that I think he was wrong in that point of view, but I am not sure I go so far as to approve of aero-planes, though they may be a military necessity. If the Almighty had meant us to fly he would have provided us with wings. Since He did not it is plain he meant us to stick to the solid earth. At any rate, you will never see *me*, Mrs. Dr. dear, cavorting through the sky in an aeroplane."

"But you won't refuse to cavort a bit in father's new auto-mobile when it comes, will you, Susan?" teased Rilla.

"I do not expect to trust my old bones in automobiles, either," retorted Susan. "But I do not look upon them as some narrow-minded people do. Whiskers-on-the-moon says the Government should be turned out of office for permitting them to run on the Island at all. He foams at the mouth, they tell me, when he sees one. The other day he saw one coming along that narrow side-road by his wheat field, and Whiskers bounded over the fence and stood right in the middle of the road, with his pitchfork. The man in the machine was an agent of some kind, and Whiskers hates agents as much as he hates automobiles. He made the car come to a halt, because there was not room to pass him on either side, and the agent could not actually run over him. Then he raised his pitchfork and shouted, 'Get out of this with your devil-machine or I will run this pitchfork clean through you.' And Mrs. Dr. dear, if you will believe me, that poor agent had to back his car clean out to the Lowbridge road, nearly a mile, Whiskers following him every step, shaking his pitchfork and bellowing insults. Now, Mrs. Dr. dear, *I* call such conduct unreasonable; but all the same," added Susan, with a sigh, "what with aero-planes and automobiles and all the rest of it, this Island is not what it used to be."

The aeroplane soared and dipped and circled, and soared again, until it became a mere speck far over the sun-set hills.

> "'*With the majesty of pinion*
> *Which the Theban eagles bear,*

Sailing with supreme dominion
Through the azure fields of air,'"

quoted Anne Blythe dreamily.

"I wonder," said Miss Oliver, "if humanity will be any *happier* because of aeroplanes. It seems to me that the *sum* of human happiness remains much the same from age to age, no matter how it may vary in distribution, and that all the 'many inventions' neither lessen nor increase it."

"After all, the 'kingdom of heaven is within you,'" said Mr. Meredith, gazing after the vanishing speck which symbolized man's latest victory in a world-old struggle. "It does not depend on material achievements and triumphs."

"Nevertheless, an aeroplane is a fascinating thing," said the doctor. "It has always been one of humanity's favourite dreams—the dream of flying. Dream after dream comes true—or rather is *made* true by persevering effort. I should like to have a flight in an aeroplane myself."

"Shirley wrote me that he was dreadfully disappointed in his first flight," said Rilla. "He had expected to experience the sensation of soaring up from the earth like a bird—and instead he just had the feeling that he wasn't moving at all, but that the earth was *dropping away* under him. And the first time he went up alone he suddenly felt *terribly homesick*. He had never felt like that before; but all at once, he said, he felt as if he were adrift in *space*—and he had a wild desire to *get back home* to the old planet and the companionship of fellow creatures. He soon got over that feeling, but he says his first flight alone was a nightmare to him because of that dreadful sensation of ghastly loneliness."

The aeroplane disappeared. The doctor threw back his head with a sigh.

"When I have watched one of those bird-men out of sight I come back to earth with an odd feeling of being merely a crawling insect. Anne," he said, turning to his wife, "do you remember the first time I took you for a buggy ride in Avonlea—that night we went to the Carmody concert, the first fall you taught in Avonlea? I had our little black mare with the white star on her forehead, and a shining brand-new buggy,—and I was the proudest fellow in the world, barring none. I suppose our grandson will be taking his sweetheart out quite casually for an evening 'fly' in his aeroplane."

"An aeroplane won't be as nice as little Silverspot was," said Anne. "A machine is simply a machine,—but Silverspot, why she was a personality, Gilbert. A drive behind her had something in it that not even a flight among sunset clouds could have. No, I don't envy my grandson's sweetheart, after all. Mr. Meredith is right. 'The Kingdom of Heaven'—and of love—and of happiness—doesn't depend on externals."

"Besides," said the doctor gravely, "our said grandson will have to give most of his attention to the aeroplane—he won't be able to let the reins lie on its back while he gazes into his lady's eyes. And I have an awful suspicion that you can't run an aeroplane with one arm. No"—the doctor shook his head—"I believe I'd still prefer Silverspot after all."

The Russian line broke again that summer and Susan said bitterly that she had expected it ever since Kerensky had gone and got married.

"Far be it from me to decry the holy state of matrimony, Mrs. Dr. dear, but I felt that when a man was running a revolution he had his hands full and should have postponed marriage until a more fitting season. The Russians are done for this time and there would be no sense in shutting our eyes to the fact. But have you seen Woodrow Wilson's reply to the

Pope's peace proposals? It is magnificent. I really could not have expressed the rights of the matter better myself. I feel that I can forgive Wilson everything for it. He knows the meaning of words and that you may tie to. Speaking of meanings, have you heard the latest story about Whiskers-on-the-moon, Mrs. Dr. dear? It seems he was over at the Lowbridge Road school the other day and took a notion to examine the fourth class in spelling. They have the summer term there yet, you know, with the spring and fall vacations, being rather backward people on that road. My niece, Ella Baker, goes to that school and she it was who told me the story. The teacher was not feeling well, having a dreadful headache, and she went out to get a little fresh air while Mr. Pryor was examining the class. The children got along all right with the spelling but when Whiskers began to question them about the meanings of the words they were all at sea, because they had not learned them. Ella and the other big scholars felt terrible over it. They love their teacher so, and it seems Mr. Pryor's brother, Abel Pryor, who is a trustee of that school, is against her and has been trying to turn the other trustees over to his way of thinking. And Ella and the rest were afraid that if the fourth class couldn't tell Whiskers the meanings of the words he would think the teacher was no good and tell Abel so, and Abel would have a fine handle. But little Sandy Logan saved the situation. He is a Home boy, but he is as smart as a steel trap, and he sized up Whiskers-on-the-moon right off. 'What does "anatomy" mean?' Whiskers demanded. 'A pain in your stomach,' Sandy replied, quick as a flash and never batting an eyelid. Whiskers-on-the-moon is a very ignorant man, Mrs. Dr. dear; he didn't know the meaning of the words himself, and he said 'Very good—very good.' The class caught right on—at least three or four of the brighter ones did—and they kept up the fun. Jean Blane said that 'acoustic' meant 'a religious squabble,' and Muriel Baker said that an agnostic was a man who had indigestion, and Jim Carter said that 'acerbity' meant that you ate nothing but vegetable food, and so on all down the list. Whiskers swallowed it all, and kept saying 'Very good—very good' until Ella thought that die she would trying to keep a straight face. When the teacher came in, Whiskers complimented her on the splendid understanding the children had of their lesson, and said he meant to tell her trustees what a jewel they had. It was 'very unusual' he said, to find a fourth class who could answer up so prompt when it came to explaining what words meant. He went off beaming. But Ella told me this as a great secret, Mrs. Dr. dear, and we must keep it as such, for the sake of the Lowbridge Road teacher. It would likely be the ruin of her chances of keeping the school if Whiskers should ever find out how he had been bamboozled."

Mary Vance came up to Ingleside that same afternoon to tell them that Miller Douglas, who had been wounded when the Canadians took Hill 70, had had to have his leg amputated. The Ingleside folks sympathized with Mary, whose zeal and patriotism had taken some time to kindle but now burned with a glow as steady and bright as any one's.

"Some folks have been twitting me about having a husband with only one leg. But," said Mary, rising to a lofty height, "I would rather have Miller with only one leg than any other man in the world with a dozen—unless," she added as an after-thought, "unless it was Lloyd George. Well, I must be going. I thought you'd be interested in hearing about Miller, so I run up from the store, but I must hustle home for I promised Luke MacAllister I'd help him build his grain stack this evening. It's up to us girls to see that the harvest is got in, since the boys are so scarce. I've got overalls and I can tell you they're real becoming. Mrs. Alec Davis says they're indecent and shouldn't be allowed, and even Mrs. Elliott kinder looks askance at them. But bless you, the world moves, and anyhow there's no fun for me like shocking Kitty Alec."

"By the way, father," said Rilla, "I'm going to take Jack Flagg's place in his father's store for a month. I promised him today that I would, if you didn't object. Then he can help the farmers get the harvest in. I don't think I'd be much use in a harvest field myself—though lots of the girls are—but I can set Jack free while I do his work. Jims isn't much bother in the day-time now, and I'll always be home at night."

"Do you think you'll like weighing out sugar and beans, and trafficking in butter and eggs?" said the doctor, twinkling.

"Probably not. That isn't the question. It's just one way of doing my bit."

So Rilla went behind Mr. Flagg's counter for a month; and Susan went into Albert Crawford's oat fields.

"I am as good as any of them yet," she said proudly. "Not a man of them can beat me when it comes to building a stack. When I offered to help Albert looked doubtful. 'I am afraid the work will be too hard for you,' he said. 'Try me for a day and see,' said I. 'I will do my darnedest.'"

None of the Ingleside folks spoke for just a moment. Their silence meant that they thought Susan's pluck in "working out" quite wonderful. But Susan mistook their meaning and her sunburned face grew red.

"This habit of swearing seems to be growing on me, Mrs. Dr. dear," she said apologetically. "To think that I should be acquiring it at my age! It is such a dreadful example to the young girls. I am of the opinion it comes of reading the news-papers so much. They are so full of profanity and they do not spell it with stars either, as used to be done in my young days. This war is demoralizing everybody."

Susan, standing on a load of grain, her grey hair whipping in the breeze and her skirt kilted up to her knees for safety and convenience—no overalls for Susan, if you please—was neither a beautiful nor a romantic figure; but the spirit that animated her gaunt arms was the self-same one that captured Vimy Ridge and held the German legions back from Verdun.

It is not the least likely, however, that this consideration was the one which appealed most strongly to Mr. Pryor when he drove past one afternoon and saw Susan pitching sheaves gamely.

"Smart woman that," he reflected. "Worth two of many a younger one yet. I might do worse—I might do worse. If Milgrave comes home alive I'll lose Miranda and hired house-keepers cost more than a wife and are liable to leave a man in the lurch any time. I'll think it over."

A week later Mrs. Blythe, coming up from the village late in the afternoon, paused at the gate of Ingleside in an amazement which temporarily bereft her of the power of motion. An extraordinary sight met her eyes. Around the end of the kitchen burst Mr. Pryor, running as stout, pompous Mr. Pryor had not run for years, with terror imprinted on every lineament,—a terror quite justifiable, for behind him, like an avenging fate, came Susan, with a huge, smoking iron pot grasped in her hands, and an expression in her eye that boded ill to the object of her indignation, if she should overtake him. Pursuer and pursued tore across the lawn. Mr. Pryor reached the gate a few feet ahead of Susan, wrenched it open, and fled down the road, without a glance at the transfixed lady of Ingleside.

"Susan," gasped Anne.

Susan halted in her mad career, set down her pot, and shook her fist after Mr. Pryor, who had not ceased to run, evidently believing that Susan was still in full cry after him.

"Susan, *what* does this mean?" demanded Anne, a little severely.

"You may well ask that, Mrs. Dr. dear," Susan replied wrathfully. "I have not been so upset in years. That—that—that *pacifist* has actually had the audacity to come up here and, in my own kitchen, to ask me to *marry him*. HIM!"

Anne choked back a laugh.

"But—Susan! Couldn't you have found a—well, a less spectacular method of refusing him? Think what a gossip this would have made if any one had been going past and had seen such a performance."

"Indeed, Mrs. Dr. dear, you are quite right. I did not think of it because I was quite past thinking rationally. I was just clean mad. Come in the house and I will tell you all about it."

Susan picked up her pot and marched into the kitchen, still trembling with wrathful excitement. She set her pot on the stove with a vicious thud.

"Wait a moment until I open all the windows to air this kitchen well, Mrs. Dr. dear. There, that is better. And I must wash my hands, too, because I shook hands with Whiskers-on-the-moon when he came in—not that I wanted to, but when he stuck out his fat, oily hand I did not know just what else to do at the moment. I had just finished my afternoon cleaning and thanks be, everything was shining and spotless; and thought I 'now that dye is boiling and I will get my rug rags and have them nicely out of the way before supper.' Just then a shadow fell over the floor and looking up I saw Whiskers-on-the-moon, standing in the doorway, dressed up and looking as if he had just been starched and ironed. I shook hands with him, as aforesaid, Mrs. Dr. dear, and told him you and the doctor were both away. But he said,

"'I have come to see *you*, Miss Baker.'

"I was dumbfoundered, for not a notion of his design occurred to me, and what he wanted of me I could not imagine. But I asked him to sit down, for the sake of my own manners, and then I stood there right in the middle of the floor and gazed at him as contemptuously as I could. In spite of his brazen assurance this seemed to rattle him a little; but he began trying to look sentimental at me out of his little piggy eyes, and all at once an awful suspicion flashed into my mind. Something told me, Mrs. Dr. dear, that I was about to receive my first proposal. I have always thought that I would like to have just one offer of marriage to reject, so that I might be able to look other women in the face, but you will not hear me bragging of *this*. I consider it an insult and if I could have thought of any way of preventing it I would. But just then, Mrs. Dr. dear, you will see I was at a disadvantage, being taken so completely by surprise. *Some* men, I am told, consider a little preliminary courting the proper thing before a proposal, if only to give fair warning of their intentions; but Whiskers-on-the-moon probably thought it was any port in a storm for *me* and that I would jump at him. Well, he is undeceived—yes, he is undeceived, Mrs. Dr. dear. I wonder if he has stopped running yet."

"I understand that you don't feel flattered, Susan. But *couldn't* you have refused him a little more delicately than by chasing him off the premises in such a fashion?"

"Well, maybe I might have, Mrs. Dr. dear, and I intended to, but one remark he made aggravated me beyond my powers of endurance. If it had not been for that I would not have chased him with my dye-pot, although of course I would never have dreamed of accepting him. I will tell you the whole interview. Whiskers sat down, as I have said and right beside him on another chair Doc was lying. The animal was pretending to be asleep but I knew very well he was not, for he has been Hyde all day and Hyde never sleeps. By the way, Mrs. Dr. dear, have you noticed that that cat is far oftener Hyde than Jekyll now? The more victories Germany wins the *Hyder* he becomes. I leave you to draw your own conclusions from that. I suppose Whiskers thought he might curry favour with me by praising the creature, little dreaming what my real sentiments towards it were, so he stuck out his pudgy hand and stroked Mr. Hyde's back. 'What a nice cat,' he said. The nice cat flew at him and bit him. Then it gave a fearful yowl, and bounded out of the door. Whiskers looked after it quite amazed. 'That is a queer kind of a varmint,' he said. I agreed with him on that point, but I was not going to let him see it. Besides, what business had he to call *our* cat a varmint? 'It may be a varmint or it may not,' I said, 'but it knows the difference between a Canadian and a Hun.' You would have thought, would you not, Mrs. Dr. dear, that a hint like that would have been enough for him! But it went no deeper than his skin. I saw him settling back quite comfortable, as if for a good talk, and thought I, 'If there is anything coming it may as well come soon and be done with, for with all these rags to dye before supper I have not time to waste in flirting,' so I spoke right out. 'If you have anything particular to discuss with me, Mr. Pryor, I would feel obliged if you would mention it without loss of time, because I am very busy this afternoon.' He fairly beamed at me out of that circle of red whisker, and said, 'You are a business-like woman and I agree with you. There is no use in wasting time beating around the bush. I came up here today to ask you to marry me.' So there it was,

Mrs. Dr. dear. I had a proposal at last, after waiting sixty-four years for one.

"I just glared at that presumptuous creature and I said, 'I would not marry you if you were the last man on earth, Josiah Pryor. So there you have my answer and you can take it away forthwith.' You never saw a man so taken aback as he was, Mrs. Dr. dear. He was so flabbergasted that he just blurted out the truth. 'Why, I thought you'd be only too glad to get a chance to be married,' he said. That was when I lost my head, Mrs. Dr. dear. Do you not think I had a good excuse, when a Hun and a pacifist made such an insulting remark to me? 'Go,' I thundered, and I just caught up that iron pot. I could see that he thought I had suddenly gone insane, and I suppose he considered an iron pot full of boiling dye was a dangerous weapon in the hands of a lunatic. At any rate he went, and stood not upon the order of his going, as you saw for yourself. And I do not think we will see him back here proposing to us again in a hurry. No, I think he has learned that there is at least one single woman in Glen St. Mary who has no hankering to become Mrs. Whiskers-on-the-moon."

CHAPTER XXVII

*W*aiting

"INGLESIDE,
"November 1st, 1917

"It is November—and the Glen is all grey and brown, except where the Lombardy poplars stand up here and there like great golden torches in the sombre landscape, although every other tree has shed its leaves. It has been very hard to keep our courage alight of late. The Caporetto disaster is a dreadful thing and not even Susan can extract much consolation out of the present state of affairs. The rest of us don't try. Gertrude keeps saying desperately, 'They *must* not get Venice—they must *not* get Venice,' as if by saying it often enough she can prevent them. But what is to prevent them from getting Venice I cannot see. Yet, as Susan fails not to point out, there was seemingly nothing to prevent them from getting to Paris in 1914, yet they did not get it, and she affirms they shall not get Venice either. Oh, how I hope and pray they will not—Venice the beautiful Queen of the Adriatic. Although I've never seen it I feel about it just as Byron did—I've always loved it—it has always been to me 'a fairy city of the heart.' Perhaps I caught my love of it from Walter, who worshipped it. It was always one of his dreams to see Venice. I remember we planned once—down in Rainbow Valley one evening just before the war broke out—that some time we would go together to see it and float in a gondola through its moonlit streets.

"Every fall since the war began there has been some terrible blow to our troops,—Antwerp in 1914, Serbia in 1915; last fall, Roumania, and now Italy, the worst of all. I think I would give up in despair if it were not for what Walter said in his dear last letter—that 'the dead as well as the living were fighting on our side and such an army cannot be defeated.' No, it *cannot*. We *will* win in the end. I will not doubt it for one moment. To let myself doubt would be to 'break faith.'

"We have all been campaigning furiously of late for the new Victory Loan. We Junior Reds canvassed diligently and landed several tough old customers who had at first flatly refused to invest. I—even I—tackled Whiskers-on-the-moon. I expected a bad time and a refusal. But to my amazement he was quite agreeable and promised on the spot to take a thousand dollar bond. He may be a pacifist, but he knows a good investment when it is handed out to him. Five and a half per cent. is five and half per cent. even when a militaristic government pays it.

"Father, to tease Susan, says it was her speech at the Victory Loan Campaign meeting that converted Mr. Pryor. I don't think that at all likely, since Mr. Pryor has been publicly very bitter against Susan ever since her quite unmistakable rejection of his lover-like advances. But Susan did make a speech—and the best one made at the meeting, too. It was the first time she ever did such a thing and she vows it will be the last. Everybody in the Glen was at the meeting, and quite a number of speeches were made, but somehow things were a little flat and no especial enthusiasm could be worked up. Susan was quite dismayed at the lack of zeal, because she has been burningly anxious that the Island should go over the top in regard to its quota. She kept whispering viciously to Gertrude and me that there was 'no ginger' in the speeches;

and when nobody went forward to subscribe to the loan at the close Susan 'lost her head.' At least, that is how she describes it herself. She bounded to her feet, her face grim and set under her bonnet—Susan is the only woman in Glen St. Mary who still wears a bonnet—and said sarcastically and loudly, 'No doubt it is much cheaper to *talk* patriotism than it is to *pay* for it. And we are asking *charity*, of course—we are asking you to lend us your money for nothing! No doubt the Kaiser will feel quite downcast when he hears of this meeting!'

"Susan has an unshaken belief that the Kaiser's spies—presumably represented by Mr. Pryor—promptly inform him of every happening in our Glen.

"Norman Douglas shouted out 'Hear! Hear!' and some boy at the back said, 'What about Lloyd George?' in a tone Susan didn't like. Lloyd George is her pet hero, now that Kitchener is gone.

"'I stand behind Lloyd George every time,' retorted Susan.

"'I suppose that will hearten him up greatly,' said Warren Mead, with one of his disagreeable 'haw-haws.'

"Warren's remark was spark to powder. Susan just 'sailed in' as she puts it, and 'said her say.' She said it remarkably well, too. There was no lack of 'ginger' in *her* speech, anyhow. When Susan is warmed up she has no mean powers of oratory, and the way she trimmed those men down was funny and wonderful and effective all at once. She said it was the likes of her, millions of her, that *did* stand behind Lloyd George, and *did* hearten him up. That was the key-note of her speech. Dear old Susan! She is a perfect dynamo of patriotism and loyalty and contempt for slackers of all kinds, and when she let it loose on that audience in her one grand outburst she electrified it. Susan always vows she is no suffragette, but she gave womanhood its due that night, and she literally made those men cringe. When she finished with them they were ready to eat out of her hand. She wound up by ordering them—yes, ordering them—to march up to the platform forthwith and subscribe for Victory Bonds. And after wild applause most of them did it, even Warren Mead. When the total amount subscribed came out in the Charlottetown dailies the next day we found that the Glen led every district on the Island—and certainly Susan has the credit for it. She, herself, after she came home that night was quite ashamed and evidently feared that she had been guilty of conduct unbecoming an unmarried woman: she confessed to mother that she had been 'rather unladylike.'

"We were all—except Susan—out for a trial ride in father's new automobile tonight. A very good one we had, too, though we did get ingloriously ditched at the end, owing to a certain grim old dame—to wit, Miss Elizabeth Carr of the Upper Glen—who *wouldn't* rein her horse out to let us pass, honk as we might. Father was quite furious; but in my heart I believe I sympathized with Miss Elizabeth. If I had been a spinster lady, driving along behind my own old nag, in maiden meditation fancy free, I wouldn't have lifted a rein when an obstreperous car hooted blatantly behind me. I should just have sat up as dourly as she did and said 'Take the ditch if you are determined to pass.'

"We *did* take the ditch—and got up to our axles in sand—and sat foolishly there while Miss Elizabeth clucked up her horse and rattled victoriously away from us.

"Jem will have a laugh when I write him this. He knows Miss Elizabeth of old.

"But—will—Venice—be—saved?"

"November 19, 1917

"It is not saved yet—it is still in great danger. But the Italians are making a stand at last on the Piave line. To be sure military critics say they cannot possibly hold it and must retreat to the Adige. But Susan and Gertrude and I say they *must* hold it, because Venice *must* be saved, so what are the military critics to do?

"Oh, if I could only *believe* that they *can* hold it!

"Our Canadian troops have won another great victory— they have stormed the Passchendaele Ridge and held it in the face of all counter attacks. None of our boys were in the battle—but oh, the casualty list of other people's boys! Joe Milgrave was in it but came through safe. Miranda had some bad days until she got word from him. But it is wonderful how Miranda has bloomed out since her marriage. She isn't the same girl at all. Even her eyes seem to have darkened and deepened—though I suppose that is just because they glow with the greater intensity that has come to her. She makes her father stand round in a perfectly amazing fashion; she runs up the flag whenever a yard of trench on the western front is taken; and she comes up regularly to our Junior Red Cross; and she does—yes, she does—put on funny little 'married woman' airs that are quite killing. But she is the only war bride in the Glen and surely nobody need grudge her the satisfaction she gets out of it.

"The Russian news is bad, too—Kerensky's government has fallen and Lenine is dictator of Russia. Somehow, it is very hard to keep up courage in the dull hopelessness of these grey autumn days of suspense and boding news. But we are beginning to 'get in a low,' as old Highland Sandy says, over the approaching election. Conscription is the real issue at stake and it will be the most exciting election we have ever had. All the women 'who have got de age'—to quote Jo Poirier, and who have husbands, sons and brothers at the front, can vote. Oh, if I were only twenty-one! Gertrude and Susan are both furious because they can't vote.

"'It is not fair,' Gertrude says passionately. 'There is Agnes Carr who can vote because her husband went. She did everything she could to prevent him from going, and now she is going to vote *against* the Union Government. Yet *I* have no vote, because my man at the front is only my sweetheart and not my husband!'

"As for Susan, when she reflects that *she* cannot vote, while a rank old pacifist like Mr. Pryor can—and *will*—her comments are sulphurous.

"I really feel sorry for the Elliotts and Crawfords and MacAllisters over-harbour. They have always lined up in clearly divided camps of Liberal and Conservative, and now they are torn from their moorings—I know I'm mixing my metaphors dreadfully—and set hopelessly adrift. It will kill some of those old Grits to vote for Sir Robert Borden's side—and yet they have to because they believe the time has come when we must have conscription. And some poor Conservatives who are against conscription must vote for Laurier, who always has been anathema to them. Some of them are taking it terribly hard. Others seem to be in much the same attitude as Mrs. Marshall Elliott has come to be regarding Church Union.

"She was up here last night. She doesn't come as often as she used to. She is growing too old to walk this far—dear old 'Miss Cornelia.' I hate to think of her growing old—we have always loved her so and she has always been so good to us Ingleside young fry.

"She used to be so bitterly opposed to Church Union. But last night, when father told her it was practically decided, she said in a resigned tone,

"'Well, in a world where everything is being rent and torn what matters one more rending and tearing? Anyhow, compared with Germans even Methodists seem attractive to me.'

"Our Junior R.C. goes on quite smoothly, in spite of the fact that Irene has come back to it—having fallen out with the Lowbridge society, I understand. She gave me a sweet little jab last meeting—about knowing me across the square in Charlottetown 'by my green velvet hat.' Everybody *does* know me by that detestable and detested hat. This will be my fourth season for it. Even mother wanted me to get a new one this fall; but I said, 'no.' As long as the war lasts so long do I wear that velvet hat in winter."

"November 23, 1917

"The Piave line still holds—and General Byng has won a splendid victory at Cambrai. I *did* run up the flag for that—but Susan only said 'I shall set a kettle of water on the kitchen range tonight. I notice little Kitchener always has an attack of croup after any British victory. I do hope he has no pro-German blood in his veins. Nobody knows much about his father's people.'

"Jims has had a few attacks of croup this fall—just the ordinary croup—not that terrible thing he had last year. But whatever blood runs in his little veins it is good, healthy blood. He is rosy and plump and curly and cute; and he says such funny things and asks such comical questions. He likes very much to sit in a special chair in the kitchen; but that is

Susan's favourite chair, too, and when she wants it, out Jims must go. The last time she put him out of it he turned around and asked solemnly, 'When you are dead, Susan, can I sit in that chair?' Susan thought it quite dreadful, and I think that was when she began to feel anxiety about his possible ancestry. The other night I took Jims with me for a walk down to the store. It was the first time he had ever been out so late at night, and when he saw the stars he exclaimed, 'Oh, Willa, see the big moon and *all the little moons*!' And last Wednesday morning, when he woke up, my little alarm clock had stopped because I had forgotten to wind it up. Jims bounded out of his crib and ran across to me, his face quite aghast above his little blue flannel pajamas. 'The clock is dead,' he gasped, 'oh Willa, the clock is dead.'

"One night he was quite angry with both Susan and me because we would not give him something he wanted very much. When he said his prayers he plumped down wrathfully, and when he came to the petition 'Make me a good boy' he tacked on emphatically, 'and please make Willa and Susan good, 'cause they're *not.*'

"I don't go about quoting Jims' speeches to all I meet. That always bores me when other people do it! I just enshrine them in this old hotch-potch of a journal!

"This very evening as I put Jims to bed he looked up and asked me gravely, 'Why can't yesterday come back, Willa?'

"Oh, why can't it, Jims? That beautiful 'yesterday' of dreams and laughter—when our boys were home—when Walter and I read and rambled and watched new moons and sunsets together in Rainbow Valley. If it could just come back! But the yesterdays never come back, little Jims—and the todays are dark with clouds—and we dare not think about the tomorrows."

"December 11th, 1917

"Wonderful news came today. The British troops captured Jerusalem yesterday. We ran up the flag and some of Gertrude's old sparkle came back to her for a moment. "'After all,' she said, 'it is worth while to live in the days which see the object of the Crusades attained. The ghosts of all the old Crusaders must have crowded the walls of Jerusalem last night, with Coeur-de-lion at their head.'

"Susan had cause for satisfaction also.

"'I am so thankful I can pronounce Jerusalem and Hebron,' she said. 'They give me a real comfortable feeling after Przemysl and Brest-Litovsk! Well, we have got the Turks on the run, at least, and Venice is safe and Lord Lansdowne is not to be taken seriously; and I see no reason why we should be downhearted.'

"Jerusalem! The 'meteor flag of England' floats over you—the Crescent is gone. How Walter would have thrilled over that!"

"December 18th, 1917

"Yesterday the election came off. In the evening mother and Susan and Gertrude and I foregathered in the living room and waited in breathless suspense, father having gone down to the village. We had no way of hearing the news, for Carter Flagg's store is not on our line, and when we tried to get it Central always answered that the line 'was busy'—as no doubt it was, for everybody for miles around was trying to get Carter's store for the same reason we were.

"About ten o'clock Gertrude went to the 'phone and happened to catch some one from over-harbour talking to

Carter Flagg. Gertrude shamelessly listened in and got for her comforting what eaves-droppers are proverbially supposed to get—to wit, unpleasant hearing; the Union government had 'done nothing' in the West.

"We looked at each other in dismay. If the Government had failed to carry the West, it was defeated.

"'Canada is disgraced in the eyes of the world,' said Gertrude bitterly.

"'If everybody was like the Mark Crawfords over-harbour this would not have happened,' groaned Susan. 'They locked their Uncle up in the barn this morning and would not let him out until he promised to vote Union. That is what I call effective argument, Mrs. Dr. dear.'

"Gertrude and I couldn't rest at all after that. We walked the floor until our legs gave out and we had to sit down perforce. Mother knitted away as steadily as clockwork and pretended to be calm and serene—pretended so well that we were all deceived and envious until next day, when I caught her raveling out four inches of her sock. She had knit that far past where the heel should have begun!

"It was twelve before father came home. He stood in the doorway and looked at us and we looked at him. We did not dare ask him what the news was. Then he said that it was Laurier who had 'done nothing' in the West, and that the Union Government was in with a big majority. Gertrude clapped her hands. I wanted to laugh and cry, mother's eyes flashed with their old-time starriness and Susan emitted a queer sound between a gasp and a whoop.

"'This will not comfort the Kaiser much,' she said.

"Then we went to bed, but were too excited to sleep. Really, as Susan said solemnly this morning, 'Mrs. Dr. dear, I think politics are too strenuous for women.'"

"December 31st, 1917

"Our fourth War Christmas is over. We are trying to gather up some courage wherewith to face another year of it. Germany has, for the most part, been victorious all summer. And now they say she has all her troops from the Russian front ready for a 'big push' in the spring. Sometimes it seems to me that we just cannot live through the winter waiting for *that*.

"I had a great batch of letters from overseas this week. Shirley is at the front now, too, and writes about it all as coolly and matter-of-factly as he used to write of football at Queen's. Carl wrote that it had been raining for weeks and that nights in the trenches always make him think of the night of long ago when he did penance in the graveyard for running away from Henry Warren's ghost. Carl's letters are always full of jokes and bits of fun. They had a great rat-hunt the night before he wrote—spearing rats with their bayonets—and he got the best bag and won the prize. He has a tame rat that knows him and sleeps in his pocket at night. Rats don't worry Carl as they do some people—he was always chummy with all little beasts. He says he is making a study of the habits of the trench rat and means to write a treatise on it some day that will make him famous.

"Ken wrote a short letter. His letters are all rather short now—and he doesn't *often* slip in those dear little sudden sentences I love so much. Sometimes I think he has forgotten all about the night he was here to say good-bye—and then there will be just a line or a word that makes me think he remembers and always will remember. For instance today's letter hadn't a thing in it that mightn't have been written to any girl, except that he signed himself 'Your Kenneth,' instead of 'Yours, Kenneth,' as he usually does. Now, *did* he leave that 's' off intentionally or was it only carelessness? I shall lie awake half the night wondering. He is a captain now. I am glad and proud—and yet 'Captain Ford' sounds so horribly far away and high up. 'Ken' and 'Captain Ford' seem like two different persons. I *may* be practically engaged to Ken—mother's opinion on that point is my stay and bulwark—but I *can't* be to 'Captain Ford'!

"And Jem is a lieutenant now—won his promotion on the field. He sent me a snapshot, taken in his new uniform. He looked thin and old—*old*—my boy-brother Jem. I can't forget mother's face when I showed it to her. '*That*—my Little Jem,—the baby of the old House of Dreams?' was all she said.

"There was a letter from Faith, too. She is doing V.A.D. work in England and writes hopefully and brightly. I think she is almost happy—she saw Jem on his last leave and she is so near him she could go to him, if he were wounded. That means so much to her. Oh, if I were only with her! But my work is here at home. I know Walter wouldn't have wanted me to leave mother and in everything I try to 'keep faith' with him, even to the little details of daily life. Walter died for Canada—I must live for her. That is what he asked me to do."

"January 28th, 1918

"'I shall anchor my storm-tossed soul to the British fleet and make a batch of bran biscuits,' said Susan today to Cousin Sophia, who had come in with some weird tale of a new and all-conquering submarine, just launched by Germany. But Susan is a somewhat disgruntled woman at present, owing to the regulations regarding cookery. Her loyalty to the Union Government is being sorely tried. It surmounted the first strain gallantly. When the order about flour came Susan said, quite cheerfully,

"'I am an old dog to be learning new tricks, but I shall learn to make war bread if it will help defeat the Huns.'

"But the later suggestions went against Susan's grain. Had it not been for father's decree I think she would have snapped her fingers at Sir Robert Borden.

"'Talk about trying to make bricks without straw, Mrs. Dr. dear! How am I to make a cake without butter or sugar? It cannot be done—not cake that *is* cake. Of course one can make a *slab*, Mrs. Dr. dear. And we cannot even camooflash it with a little icing! To think that I should have lived to see the day when a government at Ottawa should step into *my* kitchen and put me on rations!'

"Susan would give the last drop of her blood for her 'king and country,' but to surrender her beloved recipes is a very different and much more serious matter.

"I had letters from Nan and Di too—or rather notes. They are too busy to write letters, for exams are looming up. They will graduate in Arts this spring. I am evidently to be the dunce of the family. But somehow I never had any hankering for a college course, and even now it doesn't appeal to me. I'm afraid I'm rather devoid of ambition. There is only *one thing* I really want to be—and I don't know if I'll ever be it or not. If not—I don't want to be *anything*. But I shan't write it down. It is all right to think it; but, as Cousin Sophia would say, it might be brazen to write it down.

"I *will* write it down. I won't be cowed by the conventions and Cousin Sophia! I want to be Kenneth Ford's wife! There, now!

"I've just looked in the glass, and I hadn't the sign of a blush on my face. I suppose I'm not a properly constructed damsel at all.

"I was down to see Little Dog Monday today. He has grown quite stiff and rheumatic but there he sat, waiting for the train. He thumped his tail and looked pleadingly into my eyes. 'When will Jem come?' he seemed to say. Oh, Dog Monday, there is no answer to that question; and there is, as yet, no answer to the other which we are all constantly asking, 'What will happen when Germany strikes again on the western front—her one great, last blow for victory!'"

"March 1st, 1918

"'What will spring bring?' Gertrude said today. 'I dread it as I never dreaded spring before. Do you suppose there will *ever* again come a time when life will be free from fear? For almost four years we have lain down with fear and risen up with it. It has been the unbidden guest at every meal, the unwelcome companion at every gathering.'

"'Hindenburg says he will be in Paris on April first,' sighed Cousin Sophia.

"'Hindenburg!' There is no power in pen and ink to express the contempt which Susan infused into that name. 'Has he forgotten what day the first of April is?'

"'Hindenburg has kept his word hitherto,' said Gertrude, as gloomily as Cousin Sophia herself could have said it.

"'Yes, fighting against Russians and Roumanians,' retorted Susan. 'Wait you till he comes up against the British and French, not to speak of the Yankees, who are getting there as fast as they can and will no doubt give a good account of themselves.'

"'You said just the same thing before Mons, Susan,' I reminded her.

"'Hindenburg says he will spend a million lives to break the Allied front,' said Gertrude. 'At such a price he *must* purchase some successes and how can we live through *them*, even if he is baffled in the end. These past two months when we have been crouching and waiting for the blow to fall have seemed as long as all the preceding months of the war put together. I work all day feverishly and waken at three o'clock at night to wonder if the iron legions have struck at last. I wish there was no such hour as three o'clock at night. It is then I see Hindenburg in Paris and Germany triumphant. I never see her so at any other time than that accursed hour.'

"Susan looked dubious over Gertrude's adjective, but evidently concluded that the 'a' saved the situation.

"'I wish it were possible to take some magic draught and go to sleep for the next three months—and then waken to find Armageddon over,' said mother, almost impatiently.

"It is not often that mother slumps into a wish like that—or at least the verbal expression of it. Mother has changed a great deal since that terrible day in September when we knew that Walter would not come back; but she has always been brave and patient. Now it just seemed as if even she had reached the limit of her endurance.

"Susan went over to mother and touched her shoulder.

"'Do not you be frightened or downhearted, Mrs. Dr. dear,' she said gently. 'I felt somewhat that way myself last night, and I rose from my bed and lighted my lamp and opened my Bible; and what do you think was the first verse my eyes lighted upon? It was 'And they shall fight against thee but they shall not prevail against thee, for I am with thee, saith the Lord of Hosts, to deliver thee.' I am not gifted in the way of dreaming, as Miss Oliver is, but I knew then and there, Mrs. Dr. dear, that it was a manifest leading, and that Hindenburg will never see Paris. So I read no further but went back to my bed, and I did not waken at three o'clock or any other hour before morning.'

"I say that verse Susan read over and over again to myself. The Lord of Hosts *is* with us—and the spirits of all just men made perfect—and even the legions and guns that Germany is massing on the western front *must* break against such a barrier. This is in certain uplifted moments; but when other moments come I feel, like Gertrude, that I *cannot* endure any longer this awful and ominous hush before the coming storm."

"March 23rd, 1918

"Armageddon has begun!—'the last great fight of all!' Is it, I wonder? Yesterday I went down to the Post Office for the mail. It was a dull, bitter day. The snow was gone but the grey, lifeless ground was frozen hard and a biting wind was blowing. The whole Glen landscape was ugly and hopeless.

"Then I got the paper with its big black headlines. Germany struck on the twenty-first. She makes big claims of guns and prisoners taken. General Haig reports that 'severe fighting continues.' I don't like the sound of that last expression.

"We all find we cannot do any work that requires concentration of thought. So we all knit furiously, because we can do that mechanically. At least the dreadful waiting is over—the horrible wondering where and when the blow will fall. It *has* fallen—but they shall not prevail against us!

"Oh, what is happening on the western front tonight as I write this, sitting here in my room with my journal before me? Jims is asleep in his crib and the wind is wailing around the window; over my desk hangs Walter's picture, looking at me with his beautiful deep eyes; the Mona Lisa he gave me the last Christmas he was home hangs on one side of it, and on the other a framed copy of 'The Piper.' It seems to me that I can *hear* Walter's voice repeating it—that little poem into which he put his soul, and which will therefore live forever, carrying Walter's name on through the future of our land. Everything about me is calm and peaceful and 'homey.' Walter seems very near me—if I could just sweep aside the thin wavering little veil that hangs between, I could *see* him—just as *he* saw the Pied Piper the night before Courcelette.

"Over there in France tonight—*does the line hold?*"

CHAPTER XXVIII

$\mathcal{B}$lack Sunday

In March of the year of grace 1918 there was one week into which must have crowded more of searing human agony than any seven days had ever held before in the history of the world. And in that week there was one day when all humanity seemed nailed to the cross; on that day the whole planet must have been agroan with universal convulsion; everywhere the hearts of men were failing them for fear.

It dawned calmly and coldly and greyly at Ingleside. Mrs. Blythe and Rilla and Miss Oliver made ready for church in a suspense tempered by hope and confidence. The doctor was away, having been summoned during the wee sma's to the Marwood household in the Upper Glen, where a little war bride was fighting gallantly on her own battle-ground to give life, not death, to the world. Susan announced that she meant to stay home that morning—a rare decision for Susan.

"But I would rather not go to church this morning, Mrs. Dr. dear," she explained. "If Whiskers-on-the-moon were there and I saw him looking holy and pleased, as he always looks when he thinks the Huns are winning, I fear I would lose my patience and my sense of decorum and hurl a Bible or hymn-book at him, thereby disgracing myself and the sacred edifice. No, Mrs. Dr. dear, I shall stay home from church till the tide turns and pray hard here."

"I think I might as well stay home, too, for all the good church will do me today," Miss Oliver said to Rilla, as they walked down the hard-frozen red road to the church. "I can think of *nothing* but the question, 'Does the line still hold?'"

"Next Sunday will be Easter," said Rilla. "Will it herald death or life to our cause?"

Mr. Meredith preached that morning from the text, "He that endureth to the end shall be saved," and hope and confidence rang through his inspiring sentences. Rilla, looking up at the memorial tablet on the wall above their pew, "sacred to the memory of Walter Cuthbert Blythe," felt herself lifted out of her dread and filled anew with courage. Walter could not have laid down his life for naught. His had been the gift of prophetic vision and he had foreseen victory. She would cling to that belief—the line *would* hold.

In this renewed mood she walked home from church almost gaily. The others, too, were hopeful, and all went smiling into Ingleside. There was no one in the living room, save Jims, who had fallen asleep on the sofa, and Doc, who sat "hushed in grim repose" on the hearth-rug, looking very Hydeish indeed. No one was in the dining room either,—and, stranger still, no dinner was on the table, which was not even set. Where was Susan?

"Can she have been taken ill?" exclaimed Mrs. Blythe anxiously. "I thought it strange that she did not want to go to church this morning."

The kitchen door opened and Susan appeared on the threshold with such a ghastly face that Mrs. Blythe cried out in sudden panic,

"Susan, what is it?"

"The British line is broken and the German shells are falling on Paris," said Susan dully.

The three women stared at each other, stricken.

"It's not true—it's *not*," gasped Rilla.

"The thing would be—ridiculous," said Gertrude Oliver—and then she laughed horribly.

"Susan, who told you this—when did the news come?" asked Mrs. Blythe.

"I got it over the long-distance 'phone from Charlotte-town half an hour ago," said Susan. "The news came to town late last night. It was Dr. Holland 'phoned it out and he said it was only too true. Since then I have done nothing, Mrs. Dr. dear. I am very sorry dinner is not ready. It is the first time I have been so remiss. If you will be patient I will soon have something for you to eat. But I am afraid I let the potatoes burn."

"Dinner! Nobody wants any dinner, Susan," said Mrs. Blythe wildly. "Oh, this thing is unbelievable—it must be a nightmare."

"Paris is lost—France is lost—the war is lost," gasped Rilla, amid the utter ruins of hope and confidence and belief.

"Oh God—oh God," moaned Gertrude Oliver, walking about the room and wringing her hands. "Oh—God!"

Nothing else—no other words—nothing but that age-old plea—the old, old cry of supreme agony and appeal, from the human heart whose every human staff has failed it.

"Is God dead?" asked a startled little voice from the doorway of the living room. Jims stood there, flushed from sleep, his big brown eyes filled with dread. "Oh, Willa—oh, Willa, is God dead?"

Miss Oliver stopped walking and exclaiming, and stared at Jims, in whose eyes tears of fright were beginning to gather. Rilla ran to his comforting, while Susan bounded up from the chair upon which she had dropped.

"No," she said briskly, with a sudden return of her real self. "No, God isn't dead—nor Lloyd George either. We were forgetting that, Mrs. Dr. dear. Don't cry, little Kitchener. Bad as things are, they might be worse. The British line may be broken but the British navy is not. Let us tie to that. I will take a brace and get up a bite to eat, for strength we must have."

They made a pretence of eating Susan's "bite," but it was only a pretence. Nobody at Ingleside ever forgot that black afternoon. Gertrude Oliver walked the floor—they all walked the floor; except Susan, who got out her grey war sock.

"Mrs. Dr. dear, I *must* knit on Sunday at last. I have never dreamed of doing it before for, say what might be said, I have considered it was a violation of the third commandment. But whether it is or whether it is not I must knit today or I shall go mad."

"Knit if you can, Susan," said Mrs. Blythe restlessly. "I would knit if I could—but I cannot—I cannot."

"If we could only get fuller information," moaned Rilla. "There might be something to encourage us—if we knew all."

"We know that the Germans are shelling Paris," said Miss Oliver bitterly. "In that case they must have smashed through everywhere and be at the very gates. No, we have lost—let us face the fact as other peoples in the past have had to face it. Other nations with right on their side have given their best and bravest—and gone down to defeat in spite of it. Ours is

'but one more
To baffled millions who have gone before.'"

"I won't give up like that," cried Rilla, her pale face suddenly flushing. "I won't despair. We are not conquered— no, if Germany overruns all France we are not conquered. I am ashamed of myself for this hour of despair. You won't see me slump again like that. I'm going to ring up town at once and ask for particulars."

But town could not be got. The long-distance operator there was submerged by similar calls from every part of the distracted country. Rilla finally gave up and slipped away to Rainbow Valley. There she knelt down on the withered grey grasses in the little nook where she and Walter had had their last talk together, with her head bowed against the mossy trunk of a fallen tree. The sun had broken through the black clouds and drenched the valley with a pale golden splendour. The bells on the Tree Lovers twinkled elfinly and fitfully in the gusty March wind.

"Oh God, give me strength," Rilla whispered. "Just strength—and courage." Then like a child, she clasped her hands together and said, as simply as Jims could have done, "*Please* send us better news tomorrow."

She knelt there a long time, and when she went back to Ingleside she was calm and resolute. The doctor had arrived home, tired but triumphant, little Douglas Haig Marwood having made a safe landing on the shores of time. Gertrude was still pacing restlessly but Mrs. Blythe and Susan had reacted from the shock, and Susan was already planning a new line of defence for the channel ports.

"As long as we can hold *them*," she declared, "the situation is saved. Paris has really no military significance."

"Don't," cried Gertrude sharply, as if Susan had run something into her. She thought the old worn phrase, 'no military significance' nothing short of ghastly mockery under the circumstances, and more terrible to endure than the voice of despair would have been.

"I heard up at Marwood's of the line being broken," said the doctor, "but this story of the Germans shelling Paris seems to be rather incredible. Even if they broke through they were fifty miles from Paris at the nearest point and how could they get their artillery close enough to shell it in so short a time? Depend upon it, girls, that part of the message can't be true. I'm going to try a long-distance call to town myself."

The doctor was no more successful than Rilla had been, but his point of view cheered them all a little, and helped them through the evening. And at nine o'clock a long-distance message came through at last, that helped them through the night.

"The line broke only in one place, before St. Quentin," said the doctor, as he hung up the receiver, "and the British troops are retreating in good order. That's not so bad. And as for the shells that are falling on Paris, they are coming from a distance of seventy miles—from some amazing long-range gun the Germans have invented and sprung with the opening of the offensive. That is all the news to date, and Dr. Holland says it is reliable."

"It would have been dreadful news yesterday," said Gertrude, "but compared to what we heard this morning it is almost like good news. But still," she added, trying to smile, "I am afraid I will not sleep much tonight."

"There is one thing to be thankful for at any rate, Miss Oliver, dear," said Susan, "and that is that Cousin Sophia did not come in today. I really could not have endured *her* on top of all the rest."

CHAPTER XXIX

"Wounded and Missing"

"Battered but not broken," was the headline in Monday's paper, and Susan repeated it over and over to herself as she went about her work. The gap caused by the St. Quentin disaster had been patched up in time, but the Allied line was being pushed relentlessly back from the territory they had purchased in 1917 with half a million lives. On Wednesday the headline was "British and French check Germans"; but still the retreat went on. Back—and back—and back! Where would it end? Would the line break again—this time disastrously?

On Saturday the headline was "Even Berlin Admits Offensive Checked," and for the first time in that terrible week the Ingleside folks dared to draw a long breath.

"Well, we have got one week over—now for the next," said Susan staunchly.

"I feel like a prisoner on the rack when they stopped turning it," Miss Oliver said to Rilla, as they went to church on Easter Morning. "But I am not off the rack. The torture may begin again at any time."

"I doubted God last Sunday," said Rilla, "but I don't doubt Him today. Evil cannot win. Spirit is on our side and it is bound to outlast flesh."

Nevertheless her faith was often tried in the dark spring that followed. Armageddon was not, as they had hoped, a matter of a few days. It stretched out into weeks and months. Again and again Hindenburg struck his savage, sudden blows, with alarming, though futile success. Again and again the military critics declared the situation extremely perilous. Again and again Cousin Sophia agreed with the military critics.

"If the Allies go back three miles more the war is lost," she wailed.

"Is the British navy anchored in those three miles?" demanded Susan scornfully.

"It is the opinion of a man who knows all about it," said Cousin Sophia solemnly.

"There is no such person," retorted Susan. "As for the military critics, they do not know one blessed thing about it, any more than you or I. They have been mistaken times out of number. Why do you always look on the dark side, Sophia Crawford?"

"Because there ain't any bright side, Susan Baker."

"Oh, is there not? It is the twentieth of April, and Hindy is not in Paris yet, although he said he would be there by April first. Is that not a bright spot at least?"

"It is my opinion that the Germans will be in Paris before very long and more than that, Susan Baker, they will be in Canada."

"Not in this part of it. The Huns shall never set foot in Prince Edward Island as long as I can handle a pitchfork," declared Susan, looking and feeling quite equal to routing the entire German army single-handed. "No, Sophia Crawford, to tell you the plain truth I am sick and tired of your gloomy predictions. I do not deny that some mistakes have been made. The Germans would never have got back Passchendaele if the Canadians had been left there; and it was bad business trusting to those Portuguese at the Lys River. But that is no reason why you or any one should go about proclaiming the war is lost. I do not want to quarrel with you, least of all at such a time as this, but our morale must be kept up, and I am going to speak my mind out plainly and tell you that if you cannot keep from such croaking your room is better than your company."

Cousin Sophia marched home in high dudgeon to digest her affront, and did not reappear in Susan's kitchen for many weeks. Perhaps it was just as well, for they were hard weeks, when the Germans continued to strike, now here, now there, and seemingly vital points fell to them at every blow. And one day in early May, when wind and sunshine frolicked in Rainbow Valley and the maple grove was golden-green and the harbour all blue and dimpled and white-capped, the news came about Jem.

There had been a trench raid on the Canadian front—a little trench raid so insignificant that it was never even mentioned in the dispatches and when it was over Lieutenant James Blythe was reported "wounded and missing."

"I think this is even worse than news of his death would have been," moaned Rilla through her white lips, that night.

"No—no—'missing' leaves a little hope, Rilla," urged Gertrude Oliver.

"Yes—torturing, agonized hope that keeps you from ever becoming quite resigned to the worst," said Rilla. "Oh, Miss Oliver—must we go for weeks and months,—not knowing whether Jem is alive or dead? Perhaps we will never know. I—I *cannot* bear it—I *cannot*. Walter—and now Jem. This will kill mother,—look at her face, Miss Oliver, and you will see that. And Faith—poor Faith—how can she bear it?"

Gertrude shivered with pain. She looked up at the pictures hanging over Rilla's desk and felt a sudden hatred of Mona Lisa's endless smile.

"Will not even this blot it off your face?" she thought savagely.

But she said gently,

"No, it won't kill your mother. She's made of finer mettle than that. Besides, she refuses to believe Jem is dead; she will cling to hope and we must all do that. Faith, you may be sure, will do it."

"I cannot," moaned Rilla. "Jem was wounded,—what chance would he have? Even if the Germans found him—we know how they have treated wounded prisoners. I wish I *could* hope, Miss Oliver—it would help, I suppose. But hope seems dead in me. I can't hope without some *reason* for it—and there is no reason."

When Miss Oliver had gone to her own room and Rilla was lying on her bed in the moonlight, praying desperately for a little strength, Susan stepped in like a gaunt shadow and sat down beside her.

"Rilla, dear, do not you worry. Little Jem is *not* dead."

"Oh, how can you believe that, Susan?"

"Because I *know*. Listen you to me. When that word came this morning the first thing I thought of was Dog Monday. And tonight, as soon as I got the supper dishes washed and the bread set, I went right down to the station. There was Dog Monday, waiting for the night train, just as patient as usual. Now, Rilla dear, that trench raid was four days ago—last Monday—and I said to the station agent, 'Can you tell me if that dog howled or made any kind of a fuss last Monday night?' He thought it over a bit, and then he said, 'No, he did not.' 'Are you sure?' I said. 'There's more depends on it than you think!' 'Dead sure,' he said. 'I was up all night last Monday night because my mare was sick, and there was never a sound out of him. I would have heard it if there had been, for the stable door was open all the time and his kennel is right across from it!' Now, Rilla dear, those were the man's very words. And you know how that poor little dog howled all night after the battle of Courcelette. Yet he did not love Walter as much as he loved Jem. If he mourned for Walter like that, do you suppose he would sleep sound in his kennel the night after Jem had been killed? No, Rilla dear, Little Jem is *not* dead, and that you may tie to. If he were, Dog Monday would have known, just as he knew before, and he would not be still waiting for the trains."

It was absurd—and irrational—and impossible. But Rilla believed it, for all that; and Mrs. Blythe believed it; and the doctor, though he smiled faintly in pretended derision, felt an odd confidence replace his first despair; and foolish and absurd or not, they all plucked up heart and courage to carry on, just because a faithful little dog at the Glen station was still watching with unbroken faith for his master to come home. Common sense might scorn—incredulity might mutter "Mere superstition"—but in their hearts the folk of Ingleside stood by their belief that Dog Monday knew.

CHAPTER XXX

The Turning of the Tide

Susan was very sorrowful when she saw the beautiful old lawn of Ingleside ploughed up that spring and planted with potatoes. Yet she made no protest, even when her beloved peony bed was sacrificed. But when the Government passed the Daylight Saving law Susan balked. There was a Higher Power than the Union Government, to which Susan owed allegiance.

"Do you think it right to meddle with the arrangements of the Almighty?" she demanded indignantly of the doctor. The doctor, quite unmoved, responded that the law must be observed, and the Ingleside clocks were moved on accordingly. But the doctor had no power over Susan's little alarm.

"I bought that with my own money, Mrs. Dr. dear," she said firmly, "and it shall go on God's time and not Borden's time."

Susan got up and went to bed by "God's time," and regulated her own goings and comings by it. She served the meals, under protest, by Borden's time, and she had to go to church by it, which was the crowning injury. But she said her prayers by her own clock, and fed the hens by it; so that there was always a furtive triumph in her eye when she looked at the doctor. She had got the better of him by so much at least.

"Whiskers-on-the-moon is very much delighted with this daylight saving business," she told him one evening. "Of course he naturally would be, since I understand that the Germans invented it. I hear he came near losing his entire wheat crop lately. Warren Mead's cows broke into the field one day last week—it was the very day the Germans captured the Chemang-de-dam, which may have been a coincidence or may not—and were making fine havoc of it when Mrs. Dick Clow happened to see them from her attic window. At first she had no intention of letting Mr. Pryor know. She told me she just *gloated* over the sight of those cows pasturing on his wheat. She felt it served him exactly right. But presently she reflected that the wheat crop was a matter of great importance and that 'save and serve' meant that those cows must be routed out as much as it meant anything. So she went down and 'phoned over to Whiskers about the matter. All the thanks she got was that he said something queer right out to her. She is not prepared to state that it was actually swearing, for you cannot be sure just what you hear over the 'phone; but she has her own opinion, and so have I, but I will not express it for here comes Mr. Meredith, and Whiskers is one of his elders, so we must be discreet."

"Are you looking for the new star?" asked Mr. Meredith, joining Miss Oliver and Rilla, who were standing among the blossoming potatoes gazing skyward.

"Yes—we have found it—see, it is just above the tip of that tallest old pine."

"It's wonderful to be looking at something that happened three thousand years ago, isn't it?" said Rilla. "That is when astronomers think the collision took place which produced this new star. It makes me feel horribly insignificant," she added under her breath.

"Even this event cannot dwarf into what may be the proper perspective in star systems the fact that the Germans are again only one leap from Paris," said Gertrude restlessly.

"I think I would like to have been an astronomer," said Mr. Meredith dreamily, gazing at the star.

"There must be a strange pleasure in it," agreed Miss Oliver, "an *unearthly* pleasure, in more senses than one. I would like to have a few astronomers for my friends."

"Fancy talking the gossip of the hosts of heaven," laughed Rilla.

"I wonder if astronomers feel a very deep interest in earthly affairs?" said the doctor. "Perhaps students of the canals of Mars would not be so keenly sensitive to the significance of a few yards of trenches lost or won on the western front."

"I have read somewhere," said Mr. Meredith, "that Ernest Renan wrote one of his books during the siege of Paris in 1870 and 'enjoyed the writing of it very much.' I suppose one would call him a philosopher."

"I have read also," said Miss Oliver, "that shortly before his death he said that his only regret in dying was that he must die before he had seen what that 'extremely interesting young man, the German Emperor,' would do in his life. If Ernest Renan 'walked' today and saw what that interesting young man had done to his beloved France, not to speak of the world, I wonder if his mental detachment would be as complete as it was in 1870."

"I wonder where Jem is tonight," thought Rilla, in a sudden bitter inrush of remembrance.

It was over a month since the news had come about Jem. Nothing had been discovered concerning him, in spite of all efforts. Two or three letters had come from him, written before the trench raid, and since then there had been only unbroken silence. Now the Germans were again at the Marne, pressing nearer and nearer Paris; now rumours were coming of another Austrian offensive against the Piave line. Rilla turned away from the new star, sick at heart. It was one of the moments when hope and courage failed her utterly,—when it seemed impossible to go on even one more day. If only they *knew* what had happened to Jem—you can face anything you *know*. But a beleaguerment of fear and doubt and suspense is a hard thing for the morale. Surely, if Jem were alive, some word would have come through. He *must* be dead. Only—they would never know—they could never be quite sure; and Dog Monday would wait for the train until he died of old age. Monday was only a poor, faithful, rheumatic little dog, who knew nothing more of his master's fate than they did.

Rilla had a "white night" and did not fall asleep until late. When she wakened Gertrude Oliver was sitting at her window leaning out to meet the silver mystery of the dawn. Her clever, striking profile, with the masses of black hair behind it, came out clearly against the pallid gold of the eastern sky. Rilla remembered Jem's admiration of the curve of Miss Oliver's brow and chin, and she shuddered. Everything that reminded her of Jem was beginning to give intolerable pain. Walter's death had inflicted on her heart a terrible wound. But it had been a clean wound and had healed slowly, as such wounds do, though the scar must remain forever. But the torture of Jem's disappearance was another thing: there was a poison in it that kept it from healing. The alternations of hope and despair, the endless watching each day for the letter that never came—that might never come—the newspaper tales of ill-usage of prisoners—the bitter wonder as to Jem's wound—all were increasingly hard to bear.

Gertrude Oliver turned her head. There was an odd brilliancy in her eyes.

"Rilla, I've had another dream."

"Oh, no—no," cried Rilla, shrinking. Miss Oliver's dreams had always foretold coming disaster.

"Rilla, it was a good dream. Listen—I dreamed just as I did four years ago, that I stood on the veranda steps and looked down the Glen. And it was still covered by waves that lapped about my feet. But as I looked the waves began to ebb—and they ebbed as swiftly as, four years ago, they rolled in—ebbed out and out, to the gulf; and the Glen lay before me, beautiful and green, with a rainbow spanning Rainbow Valley—a rainbow of such splendid colour that it dazzled me—and I woke. Rilla—Rilla Blythe—the tide has turned."

"I wish I could believe it," sighed Rilla.

"'Sooth was my prophecy of fear
Believe it when it augurs cheer,'"

quoted Gertrude, almost gaily. "I tell you I have no doubt."

Yet, in spite of the great Italian victory at the Piave that came a few days later, she *had* doubt many a time in the hard month that followed; and when in mid-July the Germans crossed the Marne again despair came sickeningly. It was idle, they all felt, to hope that the miracle of the Marne would be repeated.

But it was: again, as in 1914, the tide turned at the Marne. The French and the American troops struck their sudden smashing blow on the exposed flank of the enemy and, with the almost inconceivable rapidity of a dream, the whole aspect of the war changed.

"The Allies have won two tremendous victories," said the doctor on the twentieth of July.

"It is the beginning of the end—I feel it—I feel it," said Mrs. Blythe.

"Thank God," said Susan, folding her trembling old hands. Then she added, under her breath, "but it won't bring our boys back."

Nevertheless she went out and ran up the flag, for the first time since the fall of Jerusalem. As it caught the breeze and swelled gallantly out above her, Susan lifted her hand and saluted it, as she had seen Shirley do. "We've all given something to keep you flying," she said. "Four hundred thousand of our boys gone overseas—fifty thousand of them killed. But—you are worth it!" The wind whipped her grey hair about her face and the gingham apron that shrouded her from head to foot was cut on lines of economy, not of grace; yet, somehow, just then Susan made an imposing figure. She was one of the women—courageous, unquailing, patient, heroic—who had made victory possible. In her, they all saluted the symbol for which their dearest had fought. Something of this was in the doctor's mind as he watched her from the door.

"Susan," he said, when she turned to come in, "from first to last of this business you have been a brick!"

$\mathcal{M}$rs. Matilda Pitman

Rilla and Jims were standing on the rear platform of their car when the train stopped at the little Millward siding. The August evening was so hot and close that the crowded cars were stifling. Nobody ever knew just why trains stopped at Millward siding. Nobody was ever known to get off there or get on. There was only one house nearer to it than four miles, and it was surrounded by acres of blueberry barrens and scrub spruce trees.

Rilla was on her way into Charlottetown to spend the night with a friend and the next day in Red Cross shopping; she had taken Jims with her, partly because she did not want Susan or her mother to be bothered with his care, partly because of a hungry desire in her heart to have as much of him as she could before she might have to give him up forever. James Anderson had written to her not long before this; he was wounded and in the hospital; he would not be able to go back to the front and as soon as he was able he would be coming home for Jims.

Rilla was heavy-hearted over this, and worried also. She loved Jims dearly and would feel deeply giving him up in any case; but if Jim Anderson were a different sort of a man, with a proper home for the child, it would not be so bad. But to give Jims up to a roving, shiftless, irresponsible father, however kind and good-hearted he might be—and she knew Jim Anderson *was* kind and good-hearted enough—was a bitter prospect to Rilla. It was not even likely Anderson would stay in the Glen; he had no ties there now; he might even go back to England. She might never see her dear, sunshiny, carefully-brought-up little Jims again. With such a father what might his fate be? Rilla meant to beg Jim Anderson to leave him with her, but, from his letter, she had not much hope that he would.

"If he would only stay in the Glen, where I could keep an eye on Jims and have him often with me I wouldn't feel so worried over it," she reflected. "But I feel sure he won't—and Jims will never have any chance. And he is such a bright little chap—he has ambition, wherever he got it—and he isn't lazy. But his father will never have a cent to give him any education or start in life. Jims, my little war baby, whatever is going to become of you?"

Jims was not in the least concerned over what was to become of him. He was gleefully watching the antics of a striped chipmunk that was frisking over the roof of the little siding. As the train pulled out Jims leaned eagerly forward for a last look at Chippy, pulling his hand from Rilla's. Rilla was so engrossed in wondering what was to become of Jims in the future that she forgot to take notice of what was happening to him in the present. What did happen was that Jims lost his balance, shot headlong down the steps, hurtled across the little siding platform, and landed in a clump of bracken fern on the other side.

Rilla shrieked and lost her head. She sprang down the steps and jumped off the train.

Fortunately, the train was still going at a comparatively slow speed; fortunately also, Rilla retained enough sense to jump the way it was going; nevertheless, she fell and sprawled helplessly down the embankment, landing in a ditch full of a rank growth of golden-rod and fireweed.

Nobody had seen what had happened and the train whisked briskly away around a curve in the barrens. Rilla picked herself up, dizzy but unhurt, scrambled out of the ditch, and flew wildly across the platform, expecting to find Jims dead or broken in pieces. But Jims, except for a few bruises, and a big fright, was quite uninjured. He was so badly scared that he didn't even cry, but Rilla, when she found that he was safe and sound, burst into tears and sobbed wildly.

"Nasty old twain," remarked Jims in disgust. "And nasty old God," he added, with a scowl at the heavens.

A laugh broke into Rilla's sobbing, producing something very like what her father would have called hysterics. But she caught herself up before the hysteria could conquer her.

"Rilla Blythe, I'm ashamed of you. Pull yourself together immediately. Jims, you shouldn't have said anything like that."

"God frew me off the twain," declared Jims defiantly. "*Somebody* frew me; *you* didn't frow me; so it was God."

"No, it wasn't. You fell because you let go of my hand and bent too far forward. I told you not to do that. So that it was your own fault."

Jims looked to see if she meant it; then glanced up at the sky again.

"Excuse me, then, God," he remarked airily.

Rilla scanned the sky also; she did not like its appearance; a heavy thundercloud was rising in the north-west. What in the world was to be done? There was no other train that night, since the nine o'clock special ran only on Saturdays. Would it be possible for them to reach Hannah Brewster's house, two miles away, before the storm broke? Rilla thought she could do it alone easily enough, but with Jims it was another matter. Were his little legs good for it?

"We've got to try it," said Rilla desperately. "We might stay in the siding until the thunderstorm is over; but it may keep on raining all night and anyway it will be pitch dark. If we can get to Hannah's she will keep us all night."

Hannah Brewster, when she had been Hannah Crawford, had lived in the Glen and gone to school with Rilla. They had been good friends then, though Hannah had been three years the older. She had married very young and had gone to live in Millward. What with hard work and babies and a ne'er-do-well husband, her life had not been an easy one, and Hannah seldom revisited her old home. Rilla had visited her once soon after her marriage, but had not seen her or even heard of her for years; she knew, however, that she and Jims would find welcome and harbourage in any house where rosy-faced, open-hearted, generous Hannah lived.

For the first mile they got on very well but the second one was harder. The road, seldom used, was rough and deep-rutted. Jims grew so tired that Rilla had to carry him for the last quarter. She reached the Brewster house, almost exhausted, and dropped Jims on the walk with a sigh of thankfulness. The sky was black with clouds; the first heavy drops were beginning to fall; and the rumble of thunder was growing very loud. Then she made an unpleasant discovery. The blinds were all down and the doors locked. Evidently the Brewsters were not at home. Rilla ran to the little barn. It, too, was locked. No other refuge presented itself. The bare whitewashed little house had not even a veranda or porch.

It was almost dark now and her plight seemed desperate.

"I'm going to get in if I have to break a window," said Rilla resolutely. "Hannah would want me to do that. She'd never get over it if she heard I came to her house for refuge in a thunderstorm and couldn't get in."

Luckily she did not have to go to the length of actual housebreaking. The kitchen window went up quite easily. Rilla lifted Jims in and scrambled through herself, just as the storm broke in good earnest.

"Oh, see all the little pieces of thunder," cried Jims in delight, as the hail danced in after them. Rilla shut the window and with some difficulty found and lighted a lamp. They were in a very snug little kitchen. Opening off it on one side was a trim, nicely furnished parlour, and on the other a pantry, which proved to be well stocked.

"I'm going to make myself at home," said Rilla. "I know that is just what Hannah would want me to do. I'll get a little snack for Jims and me, and then if the rain continues and nobody comes home I'll just go upstairs to the spare room and go to bed. There is nothing like acting sensibly in an emergency. If I had not been a goose when I saw Jims fall off the train I'd have rushed back into the car and got some one to stop it. Then I wouldn't have been in this scrape. Since I am in it I'll make the best of it.

"This house," she added, looking around, "is fixed up much nicer than when I was here before. Of course Hannah and Ted were just beginning housekeeping then. But somehow I've had the idea that Ted hasn't been very prosperous. He must have done better than I've been led to believe, when they can afford furniture like this. I'm awfully glad for Hannah's sake."

The thunderstorm passed, but the rain continued to fall heavily. At eleven o'clock Rilla decided that nobody was coming home. Jims had fallen asleep on the sofa; she carried him up to the spare room and put him to bed. Then she undressed, put on a nightgown she found in the washstand drawer, and scrambled sleepily in between very nice lavendarscented sheets. She was so tired, after her adventures and exertions, that not even the oddity of her situation could keep her awake; she was sound asleep in a few minutes.

Rilla slept until eight o'clock the next morning and then wakened with startling suddenness. Somebody was saying in a harsh, gruff voice,

"Here, you two, wake up. I want to know what this means."

Rilla did wake up, promptly and effectually. She had never in all her life wakened up so thoroughly before. Standing in the room were three people, one of them a man, who were absolute strangers to her. The man was a big fellow with a bushy black beard and an angry scowl. Beside him was a woman—a tall, thin, angular person, with violently red hair and an indescribable hat. She looked even crosser and more amazed than the man, if that were possible. In the background was another woman—a tiny old lady who must have been at least eighty. She was, in spite of her tinyness, a very striking-looking personage; she was dressed in unrelieved black, had snow-white hair, a dead-white face, and snapping, vivid, coal-black eyes. She looked as amazed as the other two, but Rilla realized that she didn't look cross.

Rilla also was realizing that something was wrong—fearfully wrong. Then the man said, more gruffly than ever,

"Come now. Who are you and what business have you here?"

Rilla raised herself on one elbow, looking and feeling hopelessly bewildered and foolish. She heard the old black-and-white lady in the background chuckle to herself. "*She* must be real," Rilla thought, "I can't be dreaming *her*." Aloud she gasped,

"Isn't this Theodore Brewster's place?"

"No," said the big woman, speaking for the first time, "this place belongs to us. We bought it from the Brewsters last fall. They moved to Greenvale. Our name is Chapley."

Poor Rilla fell back on her pillow, quite overcome.

"I beg your pardon," she said. "I—I—thought the Brewsters lived here. Mrs. Brewster is a friend of mine. I am Rilla Blythe,—Dr. Blythe's daughter from Glen St. Mary. I—I was going to town with my—my—this little boy—and he fell off the train—and I jumped off after him—and nobody knew of it. I knew we couldn't get home last night and a storm was coming up—so we came here and when we found nobody at home—we—we—just got in through the window and—and—made ourselves at home."

"So it seems," said the woman sarcastically.

"A likely story," said the man.

"We weren't born yesterday," added the woman.

Madam Black-and-White didn't say anything; but when the other two had made their pretty speeches she doubled up in a silent convulsion of mirth, shaking her head from side to side and beating the air with her hands.

Rilla, stung by the disagreeable attitude of the Chapleys, regained her self-possession and lost her temper. She sat up in bed and said in her haughtiest voice,

"I do not know when you were born, or where, but it must have been somewhere where very peculiar manners were taught. If you will have the decency to leave my room—er—*this* room—until I can get up and dress I shall not transgress upon your hospitality"—Rilla was killingly sarcastic—"any longer. And I shall pay you amply for the food we have eaten and the night's lodging I have taken."

The black-and-white apparition went through the motion of clapping her hands, but not a sound did she make. Perhaps Mr. Chapley was cowed by Rilla's tone—or perhaps he was appeased at the prospect of payment; at all events, he spoke more civilly.

"Well, that's fair. If you pay up it's all right."

"She shall do no such thing as pay you," said Madam Black-and-White in a surprisingly clear, resolute, authoritative tone of voice. "If you haven't got any shame for yourself, Robert Chapley, you've got a mother-in-law who can be ashamed for you. No strangers shall be charged for food and lodging in any house where Mrs. Matilda Pitman lives. Remember that, though I may have come down in the world, I haven't quite forgot all decency for all that. I knew you was a skinflint when Amelia married you, and you've made her as bad as yourself. But Mrs. Matilda Pitman has been boss for a long time, and Mrs. Matilda Pitman will remain boss. Here you, Robert Chapley, take yourself out of here and let that girl get dressed. And you, Amelia, go downstairs and cook a breakfast for her."

Never, in all her life, had Rilla seen anything like the abject meekness with which those two big people obeyed that mite. They went without word or look of protest. As the door closed behind them Mrs. Matilda Pitman laughed silently, and rocked from side to side in her merriment.

"Ain't it funny?" she said. "I mostly lets them run the length of their tether, but sometimes I has to pull them up, and then I does it with a jerk. They don't dast aggravate me, because I've got considerable hard cash, and they're afraid I won't leave it all to them. Neither I will. I'll leave 'em some, but some I won't, just to vex 'em. I haven't made up my mind where I will leave it but I'll have to, soon, for at eighty a body is living on borrowed time. Now, you can take your time about dressing, my dear, and I'll go down and keep them mean scalawags in order. That's a handsome child you have there. Is he your brother?"

"No, he's a little war baby I've been taking care of, because his mother died and his father was overseas," answered Rilla in a subdued tone.

"War baby! Humph! Well, I'd better skin out before he wakes up or he'll likely start in crying. Children don't like me—never did. I can't recollect any youngster ever coming near me of its own accord. Never had any of my own. Amelia was my stepdaughter. Well, it's saved me a world of bother. If kids don't like me I don't like them, so that's an even score. But that certainly is a handsome child."

Jims chose this moment for waking up. He opened his big brown eyes and looked at Mrs. Matilda Pitman unblinkingly. Then he sat up, dimpled deliciously, pointed to her and said solemnly to Rilla,

"Pwitty lady, Willa—pwitty lady."

Mrs. Matilda Pitman smiled. Even eighty-odd is sometimes vulnerable in vanity.

"I've heard that children and fools tell the truth," she said. "I was used to compliments when I was young—but they're scarcer when you get as far along as I am. I haven't had one for years. It tastes good. I s'pose now, you monkey, you wouldn't give me a kiss."

Then Jims did a quite surprising thing. He was not a demonstrative youngster and was chary with kisses even to the Ingleside people. But without a word he stood up in bed, his plump little body encased only in his undershirt, ran to the footboard, flung his arms about Mrs. Matilda Pitman's neck, and gave her a bear hug, accompanied by three or four hearty, ungrudging smacks.

"Jims," protested Rilla, aghast at this liberty.

"You leave him be," ordered Mrs. Matilda Pitman, setting her bonnet straight. "Laws I like to see some one that isn't skeered of me. Everybody is—*you* are, though you're trying to hide it. And why? Of course Robert and Amelia are because I make 'em skeered on purpose. But folks always are—no matter how civil I be to them. Are you going to keep this child?"

"I'm afraid not. His father is coming home before long."

"Is he any good—the father, I mean?"

"Well—he's kind and nice—but he's poor—and I'm afraid he always will be," faltered Rilla.

"I see—shiftless—can't make or keep. Well, I'll see—I'll see. I have an idea. It's a good idea, and besides it will make Robert and Amelia squirm. That's its main merit in my eyes, though I like that child, mind you, because he ain't skeered of me. *He's* worth some bother. Now, you get dressed, as I said before, and come down when you're good and ready."

Rilla was stiff and sore after her tumble and walk of the night before, but she was not long in dressing herself and Jims. When she went down to the kitchen she found a smoking hot breakfast on the table. Mr. Chapley was nowhere in sight and Mrs. Chapley was cutting bread with a sulky air. Mrs. Matilda Pitman was sitting in an armchair, knitting a grey army sock. She still wore her bonnet and her triumphant expression.

"Set right in, dears, and make a good breakfast," she said.

"I am not hungry," said Rilla almost pleadingly. "I don't think I can eat anything. And it is time I was starting for the station. The morning train will soon be along. Please excuse me and let us go—I'll take a piece of bread and butter for Jims."

Mrs. Matilda Pitman shook a knitting needle playfully at Rilla.

"Sit down and take your breakfast," she said. "Mrs. Matilda Pitman commands you. Everybody obeys Mrs. Matilda Pitman—even Robert and Amelia. You must obey her too."

Rilla did obey her. She sat down and, such was the influence of Mrs. Matilda Pitman's mesmeric eye, she ate a tolerable breakfast. The obedient Amelia never spoke; Mrs. Matilda Pitman did not speak either; but she knitted furiously and chuckled. When Rilla had finished, Mrs. Matilda Pitman rolled up her sock.

"Now you can go if you want to," she said, "but you don't have to go. You can stay here as long as you want to and I'll make Amelia cook your meals for you."

The independent Miss Blythe, whom a certain clique of Junior Red Cross girls accused of being domineering and "bossy," was thoroughly cowed.

"Thank you," she said meekly, "but we must really go."

"Well, then," said Mrs. Matilda Pitman, throwing open the door, "your conveyance is ready for you. I told Robert he must hitch up and drive you to the station. I enjoy making Robert do things. It's almost the only sport I have left. I'm over eighty and most things have lost their flavour except bossing Robert."

Robert sat before the door on the front seat of a trim, double-seated, rubber-tired buggy. He must have heard every word his mother-in-law said but he gave no sign.

"I do wish," said Rilla, plucking up what little spirit she had left, "that you would let me—oh—ah—" then she quailed again before Mrs. Matilda Pitman's eye—"recompense you for—for—"

"Mrs. Matilda Pitman said before—and meant it—that she doesn't take pay for entertaining strangers, nor let other people where she lives do it, much as their natural meanness would like to do it. You go along to town and don't forget to call the next time you come this way. Don't be scared. Not that you *are* scared of much, I reckon, considering the way you sassed Robert back this morning. I like your spunk. Most girls nowadays are such timid, skeery creeturs. When I was girl I wasn't afraid of nothing nor nobody. Mind you take good care of that boy. *He* ain't any common child. And make Robert drive around all the puddles in the road. I won't have that new buggy splashed."

As they drove away Jims threw kisses at Mrs. Matilda Pitman as long as he could see her, and Mrs. Matilda Pitman waved her sock back at him. Robert spoke no word, either good or bad, all the way to the station, but he remembered the puddles. When Rilla got out at the siding she thanked him courteously. The only response she got was a grunt as Robert turned his horse and started for home.

"Well"—Rilla drew a long breath—"I must try to get back into Rilla Blythe again. I've been somebody else these past few hours—I don't know just who—some creation of that extraordinary old person's. I believe she hypnotized me. What an adventure this will be to write the boys."

And then she sighed. Bitter remembrance came that there were only Jerry and Carl and Shirley to write it to now. Jem—who would have appreciated Mrs. Matilda Pitman keenly—where was Jem?

CHAPTER XXXII

*W*ord from Jem

"August 4th, 1918

"It is four years tonight since the dance at the lighthouse—four years of war. It seems like three times four. I was fifteen then. I am nineteen now. I expected that these past four years would be the most delightful years of my life and they have been years of war—years of fear and grief and worry,—but I humbly hope, of a little growth in strength and character as well.

"Today I was going through the hall and I heard mother saying something to father about me. I didn't mean to listen—I couldn't help hearing her as I went along the hall and upstairs—so perhaps that is why I heard what listeners are said never to hear—something good of myself. And because it was mother who said it I'm going to write it here in my journal, for my comforting when days of discouragement come upon me, in which I feel that I am vain and selfish and weak and that there is no good thing in me.

"'Rilla has developed in a wonderful fashion these past four years. She used to be such an irresponsible young creature. She has changed into a capable, womanly girl and she is such a comfort to me. Nan and Di have grown a little away from me—they have been so little at home—but Rilla has grown closer and closer to me. We are *chums*. I don't see how I could have got through these terrible years without her, Gilbert.'

"There, that is just what mother said—and I feel glad—

and sorry—and proud—and humble! It's beautiful to have my mother think that about me—but I don't deserve it quite. I'm not as good and strong as all that. There are heaps of times when I have felt cross and impatient and woeful and despairing. It is mother and Susan who have been this family's backbone. But I have helped a little, I believe, and I am so glad and thankful.

"The war news has been good right along. The French and Americans are pushing the Germans back and back and back. Sometimes I am afraid it is too good to last—after nearly four years of disasters one has a feeling that this constant success is unbelievable.

"We don't rejoice noisily over it. Susan keeps the flag up but we go softly. The price paid has been too high for jubilation. We are just thankful that it has not been paid in vain.

"No word has come from Jem. We hope—because we dare not do anything else. But there are hours when we *all* feel—though we never say so—that such hoping is foolishness. These hours come more and more frequently as the weeks go by. And we may never *know*. That is the most terrible thought of all. I wonder how Faith is bearing it. To judge from her letters she has never for a moment given up hope, but she must have had her dark hours of doubt like the rest of us."

"August 20th, 1918

"The Canadians have been in action again and Mr. Meredith had a cable today saying that Carl had been slightly wounded and is in the hospital. It did not say where the wound was, which is unusual, and we all feel worried.

"There is news of a fresh victory every day now."

"August 30th, 1918

"The Merediths had a letter from Carl today. His wound was 'only a slight one'—but it was in his right eye and the sight is gone forever!

"'One eye is enough to watch bugs with,' Carl writes cheerfully. And we know it might have been oh so much worse! If it had been both eyes! But I cried all the afternoon after I saw Carl's letter. Those beautiful, fearless blue eyes of his!

"There is one comfort—he will not have to go back to the front. He is coming home as soon as he is out of the hospital—the first of our boys to return. When will the others come?

"And there is one who will never come. At least we will not see him if he does. But, oh, I think he will be there—when our Canadian soldiers return there will be a shadowy army with them—the army of the fallen. We will not *see* them—but they will be there!"

"September 1st, 1918

"Mother and I went into Charlottetown yesterday to see the moving picture, 'Hearts of the World.' I made an awful goose of myself—father will never stop teasing me about it for the rest of my life. But it all seemed so horribly *real*—and I was so intensely interested that I forgot *everything* but the scenes I saw enacted before my eyes. And then, quite near the last, came a terribly exciting one. The heroine was struggling with a horrible German soldier who was trying to drag her away. I *knew* she had a knife—I had seen her hide it, to have it in readiness—and I couldn't understand *why* she didn't produce it and finish the brute. I thought *she must have forgotten it*, and just at the tensest moment of the scene I lost my head altogether. I just stood right up on my feet in that crowded house and shrieked at the top of my voice—*'The knife is in your stocking—the knife is in your stocking!'*

"I created a sensation!

"The funny part was, that just as I said it, the girl *did* snatch out the knife and stab the soldier with it!

"Everybody in the house laughed. I came to my senses and fell back in my seat, overcome with mortification. Mother was shaking with laughter. *I* could have shaken *her*. Why hadn't she pulled me down and choked me before I had made such an idiot of myself. She protests that there wasn't time.

"Fortunately the house was dark, and I don't believe there was anybody there who knew me. And I thought I was becoming sensible and self-controlled and womanly! It is plain I have some distance to go yet before I attain that devoutly desired consummation."

"September 20th, 1918

"In the east Bulgaria has asked for peace, and in the west the British have smashed the Hindenburg line; and right here in Glen St. Mary little Bruce Meredith has done something that I think wonderful—wonderful because of the love behind it. Mrs. Meredith was here tonight and told us about it—and mother and I cried, and Susan got up and clattered the things about the stove.

"Bruce always loved Jem very devotedly, and the child has never forgotten him in all these years. He has been as faithful in his way as Dog Monday was in his. We have always told him that Jem would come back. But it seems that he was in Carter Flagg's store last night and he heard his Uncle Norman flatly declaring that Jem Blythe would never come back and that the Ingleside folks might as well give up hoping he would. Bruce went home and cried himself to sleep. This morning his mother saw him going out of the yard, with a very sorrowful and determined look, carrying his pet kitten. She didn't think much more about it until later on he came in, with the most tragic little face, and told her, his little body shaking with big sobs, that he had drowned Stripey.

"'Why did you do that?' Mrs. Meredith exclaimed.

"'To bring Jem back,' sobbed Bruce. 'I thought if I sacrificed Stripey God would send Jem back. So I drownded him—and, oh mother, it was *awful* hard—but surely God will send Jem back now, 'cause Stripey was the dearest thing I had. I just told God I would give Him Stripey if He would send Jem back. And He will, won't He, mother?'

"Mrs. Meredith didn't know what to say to the poor child. She just could *not* tell him that perhaps his sacrifice wouldn't bring Jem back—that God didn't work that way. She told him that he mustn't expect it right away—that perhaps it would be quite a long time yet before Jem came back. But Bruce said,

"'It oughtn't to take longer'n a week, mother. Oh, mother, Stripey was such a nice little cat. He purred so pretty. Don't you think God *ought* to like him enough to let us have Jem?'

"Mr. Meredith is worried about the effect on Bruce's faith in God, and Mrs. Meredith is worried about the effect on Bruce himself if his hope isn't fulfilled. And I feel as if I must cry every time I think of it. It was so splendid—and sad—and beautiful. The dear, devoted little fellow! He worshipped that kitten. And if it all goes for nothing—as so many sacrifices *seem* to go for nothing—he will be broken-hearted, for he isn't old enough to understand that God doesn't answer our prayers just as we hope—and doesn't make bargains with us when we yield something we love up to Him."

"September 24th, 1918

"I have been kneeling at my window in the moonshine for a long time, just thanking God over and over again. The joy of last night and today has been so great that it seemed half pain—as if our hearts weren't big enough to hold it.

"Last night I was sitting here in my room at eleven o'clock, writing a letter to Shirley. Everyone else was in bed, except father, who was out. I heard the telephone ring and I ran out to the hall to answer it, before it should waken mother. It was long-distance calling, and when I answered it said 'This is the telegraph company's office in Charlottetown. There is an overseas cable for Dr. Blythe.'

"I thought of Shirley—my heart stood still—and then I heard him saying, 'It's from Holland.'

"The message was

"'Just arrived. Escaped from Germany. Quite well. Writing.
'James Blythe.'

"I didn't faint or fall or scream. I didn't feel glad or surprised. I didn't feel *anything*. I felt numb, just as I did when I heard Walter had enlisted. I hung up the receiver and turned round. Mother was standing in her doorway. She wore her old rose kimono, and her hair was hanging down her back in a long thick braid, and her eyes were shining. She looked just like a young girl.

"'There is word from Jem?' she said.

"How did she know? I hadn't said a word at the 'phone except 'Yes—yes—yes.' She says she doesn't know how she knew, but she *did* know. She was awake and she heard the ring and she knew that there was word from Jem.

"'He's alive—he's well—he's in Holland,' I said.

"Mother came out into the hall and said,

"'I must get your father on the 'phone and tell him. He is in the Upper Glen.'

"She was very calm and quiet—not a bit like I would have expected her to be. But then I wasn't either. I went and woke up Gertrude and Susan and told them. Susan said 'Thank God,' firstly, and secondly she said 'Did I not tell you Dog Monday knew?' and thirdly, 'I'll go down and make a cup of tea,'—and she stalked down in her nightdress to make it. She did make it—and made mother and Gertrude drink it—but I went back to my room and shut my door and locked it, and knelt by my window and cried—just as Gertrude did when her great news came.

"I think I know at last exactly what I shall feel like on the resurrection morning."

"October 4th, 1918

"Today Jem's letter came. It has been in the house only six hours and it is almost read to pieces. The post-mistress told everybody in the Glen it had come, and everybody came up to hear the news.

"Jem was badly wounded in the thigh—and he was picked up and taken to prison, so delirious with fever that he didn't know what was happening to him or where he was. It was weeks before he came to his senses and was able to write. Then he did write—but it never came. He wasn't treated at all badly at his camp—only the food was poor. He had nothing to eat but a little black bread and boiled turnips and now and then a little soup with black peas in it. And we sat down every one of those days to three good square luxurious meals! He wrote us as often as he could but he was afraid we were not getting his letters because no reply came. As soon as he was strong enough he tried to escape, but was caught and brought back; a month later he and a comrade made another attempt and succeeded in reaching Holland.

"Jem can't come home right away. He isn't *quite* so well as his cable said, for his wound has not healed properly and he has to go into a hospital in England for further treatment. But he says he will be all right eventually, and we know he is safe and will be back home sometime, and oh, the difference it makes in *everything*!

"I had a letter from Jim Anderson today, too. He *has married an English girl*, got his discharge, and is coming right home to Canada with his bride. I don't know whether to be glad or sorry. It will all depend on what kind of a woman she is. I had a second letter also of a somewhat mysterious tenor. It is from a Charlottetown lawyer, asking me to go in to see him at my earliest convenience in regard to a certain matter connected with the estate of the 'late Mrs. Matilda Pitman.'

"I read a notice of Mrs. Pitman's death—from heart-failure—in the *Enterprise* a few weeks ago. I wonder if this summons has anything to do with Jims."

"October 4th, 1918

"I went into town this morning and had an interview with Mrs. Pitman's lawyer,—a little thin, wispy man, who spoke of his late client with such profound respect that it is evident that he was as much under her thumb as Robert and Amelia were. He drew up a new will for her a short time before her death. She was worth thirty thousand dollars, the bulk of which was left to Amelia Chapley. But she left five thousand to me in trust for Jims. The interest is to be used as I see fit for his education, and the principal is to be paid over to him on his twentieth birthday. Certainly Jims was born lucky. I saved him from slow extinction at the hands of Mrs. Conover,—Mary Vance saved him from death by diphtheritic croup,—his star saved him when he fell off the train. And he tumbled not only into a clump of bracken, but right into this nice little legacy. Evidently, as Mrs. Matilda Pitman said, and as I have always believed, he is no common child and has no common destiny in store for him.

"At all events he is provided for, and in such a fashion that Jim Anderson can't squander his inheritance if he wanted to. Now, if the new English stepmother is only a good sort I shall feel quite easy about the future of my war baby.

"I wonder what Robert and Amelia think of it. I fancy they will nail down their windows when they leave home after this!"

$\mathscr{V}$ictory!!

A day "of chilling winds and gloomy skies," Rilla quoted one Sunday afternoon,—the sixth of October to be exact. It was so cold that they had lighted a fire in the living room and the merry little flames were doing their best to counteract the outside dourness. "It's more like November than October— November is such an ugly month."

Cousin Sophia was there, having again forgiven Susan, and Mrs. Martin Clow, who was not visiting on Sunday but had dropped in to borrow Susan's cure for rheumatism—that being cheaper than getting one from the doctor.

"I'm afeared we're going to have an airly winter," foreboded Cousin Sophia. "The muskrats are building awful big houses around the pond, and that's a sign that never fails. Dear me, how that child has grown!" Cousin Sophia sighed again, as if it were an unhappy circumstance that a child should grow. "When do you expect his father?"

"Next week," said Rilla.

"Well, I hope the stepmother won't abuse the pore child," sighed Cousin Sophia, "but I have my doubts—I have my doubts. Anyhow, he'll be sure to feel the difference between his usage here and what he'll get anywhere else. You've spoiled him so, Rilla, waiting on him hand and foot the way you've always done."

Rilla smiled and pressed her cheek to Jims' curls. She knew sweet-tempered, sunny, little Jims was not spoiled. Nevertheless her heart was anxious behind her smile. She, too, thought much about the new Mrs. Anderson and wondered uneasily what she would be like.

"I *can't* give Jims up to a woman who won't love him," she thought rebelliously.

"I b'lieve it's agoing to rain," said Cousin Sophia. "We have had an awful lot of rain this fall already. It's going to make it awful hard for people to get their roots in. It wasn't so in my young days. We gin'rally had beautiful Octobers then. But the seasons is altogether different now from what they used to be."

Clear across Cousin Sophia's doleful voice cut the telephone bell. Gertrude Oliver answered it. "Yes—what? *What?* Is it true—is it official? Thank you—thank you."

Gertrude turned and faced the room dramatically, her dark eyes flashing, her dark face flushed with feeling. All at once the sun broke through the thick clouds and poured through the big crimson maple outside the window. Its reflected glow enveloped her in a weird, immaterial flame. She looked like a priestess performing some mystic, splendid rite.

"Germany and Austria are suing for peace," she said.

Rilla went crazy for a few minutes. She sprang up and danced around the room, clapping her hands, laughing, crying.

"Sit down, child," said Mrs. Clow, who never got excited over anything, and so had missed a tremendous amount of trouble and delight in her journey through life.

"Oh," cried Rilla, "I have walked the floor for hours in despair and anxiety in these past four years. Now let me walk it in joy. It was worth living long dreary years for this minute, and it would be worth living them again just to look back to it. Susan, let's run up the flag—and we must 'phone the news to every one in the Glen."

"Can we have as much sugar as we want to now?" asked Jims eagerly.

It was a never-to-be-forgotten afternoon. As the news spread excited people ran about the village and dashed up to Ingleside. The Merediths came over and stayed to supper and everybody talked and nobody listened. Cousin Sophia tried to protest that Germany and Austria were not to be trusted and it was all part of a plot, but nobody paid the least attention to her.

"This Sunday makes up for that one in March," said Susan.

"I wonder," said Gertrude dreamily, apart to Rilla, "if things won't seem rather flat and *insipid* when peace really comes. After being fed for four years on horrors and fears, terrible reverses, amazing victories, won't anything less be tame and uninteresting? How strange—and blessed—and *dull* it will be not to dread the coming of the mail every day."

"We must dread it for a little while yet, I suppose," said Rilla. "Peace won't come—can't come—for some weeks yet. And in those weeks dreadful things may happen. My excitement is over. We have won the victory—but oh, what a price we have paid!"

"Not too high a price for freedom," said Gertrude softly. "Do you think it was, Rilla?"

"No," said Rilla, under her breath. She was seeing a little white cross on a battlefield of France. "No—not if those of us who live will show ourselves worthy of it—if we 'keep faith.'"

"We *will* keep faith," said Gertrude. She rose suddenly. A silence fell around the table, and in the silence Gertrude repeated Walter's famous poem "The Piper." When she finished Mr. Meredith stood up and held up his glass.

"Let us drink," he said, "to the silent army,—to the boys who followed when the Piper summoned. 'For our tomorrow they gave their today'—theirs is the victory!"

$\mathcal{M}$r. Hyde Goes to His Own Place and Susan Takes a Honeymoon

Early in November Jims left Ingleside. Rilla saw him go with many tears but a heart free from boding. Mrs. Jim Anderson, Number Two, was such a nice little woman that one was rather inclined to wonder at the luck which bestowed her on Jim. She was rosy-faced and blue-eyed and wholesome, with the roundness and trigness of a geranium leaf. Rilla saw at first glance that she was to be trusted with Jims.

"I'm fond of children, miss," she said heartily. "I'm used to them—I've left six little brothers and sisters behind me. Jims is a dear child and I must say you've done wonders in bringing him up so healthy and handsome. I'll be as good to him as if he was my own, miss. And I'll make Jim toe the line all right. He's a good worker—all he needs is some one to keep him at it, and to take charge of his money. We've rented a little farm just out of the village, and we're going to settle down there. Jim wanted to stay in England but I says 'No.' I hankered to try a new country and I've always thought Canada would suit me."

"I'm so glad you are going to live near us. You'll let Jims come here often, won't you? I love him dearly."

"No doubt you do, miss, for a lovabler child I never did see. We understand, Jim and me, what you've done for him, and you won't find us ungrateful. He can come here whenever you want him and I'll always be glad of any advice from you about his bringing-up. He is more your baby than any one else's I should say, and I'll see that you get your fair share of him, miss."

So Jims went away—with the soup tureen, though not in it. Then the news of the armistice came, and even Glen St. Mary went mad. That night the village had a bonfire, and burned the Kaiser in effigy. The fishing village boys turned out and burned all the sandhills off in one grand glorious conflagration that extended for seven miles. Up at Ingleside Rilla ran laughing to her room.

"Now I'm going to do a most unladylike and inexcusable thing," she said, as she pulled her green velvet hat out of its box. "I'm going to kick this hat about the room until it is without form and void; and I shall never as long as I live wear anything of that shade of green again."

"You've certainly kept your vow pluckily," laughed Miss Oliver.

"It wasn't pluck—it was sheer obstinacy—I'm rather ashamed of it," said Rilla, kicking joyously. "I just wanted to show mother. It's mean to want to show your mother—most unfilial conduct! But I *have* shown her. And I've shown myself a few things! Oh, Miss Oliver, just for one moment I'm really feeling quite young again—young and frivolous and silly. Did I ever say November was an ugly month? Why it's the most beautiful month in the whole year. Listen to the bells ringing in Rainbow Valley! I never heard them so clearly. They're ringing for peace—and new happiness—and all the dear, sweet, sane *homey* things that we can have again now, Miss Oliver. Not that *I* am sane just now—I don't pretend to be. The whole world is having its little crazy spell today. Soon we'll sober down—and 'keep faith'—and begin to build up our new world. But just for today let's be mad and glad."

Susan came in from the outdoor sunlight looking supremely satisfied.

"Mr. Hyde is gone," she announced.

"Gone! Do you mean he is dead, Susan?"

"No, Mrs. Dr. dear, that beast is not dead. But you will never see him again I feel sure of that."

"Don't be so mysterious, Susan. What has happened to him?"

"Well, Mrs. Dr. dear, he was sitting out on the back steps this afternoon. It was just after the news came that the armistice had been signed and he was looking his Hydest. I can assure you he was an awesome looking beast. All at once, Mrs. Dr. dear, Bruce Meredith came around the corner of the kitchen walking on his stilts. He has been learning to walk on them lately and came over to show me how well he could do it. Mr. Hyde just took a look and one bound carried him over the yard fence. Then he went tearing through the maple grove in great leaps with his ears laid back. You never saw a creature so terrified, Mrs. Dr. dear. He has never returned."

"Oh, he'll come back, Susan, probably chastened in spirit by his fright."

"We will see, Mrs. Dr. dear—we will see. Remember, *the armistice has been signed*. And *that* reminds me that Whiskers-on-the-moon had a paralytic stroke last night. I am not saying it is a judgment on him, because I am not in the counsels of the Almighty, but one can have one's own thoughts about it. Neither Whiskers-on-the-moon or Mr. Hyde will be much more heard of in Glen St. Mary, Mrs. Dr. dear, and that you may tie to."

Mr. Hyde certainly was heard of no more. As it could hardly have been his fright that kept him away the Ingleside folks decided that some dark fate of shot or poison had descended on him—except Susan, who believed and continued to affirm that he had merely "gone to his own place." Rilla lamented him, for she had been very fond of her stately golden pussy, and had liked him quite as well in his weird Hyde moods as in his tame Jekyll ones.

"And now, Mrs. Dr. dear," said Susan, "since the fall house-cleaning is over and the garden truck is all safe in cellar, I am going to take a honeymoon to celebrate the peace."

"A *honeymoon*, Susan?"

"Yes, Mrs. Dr. dear, a honeymoon," repeated Susan firmly. "I shall never be able to get a husband but I am not going to be cheated out of everything and a honeymoon I intend to have. I am going to Charlottetown to visit my married brother and his family. His wife has been ailing all the fall, but nobody knows whether she is going to die or not. She never *did* tell any one what she was going to do until she did it. That is the main reason why she was never liked in our family. But to be on the safe side I feel that I should visit her. I have not been in town for over a day for twenty years and I have a feeling that I might as well see one of these moving pictures there is so much talk of, so as not to be wholly out of the swim. But have no fear that I shall be carried away with them, Mrs. Dr. dear. I shall be away a fortnight if you can spare me so long."

"You certainly deserve a good holiday, Susan. Better take a month—that is the proper length for a honeymoon."

"No, Mrs. Dr. dear, a fortnight is all I require. Besides, I must be home for at least three weeks before Christmas to make the proper preparations. We will have a Christmas that *is* a Christmas this year, Mrs. Dr. dear. Do you think there is any chance of our boys being home for it?"

"No, I think not, Susan. Both Jem and Shirley write that they don't expect to be home before spring—it may be even midsummer before Shirley comes. But Carl Meredith will be home, and Nan and Di, and we *will* have a grand celebration once more. We'll set chairs for all, Susan, as you did our first war Christmas,—yes, for *all*—for my dear lad whose chair must always be vacant, as well as for the others, Susan."

"It is not likely I would forget to set *his* place, Mrs. Dr. dear," said Susan, wiping her eyes as she departed to pack up for her "honeymoon."

CHAPTER XXXV

"𝓡illa-my-Rilla!"

Carl Meredith and Miller Douglas came home just before Christmas and Glen St. Mary met them at the station with a brass band borrowed from Lowbridge and speeches of home manufacture. Miller was brisk and beaming in spite of his wooden leg; he had developed into a broad-shouldered, imposing looking fellow and the D.C. medal he wore reconciled Miss Cornelia to the shortcomings of his pedigree to such a degree that she tacitly recognized his engagement to Mary. The latter put on a few airs—especially when Carter Flagg took Miller into his store as head clerk—but nobody grudged them to her.

"Of course farming's out of the question for us now," she told Rilla, "but Miller thinks he'll like store keeping fine once he gets used to a quiet life again, and Carter Flagg will be a more agreeable boss than old Kitty. We're going to be married in the fall and live in the old Mead house with the bay windows and the mansard roof. I've always thought that the handsomest house in the Glen, but never did I dream I'd ever live there. We're only renting it, of course, but if things go as we expect and Carter Flagg takes Miller into partnership we'll own it some day. Say, I've got on some in society, haven't I, considering what I come from? I never aspired to being a storekeeper's wife. But Miller's real ambitious and he'll have a wife that'll back him up. He says he never saw a French girl worth looking at twice and that his heart beat true to me every moment he was away."

Jerry Meredith and Joe Milgrave came back in January, and all winter the boys from the Glen and its environs came home by two and threes. None of them came back just as they went away, not even those who had been so fortunate as to escape any injury.

One spring day, when the daffodils were blowing on the Ingleside lawn, and the banks of the brook in Rainbow Valley were sweet with white and purple violets, the little, lazy afternoon accommodation train pulled into the Glen station. It was very seldom that passengers for the Glen came by that train, so nobody was there to meet it except the new station agent and a small black and yellow dog, who for four and a half long years had met every train that had steamed into Glen St. Mary. Thousands of trains had Dog Monday met and never had the boy he waited and watched for returned. Yet still Dog Monday watched on with eyes that never quite lost hope. Perhaps his dog-heart failed him at times; he was growing old and rheumatic; when he walked back to his kennel after each train had gone his gait was very sober now— he never trotted but went slowly with a drooping head and a depressed tail that had quite lost its old saucy uplift.

One passenger stepped off the train—a tall fellow in a faded lieutenant's uniform, who walked with a barely perceptible limp. He had a bronzed face and there were some grey hairs in the ruddy curls that clustered around his forehead. The new station agent looked at him anxiously. He was used to seeing the khaki-clad figures come off the train, some met by a tumultuous crowd, others, who had sent no word of their coming, stepping off quietly like this one. But there was a certain distinction of bearing and features in this soldier that caught his attention and made him wonder a little more interestedly who he was.

A black and yellow streak shot past the station agent. Dog Monday stiff? Dog Monday rheumatic? Dog Monday old? Never believe it. Dog Monday was a young pup, gone clean mad with rejuvenating joy.

He flung himself against the tall soldier, with a bark that choked in his throat from sheer rapture. He flung himself on the ground and writhed in a frenzy of welcome. He tried to climb the soldier's khaki legs and slipped down and grovelled in an ecstasy that seemed as if it must tear his little body in pieces. He licked his boots and when the lieutenant had, with laughter on his lips and tears in his eyes, succeeded in gathering the little creature up in his arms Dog Monday laid his head on the khaki shoulder and licked the sunburned neck, making queer sounds between barks and sobs.

The station agent had heard the story of Dog Monday. He knew now who the returned soldier was. Dog Monday's long vigil was ended. Jem Blythe had come home.

"We are all very happy—and sad—and thankful," wrote Rilla in her diary a week later, "though Susan has not yet recovered—never will recover, I believe—from the shock of having Jem come home the very night she had, owing to a strenuous day, prepared a 'pick up' supper. I shall never forget the sight of her, tearing madly about from pantry to cellar, hunting out stored away goodies. Just as if anybody cared what was on the table—none of us could eat, anyway. It was meat and drink just to look at Jem. Mother seemed afraid to take her eyes off him lest he vanish out of her sight. It is wonderful to have Jem back—and Little Dog Monday. Monday refuses to be separated from Jem for a moment. He sleeps on the foot of his bed and squats beside him at meal times. And on Sunday he went to church with him and insisted on going right into our pew, where he went to sleep on Jem's feet. In the middle of the sermon he woke up and seemed to think he must welcome Jem all over again, for he bounced up with a series of barks and wouldn't quiet down until Jem took him up in his arms. But nobody seemed to mind, and Mr. Meredith came and patted his head after the service and said,

"'Faith and affection and loyalty are precious things wherever they are found. That little dog's love is a treasure, Jem.'

"One night when Jem and I were talking things over in Rainbow Valley, I asked him if he had ever felt afraid at the front.

"Jem laughed.

"'Afraid! I was afraid scores of times—sick with fear,—I who used to laugh at Walter when he was frightened. Do you know, Walter was *never* frightened after he got to the front. *Realities* never scared him—only his imagination could do that. His colonel told me that Walter was the bravest man in the regiment. Rilla, I never *realized* that Walter was dead till I came back home. You don't know how I miss him now—you folks here have got used to it in a sense—but it's all fresh to me. Walter and I grew up together—we were chums as well as brothers—and now here, in this old valley we loved when we were children, it has come home to me that I'm not to see him again.'

"Jem is going back to College in the fall and so are Jerry and Carl. I suppose Shirley will, too. He expects to be home in July. Nan and Di will go on teaching. Faith doesn't expect to be home before September. I suppose she will teach then, too, for she and Jem can't be married until he gets through his course in medicine. Una Meredith has decided, I think, to take a course in Household Science at Kingsport—and

Gertrude is to be married to her Major and is frankly happy about it,—'shamelessly happy' she says; but I think her attitude is very beautiful. They are all talking of their plans and hopes—more soberly than they used to do long ago, but still with interest, and a determination to carry on and make good in spite of lost years.

"'We're in a new world,' Jem says, 'and we've got to make it a better one than the old. That isn't done yet, though some folks seem to think it ought to be. The job isn't finished—it isn't really begun. The old world is destroyed and we must build up the new one. It will be the task of years. I've seen enough of war to realize that we've got to make a world where wars can't happen. We've given Prussianism its mortal wound,—but it isn't dead yet and it isn't confined to Germany either. It isn't enough to drive out the old spirit— we've got to bring in the new.'

"I'm writing down those words of Jem's in my diary so that I can read them over occasionally and get courage from them, when moods come when I find it not so easy to 'keep faith.'"

Rilla closed her journal with a little sigh. Just then she was not finding it easy to keep faith. All the rest seemed to have some special aim or ambition about which to build up their lives—she had none. And she was very lonely, horribly lonely. Jem had come back—but he was not the laughing boy-brother who had gone away in 1914 and he belonged to Faith. Walter would never come back. She had not even Jims left. All at once her world seemed wide and empty—that is, it had seemed wide and empty from the moment yesterday when she had read in a Montreal paper a fortnight-old list of returned soldiers in which was the name of Captain Kenneth Ford.

So Ken was home—and he had not even written her that he was coming. He had been in Canada two weeks and she had not had a line from him. Of course he had forgotten—if there was ever anything to forget—a handclasp—a kiss—a look—a promise asked under the influence of a passing emotion. It was all absurd—she had been a silly, romantic, inexperienced goose. Well, she would be wiser in the future,—very wise,—and very discreet—and very contemptuous of men and their ways.

"I suppose I'd better go with Una and take up Household Science, too," she thought, as she stood by her window and looked down through a delicate emerald tangle of young vines on Rainbow Valley, lying in a wonderful lilac light of sunset. There did not seem anything very attractive just then about Household Science, but, with a whole new world waiting to be built, a girl must do something.

The door bell rang. Rilla turned reluctantly stairwards. She must answer it—there was no one else in the house; but she hated the idea of callers just then. She went downstairs very slowly, and opened the front door.

A man in khaki was standing on the steps—a tall fellow, with dark eyes and hair, and a narrow white scar running across his brown cheek. Rilla stared at him foolishly for a moment. Who was it?

She ought to know him—there was certainly something very familiar about him,—

"Rilla-my-Rilla," he said.

"Ken," gasped Rilla. Of course, it was Ken—but he looked so much older—he was so much changed—that scar—the lines about his eyes and lips—her thoughts went whirling helplessly.

Ken took the uncertain hand she held out, and looked at her. The slim Rilla of four years ago had rounded out into symmetry. He had left a schoolgirl, and he found a woman—

a woman with wonderful eyes and a dented lip, and rose-bloom cheek,—a woman altogether beautiful and desirable—the woman of his dreams.

"*Is* it Rilla-*my*-Rilla?" he asked, meaningly.

Emotion shook Rilla from head to foot. Joy—happiness—sorrow—fear—every passion that had wrung her heart in those four long years seemed to surge up in her soul for a moment as the deeps of being were stirred. She tried to speak; at first voice would not come. Then—

"Yeth," said Rilla.

THE END

CANADIAN WOMEN'S POETRY OF THE FIRST WORLD WAR

L.M. Montgomery did not include the full text of Walter Blythe's poem "The Piper" in *Rilla of Ingleside*, but she would have expected readers to recognize the allusion to John McRae's "In Flanders Fields," which had circulated worldwide since its publication in 1915 and which remains well known today, particularly in Canada. Although she had published over 360 poems by the time the First World War ended, only one referred directly to the events of the war. "Our Women" appeared in *Canadian Poems of the Great War*, an anthology edited by John W. Garvin and published by McClelland and Stewart (Montgomery's Canadian publisher) in 1918. It was likely in this anthology that Montgomery came across the poem "The Young Knights" by fellow Ontario writer Virna Sheard (ca. 1865–1943), which had first been published in Sheard's collection *Carry On!*, published by Warwick Bros. & Rutter (Toronto) in 1917 and which Montgomery quoted in her epigraph to *Rilla of Ingleside*. Both poems are significant because of their focus not on men's experiences in the trenches but on the women at home who watched husbands, sons, and brothers go off to fight, the same focus that can be found in *Rilla of Ingleside*.

OUR WOMEN
by L.M. Montgomery

Bride of a day, your eye is bright,
And the flower of your cheek is red.
"He died with a smile on a field of France—
I smile for his sake," she said.

Mother of one, the babe you bore
Sleeps in a chilly bed.
"He gave himself with a gallant pride—
Shall I be less proud?" she said.

Woman, you weep and sit apart,
Whence is your sorrow fed?
"I have none of love or kin to go—
I am shamed and sad," she said.

THE YOUNG KNIGHTS
by Virna Sheard

Now they remain to us forever young
Who with such splendor gave their youth away;
Perpetual Spring is their inheritance,
Though they have lived in Flanders and in France
A round of years, in one remembered day.

They drained life's goblet as a joyous draught
    And left within the cup no bitter lees.
Sweetly they answered to the King's behest,
    And gallantly fared forth upon a quest,
Beset by foes on land and on the seas.

So in the ancient world hath bloomed again
    The rose of old romance—red as of yore;
The flower of high emprise hath whitely blown
    Above the graves of those we call our own,
And we will know its fragrance evermore.

Now if their deeds were written with the stars,
    In golden letters on the midnight sky
They would not care. They were so young, and dear,
    They loved the best the things that were most near,
And gave no thought to glory far and high.

They need no shafts of marble pure and cold—
    No painted windows radiantly bright;
Across our hearts their names are carven deep—
    In waking dreams, and in the dreams of sleep,
They bring us still ineffable delight.

Methinks heaven's gates swing open very wide
    To welcome in a host so fair and strong;
Perchance the unharmed angels as they sing,
    May envy these the battle-scars they bring,
And sigh e'er they take up the triumph song!

GLOSSARY

"ABLE-BODIED MEN ... EIGHTEEN AND FORTY-FIVE" Canada's require-
ments for military volunteers. Volunteers had to meet these age limits and
be medically fit for active service.

"ACTIVE SERVICE" Soldiers on war service in the field, in the air, or at sea.

ADENOIDS Tissue found in the airway between the nose and the back of
the throat. Enlarged or infected adenoids caused the sufferer to breathe
through the mouth, often noisily.

THE ADIGE The second-longest river in Italy. In November 1917, after
their disastrous defeat in the Battle of Caporetto, the Italians retreated to
the Piave River, just 18 miles north of Venice. Rilla and Gertrude are afraid
that the Axis armies will force the Italian army to retreat again to the Adige
River, south of Venice, thus losing Venice to the enemy.

AERIAL, CELESTIAL MUSIC ... IN MILTON'S EDEN Properly, "when /
Cherubick songs by night from neighbouring hills / Aereal musick send."
From *Paradise Lost* (1667), by English poet John Milton.

AEROPLANE First World War airplanes were usually biplanes (double-
winged planes), built of wood and canvas with metal struts. They were first
used to observe enemy trench and artillery locations, but fighter models
soon resulted in a literal "war in the air." Flying may have been, as Susan
comments, a "clean" job, but the life expectancy for a British pilot on the
western front in 1917 was a mere six weeks. See also *strafing*.

AISNE, BATTLE OF After the Battle of the Marne in September 1914, the
British and French armies drove the Germans back across the River Aisne
in France, but neither side could advance farther. This battle defined the
trench lines on this area of the front for the succeeding years of the war. See
also *Marne, Battle of*.

ALLIES Britain, France, Russia, Belgium, Serbia, and the other countries
who allied to fight against Germany, Austria-Hungary, and Turkey. Canada,
Newfoundland, Australia, New Zealand, and all other countries and terri-
tories under British dominion were also automatically at war on the Allied

side. Many other countries joined the original Allies, including Italy, the United States, Japan, Romania, and other small countries.

AMERICA   See *United States*.

"AND SO, GOODNIGHT"   Properly, "and so, good-night!" From *Trilby* (1894), by French-born English writer George Du Maurier.

"AND THEY SHALL FIGHT ... TO DELIVER THEE"   Properly, "And they shall fight against thee; but they shall not prevail against thee; for I am with thee, saith the LORD, to deliver thee." From the Bible, Jeremiah 1:19.

ANTI-CHRIST SPOKE OF IN REVELATIONS   The term *antichrist*, referring in the Christian tradition to a false or adversarial Christ, appears in 1 John 2:18, 1 John 2:22, 1 John 4:3, and 2 John 1:7. Related terms mentioned in the Book of Revelation include the Beast, the Dragon, and the False Prophet.

ANTWERP   Antwerp, a city in Belgium ringed by forts and a major port on the North Sea coast, was besieged by the Germans in late September 1914 and surrendered to them on October 10 after a gallant defence by the small Belgian army. Antwerp's capture threatened other seaports vital to British supply lines and caused the series of battles known as "the Race to the Sea" in the fall of 1914. Although some Belgian ports were occupied by the Germans, the French ports remained in Allied hands. Antwerp was occupied by the Germans until the end of the war.

ANZACS   Australian and New Zealand Army Corps.

THE APPLE OF HER EYE   Properly, "he kept him as the apple of his eye." From the Bible, Deuteronomy 32:10.

ARCHDUKE FERDINAND (FRANZ FERDINAND)   See *Franz Ferdinand*.

ARMAGEDDON   In the Christian tradition, the place of the final battle on the Last Day of Judgment. Commonly used to refer to a final, decisive conflict on a grand scale. From the Bible, Revelation 16:16.

ARMISTICE   Fighting officially ended between Germany and the Allies at the 11th hour of the 11th day of November, 1918. Canada now observes Remembrance Day on this day each year.

HERBERT ASQUITH   Prime minister of Britain from 1908 to December 1916. Asquith, a Liberal, formed a coalition government with the Conservatives in 1915 to manage the war effort, but his leadership was questioned throughout 1916.

AUSTRIA; AUSTRO-HUNGARIAN EMPIRE   Ruled over by Emperor Franz Joseph until his death in November 1916, Austria had sovereignty over neighbouring Hungary, the Balkan states of Bosnia and Herzogovina, and parts of Poland, which it turned into the Austrian province of Galicia. Emperor Franz Joseph's son predeceased him, leaving Archduke Franz Ferdinand, his brother's son, as the heir to the Empire in 1914. Austria declared war on Serbia on July 28, 1914, thus instigating the events that drew the great European powers into the First World War. See "The Origins of the First World War"; see also *Allies*; *Central Powers*; *Franz Ferdinand*; *Franz Josef*; *Serbia*.

AUTOMOBILE   Prince Edward Island banned cars from its roads in 1908 because of their noise, smells, and speed; the argument against them was that they scared the horses. In 1913, P.E.I. allowed cars on the roads on Mondays, Wednesdays, Thursdays, and Saturdays, chosen to avoid market days and church days. The war and the need for fast transport of troops and goods caused the ban to be relaxed further.

AXIS   See *Central Powers*.

BAGDAD; BAGHDAD   Southern capital of the Turkish Ottoman Empire, located on the Mesopotamian front, near Kut. Captured by the British in March 1917.

BALKAN STATES   Small Slavic countries—Serbia, Bosnia, Herzogovina, Greece, Romania, Bulgaria, and Montenegro—that fought for their independence from or were fought over by Russia, Austria, and Turkey in the nineteenth and early twentieth century. See also *Austria*; *Balkan war*; *Bulgaria*; *Constantine of Greece*; *Romania*; *Serbia*.

BALKAN WAR   The Balkan countries were in a constant state of unrest during the nineteenth and early twentieth centuries, as Russia, Turkey, and Austria fought for sovereignty over them. In 1912, Serbia, Bulgaria, Greece, and Montenegro allied, with Russia's encouragement, to form the Balkan League, which declared war on Turkey (the Ottoman Empire) in October. The League was successful, and peace was declared in December. However, war was resumed in January 1913, with the League again victorious; Turkey lost most of its European possessions in what is now called the First Balkan War. The Second Balkan War began when the League quarrelled over the division of territory, resulting in Serbia and Greece declaring war on Bulgaria in June 1913. Serbia and Greece were victorious, and Bulgaria was forced to sign a peace treaty in August.

BANSHEE   In Irish mythology, a female spirit who acts as an omen of death or a messenger from the Otherworld.

BAPAUME   A village on the Somme front that the Allies captured from the Germans in 1917.

BATTALION   A military unit composed of headquarters staff and several companies. Companies, usually commanded by captains, were divided into small platoons, each commanded by a lieutenant or second lieutenant.

BATTALION RUNNER   Communication between Battalion Headquarters and troops in battle was essential, but temporary telephone lines were often cut by artillery shells. Battalion runners physically carried orders and messages back and forth across open ground between the attacking troops and headquarters staff, a very dangerous task because of enemy shelling and machine-gun fire.

BAYONET   A sharp, dagger-like instrument that was fixed to the end of a rifle. Used to stab the enemy through the body during hand-to-hand fighting.

BEAUX   Plural form of "beau," referring to suitors. In modern terms, potential boyfriends.

BELGIUM   A small country adjoining France, ruled by King Albert (King of the Belgians) in 1914. Belgium's tiny army, many times outnumbered by the German army, earned the admiration of the world for its determined fighting, while the German army earned a reputation for barbarism during the Belgian invasion by pursuing a deliberate policy of "frightfulness" to try to force the country to submit. Most of Belgium was occupied by the Germans for the duration of the war. Those who lived in the free area suffered much hardship because of the fighting; farms were destroyed and crops could not be harvested, causing food shortages. Aid for the "starving Belgians" became a popular cause throughout North America in late 1914 and 1915. Rilla's Red Cross concert to raise funds for Belgian relief reflects how this cause captured the public imagination. See "The Origins of the First World War"; see also *German atrocities*; *Louvain*; *Rheims*.

BELGRADE   A city in Serbia on the Danube River.

JOHANN VON BERNSTORFF; "BERNSTOFF"   German ambassador to the United States and Mexico during the First World War.

"BE TOO PROUD TO FIGHT THEN"   Reference to U.S. President Woodrow Wilson's "Address to Foreign-Born Citizens," made on May 10, 1915, defending the U.S.'s neutrality toward the war: "There is such a thing as a man being too proud to fight."

THE BIG PUSH   The anticipated Allied strike on the enemy that would end the stalemate of trench warfare, smash through the German lines, and win the war.

"BLACK SUNDAY"   March 24, 1918, the Sunday before Easter. Hindenburg launched the last great German offensive on the western front on March 21, 1918, before the American troops could begin fighting overseas in force. In the first of five major attacks that spring and summer, the German forces smashed through the Allied line at St. Quentin and advanced for several miles. Montgomery's account of shells falling on Paris from a long-range gun is quite accurate. Although the immediate German advance was checked by Easter Sunday, the Germans continued to advance throughout the spring and early summer, though never on the same scale as those first few days.

BLATANT BEAST   Properly, "The Blattant Beast." From *The Faerie Queene* (1590; 1596), by English poet Edmund Spenser.

BOER WAR   The South African War of 1899–1902, which pitted the British against the descendants of the Dutch Settlers, known as the Boers. Canada, for the first time, sent troops to aid Britain.

BOIL   A local infection or sore. Because antibiotics weren't available, even a small infection could become serious. Treatment was to place hot wrung-out cloths over the boil to draw out the poison.

BOLSHEVIKS   The Russian Communist Party, also known as the Red Army, led by Vladimir Lenin. See also *Lenin*; *Nicholas II*; *Russia*.

SIR ROBERT BORDEN   Canadian prime minister and leader of the Conservative Party. In 1917, Borden formed a coalition between his Conservative Party and members of the Liberal Party who favoured introducing conscription, thus creating the "Union Government." See also *Canadian election, 1917*; *Food Board*; *Union Government*.

"THE BRAVE MAN ... ITS FEAR SUBDUES"   Properly, "The brave man is not he who feels no fear, / For that were stupid and irrational / But he, whose noble soul its fear subdues / And bravely dares the danger nature shrinks from." From *Count Basil: A Tragedy* (1798), by Scottish poet and playwright Joanna Baillie.

"BREAK FAITH"; "BROKEN FAITH"   Allusions to John McCrae's 1915 war poem, "In Flanders Fields": "If ye break faith with us who die / We shall not sleep, though poppies grow / In Flanders fields." See also *Flanders*; *"The Piper."*

BREST-LITOVSK   The Polish city, deep behind the German lines, where Germany and Austria chose to sign the peace treaty (Treaty of Brest-Litovsk) with Russia in March 1918. See also *Russia*.

BRICKS WITHOUT STRAW   See the Bible, Exodus 5.

ALEKSEI BRUSILOV; "BRUSILOFF"   An innovative Russian commander who launched a successful offensive on the eastern front, beginning in June 1916 and ending in September. His victories against the Austrian army forced them to halt their attacks on Italy.

BRUSSELS   The principal city of Belgium, Brussels fell to the Germans in the autumn of 1914 and was occupied by enemy troops until the war's end.

BUCHAREST   Capital city of Romania. Lost to the Germans in 1916.

BULGARIA   One of the Balkan states. Joined Germany and Austria by declaring war on Serbia in October 1915.

"BUT ONE MORE ... HAVE GONE BEFORE"   Properly, "I am one the more / To baffled millions which have gone before." From "Epistle to Augusta" (1830), by George Gordon, Lord Byron.

SIR JULIAN BYNG; GENERAL BYNG   Commander of the Allied Third Army, including the Canadians. Won a victory using tanks to support the infantry (foot soldiers) at Cambrai, France, in November 1917.

BZURA   A river in Poland on the eastern front, considered a natural defence for the city of Warsaw.

CALAIS   A seaport in northern France, only 21 miles by sea from Dover, England. German forces tried to drive through the Allied lines at Ypres in October and November 1914 to reach the seaports of Boulogne, Dunkirk, and Calais, vital to British supply routes across the Straits of Dover and the English Channel. See also *Ypres*.

CAMBRAI, BATTLE OF   On November 20, 1917, the Allied Third Army, under Sir Julian Byng, successfully initiated the use of massed tanks attacking alongside the infantry, breaking the German line across a wide front. Unfortunately, reinforcements and supply lines prevented the attack from advancing further.

CANADIAN ELECTION, 1917   Also known as the "khaki election." In 1917, Sir Robert Borden, Canada's prime minister and leader of the Conservative Party, introduced the Military Service Act, which required every physically fit Canadian man between the ages of twenty and forty-five to register for the military, subject to specific exemptions. A nation-wide controversy exploded that dominated the December 1917 election. Borden's Conservatives allied with pro-conscription Liberals to form a Union Government; Sir Wilfrid Laurier, former prime minister and leader of the Liberal Party, campaigned against conscription. Before the election, Borden passed the Wartime Elections Bill, which for the first time gave Canadian women the vote—but only those with an immediate relative, "living or dead," with the Canadian or Allied forces. Naturalized Canadian citizens who had been born in an enemy country and arrived in Canada after 1902 were disenfranchised, as were conscientious objectors. The Union Government won a majority of votes in the Maritimes, Ontario, and the West, but won only three seats of sixty-five in Quebec, sowing the seeds of Quebec separatism. Ironically, only about 25,000 drafted men reached the battlefields; more than 300,000 men applied for and were exempted from the draft. Montgomery, a life-long Liberal, cast her first vote, for Borden and the Union Government. Her half-brother, Hugh Carlyle "Carl" Montgomery, served with the Canadian army, making her eligible for the vote.

CAPORETTO, BATTLE OF   In October 1917, the combined German and Austro-Hungarian armies attacked the Italian army at Caporetto, Italy, winning a resounding victory, breaking the Italian line, and causing 300,000 casualties, mostly prisoners. The Italians retreated to the River Piave, only 18 miles north of Venice. The defeat shocked the other Allied countries, causing Britain to send troops to reinforce the Italians.

"CARRY ON"   A military command that meant "carry on as usual." Officers used it in diverse situations, from inspecting the cooking of the men's dinner ("Carry on, Cook") to ensuring sentries were awake ("Carry on, Soldier"). In civilian speech, however, the term became synonymous with doing one's duty in abnormal circumstances, regardless of sacrifice.

CASSANDRA-LIKE CROAKINGS   In Greek mythology, the beautiful Cassandra, daughter of King Priam and Queen Hecuba of Troy, was given the gift of prophecy by Apollo. When she deceived him, he decreed that no one should believe her prophecies of doom.

CASUALTY LISTS   The names of soldiers killed on active service, wounded, captured, or who died of illness were published each day in the newspapers. Families of the men affected often saw these newspaper accounts before receiving official notification by government telegram. The extent and severity of the fighting could be judged by the length of the daily casualty list.

CATAWAMPUS   Gone askew or awry.

CENTRAL   The Central telephone exchange, where an operator routed requests for calls to the correct numbers.

CENTRAL POWERS   Germany and Austria-Hungary, who declared war on Britain, France, Russia, Serbia, and their allies. Turkey was the third major country to join Germany and Austria-Hungary, and smaller countries, such as Bulgaria, also declared for the German side. See also *Allies.*

CHARLOTTETOWN   Capital city of Prince Edward Island, with a population of approximately 10,000 people in 1914.

CHEMANG-DE-DAM   Montgomery is probably referring to the battlefield of Chemin des Dames in France, located between Soissons and Rheims, and the scene of major battles between the French and German armies in 1914, 1917, and 1918.

"CHILLING WINDS AND GLOOMY SKIES"   From "Heaven" (1883), by American poet Nancy Amelia Woodbury Priest.

CHURCH UNION   The Methodist and Presbyterian churches discussed uniting as one church, but did not do so until 1925. See Montgomery's journals for the 1920s for a full account of the union's consequences.

COAL OIL   The fuel used to burn lamps, commonly used to light houses before electricity.

COEUR-DE-LION   Richard I of England, known as Richard the Lion-Heart, reigned from 1189 to 1199. On his 1190 crusade to the Holy Land, he almost captured Jerusalem, the Holy City, twice.

"COME OUT OF" ... A DUBIOUS "HERE"   Properly, "Where did you come from, baby dear? / Out of the everywhere into here." From *At the Back of the North Wind* (1871), by Scottish novelist George MacDonald.

"COMES HE SLOW ... COMES AT LAST"   Properly, "And come he slow, or come he fast, / It is but death who comes at last." From *Marmion* (1808), by Scottish poet and novelist Sir Walter Scott.

COMMISSION   Accepting the rank of an officer in the army. College-educated young men, such as Kenneth, were considered prime officer material, though some, like Jem and Jerry, enlisted as privates, or ordinary infantry (foot) soldiers.

CONSCRIPTION   Compulsory drafting of a person into the military. See also *Canadian election, 1917.*

CONSTANTINE OF GREECE   King Constantine I of Greece was married to Kaiser Wilhelm's sister Sophia, so was pro-German, but his prime minister, Eleutherios Venizelos, favoured the Allies. Constantine kept Greece neutral, but the country grew increasingly divided over the question of the war. In 1916, Venizelos, who had resigned over this disagreement with Constantine, gained control of half of the country with the Allies' support. Constantine abdicated in 1917, but returned to his throne in 1920 at the request of the populace. See also *Eleutherios Venizelos*.

CONSUMPTION   Tuberculosis.

COOTIES; "COOTIE SARKS"   Lice or fleas, unavoidable in trench conditions. Soldiers rarely had the chance to bathe and often wore the same clothing for days or weeks. Women made special vests for soldiers to prevent lice, but they were not effective. In normal conditions, lice were considered a sign of poverty and lack of cleanliness.

COURCELETTE, BATTLE OF   The Battle of Flers-Courcelette opened on September 15, 1916, as part of the Somme offensive. The British and Canadians introduced the first tanks during this battle, and the villages of Flers, Martenpuich, and Courcelette were won, a gain of 2000 yards. The advance was halted by poor weather and strong German reinforcements. Montgomery's half-brother, Carl, fought in this battle.

CROUP   A virus that attacks infants and young children. Usually mild, but in severe cases, the airways can swell and be blocked by mucus. Even today, a child with Jims's symptoms would be taken to hospital for emergency treatment.

CROWN PRINCE   Crown Prince Wilhelm of Germany, the eldest of Kaiser Wilhelm's six sons. He survived the war.

CZAR NICHOLAS   See *Nicholas II*.

D—   "Damn," considered profane.

"DAILY LIST OF CASUALTIES"   See *casualty lists*.

DARDANELLES   See *Gallipoli*.

DAVID AND THE BETHLEHEM WATER   From the Bible, 2 Samuel 23:15, 1 Chronicles 11:17.

DAYLIGHT SAVING LAW   Daylight Saving was adopted in Germany in 1915, explaining Susan's reluctance to follow it when Sir Robert Borden's government introduced it in Canada in 1918. Moving clocks forward an hour in the spring and back one hour in the fall allowed farmers an extra hour of daylight during the growing season.

A DELUSION AND A SNARE   Properly, "a delusion, a mockery, and a snare." From British judge and politician Thomas Denman, in his judgment on the case of Daniel O'Connel v. The Queen (1844).

DEVOUTEDLY DESIRED CONSUMMATION   Properly, "a consummation / Devoutly to be wished." From *Hamlet* (ca. 1600), by William Shakespeare.

DISTINGUISHED CONDUCT MEDAL; D.C. MEDAL; D.C.M.   Awarded for "distinguished conduct in the field." The second-highest award for gallantry after the Victoria Cross.

DITTO   A dinner of plain boiled mutton, served regularly at the Meredith household in *Rainbow Valley*.

DOBRUJA   A region on the Balkan peninsula, partly in Bulgaria and partly in Romania.

DOG MONDAY   Variation on "Man Friday," a character in the novel *Robinson Crusoe* (1719), by Daniel Defoe, a term also used to refer to a male servant or assistant.

DOWN INTO THE VALLEY OF THE SHADOW   Properly, "the valley of the shadow of death." From the Bible, Psalm 23:4.

DROP HIS HANDKERCHIEF   To invite courtship, or signal romantic interest.

THE EDEN SECRET ... NAKED AND UNASHAMED   Properly, "And they were both naked ... and were not ashamed." From the Bible, Genesis 2:25.

ELDER   Each Presbyterian parish was administered by a committee of elders, men of good standing in the church.

ERZERUM   A fortress city under Turkish control in Armenia on the Mesopotamian front. Czar Nicholas II transferred his uncle, Grand Duke Nicholas, to command the Russian army in Mesopotamia in 1915. The Grand Duke's strategies succeeded in capturing Erzerum in February 1916, a key victory in the Allies' successful campaign in this region. Susan is probably referring to the Czar's mistake in banishing his capable uncle to the seeming obscurity of the Mesopotamian front.

EVENING HATE WITH THE WEEDS   An example of how military diction invaded everyday conversation. The armies on the western front often exchanged shells at nightfall, which became known as "evening hate."

"A FAIRY CITY OF THE HEART"   From *Childe Harold's Pilgrimage* (1818), by George Gordon, Lord Byron.

THE FAT OF THE LAND   From the Bible, Genesis 45:18.

FIDDLER'S INVITATION   An invitation made at the last minute to a person who wasn't on the original guest list.

FIFTH READER   One of a series of textbooks containing poems, essays, and other literature set for the P.E.I. school curriculum.

FLANDERS   A low-lying area of Belgium on the western front, subject to much trench fighting throughout the war. Made into an enduring cultural symbol of the war by Canadian John McCrae's poem "In Flanders Fields," which was published in December 1915. See also *"break faith."*

FLOUNCE   A gathered ruffle that adorned the skirt of a dress.

FERDINAND FOCH   A French commander, General Foch was appointed Supreme Commander of the Allied Forces in 1918 to provide a coordinated military strategy for the Allies.

FOOD BOARD   The Canadian Food Board published guidelines recommending voluntary rationing of butter, sugar, wheat, and meat. Although rationing was never mandatory in Canada, posters and propaganda successfully encouraged meatless days, eliminating or reducing use of certain foods, and using potatoes and other grains as wheat substitutes. By 1918, citizens were also encouraged to use their lawns and gardens to grow potatoes and other produce, as the Blythes do. Wheat and other foods were exported to Britain to help feed the troops and the civilian population.

HENRY FORD   The famous American carmaker sailed to Europe in December 1915 with the self-declared intention of negotiating peace among the warring countries. He was unsuccessful.

FRANZ FERDINAND   Archduke Franz Ferdinand, heir to the Austro-Hungarian throne. He and his morganatic wife, Sophie, were assassinated by a Serbian student in Sarajevo, Bosnia, on June 28, 1914. His death instigated the events that led to the war. See also *Austria.*

FRANZ JOSEF; "FRANCIS JOSEPH"   Franz Josef I, Emperor of Austria and King of Hungary from 1848 until his death in November 1916. See also *Austria.*

SIR JOHN FRENCH; "GENERAL FRENCH"   Commander-in-Chief of the British army until he was replaced by Sir Douglas Haig in December 1915.

FRONT   A major theatre of war. Montgomery refers most frequently to the western front, which encompassed the trenches that stretched from the Belgian seaports across France to the Swiss border, including the

Somme and Ypres, and the eastern front, which encompassed the fighting in Russia, Poland, and the Slavic countries. The war was also fought in the Mediterranean and the Dardanelles, and the Middle East, with troops and medical staff posted as far away as Africa and Lemnos.

FRUITATIVES   A type of patent medicine made in Ottawa and sold as Fruit-a-tives. Advertised in major newspapers as a tonic to ensure sound digestion and to purify the blood, it claimed to be "the only medicine in the world made of fruit juices," so children might find its taste appealing. Sold in tablet form for 50 cents per box.

GALLIPOLI   In 1915, the Allies planned to capture the Dardanelles, a 37-mile strait between Europe and Asiatic Turkey overlooked by the cliffs of the Gallipoli peninsula, to open a way from the Mediterranean Sea to the Black Sea and Russia. British, Australian, and New Zealand troops tried to land on April 25, but the Turks had fortified the hills and cliffs, and many soldiers were killed even before they had reached land. The Allied troops did battle their way to a precarious position on the peninsula and continued to attack over the summer, but heavy casualties from battle and illness and lack of progress led to all troops being evacuated during December 1915 and January 1916.

GEORGE V; "KING GEORGE"   George V, King of Great Britain from 1910 to 1936. Grandson of Queen Victoria; cousin to Kaiser Wilhelm II of Germany and to Nicholas II, Czar of Russia. The British royal family was named the House of Saxe-Coburg-Gotha when the war began; for patriotic reasons, it was changed to the House of Windsor during the war.

DAVID LLOYD GEORGE   In 1915, Lloyd George became Minister of Munitions in the British Cabinet. He resolved the shell shortage that hampered the British army in the fall of 1915. Originally a Liberal, Lloyd George joined the Conservatives in late 1916, and replaced Herbert Asquith as prime minister on December 7, 1916.

GEORGETTE   A lightweight, crinkled fabric with a graceful drape. In her January 5, 1917, journal entry, Montgomery recalls her youthful self as dressed in "georgette crepe and silk stockings"—just like Rilla.

GERMAN ATROCITIES   Germany's policy in 1914 was to deliberately practise "frightfulness" on civilian populations of captured towns. Civilians were taken hostage, and public buildings and homes were looted and destroyed. Because mass shootings of Belgian civilians did take place in Louvain, those who supported the Allies were prone to believing later reports of atrocities that took place in Belgium. The cynicism engendered by the deliberate use of such negative propaganda during the First World War led to disbelief about reports of Nazi treatment of Jewish people and other populations during the Second World War. See also *Belgium*; *Louvain*.

A GIANT REFRESHED   From the Book of Common Prayer, Psalm 78.

GIMP   Courage or "guts."

GIRD UP OUR LOINS AND PITCH IN   To prepare for action. From the Bible, Job 38:3.

"GOD IS LOVE"   From the Bible, 1 John 4:8.

"GONE TO HIS OWN PLACE"   From the Bible, 1 Samuel 5:11.

GOOSEBERRY   An unwanted chaperone or companion who makes a trio out of a couple.

THE GREAT FLEET ... ACROSS THE OCEAN   The First Canadian Contingent, comprising 25,000 soldiers and medical staff, including nurses, sailed in convoy on October 3, 1914, arriving in Plymouth, England, on October 14. The soldiers spent the fall and winter training on Salisbury Plain, England, then embarked for the trenches in France in early February 1915. See also *Salisbury Plain*.

GREEK TANGLE   See *Constantine of Greece*.

SIR EDWARD GREY   Britain's foreign secretary in 1914. Famous for saying, when Britain declared war on Germany, "The lamps are going out all over Europe; we shall not see them lit again in our lifetime."

GRITS   Plural form of "Grit," referring to someone who votes Liberal.

SIR DOUGLAS HAIG; GENERAL HAIG   Replaced Sir John French as Commander-in-Chief of the British army in December 1915. A controversial commander because his military strategy consisted of having the British make a series of frontal assaults on German trenches on the western front, causing enormous casualties for small gains in territory. For instance, 60,000 British men became casualties on the first day of the Battle of the Somme on July 1, 1916.

"HEARTS OF THE WORLD"   D.W. Griffith's popular First World War silent film, released in 1918 and starring Lillian Gish as a French girl caught in a village overrun by the Germans. In the scene Rilla describes, a brutal German soldier beats Gish and threatens to sexually assault her. Silent films, known as "moving pictures," were an increasingly respectable and popular entertainment form that Montgomery enjoyed very much.

Montgomery reported in her journal that her cousin, Frederica Campbell MacFarlane, did exactly what Rilla does here.

"HE GOES TO DO ... BEEN HIS SON" Properly, "He goes to do—what I had done, / Had Douglas' daughter been his son!" From *The Lady of the Lake* (1810), by Sir Walter Scott.

"HE THAT ENDURETH ... SHALL BE SAVED" From the Bible, Matthew 10:22; see also Matthew 24:13, Mark 13:13.

HE WENT ... HIS GOING Properly, "Stand not upon the order of your going." From *Macbeth* (1623), by William Shakespeare.

"HE WHOSE NOBLE SOUL ... SUBDUES" See *"the brave man" ... "its fear subdues."*

HIGHER POWER THAN THE UNION GOVERNMENT Susan refers to God here, claiming that her religion takes precedence over the Canadian government. Montgomery mentions in her journal that she and her husband had to check to see if a household ran on Borden's time or God's time before arriving for tea or supper—not wanting to be an hour early or late. See also *Daylight Saving law*; *Union Government*.

HILL 70 The Canadians captured Hill 70 (on the Arras front) in France during the August 15–25, 1917, battle, extending the territory they had won at Vimy Ridge in April.

PAUL VON HINDENBURG; "HINDY" Commander of East Prussia in 1914, Hindenburg became, in turn, Commander-in-Chief of the German armies in the East, Field Marshal, then Army Chief of Staff in August 1916. He and his close aide, Ludendorff, defeated Romania, then Russia, and finally undertook the German offensive and advance in the spring of 1918.

HIS PROTESTS AVAILED HIM NOTHING Properly, "Yet all this availeth me nothing." From the Bible, Esther 5:13.

HOLLAND Holland, as one of the few neutral European countries, was the goal for many prisoners of war escaping from camps in Germany. Though Montgomery does not give details of Jem's escape, many escaped prisoners of war hiked across Germany to the Dutch border, scrounging for food along the way, and were then repatriated to England. Successful escapers were rightly considered heroes.

HOLY WRIT The Bible.

HOME BOY A boy from an orphanage.

HOPETOWN A fictional orphan asylum in Nova Scotia.

HOUSEHOLD SCIENCE   Domestic science (home economics) grew out of the belief, encouraged by the Canadian and provincial governments, that healthy households and knowledgeable mothers contributed to a healthy nation. Girls and young women studied scientific subjects relevant to nutrition, food composition, sanitation, and illness; they also learned food preparation. Montgomery's cousin Frederica Campbell graduated from the Domestic Science course at Macdonald College, outside Montreal, in 1912.

HOW COULD MEN ... OF THEIR GODS   Properly, "And how can man die better / Than facing fearful odds, / For the ashes of his fathers, / And the temples of his Gods?" From "Horatius," part of *Lays of Ancient Rome* (1842), by British poet, historian, and politician Thomas Babington Macaulay.

SIR SAMUEL HUGHES; "SIR SAM HUGHES"   Canadian Minister of Militia and Defence from October 1911 to November 1916, when Prime Minister Robert Borden forced him to resign. Hughes was responsible for successfully building Valcartier, the training camp for Canadian soldiers, but he also caused great confusion in troop training, embarkation, and equipment. He insisted that Canadians be equipped with the Ross rifle, for instance, even though it jammed during rapid firing.

HUNS   Nickname for German soldiers. People of the Allied nations likened Kaiser Wilhelm II to Attila the Hun, known as "the Scourge of God." Attila, king and general of the Hun empire in Roman times, created a feared army that plundered and laid waste to all in its path.

"HUSH! HARK! ... A RISING KNELL"   From *Childe Harold's Pilgrimage* (1818), by George Gordon, Lord Byron.

"HUSHED IN GRIM REPOSE"   From "The Bard" (1757), by English poet and scholar Thomas Gray.

MR. HYDE   See *Dr. Jekyll*.

HYDROPHOBIA   Rabies, for which there was then no cure.

THE ILIAD   *The Iliad* (ca. 8th century B.C.E.), an epic poem whose authorship is generally attributed to Homer.

INFLATION   On February 24, 1917, the *Toronto Star* announced that a housewife would need to spend $1.75 to purchase the same goods that would have cost $1 in November 1914. Butter had gone from 30 cents per pound to 50 cents a pound, a dozen eggs from 38 cents to 65 cents, and, shockingly, a peck of potatoes from 14 cents to 75 cents. Meat averaged a 58 percent increase in price across all types.

ITALY   Italy formed the third member of the Triple Alliance with Germany and Austria-Hungary in 1914, but remained neutral until May 1915, when it entered the war on the Allied side. See also *Caporetto, Battle of.*

"IT'S A LONG, LONG WAY TO TIPPERARY"   A 1912 British music hall song that became a popular marching song in 1914.

DR. JEKYLL; MR. HYDE   Characters from *Strange Case of Dr. Jekyll and Mr. Hyde* (1886), a novella by Robert Louis Stevenson, who represent polar opposites of a split personality.

JERUSALEM   The Turkish Ottoman Empire controlled Jerusalem from the sixteenth century until 1917, when Sir Edmund Allenby's British troops captured it on December 10 and entered the city the following day. The Turks launched a determined counterattack later that month, but failed to recapture the city. See also *"meteor flag of England."*

JOSEPH JOFFRE; "JOFFER"; "PAPA JOFFRE"   Commander-in-Chief of the French army from the war's beginning until December 1916, when he was made a Marshal of France and effectively removed from command because of the initial German success at Verdun. He remained a popular figure and was affectionately nicknamed "Papa Joffre." Montgomery's use of "Joffer" signals Susan's awkward attempts to pronounce French.

"JOSEPH IS NOT ... TAKE BENJAMIN AWAY"   From the Bible, Genesis 42:36. In the Hebrew Bible, Joseph, Simeon, and Benjamin are three of the twelve sons of Jacob, referred to here as the "old Patriarch."

"JOY CAME IN THE MORNING"   Properly, "joy cometh in the morning." From the Bible, Psalm 30:5.

JUTLAND, BATTLE OF   Both sides claimed victory in the May 31, 1916, naval Battle of Jutland. The British lost more ships, but the Germans lost larger ones, with many of their surviving ships damaged. This was the last and greatest naval battle of the war.

THE KAISER   Kaiser Wilhelm II of Germany. Grandson of Queen Victoria and cousin of King George V of Great Britain, the Kaiser reigned from 1888 until 1918, when he was forced to abdicate. The Allies characterized him as the epitome of barbarism. Burning the Kaiser's effigy was a popular way of celebrating the Armistice in 1918. See also *Central Powers; Louvain; Lusitania.*

"KEEP FAITH"   See *"break faith"; "The Piper."*

ALEXANDER KERENSKY   A member of the Socialist Revolutionary Party in Russia, Kerensky served as Minister of Justice in the Provisional Government that took power when Czar Nicholas II abdicated in March 1917. He later became head of the Provisional Government and committed Russia to continuing the war, an unpopular move. Kerensky escaped from Russia to Finland, then to England. See also *Russia*.

KHAKI   The colour of the Canadian soldier's uniform (dust coloured, or dull brownish yellow); to be "in khaki" was to have enlisted.

"KING AND COUNTRY"   A recruiting slogan found on posters that urged young men to enlist, usually as "Your King and Country Need You!"

KING GEORGE   See *George V*.

KING OF KINGS   Recurring biblical phrase referring to God; see 1 Timothy 6:15, Daniel 2:37, Ezekiel 26:7, Revelation 17:14, Revelation 19:16.

"THE KINGDOM OF HEAVEN IS WITHIN YOU"   Properly, "the kingdom of God is within you." From the Bible, Luke 17:21.

LORD KITCHENER OF KHARTOUM; "K. OF K."   British Minister of War until his death by drowning on June 5, 1916, when his ship hit a mine off the Orkneys on the way to Russia.

KITTLE CATTLE   People who are rash, capricious, or erratic in their behaviour.

"KNIT FOUR, PURL ONE"   The typical pattern for knitting ribbed socks. Socks, mufflers (scarves), and other knitted goods were packaged and sent by the Red Cross to the troops serving overseas, or sent by families to individual soldiers.

KUT; KUT-EL-AMARA   Kut, in Mesopotamia, changed hands several times. The Allies captured the town in 1915 and advanced beyond it. Losses during the advance caused them to retreat to Kut, which the Turks then successfully besieged. The British recaptured it on February 25, 1917.

LANGEMARCK   Langemarck and St. Julien were small villages in the Ypres salient that were lost to the Allies during the Second Battle of Ypres in April and May 1915. See also *Ypres*.

LANG SYNE   Long since, or long ago.

LORD LANSDOWNE   A former Governor General of Canada, Lord Lansdowne was a minister in British Prime Minister Asquith's cabinet in 1915 and 1916. Lansdowne published a letter in the *Daily Telegraph* in 1917 that called for a "statement of intention" from the Allied countries. At the time, the letter was widely read as a defeatist call for peace and contrary to the British government's policy.

"THE LAST GREAT FIGHT OF ALL!"   Properly, "In the day of Armageddon, at the last great fight of all." From "England's Answer" (1893), by English author and poet Rudyard Kipling.

SIR WILFRID LAURIER   Former Canadian prime minister and leader of the Liberal Party, one of Canada's two major parties. Laurier, from Quebec, was anti-conscription, and lost to Robert Borden's Union Government in the 1917 election. See also *Canadian election, 1917*.

LEAVE   Soldiers were granted short leaves of absence from the trenches, usually of about a week. Leaves for infantry soldiers were infrequent and irregular, and were cancelled when an attack was imminent. Like Jem, many Canadian soldiers travelled to Britain, a twenty-four-hour journey from the trenches, to visit relatives or sightsee.

VLADIMIR LENIN; "LENINE"   In October 1917, Lenin issued his "Call for Power" in Russia, which demanded the abolition of all monarchies and the end of Russia's involvement in the war; he overturned the government and came to power, removing Russia from the war. See also *Kerensky*; *Russia*.

LIÉGE; LIÈGE   A small Belgian town that fell to the Germans early in the war. See also *Namur*.

LILY OF THE FIELD   See *toil not ... lily of the field*.

LISLE; "BLACK LISLE" STOCKING   A strong cotton stocking worn with boots or sturdy shoes.

LODZ   A town about 75 miles southwest of Warsaw in Poland, on the eastern front.

LOUVAIN   A Belgian city famous for its library of antique manuscripts and early books, it was captured by the Germans in August 1914. The Germans shot many civilians, regardless of age or gender, and burned and looted the town, including the famous library, for five days. This "sacking" of the city was internationally condemned, contributing to the German army's reputation for barbarism. See also *German atrocities*.

LOVE OUR ENEMIES   Properly, "Love your enemies." From the Bible, Matthew 5:44, Luke 6:27, Luke 6:35.

LUSITANIA   The British passenger ship was torpedoed without warning off the coast of Ireland by a German U-boat (submarine) on May 7, 1915. Of the 1959 people who sailed, 1198 were lost, including many women and children. The sinking caused horror and indignation throughout the world, especially in the United States.

LYS RIVER The Lys River followed the border between Belgium and France. In April 1918, the British army in this area occupied the ground on both sides of the river. Hindenburg's second major offensive on the western front in 1918 began on April 9, with the Portuguese Division (part of the British army) taking the brunt of the attack and falling back. Allied reinforcements helped stave off the attack, but the British withdrew from Passchendaele Ridge, which the Canadians had captured at great cost in 1917.

"MACDONALDITE"; MCMONALDITE A follower of the Reverend Donald McDonald, who founded thirteen McDonaldite churches in P.E.I. His followers were sometimes known unkindly as "jumpers" or "jerkers" because he encouraged emotional frenzy and its physical expression.

FREDERICA CAMPBELL MACFARLANE (MCFARLANE) Montgomery dedicated *Rilla of Ingleside* to her closest friend and first cousin, who died of flu-pneumonia in the epidemic that swept the world during and after the Great War. Frederica, a war bride whose husband was still overseas when she died, taught household science at Macdonald College, outside Montreal. Montgomery's dedication misspells Frederica's married name. Her husband's military attestation papers spell it McFarlane.

MAIDEN MEDITATION FANCY FREE Properly, "In maiden meditation, fancy-free." From *A Midsummer Night's Dream* (ca. 1596), by William Shakespeare.

MANSE The residence maintained by the congregation for a Presbyterian minister.

"MANY INVENTIONS" From the Bible, Ecclesiastes 7:29.

MARNE, BATTLE OF; "THE MIRACLE OF THE MARNE" On August 23, 1914, the German and British armies fought their first battle, at Mons, France. Vastly outnumbered, the British fell back in a desperate fighting retreat for the next ten days, seeking to rejoin their French allies. The British and French turned to fight the Germans at the River Marne from September 6 to 10, halting the German advance and forcing them back across the River Aisne in the first real Allied victory of the war.

On July 15, 1918, Ludendorff launched the last big German offensive of the war on the Flanders front, hoping to split the French army. The Germans failed in their eastern attack, but initially broke through the French and American lines to cross the Marne. The combined Allied troops, under Supreme Commander Foch, halted this advance on July 17 and successfully counterattacked. The Germans retreated, having lost all the ground they had gained during the spring. The Second Battle of the Marne marked the definitive turning point of the war; although fierce fighting continued until the Armistice was signed on November 11, the Allies would never again suffer a major defeat. The Canadians played a significant role in capturing German strong points during the last hundred days of the war.

MARRIED AN ENGLISH GIRL   Many Canadian soldiers, like Jim Anderson, married British or European "war brides" and brought them home to Canada. Their reception was mixed; Rilla's anxiety reflects the attitude of many families whose sons or brothers brought home a foreign bride.

MARTENPUICH   See *Courcelette, Battle of*.

A MEEK AND OBEDIENT ... LONG IN THE LAND   Properly, "Honour thy father and thy mother: that thy days may be long upon the land." From the Bible, Exodus 20:12.

MESOPOTAMIA   The land area watered by the Rivers Tigris and Euphrates; today, corresponds to modern Iraq and parts of Iran, Syria, and Turkey. The British were quite successful in the Mesopotamian campaign.

"METEOR FLAG OF ENGLAND"   From "Ye Mariners of England" (1800), by Scottish poet Thomas Campbell.

METHOD IN HER MADNESS   Properly, "Though this be madness, yet there is method in't." From *Hamlet* (ca. 1600), by William Shakespeare.

METHODIST   One of the largest Protestant religious denominations in Canada, the Methodist Church in Canada envisioned social transformation through missionary work and education. Methodists were looked down upon by the more elite Presbyterians and Anglicans in the eighteenth and nineteenth centuries, an attitude that Miss Cornelia still echoes.

MILITARY AGE   In Canada, men between eighteen and forty-five years of age. At the war's beginning, a married man's wife had to agree to his enlistment, a requirement that was soon overturned. Many boys under eighteen lied about their age to enlist, as Laurie MacAllister does in chapter 21.

MLAWA   A small town on the 1914 Russian–German border, Mlawa saw heavy fighting and changed hands fourteen times during the war. It is now in modern-day Poland.

MONKEY-FACES   A type of cookie spiced with molasses.

MONROE DOCTRINE An American isolationist policy inaugurated by President James Monroe in his address to Congress in 1823, stating that America would not tolerate European interference in its affairs, nor should America intervene in European affairs.

MONS See *Marne, Battle of.*

MUSQUODOBOIT The name of a valley, a river, and a harbour community in Nova Scotia.

MUSTARD PLASTER Powdered mustard, mixed with hot water, plastered on a piece of cloth and applied to the chest to clear lung congestion.

NAMUR A series of forts near the town of Namur in Belgium. The Belgian army held up their German attackers for twelve days before surrendering the forts in August 1914, earning international accolades for their gallant defence.

NEURALGIA Pain that follows the path of a nerve. Can also cause weakness or numbness in the affected part.

NEUVE CHAPELLE, BATTLE OF; "NEW CHAPELLE" The Battle of Neuve Chapelle in northwestern France, March 10–13, 1915, was reported as an Allied victory, but when the enormous casualty lists were published, the "victory" was reassessed. The British attacked the German lines and initially succeeded in advancing, but British lack of organization and mis-communications gave the Germans time to reinforce, regroup, and counterattack. The public was shocked by the huge number of men killed and wounded for a nominal amount of territory. Canadian troops provided supporting artillery fire to the attacking British troops.

A NEW HEAVEN AND A NEW EARTH From the Bible, Revelation 21:1. See also 2 Peter 3:13, Isaiah 65:17, Isaiah 66:22.

GRAND DUKE NICHOLAS; GRAND DUKE NIKOLAI NIKOLAEVICH Commander-in-Chief of the Russian armed forces for the first year of the war. When his nephew Czar Nicholas II took over the command of the Russian army in 1915, the Grand Duke was transferred to the Mesopotamian front, where he was highly successful. See also *Erzerum*; *Nicholas II*; *Russia.*

NICHOLAS II Czar Nicholas II, a cousin of George V of Great Britain and Kaiser Wilhelm II of Germany, ruled over Russia from 1894 until March 1917, when he was forced to abdicate. Nicholas married Princess Alexandra of Hesse-Darmstadt, German by birth but a granddaughter of Queen Victoria. He took command of the Russian forces in early 1915, and his mismanagement of the war led to his abdication and the Russian Revolution. Nicholas, his wife, and their five children became prisoners of the Bolsheviks during the Revolution and were executed in July 1918. See also *Kerensky*; *Lenin*; *Russia*.

NIMBUS   A bright cloud-like formation or halo surrounding a deity or supernatural being; associated in the Christian tradition with Jesus Christ.

NO-MAN'S-LAND   The neutral territory between the two lines of enemy trenches. Varied from a few yards to approximately two miles, depending on the section of line being held. Trench lines were protected by rolls of barbed wire, and No-man's-land was often churned up by artillery shells.

"OH GOD, OUR HELP ... OUR ETERNAL HOME"   From the hymn "O God, Our Help in Ages Past," by English hymn writer Isaac Watts (1719), paraphrasing Psalm 90 in the Bible.

"OH, HEAR US ... PERIL ON THE SEA"   From the hymn "Eternal Father, Strong to Save," with lyrics by William Whiting (1860) and music added by John B. Dykes (1861). This extract paraphrases Psalm 104 in the Bible.

OLD NICK   A nickname for Satan, or the devil.

ONE CROWDED HOUR ... WITHOUT A NAME   Properly, "One crowded hour of glorious life / Is worth an age without a name." From "The Call" (1791), by British officer and poet Thomas Osbert Mordaunt.

"OUR HOUSE IS LEFT US DESOLATE"   Properly, "your house is left unto you desolate." From the Bible, Matthew 23:38, Luke 13:35.

OVERALLS   Mary Vance pioneers trousers for women in Glen St. Mary when she dons a pair of overalls to help with the harvest. By 1917, food shortages in Britain had become acute, and Canada was short of men to harvest the crops; women and schoolboys were urged to help.

OVER THE TOP   When an attack was ordered, soldiers climbed out of their trenches and advanced toward the enemy trenches across the open ground (No-man's-land) in a frontal attack. Many men were killed or wounded by machine-gun fire or shelling in such attacks.

PACIFIST   A person who does not believe in war or violence as a means to solve problems between countries. Patriotism led many people to believe, as Susan does, that pacifists like Mr. Pryor were pro-German.

PARIS   Capital city of France, Paris was never captured by the Germans, but was threatened by German advances in September 1914 and again in the spring of 1918.

PARLIAMENT BUILDINGS   The Centre Block of the Canadian Parliament Buildings in Ottawa burned down on February 3, 1916, with a loss of seven lives. Although a German incendiary was initially suspected as the cause of the fire, an investigation found it to be accidental.

PASSCHENDAELE, BELGIUM; PASSCHENDAELE RIDGE   Sir Douglas Haig, Commander of the British army, planned the Passchendaele campaign, also known as the Third Battle of Ypres, as the anticipated Allied breakthrough on the Flanders front. The battle began on July 31, 1917, and lasted until November 6. Passchendaele has come to symbolize the horrors of the war: continued heavy rains turned the battlefields to mud so deep that men drowned if they fell off the duckboard walkways, tanks stuck in the mud, and the front lines consisted of shell holes because trenches could not be dug. The Canadians, commanded by Arthur Currie, attacked Passchendaele Ridge on October 26, advancing under a creeping barrage (artillery shells falling just ahead of the troops) that accounted for the time it would take the soldiers to struggle through the morass—50 yards every four minutes. The battle ended when the Canadians captured the village of Passchendaele, with heavy casualties, on November 6, 1917. See also *Sir Douglas Haig*.

PATIENCE IS A TIRED MARE BUT SHE JOGS ON   Properly, "Though patience be a tired mare, yet she will plod." From *Henry V* (1599), by William Shakespeare.

PATRIOTIC SOCIETY   Local organizations formed to carry out war work, such as fundraising and comforts for troops overseas.

PETROGRAD   A large city in northern Russia where the 1917 Russian Revolution first broke out. Called St. Petersburg until 1914, Petrograd until 1924, then Leningrad until 1991, when it was renamed St. Petersburg. Petrograd received its food supplies by railway during the war, but the trains often broke down, causing food shortages, which led to rioting in 1917. In October 1917, the workers and citizens stormed the Winter Palace, the ex-Czar's former residence, and the Provisional Government's current residence. See also *Russia*.

PETTICOAT   An undergarment worn under a skirt. Women often wore several, especially in winter.

PIAVE LINE   When the Italians suffered a major defeat at Caporetto, Italy, in August 1917, they retreated to the River Piave, only 18 miles north of Venice. In June 1918, the Austrian army attacked the Italian and British troops here, but were driven back in a decisive Allied victory. See also *Caporetto, Battle of.*

PIPE ME "WEST"   A common euphemism for a soldier's death was "gone west." Montgomery creates a term specific to Walter by referring to the "Piper" of his poem.

THE PIPER; THE PIED PIPER   In Robert Browning's poem "The Pied Piper of Hamelin" (1862), one of numerous versions of this legend, a rat catcher lures rats away from a village with a magical pipe, and when the community refuses to pay him for his services (or "pay the piper"), he directs the magic to the children in the community, luring them to their deaths.

"THE PIPER"   The full text of Walter's poem—described here as "the one great poem of the war"—is not revealed in this book, but the recurring phrase "keep faith" and its opposite, "break faith," allude to John McCrae's famous poem "In Flanders Fields." See Introduction; see also *"break faith."*

POISON GAS   The Germans broke the Hague Convention, an international agreement that forbade specific types of weapons, by sending a cloud of poison gas over the Allied lines, beside the Canadian troops at Langemarck (near Ypres) on April 22, 1915. Those who breathed in the gas were asphyxiated. Germany later developed gas shells that efficiently targeted specific locations. The first gas used was a form of chlorine, but more deadly forms, such as mustard gas, were developed. Many veterans who survived the war died prematurely as a result of lung damage caused by being gassed. See also *Ypres.*

A POLICY OF WATCHFUL WAITING   Phrase from President Woodrow Wilson's message to the U.S. Congress on August 27, 1913, concerning the Mexican president, Victoriano Huerta.

"POTTING HUNS"   Killing German soldiers.

"POYLOOS"   Susan's pronunciation of "poilus," the nickname for French soldiers.

PRAYER-MEETING   Many Protestant churches held mid-week prayer services in addition to Sunday services.

PRESBYTERIAN   One of the largest Protestant religious denominations in Canada in the early twentieth century.

PRISONERS OF WAR   Soldiers taken prisoner were subjected to varied treatment. By 1918, Germany barely had enough food for its troops and was short of medicines and other commodities. Jem's diet, mentioned in his letter, was as much as many German civilians obtained at the time.

PRIVATE; PTE. The lowest rank in the army. Many educated young men, such as Jem Blythe and Jerry Meredith, enlisted as privates instead of waiting for commissions as officers. Jem was "promoted on the field," which meant that he was selected from the ranks of ordinary soldiers as worthy of becoming an officer through merit and courage in battle.

PROVIDENCE; PROVIDENTIAL The protective care of the divine.

PRZEMYSL; PREMYSL A Polish fortress city in Eastern Galicia on the eastern front, under Austrian sovereignty in 1914. In August 1914, Austro-Hungarian forces checked the Russian advance on Przemysl, but Russian forces besieged the city again from November 1914 until March 15, 1915, when its commanders surrendered the city. The Austro-Hungarian army recaptured the city from the Russians in June 1915. In November 1918, Przemysl became free of Austrian sovereignty and regained its Polish identity. It is now part of modern-day Poland.

PURGE THE GARNER Properly, "he will thoroughly purge his floor, and gather his wheat into the garner." From the Bible, Matthew 3:12; see also Luke 3:17.

THE RACE THAT KNEW JOSEPH The expression "the race that knows Joseph," similar to "kindred spirits" in its reference to close friends of similar outlook, has its origins in the Bible, Exodus 1:8: "Now there arose up a new king over Egypt, which knew not Joseph." It is first used by Miss Cornelia in *Anne's House of Dreams*.

RANGS CATHEDRAL See *Rheims*.

RAP WOOD A charm; to touch wood was believed to avert misfortune.

RATIONS Soldiers were given rations of food daily, so the term, like many other military words, became common. Susan refers to food rationing for civilians to limit their consumption of needed food goods. See also *Food Board*.

"RAVEN OF BODE AND WOE" From *Rienzi* (1835), by English politician and writer Edward Bulwer-Lytton.

REAPING HOOK A farm instrument shaped like a scythe and used to cut grain by hand. Mowers, or mowing machines, first drawn by horses, and later by tractors, automated the process.

RECRUITING MEETINGS   Patriotic entertainments held to urge young men to voluntarily enlist in the army. Young women such as Rilla, who could not actively fight, were encouraged through propaganda to use their gender and appeal to incite men to fight for them.

RED CROSS   The voluntary organization that made and sent supplies to hospitals, soldiers, and prisoners of war overseas. Many Canadian towns and villages formed local chapters of the Red Cross, with female members meeting regularly to raise funds, sew sheets and clothing, make and roll bandages, knit, and pack bales of supplies to send overseas. L.M. Montgomery was voted President of the Leaskdale branch of the Red Cross.

REGULATIONS REGARDING COOKERY   See *Food Board*.

ERNEST RENAN   Nineteenth-century French philosopher and writer. The book referred to here is likely *La Réforme intellectuelle et morale* (1871), which included a vision for a newly organized France toward the end of the Second French Empire.

REPENT IN SACKCLOTH AND ASHES   Properly, "they would have repented long ago in sackcloth and ashes." From the Bible, Matthew 11:21.

RETURNED TO HER MUTTON; RETURN TO MY MUTTON   A literal translation of the French phrase "Revenons à nos moutons," from the anonymous play *La Farce de Maistre Pierre Pathelin* (ca. 1460), referring to a return to the subject at hand.

RHEIMS; REIMS   A city in northwestern France, in existence since Roman times, later the coronation place of many of the French kings. The thirteenth-century gothic Cathedral of Notre Dame and the city itself suffered severe destruction when the Germans captured and pillaged it early in the war. Rheims also suffered severely from shelling when the German army occupied the heights overlooking the city for the rest of the war. Many of its citizens stayed, but lived in their cellars to avoid the regular shelling. Montgomery illuminates Susan's difficulty with French by using phonetic pronunciations such as "Rangs" and "Rems."

ROMANIA; RUMANIA; "ROUMANIA"   A small country bordering Serbia, Bulgaria, and Hungary, Romania joined the Allies in August 1916, but its army was overrun by December.

RURAL LINE   Rural areas still had party lines, where a number of households shared the same telephone line and distinguished their own calls by unique ring tones. Anyone on the line could hear when a call was being made and eavesdrop on the conversation. Kenneth, who lives in Toronto, where private telephones were common, is impatient because he knows that at least a dozen people are listening to his conversation with Rilla.

RUSSIA When Austria declared war on Serbia in July 1914, Russia mobilized its troops, causing Germany, and, in turn, France to mobilize their troops. Russia was the most backward of the major powers; a limited form of constitutional monarchy was instituted only in the early twentieth century. The war effort placed many strains on the country; weapons and ammunition were scarce, and by 1917, food riots occurred because of shortages. The Czar was forced to abdicate in March 1917, and the Provisional Government took power. The Czar's abdication was heralded outside Russia as a positive change in its war effort, and as a sign of hope for its oppressed peasantry. The October Revolution (1917), led by Vladimir Lenin, then overturned Kerensky's Provisional Government, putting the Bolsheviks (Red Army) into power. By late 1917, Russia was effectively out of the war. Lenin negotiated the Treaty of Brest-Litovsk with Germany and Austria-Hungary in March 1918. See also *Kerensky*; *Lenin*; *Nicholas II*.

ST. JULIEN See *Langemarck*.

ST. QUENTIN On March 21, 1918, Germany began its great spring offensive by heavily bombarding 11 miles of the Somme front, from the Cambrai area to around St. Quentin, then sending its infantry to attack the British lines. German troops broke through at St. Quentin and advanced for several miles, but their advance was checked later in the week because of lack of supplies and reinforcements. As the result of this attack, the Allies retreated, giving up most of the territory so dearly won in 1917, including Passchendaele Ridge. This attack heralded the first of five major German offensives during the spring and early summer of 1918. See also *"Black Sunday."*

SALISBURY PLAIN The region of England where the First Canadian Contingent camped and trained from October 1914 until February 1915, when they embarked for the trenches on the western front. The weather broke shortly after the troops arrived, and it rained incessantly for the rest of their time there. The mud and damp became legendary.

"THE SAME YESTERDAY, TODAY AND FOREVER" Properly, "Jesus Christ the same yesterday, and to day, and for ever." From the Bible, Hebrews 13:8.

SARAJEVO Principal city of Bosnia, a small country in the Balkans under Austrian rule. Archduke Franz Ferdinand, the heir to the Austro-Hungarian Empire, was assassinated there in June 1914.

"SAVE AND SERVE" A popular expression from propaganda aimed at women to urge them to save wheat, sugar, fats, meat, and other household goods: "To save ... is to serve your country."

SENLIS A village near Paris that was overrun by the German army in September 1914. The mayor and six other citizens were shot by German soldiers.

SENTRY-GO A soldier's shift on watch in the trenches for an enemy attack.

SEPARATION ALLOWANCE A small payment by the Canadian government to the wives and families of soldiers to compensate for the men's lost wages. In September 1914, the payment was $20 per month per family.

SERBIA Originally called Servia, a small state in the Balkans that had won its independence from the larger powers in the early twentieth century. In October and November 1915, a combined army of Austrian, German, and Bulgarian troops decimated the small Serbian army, forcing their evacuation from Serbia. See "The Origins of the First World War"; see also *Austria*.

SHAKE ITS ACCURSED DUST FROM MY FEET Properly, "shake off the dust of your feet." From the Bible, Matthew 10:14; see also Mark 6:11, Luke 9:5.

SHEEP'S EYES To look longingly at a desired romantic partner.

SHIRKER; SHIRKING First applied to young men who avoided enlistment. Quickly became part of everyday speech applied to anyone who tried to avoid work or the sacrifices associated with war.

SHORTENING To put into short clothes. Baby Jims wore long dresses until he was "five months old," when Rilla "celebrated the anniversary" by putting him into short dresses.

SIEGE OF PARIS IN 1870 The Second French Empire, which Napoleon III had ruled since 1852, ended when Prussia defeated France in the Franco-Prussian war of 1870–71 and annexed the French provinces of Alsace and Lorraine.

SLACKER; SLACKING See *shirker*.

SLATE A portable, erasable writing board used by schoolchildren.

"SOMEWHERE IN FRANCE" Censorship prevented those on active service from communicating their location to those in Canada, so "somewhere in France" became a universal code for the western front.

SOMME A theatre of war in France on the western front; also the name of a battle that began on July 1, 1916. On the first day, the British army frontally attacked the Germans across the Somme front, losing 60,000 men, many killed or wounded by machine-gun fire as they left their trenches. The British did gain minimal ground, but no great advance took place. Casualties for both sides were enormous. In British cultural history, July 1, 1916, is now remembered as a symbol of the futility and waste of lives caused by the First World War.

"SOOTH WAS MY PROPHESY ... AUGURS CHEER" From *The Lady of the Lake* (1810), by Sir Walter Scott.

"THE SOUND OF A GOING" From the Bible, 2 Samuel 5:24.

SOUP TUREEN A large china or porcelain container for holding soup, which would then be served into individual bowls at the table.

SOPHIA OF GREECE See *Constantine of Greece*.

SOUTH AFRICAN VETERANS Soldiers who fought in the Boer War in South Africa, 1899–1902. See also *Boer War*.

THE SPIRITS OF ... MEN MADE PERFECT Properly, "the spirits of just men made perfect." From the Bible, Hebrews 12:23.

STRAFING A military term referring to machine-gunning the enemy troops on the ground from a low-flying plane.

THE "STRENGTH OF THE HILLS" From the Bible, Psalm 95:4.

"STRUGGLE OF ANTS ... MILLION OF SUNS?" Properly, "What is it all but a trouble of ants in the gleam of a million million of suns?" From "Vastness" (1895), by Alfred, Lord Tennyson.

SUFFRAGETTE A woman who supported extending the vote to women. See also *Canadian election, 1917*.

SUING FOR PEACE Although Germany and Austria began peace negotiations in early October 1918, they ordered their troops to continue fighting. Austria signed a peace treaty in late October, but German troops continued to fight until the Armistice was signed on November 11, 1918.

SUMMER TERM Some rural schools, like the Lowbridge School, still had spring and fall vacations so that the pupils could help their families with the planting and harvest. Students went to school in the winter and the summer, the less active farming seasons.

TEETH OF HER SOUL WERE SET ON EDGE Properly, "his teeth shall be set on edge." From the Bible, Jeremiah 31:30.

THAT SUBMARINE BUSINESS See *Lusitania*.

"THERE WAS A SOUND OF REVELRY BY NIGHT" From *Childe Harold's Pilgrimage* (1818), by George Gordon, Lord Byron.

"THEY SHALL NOT PASS" See *Verdun*.

THINGS NOT LAWFUL TO BE UTTERED Properly, "unspeakable words, which it is not lawful for a man to utter." From the Bible, 2 Corinthians 12:4.

"THIS, TOO, WILL PASS AWAY" Properly, "And this, too, shall pass away." Abraham Lincoln popularized this formulation of a proverb whose roots are found in medieval Persian Sufi poetry. Also "This Too Shall Pass Away" (1900), by American poet Ella Wheeler Wilcox.

THREE YEARS OR FOR THE DURATION OF THE WAR Rilla has just promised to wear her new hat for the same length of time that volunteer soldiers were sworn to serve when they enlisted.

"THUS FAR—NO FURTHER" Properly, "Hitherto shalt thou come, but no further." From the Bible, Job 38:11.

TOIL NOT ... LILY OF THE FIELD Properly, "Consider the lilies of the field, how they grow; they toil not, neither do they spin." From the Bible, Matthew 6:28.

"TOMASCOW"; TOMASZOW A town in Eastern Galicia on the eastern front, toward which the Austrians were advancing against the Russians in June 1915.

TRENCHES A series of ditches dug into the ground and reinforced to protect troops from enemy fire. Before the First World War, battles were conducted by manoeuvring armies over open ground, with cavalry (soldiers on horses) making swift flanking movements. The stalemate resulting from the Battle of the Aisne in September 1914 caused a new kind of warfare: troops living in a labyrinth of trenches, battling the other side with artillery fire, machine-gun fire, and the occasional "over the top" frontal attack. The war on the western front was fought in trenches from September 1914 until the summer of 1918. A typical "tour of duty" consisted of several days in the front-line trenches, or firing line, followed by several days in support trenches, followed by a period of (supposed) rest in billets (barns, houses, or open ground) behind the lines. Trench lines on the western front stretched from the Channel coast to Switzerland.

TRENCH RAID Isolated night attack by a small group of soldiers on the enemy's trench to take prisoners for information, gain a trench, or confuse and disrupt the enemy. The Canadians were renowned for their daring, successful trench raids.

TRENTINO A region of Italy, high in the mountains, where the Austrians attacked the Italian army in May 1916. The Austrians initially drove the Italians back a substantial distance, but the advance was finally checked.

TURKEY Joined Germany and Austria-Hungary to fight against the Allies on October 29, 1914. The Allies' Gallipoli expedition against the Turks was designed to force a supply route to Russia via the Dardanelles. See *Gallipoli*.

TURKISH BATH A hot bath used to induce perspiration, followed by washing, massage, and cooling. Imported to Europe and North America from the East.

TYPHOID A serious illness caused by drinking contaminated water.

UNION GOVERNMENT A group of Conservatives and Liberals in the Canadian Parliament, led by Prime Minister Robert Borden, who formed a coalition government based on the shared belief that conscription should be imposed. See *Canadian election, 1917*; *conscription*.

UNION JACK The British flag. As part of the British Empire, Canada flew the Union Jack until it created its own flag, the Maple Leaf, in 1965.

UNITED STATES The United States remained neutral until 1917, though many of its citizens raised money and goods for Belgian relief and other European causes. President Woodrow Wilson pursued an isolationist policy during the early years of the war. However, Wilson protested when Germany resumed unrestricted submarine warfare on all shipping in 1917. A month later, the United States discovered that Germany appeared to be conspiring to help Mexico attack the southern U.S. As a result, on April 6, 1917, the United States formally declared war on the "Imperial German government." Cousin Sophia was correct when she said that American soldiers would not join the Allies in large numbers in 1917; although a token number went overseas in 1917, the majority needed a year's training and did not go overseas until 1918.

UNTER DEN LINDEN The principal street in Berlin, Germany's capital city.

UNTIL THE DAY BREAK From the Bible, Song of Solomon 2:17.

V.A.D. Voluntary Aid Detachment. Originally referred to a unit of voluntary female workers, but came to refer to an individual untrained nurse. Thousands of voluntary nurses helped care for wounded and ill soldiers in all theatres of the war.

VALCARTIER   Valcartier, Quebec, located 25 miles north of Quebec City, where a training camp for the first contingent of Canadian volunteer soldiers was built in August 1914.

THE VALLEY OF DECISION   From the Bible, Joel 3:14.

V.C.   Victoria Cross, the highest award for gallantry.

ELEUTHERIOS VENIZELOS   Prime minister of Greece until he resigned in 1916 to protest King Constantine's commitment to neutrality and refusal to support the Allies. In 1916 and 1917, Venizelos gathered anti-monarchist forces, finally marching on Athens and causing the King's abdication. Greece then declared for the Allies, with Venizelos overseeing the Greek war effort. See also *Constantine of Greece*.

VERDUN   The French fortress town of Verdun, in existence since Roman times, became a symbol of French resistance to German oppression. In the 1870–71 Franco-Prussian War, it had been the last fortress to fall to the Prussians (Germans). On February 21, 1915, Crown Prince Wilhelm of Germany attacked Verdun in what was to become the longest battle of the war; it lasted until December 1915, ending with the French still in possession. French casualties reached 550,000 by the end of the battle.

"VERMIN SHIRTS"   See *cooties*.

VICTORY LOAN   To help pay for the war, the Canadian government sold bonds to citizens, corporations, and other organizations. The bonds were a "loan to the government" that paid good rates of interest and were redeemable after five, ten, or twenty years. Five bond campaigns were run, beginning in 1915 and continuing annually. The first campaign raised $100 million in subscriptions to fund the war effort. The country was divided into districts, each assigned an amount of money to raise (the district's "quota") to promote competition and enthusiasm.

VIMY RIDGE   The Canadians attacked Vimy Ridge, a strongly built line of German trenches on the Somme front, on April 7, 1917. Previous British attacks had failed, but by April 10, the Canadians, using innovative strategies and highly efficient preparations and support, had won all of their objectives in one of the most decisive engagements of the war, perhaps the first great Allied victory. The victory at Vimy Ridge—the first time the four Canadian Divisions had fought together—is now considered to be the battle that unified Canada and made it an independent nation. Four

Canadians won Victoria Crosses, and 3,598 men died out of over 10,000 casualties during the battle. The Vimy Ridge Monument in France now commemorates all Canadians who died during the First World War.

WAR BREAD   Bread made with a proportion of other grains and/or potatoes instead of wheat. See also *Food Board*.

WARSAW   Now the capital city of Poland, fought over repeatedly by the armies on the eastern front during the war. Warsaw fell to the Germans on August 4, 1915.

WE GO SOFTLY   Properly, "I shall go softly all my years." From the Bible, Isaiah 38:15.

"WE'LL NEVER LET THE OLD FLAG FALL"   World War I marching song about the Union Jack, first published in 1914, with music by M.F. Kelly and lyrics by Albert Erroll MacNutt.

WE SHOULD COUNT TIME BY HEART-THROBS   From *Festus* (1852), by English poet Philip James Bailey.

WESTERN FRONT   The western front comprised the trenches that stretched from the Channel coast across France to the Swiss border, including the small part of Belgium containing Ypres. Although Canadians, especially the medical staff, served in all theatres of the war, most Canadian soldiers were sent to the western front.

WHITE FEATHER   A symbol of cowardice. A small group of women in Britain and Canada began a white feather campaign, publicly handing out white feathers to young men who were not in uniform to show their contempt for them. See also *shirker*.

WHITED SEPULCHRE   From the Bible, Matthew 23:27.

"WI' A HUNDRED PIPES AND A' AND A'"   Scottish regimental march.

"WITH THE MAJESTY ... FIELDS OF AIR"   Properly, "Nor the pride, nor ample pinion, / That the Theban eagle bear / Sailing with supreme dominion / Through the azure deep of air." From "The Progress of Poesy" (1757), by English poet and scholar Thomas Gray.

WITHOUT FORM AND VOID   From the Bible, Genesis 1:2, Jeremiah 4:23.

"WITHOUT SHEDDING ... REMISSION OF SINS"   Properly, "without shedding of blood is no remission." From the Bible, Hebrews 9:22.

WOODROW WILSON   Twenty-eighth President of the United States, Wilson was elected in 1912 and re-elected by a narrow margin in 1916; his re-election campaign focused on keeping the United States neutral and out of the war. Wilson tried to negotiate peace among the warring nations by sending their governments a series of "peace notes." The country entered the war in April 1917. See also *United States*.

"THE WORLD IS ... WAXING LATE" From "The World is Very Evil," by Bernard of Morlaix (of Cluny), a twelfth-century Benedictine monk, translated from the Latin by John M. Neale in *The Rhythm of Bernard de Morlaix, Monk of Cluny* (1858).

YPRES; "YIPREZ" The Ypres salient in Belgium was considered one of the most dangerous places in the war. The Allies' last toehold on Belgian soil, so symbolically significant, the town of Ypres and its adjacent countryside were surrounded on three sides by the German army, allowing the Germans to shell the Allies constantly. Several major battles were fought over this ground; in 1914, the Germans attacked in an attempt to reach the seaports of Dunkirk, Boulogne, and Calais. On April 22, 1915, the Canadians were in the trenches at Langemarck, near Ypres, when the Germans released the first poison gas attack; the Canadians' stand saved the Allied line. A few days later, the Princess Patricia's Canadian Light Infantry's desperate stand near Ypres also saved the Allies from a major defeat. Ypres' military significance was that it guarded the seaports on the European side of the Strait of Dover, the English Channel, and the North Sea; if Ypres was captured, the main supply lines to Britain might also fall. See also *Langemarck*; *poison gas*.

ZEPPELIN A semi-rigid airship shaped like a bullet, equipped with engines and steering, and divided into gas-filled cells that kept it aloft. Developed by Germany's Count von Zeppelin in 1898, the Zeppelin airship was stable enough to travel relatively long distances by 1914. Germany used them during the war to bomb London in 1915, but later developed bomber aircraft.

FURTHER READING

Acton, Carol. *Grief in Wartime: Private Pain, Public Discourse*. New York: Palgrave Macmillan, 2007.

Adamson, Agar. *Letters of Agar Adamson, 1914 to 1919*. Edited by N.M. Christie. Nepean, ON: CEF Books, 1997.

Baetz, Joel, ed. *Canadian Poetry from World War I: An Anthology*. Don Mills, ON: Oxford University Press, 2009.

Berton, Pierre. *Vimy*. 1986. Toronto: Anchor Canada, 2001.

Bird, Will. *Ghosts Have Warm Hands*. Ottawa: CEF Books, 1997.

The Call to Duty: Canada's Nursing Sisters. Library and Archives Canada. www.collectionscanada.gc.ca.

Canada and the First World War. Canadian War Museum. www.warmuseum.ca.

Canada and the First World War. Library and Archives Canada. www.collectionscanada.gc.ca.

Canada in the First World War and the Road to Vimy Ridge. Veterans Affairs Canada. www.vac-acc.gc.ca.

Craig, Grace Morris. *But This Is Our War*. Toronto: University of Toronto Press, 1981.

Eaton's Catalogue, 1913/14, 1916, 1917. Internet Archive. www.archive.org.

Edwards, Owen Dudley. "L.M. Montgomery's *Rilla of Ingleside*: Intention, Inclusion, Implosion." In *Harvesting Thistles: The Textual Garden of L.M. Montgomery*, edited by Mary Henley Rubio, 126–36. Guelph: Canadian Children's Press, 1994.

Edwards, Owen Dudley, and Jennifer H. Litster. "The End of Canadian Innocence: L.M. Montgomery and the First World War." In *L.M. Montgomery and Canadian Culture*, edited by Irene Gammel and Elizabeth Epperly, 31–46. Toronto: University of Toronto Press, 1999.

Epperly, Elizabeth Rollins. *The Fragrance of Sweet-Grass: L.M. Montgomery's Heroines and the Pursuit of Romance*. Toronto: University of Toronto Press, 1992.

———, curator. *Picturing a Canadian Life: L.M. Montgomery's Personal Scrapbooks and Book Covers*. Confederation Art Centre, Charlottetown, PEI. lmm.confederationcentre.com.

The First World War: Canada Remembers. CBC Digital Archives. archives.cbc.ca.

firstworldwar.com. A Multimedia History of World War One.

Gwyn, Sandra. *Tapestry of War: A Private View of Canadians in the Great War*. Toronto: HarperCollins, 1992.

Hill, Colin. "Generic Experiment and Confusion in Early Canadian Novels of the Great War." *Studies in Canadian Literature/Études en littérature canadienne* 34, no. 2 (2009): 58–76.

Lefebvre, Benjamin. "'That Abominable War!': *The Blythes Are Quoted* and Thoughts on L.M. Montgomery's Late Style." In *Storm and Dissonance: L.M. Montgomery and Conflict*, edited by Jean Mitchell, 109–30. Newcastle, UK: Cambridge Scholars Publishing, 2008.

L.M. Montgomery Research Group. lmmresearch.org.

McKenzie, Andrea. "Women at War: L.M. Montgomery, the Great War, and Canadian Cultural Memory." In *Storm and Dissonance: L.M. Montgomery and Conflict*, edited by Jean Mitchell, 83–108. Newcastle, UK: Cambridge Scholars Publishing, 2008.

Montgomery, L.M. *After Green Gables: L.M. Montgomery's Letters to Ephraim Weber, 1916–1941*. Edited by Hildi Froese Tiessen and Paul Gerard Tiessen. Toronto: University of Toronto Press, 2006.

———. *The Blythes Are Quoted*. Edited by Benjamin Lefebvre. Toronto: Viking Canada, 2009.

———. *My Dear Mr. M: Letters to G.B. MacMillan from L.M. Montgomery*. Edited by Francis W.P. Bolger and Elizabeth R. Epperly. 1980. Toronto: Oxford University Press, 1992.

———. *The Selected Journals of L.M. Montgomery*. Edited by Mary Rubio and Elizabeth Waterston. 5 volumes. Toronto: Oxford University Press, 1985–2004.

Nicholson, G.W.L. *Canadian Expeditionary Force, 1914–1919: Official History of the Canadian Army in the First World War*. Ottawa: R. Duhamel, 1962.

Palmer, Svetlana, and Sarah Wallis, eds. *Intimate Voices from the First World War*. New York: William Morrow, 2003.

Toronto Star: Pages of the Past. www.pagesofthepast.ca.

Vance, Jonathan F. *Death So Noble: Memory, Meaning, and the First World War*. Vancouver: UBC Press, 1997.

Young, Alan R. "'We Throw the Torch': Canadian Memorials of the Great War and the Mythology of Heroic Sacrifice." *Journal of Canadian Studies/Revue d'études canadiennes* 24, no. 4 (Winter 1989–1990): 5–28.

ACKNOWLEDGMENTS

We are grateful to the following colleagues and friends for their help throughout this project: Mary Henley Rubio, Elizabeth Waterston, and Elizabeth Rollins Epperly, for their ongoing support of our Montgomery-related research; Joshua Ginter, for his invaluable help on the text; Hannah MacGregor, for her help in the University of Guelph archives; Jennifer H. Litster and the late Rea Wilmshurst, for their earlier work identifying literary allusions in the text; Mary Beth Cavert, who identified the initial publication of Virna Sheard's "The Young Knights" in her book *Carry On!*; Ruth Macdonald, David Macdonald, and Kate Macdonald Butler, who are the heirs of L.M. Montgomery, as well as Sally Keefe Cohen and Marian Dingman Hebb, who work with them; Ro Sheffe, for his expert eye; and Caitlin Drake and Helen Reeves at Penguin Canada, for their editorial expertise. The work on the text was completed thanks to a Discretionary Grant from the Board of Regents at the University of Winnipeg, awarded to Benjamin Lefebvre in 2007.